Modern Rustling!

"I can tell you where your cattle have been rustled lately," said Lance.

"Sidway, are you hinting that you can find out what Nels and I and Danny Mains couldn't?"

"No, I'm not hinting, I'm telling you," replied the cowboy with an engaging smile.

"You don't lack nerve," returned Gene shortly.

"Boss, I don't mean to be fresh. I just think you men have been hunting for rustlers in an old-fashioned way."

"Listen, young man, rustling is rustling. Cattle don't fly. They have to be driven. On their hoofs. And hoofs leave tracks."

"Only so far. I'll bet you tracked yours as far as a macadamized road, and no farther."

"Yes, that's true."

"Wal, it's a cinch. Your cattle were driven away in trucks!"

ZANE GREY

MAJESTY'S RANCHO

PUBLISHED BY POCKET BOOKS NEW YORK

POCKET BOOKS, a Simon & Schuster division of
GULF & WESTERN CORPORATION
1230 Avenue of the Americas, New York, N.Y. 10020

ISBN: 0-671-83506-8

First Pocket Books printing November, 1980

10 9 8 7 6 5 4 3 2 1

POCKET and colophon are trademarks of Simon & Schuster.

Cover art by Murray Tinkleman

Printed in the U.S.A.

MAJESTY'S RANCHO

1

Lance Sidway pulled himself up from the stone steps of the Natural History Museum. He laughed ruefully as he realized that this was his third visit to the institution. As on his two previous excursions, he had wandered round and round the inside halls examining the mounted specimens of wild animals. He loved four-footed creatures, and though a pang beset him to see these lifeless counterfeits of what had once been the free beasts of the wild, he yet experienced a sense of escape and peace that he had not felt since he left his Oregon range home for Hollywood.

There was, he knew now, a future in the motion picture studios for his great horse "Umpqua," and perhaps one for himself as well. But he shied at becoming an actor and hated to double for the handsome cowboy Apollos of the screen; and to hang around the studios merely as the owner of a wonderful horse, letting the spirited animal earn his living for him, did not fit his idea of a career. As a matter of fact, he had never desired a future in Hollywood under such circumstances and the immediate necessity for earning money was over. Nance, his sister, was perfectly well again after her operation and would soon be married. So in demand, indeed, had Umpqua been that Lance found himself with at least enough cash in hand to last him until he could find a job more to his liking.

1

He found himself leaning toward a horseback ride through southern California, across Arizona, perhaps into New Mexico. To be sure the cattle business was practically ruined, but the desert ranges and purple uplands of Arizona, or the silver grassed valleys of New Mexico, about which he had read so much, would be vastly wilder and infinitely freer than the old pastures he had ridden, and surely there would be some kind of a job for a husky chap who was fond of animals.

There was a singular zest in the thought of new adventure in a harder country than he had known. But the truth was, Hollywood did not let go its grip so easily. And why? Lance knew that he had no ambition to beat the movie game. Still he admitted the fascination of the gay bright whirl of the picture world. Reducing this down to the lure of feminine charm seemed another step in the right direction. Lance dubiously admitted to himself that he was afraid he had more than the ordinary male's weakness for the fair sex. But hell! he thought in self-defense, just think of Hollywood's thousands of extras, and more thousands of girls unable to find even jobs as extras, many of them exceptionally beautiful, all of them pretty! Here was a case where it was hard to break away. And he ruefully recalled the three girls to whose attraction he had succumbed—Coretta—and Virginia—and lastly Maurine. Only last night Maurine had faced him, a little pale, with dark eyes steady. "Lance, you've been swell to me," she had said. "I could lie to you, but I won't. At last I've got a break. You know what that means. I must make the grade. . . . Sure I love you. String along with me, darling, and when I'm a star. . . ."

That was Hollywood, but it was not Lance Sidway. Looked at now, in this serious moment, it seemed a deciding factor. "It'd happen again," muttered Lance, sadly. "And I might fall worse. It's coming to me. . . . I'm through!"

And he arose with springy step to gaze at the hazy Sierra Madres beyond which barrier there was an unsettled land. He strolled through a long terrace of roses, sensitive to their color and fragrance. They were beautiful, but he liked wild flowers best. Meanwhile he was revolving in mind the problem of riding Umpqua out of California. The horse was fat and needed work. He would not care much for the asphalt roads; perhaps, however, from Palm Springs south Lance could keep mostly to soft ground. Once in condition again, Umpqua was good for fifty miles a day without turning a hair.

Lance emerged from the Museum park, and presently, strolling along, he found himself on the edge of the University campus. Students of both sexes were in evidence, some chatting in groups, others moving along with books under their arms. These bare-headed boys and girls in their colorful sweaters, young and full of the joy of life, aroused memory and regret in Lance. After high school he had attended college in Corvallis for nearly a year, and outside of freshman miseries, which now seemed sweet, he had done well in his studies and better in athletics. But financial trouble had intervened and Nance's illness . . . both of which had sent him to Hollywood. This college atmosphere was something that he liked. If only his father had not died, to leave Nance and him orphans! Lance cast off the sadness. His sister was well—happy—and he had the greatest horse in the West and a new adventure in that West before him. Pretty lucky, Lance thought he should be telling himself! Reaching a cross street Lance halted to absorb more of the flash of color on the campus. He sauntered up the cross street toward some shade trees. On that side there were more students. He heard bantering voices and gay high-pitched laughter.

The shrill sound of a siren disrupted his attention, as well as that of the students. Wheeling, Lance saw a bright topless roadster turning the corner from the main street. Its driver was a bare-headed girl with hair bright as spun gold. At the moment she withdrew her extended left arm. Behind her raced the car with the loud horn. It caught up with her. One of the two

3

occupants, surely policemen, yelled for her to stop. The young woman took her time about it, and passing Lance, finally halted at the first shade trees where half a dozen students had congregated. Lance had not far to go to reach them and he strolled along, curious, expectant, and a little angry at the gruff yell of the officer. Lance was in time to hear:

"Why didn't you stop?"

"I have stopped," replied the girl, coolly.

Lance joined the group of students who had advanced to the curb. From all points on the campus others were coming, some on the run. Then Lance saw the girl at close range. Many a time in the studios and on the locations had he sustained a shock of masculine transport, but he had never seen a motion picture star who in his opinion could hold a candle to this girl.

"Majesty, what do these cops want?" queried a tall young fellow, stepping out.

"I'm not sure, Rollie," she replied, with a laugh. "But I think they want to chase me off the streets."

"What's the idea, officer?"

"If it's any of your business, freshie, she was speedin'," returned the other, a burly man, red-faced and thin-lipped, alighting from the police car. "*I* know her an' *she* knows me."

"Yeah?" queried the student, insolently.

"Yeah! She was makin' forty-five on the turn an' she didn't even hold out her hand."

"Say, ossifer, *we* saw this lady turn and she wasn't making twenty," interposed another student.

"Lay off us kids, can't you?" asked another, plaintively.

"Aren't there enough drunk drivers to keep you busy?"

"Looks a little steamed up himself."

Good-natured cat calls and boos sounded from back of the circle of students, crowding closer and denser. They sensed events. Lance gathered that the officers did not fail to grasp something inimical to their own well-being at the moment.

4

"Give the girl a ticket, Brady, and let's get going," advised the one at the wheel.

A storm of protest went up from the foremost line of students. Rollie, who evidently had some distinction on the campus, yelled for them to shut up.

"Beat it, you flat-feet!" he called, sharply. "You hang around here and run us fellows ragged. But lay off the girls. Get that? We won't stand for it."

"You shut up or I'll run you in," said Brady angrily, as he began writing the summons.

"Madge, is it coming to you?" Rollie asked.

"Not this time, Rollie, I swear," she replied. "I did run away from him some days ago. But today I wasn't making twenty."

"You tell that to the Judge," said Brady, coldly. "An' you're interferin' with an officer of the law."

"Law, hooey! Only when there's nothing in it for you. Get the hell out of here!"

The crowd of students surged over the sidewalk and pulled the officer from the running board of the car. He made the mistake of raising his fist, and striking himself free he shouted to his companion: "Send a riot call!" At that juncture a motorcycle policeman roared up to make a fringe of students in the street hop out of his way. Brady hoarsely repeated his order to him, and with his comrade, both swinging their arms, cleared a space.

Lance had been shoved off the pavement by the pushing of the students, all of them roused now and full of devilment. Rollie appeared to be the only one who took the affair seriously. The girl, Madge, acted as if she were enjoying the proceedings. But her violet eyes were ablaze. Rollie leaped on the running board and leaned close to speak low to her. Then Brady turning with red visage and bristling front jerked Rollie down.

"Young woman, get away from that wheel," he ordered, opening the door. "I'll take you for a little ride."

"Like hell you will," she rejoined, her voice as ringing as a bell. And she snapped the door shut.

5

Brady's attention veered to a charging crowd of students who pushed the officers' car down the street, while another gang, yelling like Indians, rushed the truck of a fruit and vegetable vender who had happened along. They halted him, and in gold and red streams they spilled the mounds of oranges and tomatoes into the street. Another moment saw the air full of colored missiles. Their target was the offending car of the law. A smashing of windows and clinking of glass mingled with the derisive yells of the assailants. Then the driver, who had attempted in no gentle manner to drive the students from crowding Brady, turned to roar at the slingers. A huge soft tomato struck him squarely in the face. That elicited a howl of fiendish glee from the armed force in the street. A hail of oranges and tomatoes not only halted his belligerent rush but blinded him, swamped him, knocked him flat. At the moment, then, a blare of sirens announced the arrival of reinforcements.

Lance hung by the girl's car while the students, numbering hundreds by now, rushed pell-mell into the street, whooping like a lot of Indians. What was left of the vender's ample supply of oranges and tomatoes disappeared from his truck as if by magic to take swift form of a colorful barrage right at the charging policemen. For a while they were held back, but as the supply of ammunition began to diminish, they forged forward, eventually to drive the students out of the street upon the campus. But it was not an onslaught such as Brady and his man had attempted. The students were having a wonderful time, but the officers, plainly disgusted and angered though they were, did not resort to violence. Against three hundred crazy students they could do nothing save harangue them off the street.

Lance, keenly enjoying the whole performance, was suddenly startled by a cry from the girl in the car. And as he wheeled he leaped off the curb. Brady had opened the car door.

"Move over, Blondie," he ordered, a rude hand on her shoulder.

"You dirty bum! Don't you dare paw me!"

It appeared to Lance that the officer's action exceeded his authority. Even if it had not, the girl's poignant outburst and the flash of her magnificent eyes would have been enough for Lance.

"I'm drivin' you to the station," declared Brady, shoving at her.

"You are not!" she cried, starting the engine. "Get off or I'll spread you along the street. . . . I'll drive to . . ."

Lance snatched the policeman's hand off the car and as he turned in surprise Lance hit him a not-too-gentle blow on his rather protruding abdomen. A gasping expulsion of breath followed the sodden drumlike sound. Brady began to sag. Lance reached up with powerful hand, pulled him off the running board, and then with a vicious swing of fist at the convulsed visage he laid the officer neatly in the street. In action as swift, Lance vaulted into the car.

"Step on it!" he yelled. And almost before the words passed his lips the little car shot ahead. Lance's knees came up hard under the dash. A shrill blast from the horn sent several students leaping for their lives. Then the car ate up the open street, to whirl at the corner, and speed on, describing swift half-circles in the traffic. Lance's hat went flying, and as the car grazed a trolley his hair stood up stiff. Though scared as he had never been, Lance's heart strangled a cowboy yell in his throat and his blood beat thick in his ears and he was possessed by a wild elation. The car whirled off the thoroughfare into a quiet street, on which the houses blurred in Lance's sight. Another turn, then block after block on a traffic-congested street, then a break in the speed—and at last a parking place!

"Whew!" exploded Lance, catching his breath. "We'd have shaken them—if they had chased us."

"Swell, wasn't it?" rejoined the girl, with an amazing coolness. And she uttered a low laugh.

"I'll tell the world. Say, but you can drive," burst out Lance, turning to look at her. With steady beauti-

7

ful hands, and shapely coral-tinted finger tips she was taking a gold monogrammed cigarette case from her purse.

"Thanks. Have a cigarette?"

"Don't mind."

"Did I scare you?"

"Yes—but it was a great ride."

"Well, we got the best of those cops anyway, and now we're just two fugitives from justice."

All this time Lance was gazing at the girl, conscious of a mounting exhilaration. To find pleasure in the beauty of women had been the only debt he owed Hollywood. But this visual experience seemed a magnifying of all former sensations.

"Oh, your hand!" she exclaimed, in sudden solicitude.

Then Lance became aware that he was opening and shutting his right hand, the knuckles of which were bruised. It was a big brown member, matching his brawny wrist.

"Bunged my fist—a little," he said, awkwardly. "Nothing much."

"No?—I wonder what that cop thought. I'll never forget his face. I was looking at it when you socked him. Did that tickle me?"

"Then I'm glad," returned Lance, beaming at her.

"You see he was sore at me. He's caught me before. Last time I made eyes at him, you know, and let him think. . . . I had a date and was late. Next time he spotted me I ran away from him. Today he must have been laying for me."

"So that was it? Big fathead! You'll get hauled up for this. I'm sorry. But I had to slug him. . . . I was looking at you when he . . ."

"Don't be sorry. You made me your friend for life. Rollie was mad, but he wouldn't have done that. . . . You're not a college man?"

"No. I went one year at Corvallis. Then . . . but that wouldn't interest you. I—I'd better be going."

"Don't go yet," she replied, detaining him with a hand on his sleeve. "Indeed I am interested. You're not going to walk out on me after such a romantic adventure. Are you?"

"Why, Miss Madge—I—you . . . of course, thats' up to the lady."

"It always should be, even if it isn't. Tell me about yourself. I'll bet you're from Hollywood. You have that cut."

"Yeah? You don't mean movie actor?" inquired Lance, quickly.

"No? Too bad! You're handsome enough to be one. My sorority sisters will be jealous. I'll have you out to the house to meet them."

"That'd be swell. But I'm afraid it's not possible. Thank you."

"You're not married?"

"I should say not."

"Nor in love. I know how that malady affects them," she replied, flippantly. "You'll come, won't you?"

"You're very kind. I—I have to say no."

"Well, of all things. A turn-down from a cavalier who fought for me! . . . It doesn't happen, at least never yet. . . . They always say: 'How about a date?' . . . What're you doing out in Hollywood?"

"I own a horse. He's been in pictures, not I. Oh, I've had to ride him a few times, doubling for these actors. I hated that. It's almost as tough on me as letting them ride him."

"A wonderful horse. How thrilling! I love horses."

"As much as cars?"

"More. We have a ranch and some Arabians. . . . What's his name?"

"Umpqua."

"Umpqua? Must be Indian?"

"Yes, it is. Means swift."

"Then he can run?"

"Run!—See here, little lady, Umpqua is as swift as the wind."

"I'll bet I've a horse that can beat him."

Lance laughed. Here apparently was a real western

9

girl. It did not detract from the dazzling glamour of her.

"Is he pretty—beautiful—grand, or what?" she continued.

"All of them. Umpqua has Arabian blood," replied Lance, warming to her interest. That seemed to put him on her level. "He is big and rangy. Mottled black with white feet and nose. Bright soft eyes. Spirited but gentle. And this Hollywood game hasn't done him any good. That's why I'm going to quit it and leave this place. Ump is too fine, too sweet a horse for Hollywood."

"You love him, don't you?" she said, softly, as if she understood.

"I'll say I do. Why, he saved Nance's life. . . . Nance is my sister. Umpqua was given to me when he was a colt. He's cowboy bred. On the Oregon range near Bend. And no horse ever had ten years' better breeding. . . . Well, Nance and I were left alone. We lost the ranch. I had to quit college. She fell ill. It was necessary to have special treatment for her—operations and all—to save her life. So to earn the money I brought Umpqua to Hollywood where I had been assured of a job. And did he make good? I'm telling you."

The girl's eyes were bright with interest.

"Splendid. And your sister—Nance?"

"Just fine now. She's going to be married soon."

"Swell! . . . Oh, wouldn't I love to see Umpqua? But I wouldn't dare. I'd want to buy him. I always try to buy everything I like. And you'd hate me. That wouldn't do at all. . . .. Cowboy, are you leaving town? Wouldn't you like . . . couldn't we meet again?"

"Why—I—I . . . hope to see you again," stammered Lance.

"We have a lot in common. Horses and ranches—and things," she went on, consulting her wrist watch. "Let's see. If I don't get pinched and haled into court, I can cut psych. Say two-thirty, here, tomorrow. Will that be convenient?"

"Okay by me," replied Lance, and opened the door to step out.

"Thank you for all you did. Good-by till tomorrow. And be careful. Don't forget you punched a cop. They'll be looking for you if they can remember what you look like. I won't forget."

Lance stood there rooted to the spot, watching the bright car and golden head flash out of sight. Then expecting to come down to earth with a dull thud, he found himself in the clouds. He soared while he hunted for a westbound trolley and the long ride out seemed only a few moments. Riding a block past his street augured further of his mental aberration. He strode on, out of the main zone of buildings, into the hills, and up the canyon where he had lodgings with a man who rented him a little pasture and stall for his horse. Lance went into the alfalfa-odorous barn. Umpqua nickered at him. "My God, Ump!" said Lance, as he put his arm over the noble arched neck and laid his cheek against the glossy mane. "I've fallen like a ton of bricks. Hardest ever!—No, old pard, not a movie extra or even a star. But a college girl. Another blonde, Ump! Only this one has them all backed off the lot. . . . So that's what was wrong with me when I sat dumb in her car?"

Contact with Umpqua brought Lance down to reality and to the fact that he was leaving Hollywood. Against his sober judgment he would keep the date with the girl, which would be a last sentimental gesture before he rode out toward the open ranges and to the life he was meant for.

Lance packed and tagged his outfit, walked down town to an express office, and checked it to be sent for later. Then he cashed his last check from the studio. It was still only mid-afternoon. On the boulevard he dropped into a movie theater and sat through two pictures, no details of which he could have faintly remembered afterward. Then he went to a restaurant for his supper. Even his usually keen appetite did not return to break his abstraction. Thereafter he strolled up the boulevard, knowing it would be the last time.

11

There was a premiere at the Chinese, heralded aloft by great searchlight beams, streaking up and sweeping across the heavens. Hollywood's main thoroughfare blazed with colored lights. Cars hummed to and fro, halted for the signals, rolled on again. Lance stood on the corner of Vine Street, absorbing the flash, the glitter, the roar, the vivid life of the strange city. There was a little sadness mixed with his varied feelings and he could not quite analyze the cause. He did not really want this life. Then a shining black limousine sped noiselessly by. Lance caught a fleeting glimpse of a lovely fair girl, radiant in white, lying languorously back against the black-clad shoulder of her companion. That was Hollywood. How many times Lance had seen the same sight, always with a vague envy!

He let that glimpse be the last to intrigue him, and striding back to his room, he went to bed. There, wide-awake, he lay in the dark, remembering, wondering, feeling more clearly than at any time since his adventure.

A vivid and entrancing picture of the girl appeared etched against the blackness. Her face floated there, exquisitely fair. It was oval, crowned by shining golden hair, which waved back from her broad low brow. Slender arched eyebrows marked large intent eyes, wide apart, dark, the color of violets and singularly expressive with a light of friendliness, of frank interest. The whole face had a flash, of which fixed and changeless beauty was only a part.

Feature by feature the girl's face appeared to Lance with a clearness which astonished him.

Lance shut his eyes to blot out this memory picture. But it made no difference. She was there, in his mind, on his heart. Never in all his life had he yearned for anything so dearly as to kiss those red lips. That dragged him rudely out of his trance. It would be wise not to see the girl again. With a pang he abandoned the idea. Majesty. . . . Madge, that student Rollie had called her. The first name suited her. Who was she? Where was that ranch with the Arabian horses? Somewhere in California, no doubt. That girl had class. Yet there was nothing the least snobbish about her. Too lovely, too kind and sweet to be a flirt! No need. She was rich, of course, Lance thought, remembering her clothes and her car! He remembered, too, the jeweled monogram on her cigarette case, but could recall only the letter M. And Lance rolled over to go to sleep. Aw! What the hell? He was always mooning over some pretty dame, especially a blonde, and here he had what was coming to him. Forget it, cowboy, and hit the trail.

All the same he dreamed of her and upon awakening in the morning, he began to waver in his resolution. Why be a sap? She had been grateful. He would want to know how she fared with the police and the college authorities. She would keep the date and wait for him. Lance, in the broad light of day, while he made his final preparations to leave, thought better of his resolve not to meet her. Treat a swell girl like that—stand her up on a promised date—a girl who loved horses—it just was not in him. And all the rest of the morning, at lunch, and when he took the bus downtown, he was conscious of a tingling expectance, a heat in his veins, a glamour over everything.

It amazed Lance extremely that he could not immediately find the parking place where he was to meet the girl. He had been so balmy, he thought, that he had scarcely known whether he was walking or riding. It was a good thing that he had come downtown so early. After wandering around, up one street and down another, at last he found the vacant lot which had been utilized to park cars. He was still a quarter of an hour ahead of time. An attendant, observing Lance loitering around, told him he could sit in one of the cars if he were waiting for someone. Lance promptly availed himself of this permission; in fact he took a back seat in a car standing against a building. Lance did not believe she would come at all; if she did he wanted to see her before she spied him. The buoyancy usual with Lance at a rendezvous seemed to be wanting here. This was a tremendous occasion.

He could see a large blue-handed clock in a tower

some distance away, and watching this, as the half hour neared, he gave way more and more to inexplicable feelings. If she came, that would be proof she liked him, and maybe. . . . Why not postpone his departure for Arizona? A few days or even weeks would not make any particular difference. If she wanted to see him, take him to the house to meet her friends, perhaps go out to see Umpqua—how could he ever resist that? He had always been a fool over girls. With this one he would be serious and assuredly she had only a passing fancy or interest in him. Or she might have been one of these beautiful dames who had to have a new flame every day. Maybe he had better just wait to have a farewell look at her, and not let her know he was there. But suppose she really had been struck with him! That was possible. It had happened once. In this case there would never again be any peace away from the glad light of those violet eyes.

"Gosh! I was a dumbbell for coming," he muttered, kicking himself. "She's late now. . . . She won't come —and am I glad?"

Nevertheless he lingered there, sliding down in the seat, watching with hawk eyes the passing cars, slowly succumbing to a pang in his breast. At a quarter to three he gave up hope.

Then a bright tan roadster flashed into sight. It slowed and turned in. The driver was a girl in blue. But her blue hat did not hide a gleam of gold. She had come! Lance's heart gave a leap and his blood gushed through his veins.

Then a seven-passenger car, shiny black in hue, flashed into sight, slowed and stopped outside the turn. From it leaped a slender young man, noticeably well-dressed. He waved the car on with sharp gesture and came hurrying, his piercing gaze on the blonde girl.

Lance saw her sweep a quick glance all around the parking place. She was looking for him, and the disappointment she expressed was so sweet and moving to Lance that it would have drawn him out of his hiding place but for the mien of the newcomer.

She halted at an angle from Lance's position, perhaps a dozen steps distant, and scarcely had she dismissed the polite attendant when the other man caught up to lean over the side of her car. He did not remove his soft gray hat. He had a remarkably handsome visage, pale, chiseled as if from marble, a square chin and ruthless mouth, and light gray eyes sharp as daggers. He reminded Lance of someone he knew.

"On the lam, eh, Madge? You certainly gave that driver of mine a run," he said, with an air of cool effrontery.

"Hello, Bee. What do you mean—on the lam?" she replied.

"Trying to run away from me again."

"No. I was in a hurry to keep a date. I'm too late. He's come and gone. Damn old Fuzzy-Top! It was his fault."

"Was your date with Fuzzy-Top?"

"No. You don't seem to understand my college talk any better than I do your gangster expressions. Fuzzy is one of my profs."

Gangster! Lance sustained a sudden shock. So that was it. This young man bore a remarkable resemblance to the picture star, Robert Morris, in his racketeer roles. What could the girl possibly have to do with a gangster? Plenty, thought Lance, considering that she had the imperious look of one who had an insatiable thirst for adventure.

"Madge, I haven't said nothing yet," replied the fellow, with a laugh. "Saying it with flowers is not my way. How about cocktails? Take me for a ride."

"Bee, I told you I had a date," she protested. "With a perfectly swell fellow. I'm crazy about him."

"Yeah? He doesn't seem so crazy about you. Dish the date and let's go places." With that the cool gentleman walked around the front of her car, and opening the door he slipped in and slammed it shut.

"You've got a nerve," she retorted.

"Didn't you tell me that was what you liked about me?"

"I suspect I did. You were something new, Bee."

15

"Thanks. You're a new twist on me. All women are flirts. But I went for you in a big way. And you went out with me, didn't you?"

"Yes. A couple of times. If you recall I met you at the Grove one afternoon for tea. We danced. And one other time at the Biltmore, where we quarreled because you were pretty raw."

"Cooled on me, eh?"

"Not exactly. You still pack a thrill. But you're a little too—too . . ."

"Madge, no broad ever made a sucker of Bee Uhl yet," he rejoined, with a crisp ring in his voice.

"Mr. Uhl, you're quite beyond me," said the girl, with a smile that disarmed her aloofness. "I'm afraid you're going to make me regret my—well, shall we call it playful indiscretion? I never took you for a gentleman, but I thought you a good sport. If I'm not mistaken the favors of our little flirtation were yours. . . . Where can I drop you?"

"Say, Beauty, you hate yourself, don't you? Well, I can take it. But the Honey Bee is not through buzzing around yet. . . . Let me off corner Seventh."

In another moment they were gone, leaving Lance in a queer state of mind. He hardly knew what to think, or why he had not made his presence known. Presently his romance burst like a pricked bubble. But his relief did not equal his regret. He would not be seeing Madge again. If her apparently friendly contact with a gangster had caused her to fall somewhat in his hasty estimation, that did not seem to make any difference. Almost he sympathized with Honey Bee Uhl. That was a cognomen. Lance wondered what it signified. Then his sympathy veered to the spirited girl. He seemed to grasp that it would be impossible for her to have any fun, at least with men, to follow any natural bent of conquest or coquetry, to play around and look for what and whom she wanted from life, without leaving havoc in her wake. A girl as beautiful as she was, radiant with such an intense and fatal charm, would have to go into a nunnery, or else expect a fall of Troy around her. No doubt she desired that very thing. Lance congratulated himself on his great good fortune in avoiding the meeting, yet when it was too late he wanted it otherwise.

In less than two hours Lance was riding Umpqua along the hilly backroads of Hollywood. He was on his way and saw the last of the town from a bridle path high upon a foothill. He knew every bit of soft road under the slope of the mountains and avoided the asphalt wherever possible. At nine o'clock, some twenty miles out of the city, he called it a day and sought lodgings for himself and Umpqua.

Up at dawn he made San Bernardino by nightfall and the next day Banning. This entrance to the desert pass he welcomed as an event. From there on he could keep his horse almost altogether off the paved roads. That night Lance was so tired he went to sleep when his head touched the pillow. On the following morning he headed down San Gorgonio Pass toward the great gray valley of the southernmost California desert.

He knew that arid country, having been to Palm Springs and Indio with motion-picture companies. Still, sight of the rolling wasteland with its knolls of mesquite and flats of greasewood, and the irregular barren mountains zigzagging the horizon, afforded him keen pleasure. How different this country from the golden pastures and black hills and swift streams of Oregon! Lance could not have conceived a greater contrast. And by noonday the June heat of the desert was intense. Sweat oozed out of his every pore and Umpqua was wet. But this heat was what both horse and rider needed. They were heavy from underwork and overeating. By midafternoon Lance reached a little station on the railroad above Indio, where he halted for the night. He slept on a spread of hay under a cottonwood tree; and when the red sun peeped over the Chocolate Mountains next morning Lance felt that the comfort and the lure of Hollywood had been left far behind.

From that point he began a leisurely journey down

the long sun-baked desert. Mecca, the Salton Sea, Niland were each marked by hitching up another hole in Umpqua's cinch. But the great horse, once off the automobile roads and loosened up by the heat, soon showed his sound bottom and his love of the open. He knew they were headed for new ranges. Lance struck the five mile stretch of sand dunes at sunrise, and he marveled at the smooth mounds with their knifelike crests, the scalloped vales between the dunes, the opal hues changing and playing across the sands. Umpqua did not like this region where his hoofs sank to his fetlocks. The flinty levels beyond, black and red with polished gravel, the sparse tufts of grease-wood and cactus, the volcanic peaks, and finally the dusky arrowwood-bordered road to the Colorado River—these kept Umpqua on his easy ground-covering gait. Lance's first sight of the red river justified what he had anticipated—a sullen swirling muddy flood, inimicable to horse and rider. And Yuma at night struck Lance favorably, with its wide main street and bright lights, its giant Indians and stealthily stepping Mexicans. He was across the river and this was Arizona.

That fact roused Lance at dawn. On his way again he appeared to have Arizona burst upon him in a blaze of brilliant sunlight that flooded vast wastes of barren soil and meager patches of grass, and ranges of ragged mountains asleep in the sunrise, and dim mesas and escarpments in the distance, and ghosts of purple domes hauntingly vague. Lance was a man of the open, but the great distances, the vastness, the endless reach of wasteland allured while it repelled him. He rode on, and dust, heat, wind were his portion. Ranches, service stations, hamlets stretched lonesomely across the desert. He had lost track of days and miles beyond Yuma by the time he reached Florence. Tombstone with its preserved buildings of a hard frontier past, Bisbee with its great mines and bustle, Douglas, an enterprising and progressive town marked Lance's long ride across southern Arizona. Lance meant to strike off the main highway and railroad somewhere beyond Douglas into the ever-increasing rugged grandeur and beautiful valleys of this Arizona land. But his money, which he had thought would hold out for a much longer period, had dwindled to almost nothing, and it was now necessary that he stop and look for work. A rest would do Umpqua good. Lance found a Mexican who owned a small pasture outside of town and here he left the horse. In a pinch he could pawn his watch of gun, but he would have a try at finding work before resorting to that.

Lance accosted men in service stations and stores without any success. What he wanted to encounter was a cowboy. But this type appeared remarkably scarce. One man, evidently a cattleman, laughed gruffly at Lance: "Wal, son, thet kind of two-laiged critter has been aboot washed up on this range."

"You don't say. What by?" queried Lance, blankly.

"I reckon by hard times. North of heah a ways there's some cattle left. But down heah the only successful business is bootlegging."

That discouraged Lance, and he strolled around, slowly succumbing to the need of pawning his watch. Walking in high-heeled cowboy boots was not exactly a joy. It was noon and Lance was hot. Presently he heard voices near at hand, and turning discovered that he had halted close to a big black car, from which issued sharp voices. A second glance at that car struck him singularly. How like the black car that had followed the girl Madge to the parking place where he had chosen to avoid meeting her! With a pang he realized he had not thought of her for days. He was in another world. But this car! . . . Shiny black, without a gleam of metal anywhere, a fine high-priced machine, it certainly resembled. . . .

"Hey, buddy, come here," called a voice that shot through Lance. A young man, with pale face and eyes like gimlets, was leaning out of the front seat opposite the driver. Lance recognized him immediately. The young man Madge had designated as a gangster and who had called himself Honey Bee Uhl.

19

2

Lance advanced slowly, hiding an intense curiosity. Somehow he wanted to find out all he could about this fellow.

"Hello, yourself," he replied.

"You look sort of on the loose."

"Well, I look just what I am," Lance replied.

"No offense. We're loafing here for a guy, and I just wanted to be friendly. Care for a drink?"

"Not till I have a feed."

"Broke?"

"Flat as a pancake. And I can't find a job in this slow burg."

"Say, buddy, there's plenty jobs for the right guys. Can you drive a truck?"

"Mister, I could drive two trucks," retorted Lance, boastfully.

"Yeah? Well, how'd you like to grab a century?"

"Uhuh! Sounds good to me. I'd pull almost any kind of a job for that much dough. Only I'd want to be sure I was going to get it," laughed Lance.

"Exactly. It's okay. Now who are you and what have you been doing?"

"You never heard of me, mister," said Lance, evasively. "But I'll say I've been beating it from L.A."

"Dicks after you?"

Lance laughed grimly and looked blankly silent,

and averted his face somewhat from the piercing scrutiny bent upon him.

"Come clean with me, buddy, if you want your luck to change. What you been doing in L.A.?"

"Are you asking me, mister?"

"Yes, I am. It's not for you to ask *me* questions," replied Uhl, with impatient sharpness. "Take it or leave it."

"Aw, what the hell? I'm hungry. . . . I beat it out of Portland ahead of Latzy Cork," hazarded Lance, remembering the name of a shady underworld character who had recently been eluding the police on the coast.

"That racket, eh?" flashed Uhl, snapping his fingers. And with his eyes like gray fire he turned in the seat to his companions. Lance took advantage of this moment to make certain that he would recognize the driver of the car, and the three hard-faced individuals in the back seat, if he ever saw them again. At the side of the one farthest toward the road Lance espied the muzzle of a machine gun. "Cork may have been spotting me. What do you think, Dipper?"

"Not a chance, Bee. He's been in Frisco and north for two months," replied the one addressed.

"We don't know that," said Uhl, doubtfully, and turning again he pulled out a roll of bills, the wrapper of which bore the denomination one hundred. "Here's your dough, buddy. . . . You're on the spot. But the only risk you run is if you double-cross me."

"If I undertake the job, I'll be straight," interposed Lance.

"That's how you strike me. . . . See the big canvas covered truck across there, back of the service station? Well, she's your bus. You're to take her to Tucson. She's empty, but you drive slow, as if she was loaded heavy. See? You'll be held up sooner or later, probably after dark outside of Tuscon. That'll be okay. You're dumb. You just drove the truck over and you don't know me. See?"

"I don't know whether I see or not," rejoined Lance, dubiously. "Who'll hold me up—and why?"

"Say, you won't need to fake being dumb. All you

21

got to do is stop when you're held up, See? You don't know nothing."

"Does that truck belong to you?"

"Yes."

"Rumrunner?"

"I told you it was empty," snapped Uhl. "Is it a go?"

"You bet," declared Lance, taking the proffered money. "What'll I do when I get to Tucson?"

"You'll be on the main highway. Stop at the first service station on the edge of town. Right-hand side."

"Then what?"

"If I don't meet you someone else will."

"Suppose these holdup gents take the truck away from me?"

"That won't be your loss."

"Boss," interposed the sallow-faced Dipper, "this husky bird is packin' a rod."

"Say, are you telling me? I hope he turns cowboy with it on those dopes. . . . Buddy, if you turn this trick there'll be more."

"This one doesn't strike me so hot," declared Lance, tersely. "But one at a time. I'm on my way."

As Lance strode off, carefully pocketing the money he heard Uhl say: "Dip, if he comes through we'll take him on."

"No gamble, Boss. That fellow will do. . . "

Lance passed on out of earshot. At the station he said to the operator: "That truck ready?" Upon being informed that "she's all set," Lance climbed into the driver's seat and took a look. The machine was a fine make. As he moved out of the station yard he observed that the big black car had gone. Lance did not look to see what had become of it. A block away he turned into the highway and got through Douglas without a stop. Once beyond the town he opened up to twenty-five miles an hour and faced the north with a grim realization that he was in for an adventure he never would have hazarded but for a blonde college girl named Madge who had intrigued him.

"Queer setup," soliloquized Lance, now giving rein

to his conjectures. "I hit the bull's-eye with that crack about Latzy Cork. . . . Racket? Wonder which racket? Cork was suspected of most everything up north. . . . Anyhow I got away with it. . . . And this Bee Uhl. He's a crook all right. From Chi. . . . I get it. Chicago, of course. He doesn't seem to care who knows it. And this big truck must have to do with bootlegging. Over the border, maybe. Or up from some harbor on the Gulf. . . . Nothing to me. It gets my goat, though, what this slick bozo had to do with that girl.

Lance reflected presently that he ought to have that circumstance mastered. Madge's own words testified to that. She had flirted with Uhl, obviously for the thrill of it. She certainly knew he was a gangster. Perhaps that was the secret. A girl like her must be besieged by admirers, importuned and bored until she was tired of them. Still Uhl was handsome, and perhaps his hard and insolent way might have appealed to the girl. Assuredly that had been the inception of the affair. Lance felt glad to convince himself that she had realized her mistake, and in a thoroughbred but kindly way had made it clear to Uhl.

"But what in the hell did *she* want to fall for a guy like that?" bit out Lance, jealously. "Oh, be yourself, Lance!" Just because this Majesty, the student Rollie had called her, happened to be the loveliest and most fascinating girl Lance had ever met, was no reason for him to think her on the plane of the angels.

Lance did not need to bring back the vision of her. That was limned on his memory. No use faking it, he thought—he had fallen in love with her at first sight. That was all right. But he wished the thought and beauty and charm of her would not stick so tenaciously. He could not banish her and again came the regret that he had not stood right out like a man to meet her that day. He could at least have spared her the encounter with Uhl.

All at once Lance had a disturbing thought. Uhl, gangster, racketeer, bootlegger, might have another slant to his crookedness. He might be a kidnaper. That seemed reasonable enough, and the idea grew on

Lance. The girl must belong to a rich California family. Her style, her patrician air, her talk of a ranch full of Arabian horses, surely these attested wealth. And that might explain Bee Uhl's interest in her. With the near approach of repeal of prohibition these bootleggers must work up other rackets. Already there had been a nationwide activity in kidnaping.

"Goofy or not, I take it as a hunch," muttered Lance, with finality. "Believe me, I'll get a line on that slicker with his roll of centuries, if I can." And in the stress of the moment Lance thought that if he did verify such suspicion of the gangster, it would not be beyond him to go back to Los Angeles to warn the girl. Then the realization of his sudden tumult of delight made him look aghast at himself. "Quit your romancing, kid," he said. "This is hard pay. And I'm on a job I should have passed up."

But nothing he thought or reasoned out changed the essential sentiment and presagement of the situation. The way accidents and circumstances fell across his path and what came of them had taught him to believe any strange and far-reaching adventure could befall him.

Cars and trucks going and coming passed Lance now and then, the southbound traffic being the heavier. Lance did not see the big black automobile belonging to Uhl. Once he looked back down a league-long stretch, half expecting to discover the car following. But he did not.

Driving a truck did not permit of close attention to the desert scenery, which had been his pleasure while riding Umpqua. However, that labor and his concentration on the peculiar circumstances leading to this ride, certainly made the time fly. Almost before he knew it, he was climbing the tortuous grade through Bisbee, keeping keen lookout for the holdup he had been told to expect. About midafternoon he went through picturesque Tombstone on the outskirts of which he halted for gasoline. This necessitated his breaking the hundred dollar bill Uhl had given him. The service-station man, a westerner of middle age, glanced from the bill to Lance with keen blue eyes. "Seen bills like this before—an' also that truck you're drivin'. How aboot yore company?"

"Don't savvy," returned Lance, gruffly. "What you mean by company?"

"Wal, usualy thar's two or three trucks like this one strung along. Reckon you're new to . . ."

"To what, mister?" interrupted Lance.

"Wal, I ain't sayin'," responded the operator, in cool evasion.

"Yeah? Well, as a matter of fact, I'm damn new at this job."

That little wordy byplay roused Lance anew to the possibilities that might be thickening ahead of him. Thereafter he kept keen as a whip, increasing his speed a little. It was almost dark when he passed Mescal, a desert hamlet, and he did not halt to appease thirst or hunger. He wanted to get this job over. The desert night was soft and balmy, cooling as the radiation of the day's heat passed away. Jackrabbits and coyotes leaped across the road, gray in the flash of his lamps. The headlights of cars grew from pin points in the blackness to yellow orbs, rushing at him and passing by, to leave the distant road dark again. The dry odor of dust and desert growths clogged his nostrils. Under favorable circumstances Lance would have liked closer acquaintance with that desert. The spectral arms of cactus and the dense thickets of mesquite accentuated the lonesomeness.

Some miles beyond Vail there appeared to come a brightening of the north. Soon Lance made that out to be the lights of Tucson, miles away still, but clear in the rarefied atmosphere. Lance rolling along at forty miles or more an hour, began to feel an edge for the expected holdup. Every time he caught the gleam of headlights behind he prepared for the order to halt. But so many cars passed him the next hour and so bright grew the illuminated horizon that he began to believe he might reach the first service station on the right without being stopped.

Presently a car came up behind and held its place

25

for a couple of miles. Lance anticipated that this was the one, and he forced himself to be ready. He slowed down to thirty, then to twenty. The car kept behind him, somewhat to the left. At length it slipped up alongside Lance. "Hey, you driver. Halt!" rang out a hoarse voice. Lance shut off, and applying the brakes, screeched to a stop.

"*Stick 'em up!*" came from the car. A flashlight blinded Lance.

"Okay!" he yelled, complying with the order.

Two men leaped out and a door clicked. The car moved on ahead to come to a standstill in front of the truck. Lance's door was jerked open. Light flooded his cab. Over an extended gun he caught indistinct sight of two faces, the foremost of which was masked. Lance heard footsteps running back behind his truck and the clank of bolts.

"Bud, j'ever see this one before?" queried the bandit with the gun.

"Nope. Another new one," came the laconic answer.

"Who are you?" followed the demand.

"Arizona cowpuncher," replied Lance. "Broke. Agreed to drive this truck."

"Who hired you?"

"I don't know. Five men in a black car at Douglas."

From behind clanked the hinge and there was a slap of canvas. "Empty, by God!" cried a hoarse voice, in anger. Footsteps preceded the appearance of two more men, one of whom Lance managed to distinguish despite the blinding flashlight. "Henny, we're tricked. He's made suckers out of us again. This truck is empty."

"Ah, hell no!"

"Aw, hell yes! It's a cattle car. As late as yesterday, when we picked them cars up, this one was full of steers. The other one had the . . ."

"Shut up!" yapped the leader, pounding his gun on the door. "Hey, driver, how many trucks like this have you lamped lately?"

"Off and on I've seen a good many," rejoined

Lance, glibly. "Three in a row day before yester-day."

"Goin' which way?"

"North, out of Douglas."

"Ah ha! I *told* you, Henny," yelled the enraged bandit. "An' they'll all come back full of steers. He's took to buyin' steers. What you think of that? In the cattle bizness. A blind. Ha! Ha! An' it made a sucker out of you."

"Driver, is there a short cut to El Paso without goin' through Douglas?" queried the leader, sharply.

"Yes, at Benson," replied Lance, readily. "Poor road, but passable."

The leader snapped off his flashlight. "Beat it, cow-boy, wherever you're goin'. An' tell your boss we're onto his racket."

"Henny, if there's a short cut, no matter how bad, we might head off that car," rasped the man Bud. He had a bitter raucous voice that Lance would remem-ber. The four bandits ran to pile into their car. "Turn an' step on it!" ordered the leader. In another moment their car was roaring east on the highway, and Lance had a clear road ahead. Relieved, and more interested than ever, he threw in his clutch and sped on toward Tuscon. Lance saw that he had been used merely to throw this gang off the track. The cattle slant to the business seemed a trick that would take more than one carload of bandits to beat.

The run from that lonely stretch of road to the serv-ice station designated was accomplished in short order, Lance driving at a fast clip. The truck appeared to ooze along as smoothly as a limousine. Hardly had Lance come to a halt in the station yard when two men in dark garb, slouch hats pulled down, hurried out to meet him. Lance was ready for them, and open-ing the door he stepped out with a long whew of re-lief.

"Hello. Am I glad to see you? Take her away," he said, vociferously.

"Dey stick you up?" queried one, tensely, while the other leaped into the seat.

27

"You bet. About five miles out. You should have heard Bud and Henny cuss to find her empty. I gave them a bum steer."

"Yeah? An' how bum?"

"They asked me if there was a short cut to El Paso and I told them yes, at Benson. I heard it was some road. They'll get lost."

"Thet'll go hot with the boss. How much'd you dole out for gas? He forgot thet, an' told me to square it."

Lance named the sum, which was handed to him in a five dollar note and no change wanted.

"Blick, have we got all night?" demanded the man in the driver's seat. "Cut it."

"Keep your shirt on. Honey Bee gave me an order, didn't he? . . . Driver, yer come through clean. I'm to tell you thet if you're hangin' round Douglas next run, you can get another job."

"Swell. I'll hang around, if it's not too long. When's the next run?"

"I don't know. Mebbe in a month—mebbe longer."

When they had gone Lance went into the service station, aware that his arrival and the short conference had been observed.

"How far to a hash joint? I'm sure starved," he began, genially.

"Stranger hereabouts?" the man returned, with a keen look. "Plenty grub places up the street."

"Thanks. Yes, I'm a stranger. And I don't mind telling you I drove that truck because I was broke. I was held up out here and scared stiff."

"You don't say. Well, that's not strange considerin' the company. You got off lucky."

"Yeah? What was I up against?"

"Couldn't say."

"Did you ever see that truck before?"

"Yep, an' some more like it. They been comin' and goin' every six weeks or so."

"Cattle business must be good when steers get hauled in trucks," commented Lance; then waiting a moment for an answer, which did not come, he strode up the street. In the middle of the second block he found a café, where he obtained his supper. At the next corner there was a hotel. Inquiry brought the information that he could take a bus early next morning for Douglas. Then he went to bed. Events of the day had been thought-provoking, but they did not keep him awake.

On the bus the following morning, however, he had nothing to do but think. It took Lance practically all that long ride to reason out the futility of any further interest in Uhl. Lance did not want to drive any more questionable trucks. Aside from an interesting experience, this meeting with Uhl had no warrant to absorb him. It was the singular connection with the college girl that kept him wondering and conjecturing, and thinking that he should warn her somehow. But he did not even know her last name. And to go back to Los Angeles on such a fanciful assumption seemed absurd. Nevertheless his conscience bothered him. That passed, however, leaving Lance with only the increasing pang of regret. When at Douglas he went out to see Umpqua, and quite provokingly he conceived a picture of Madge on his beautiful horse, he almost gave way to rage at his sentimentality. All the same, thought of the girl persisted, and Lance finally reconciled himself to being haunted.

Riding northeast from Douglas the Arizona desert land magnified its proportions of color and wildness and rugged grandeur to such a degree that Lance was loath to travel on and turn his back to ranges that dwarfed those he had ridden in Oregon. What a grand country he was entering! Ahead of him were mountains, peaked and lofty, purple in the distance, growing black and gray as league after league he neared them. Lance took his time stopping to ask questions, but the several little hamlets along the way failed to yield much information. He spent one night at Chiricahua, which town appeared to be in the center of a vast green and gray range surrounded by mountains. He had begun to see cattle in considerable numbers, though not one hundredth as many as the country might have supported. He rode on and on over a rolling and lovely valley.

Darkness overtook Lance. He had inquired at Apache about towns farther north. He had been told they were few and far between. It looked as though his preoccupation with the solitude and beauty of this upland valley was going to make him spend a night in the open. He did not mind that. The day had been hot and the night still remained warm. However, three hours after sunset he sighted lights ahead and soon entered a place called Bolton. Unlike most of the other towns, this one appeared to be comparatively new and located on both highway and railroad. There was a wide main street with bright lights and many parked cars, stores and cafés, a hotel and an inn, a bank and motion-picture theater. Lance rode on through to the outer zone of garages and autocamps. Umpqua, staunch as he was, had begun to tire. Lance was pleased to see several horses tethered beyond a garage off the main street, and next a livery stable. The garage, evidently, also provided the facilities of a service station and was quite modest compared to showy places Lance had passed.

"Howdy, cowboy," drawled a pleasant voice. "Git down an' come in."

"Hello, yourself," replied Lance, greeting a sturdy bowlegged young man who had appeared from somewhere. There was enough light to make out a lean tanned face from which shone narrow slits of eyes, keen and friendly.

"My Gawd!—Where'd you steal thet hawse?" queried this individual.

"Are you kidding me or is that the way horsemen are greeted here?" asked Lance.

"Shore kiddin', cowboy. We got some grand hawses in this country an' thet's why I got fresh. But on the level where *did* you find him?"

"Oregon bred. He was given us when he was a colt. And I raised him."

"You from Oregon?" went on the other, walking around the horse in a way that betrayed a love of horseflesh. It was an open sesame to Lance's friend-liness.

"Yes, rode him all the way."

"Don't tell. I'll be dog-goned. . . . Wal, lookin' him over I ain't so surprised. All hawse, cowboy, an' I'd trade you my garage for him."

"Sounds cowboy," laughed Lance.

"Shore I was—I *am* a cowboy. Been ridin' Arizona ranges all my life. But these hard times I had to make a livin' for my mother an' me."

"Gee, that's bad news. I came to Arizona to find a job with some cattle outfit."

"Wal, you're jest outa luck. Cowboys air scarce these days. As scarce as jobs. Plenty of cattle all through heah. An' the outfits thinned down to two or three riders. My job for three years before this bust-up hit us was with Gene Stewart. Finest rancher in these parts. Used to run eighty thousand haid. But of late years Gene has lost out. An' as I couldn't ride no more for nothin' I had to take this place. Pays fair, but I just hate it."

"Don't blame you. . . . How about me bedding down Umpqua in this livery stable?"

"*Umpqua?* What a name! Where'n hell did you git thet?"

"It's Indian. Name of a river in Oregon. Means swift."

"Swell handle at thet. Shore, this stable is okay. I'll go in with you. . . . What'd you say your name was? Mine's Ren Starr."

"I didn't say yet. It's Lance Sidway."

"Air you gonna hang about heah a spell?"

"Yes, if I can find work."

The livery stable man turned out to be an old fel-low with an unmistakable cattle range air about him. He was almost as enthusiastic over Umpqua as Starr had been. For the first time in a long while Lance began to feel at home with his kind.

"Ump, old boy, this barn smells good, doesn't it?" said Lance, and giving his pet a parting smack he went out with Starr. "Where can I eat and sleep?"

"Several places, but outside the hotel, you'll like Mrs. Goodman's café. Nice woman, dotes on cowboys, an' runs a swell little chuck house."

"Won't you come with me? I'd like to talk."

"Wal, shore. I've had my supper. But I can always eat. An' it's closin' time for my place anyway."

Presently Lance was ushered into a clean fragrant little shop, with more of a homey than a café look, and introduced to a portly woman of kind and genial aspect. Evidently she had a warm spot in her heart for cowboys.

"Wal, Oregon, I'd shore like to see you stop heah," said Starr, eagerly. Manifestly he had taken to Lance as Lance had to him.

"All the way up from Apache I've liked the range more and more."

"Hell, this ain't nothin'. You ought to see thet range down along the west slope of the Peloncillo Mountains. Swell deer an' antelope huntin'. Bear an' cougar up high. Trout fishin', oh boy! Grass an' sage ranges."

"Sounds more than swell. Is that where your Gene Stewart runs cattle?"

"Used to, when he had ten outfits. But now he's only got about a thousand haid left, not countin' yearlin's an' calves. He jest lets them graze around his ranch, with a couple of Mexican kids ridin' for him."

"How far away is his ranch?"

"I reckon about thirty by trail. The road runs round an' up an' down. Cars register forty-two miles. No road work this spring makes tough goin', an' I don't mean mebbe."

"Wonder what chance I'd have getting on with him? Wages no object for a while. I want to ride open country, and have a square meal often, with pasture for Umpqua. You see he was raised to fare for himself. Alfalfa and grain would spoil him."

"My idee of trainin' a hawse right. . . . I'll tell you, Sidway, there's a pretty shore chance for you out with Gene. He needs riders most damn bad. I'll give you a note to him in the mawnin'. Thet'll cinch it, if you really want a job for nothin' 'cept board. He'll be glad.

Only you gotta approach him sorta careful. . . . Sensitive fellow, Gene is, but the salt of this range. For two bits I'll sell out an' go with you."

"That'd be swell. Why don't you?"

"It'd be all right with Mom. She wants to get out of this hot country for a while. But I'm makin' money an' I reckon I ought to save plenty before hittin' the trail again."

"All right, Ren. Thanks for the hunch. I'll go. Maybe we can see each other sometimes. I'd like that."

"Me too. Shore we can. Gene would give you a Sunday off now an' then. I'd run out after you."

"What kind of ranch does Stewart own?"

"Gee whiz! I reckoned every puncher in the West had heahed of it. Close to the border. Used to belong to a Mexican named Don Carlos. He was shot long before I come to this part of Arizona. I was hardly borned then. But I've heahed the story. Durin' the Mexican Revolution around twenty-five years ago Don Carlos had thet ranch. It was a Spanish grant. An' he was sellin' contraband along the border. Gene Stewart was a tough cowboy them days. Great with the rope an' hawse—a daid shot—an' nerve, say! they didn't come no cooler than thet *hombre*. Wal, he joined up with the revolutionists. They called him *El Capitan*. After Madero was assassinated Gene come back heah. About thet time a rich girl from Noo Yoork come along. She bought Don Carlos' Ranch. Stillwell, the foreman then, corralled the hardest bunch of cowboys thet ever rode a range. But nobody could boss them until he put Gene on the job. They run Don Carlos an' his band off the range. An' they made thet ranch the finest in the West. It's as beautiful as ever, but turrible run down these last two years . . . Wal, Gene married his boss, the rich girl from the East, an' was thet a romance!"

"Darned interesting, Ren. I'm going to like Stewart."

"You shore will, an' if you turn out as good as you look—excuse me bein' personal—Gene is goin' to cotton to you. He was grand to me. An' I just love him

33

as if he was my dad. He always stops in to see me, hopin' I'll come back. But he never says so. He was in town today, worried plain about somethin'. He said it was only cause he was losin' a few cattle."

"Cattle thieves?" exclaimed Lance, quickly.

"Rustlers over heah, Sid."

"No!"

"Shore. There's still some rustlin' all over. Nothin' heah like it used to be. But you see a dozen haid to Gene now means more'n a thousand, years ago. He was sore because he couldn't find out how the cattle was stole. An' old Nels, the last of thet great outfit of cowboys, couldn't find out either."

"Too old-fashioned, maybe."

"Dog-gone, Sid. I had thet very idee."

"Say, Starr," spoke up Lance, as if with an inspiration. "Not so many days ago I drove a big truck from Douglas to Tucson. It was empty but it had been full of steers."

Lance related briefly the circumstances that made it necessary for him to earn some money, but he did not go into detail about the men he had met on that adventure.

"Wal, I'm a son-of-a-gun! . . . What kind of a truck?"

"A big one, fine make, and canvas-covered. I took the license number and the name of the owner. Which I suspect is not the name of the right owner."

"Sidway, you're sayin' things," rejoined Starr, growing cool after his excitement. "I've seen three or four trucks like thet one pass heah every month or so. One went through north four days ago."

"Did you pay any particular attention to it?"

"No. Only saw it an' was sore as usual 'cause the driver got gas from one of the other stations. You see them fellers never have bought a gallon of gas from me. Thet's okay, shore. My place is as you saw it."

"Starr, they passed you up because you were a cowboy."

"You don't say! Thet's an idee. A hot one."

"Something I heard on my drive gives me a hunch

34

now that these truck men bought cattle as a blind. Perhaps of late they *steal* cattle. All kinds of business pretty punk these days."

"Pard, you are a whiz," ejaculated Starr, intensely. "Rackin' my haid I figger thet I haven't seen them trucks go through heah *southbound* since last fall. They do go through, shore. I been told thet. But late in the night."

"We got something to work on."

"I should smile. I'll grow curious as hell. Sid, this heah is goin' to be most damn interestin' to Gene. You tell him pronto. All about them trucks."

"You bet. And, Starr, if I get in with Stewart I'll send you the receipt and money to send for my baggage in Los Angeles."

"Glad to fetch it out. . . . Wal, I reckon you ought to hit the hay. Your eyes look tired. Come on an' I'll take you to the hotel. Most as reasonable as autocamps, an' good."

On the way across the street Starr said: "There's shore a lot to tell you about Stewart, his ranch an' all. But I cain't think of everythin' all to oncet. . . . You'll find Mrs. Stewart jest swell. Still handsome an' the nicest woman! I most forgot their daughter. No wonder, 'cause I haven't seen her for nearly four years. She was only a kid then. But could she cock her eye at a man? Had all the cowboys dotty. *Me!* I reckoned I had the inside track 'cause she let me kiss her oncet. But I was wrong, Sid. Thet girl was a hells-rattler, but straight as a string. Jest full of fem. . . . Wal, Gene told me today thet she was comin' home. He was plumb excited over thet. Worships the girl! An' mebbe he was worryin' about her too. . . . Sid, if I remember thet girl she will keep you awake nights."

"Not much," declared Lance with a laugh. "Boy, I've been in Hollywood for a spell, hobnobbing with the prettiest and slickest girls in the world."

"Hollywood? My Gawd, what'll you spring on me next? Sid, you are goin' to relieve the tedium of my days. . . . Did you fall for any of them stars?"

"Ren, I fell with a dull thud for three. And not

stars, either. Just extras prettier than the stars. Harder every fall! And I can't imagine *me* falling for a ranch girl. No offense, boy. My sister is a ranch girl and she's my pride. *But* you can get what I mean, if you go to the flickers."

"You mean movies? I go every show an' sometimes twice."

"Then you know how safe I'll be on an Arizona ranch."

"Safe out heah, *if* she doesn't come home, which I don't believe she will? Pard, I wouldn't gamble on thet. . . . Wal, heah's your hotel. I'll be sayin' *adios* till mawnin'. I'm shore glad we met, Lance."

"So am I, Ren. It's just swell. See you early tomorrow. Don't forget to write that note to Stewart. Good night."

Lance went to bed glowingly excited and satisfied with the day's happenings, and its promise. Particularly was he pleased at finding the ex-cowboy, Starr. Lance thought he would be a fellow to tie to. Luck had attended this adventuring into a new and far country.

After an early breakfast next morning Lance made his first Arizona purchases, which consisted of a new riding outfit, and a much needed shaving kit and sevrly other articles. His discarded things he tied in his old coat, so that he could carry the bundle conveniently on his saddle. When he presented himself at Starr's garage, that worthy stared in comical surprise.

"Mawnin' Sid," he drawled. "What you been about? All dolled up. My Gawd! I hadn't no idee you was such a handsome galoot. On thet hawse you'll knock 'em cold. Say! I've a hunch you've either seen or heahed about Gene Stewart's daughter."

"Nope, I haven't. But I needed some clean duds and a shave," explained Lance. "Couldn't ask for a job looking like a tramp."

"I ain't so shore, Sid," returned Starr, doubtfully. "Gene likes 'em tough. Why, with thet red scarf an' all you look like Buck Jones."

"Ren, I bought the least gaudy outfit that storekeeper had," protested Lance. "If you think I should change back to . . ."

"Aw, I was half kiddin'. You look okay. In fact you look grand. But no cowpuncher can fool Gene Stewart. He'll see right through you, Sid. An' I'll bet my shop he'll take to you same as I did."

"Well, then, what the hell . . ."

"Thet's it. What the hell will come off if you run plumb into Gene's daughter? She's on her way home. Gene told my mother so yesterday."

"Ren, you certainly harp on that subject. Is the heart of Miss Stewart all you're concerned with?" queried Lance, facetiously.

"Hell no! I'm jest concerned about what'll happen to you, if she sees you. An' in this new outfit you shore stand out from the landscape."

"Like all the Arizona cowboys, aren't you?" went on Lance. "Oh, I knew a lot of them in Hollywood. Swell fellows, but simply nuts on jokes . . . . . . and girls! . . . Next to that they liked t. . . . . . . il bet you five bucks *I* don't even see your Arizona cowgirl queen. . . . Man, I've lived in Hollywood for over a year."

"So you told me before," replied Starr dryly. "Thet bet's on. Heah's your note to Gene Stewart. I shore hope you turn out half as good as my recommendation."

"Thanks, Ren. I hope I make good. Now tell me how to find this wonderful ranch."

"Go out the highway, south, of course. Take the first road—it's a dirt road—turnin' left. Stick on thet for about five miles, till you come to a bridge over a crick. Lots of green willows. Anyway, it's the first bridge you come to, so you cain't miss it. There's a trail thet follers the crick, on the right-hand side. Hit thet trail, pard, an' good luck to you."

"How'll I know the ranch when I come to it?"

"Hell! it's the only ranch out there. The house, old Spanish style, sets on a knoll among trees. Walls used to be white. But you can see it from the divide, ten miles away."

37

In very short order Lance was out of Bolton on a road that seemed to climb and lose itself in gray obscurity. Umpqua, scenting something out there, the sage and the open, perhaps, settled down to his fast ground-gaining trot. Lance saw on his right where the highway, a shining ribbon, followed the railroad and line of telegraph poles off to the southwest across the desert. On his left, beyond the green willows bordering the brook, an occasional humble ranch, or adobe Mexican house, gave life to a range gradually growing wilder as he proceeded. Ahead of him on the horizon mountain ranges stood up, some bold, others dim. Lance's quick eye caught sight of romping jack rabbits and sneaking coyotes, and the white rumps of deer-like animals he concluded were antelope.

Eventually the trail left the brook. Dwarf cedar trees and a line of pale purple marked the zone of sage. Lance was familiar with Oregon and California sage, but neither had the luxuriance and fragrance of this Arizona brand, Umpqua manifestly liked the smell of it. There seemed to be a tang and a zest in this clear air. The sun became hot on Lance's back; heat veils arose like smoke from the ground; the peaks that had been sharp against the blue appeared to dim in haze. Down to the right, toward the road Lance could still see, herds of cattle dotted the gray. The trail, however, headed more to the left, toward rising land, and rugged bits of outcropping rocks red in color, and back clumps of cedars.

By noonday Lance calculated that he had covered at least twenty miles, two thirds of the distance to Stewart's ranch; and soon he had surmounted the divide Starr had mentioned. The scene was so splendid that Lance halted to gaze and gaze spellbound. He saw a moving dust line from a car creeping across this vast gray-purple bowl under him which must be the southern end of Bernardino Valley. Rocky areas and clumps of cedars and darker patches of trees relieved the monotony of that range, sweeping away and upward to the mountains that must be the Peloncillos. Then Lance's keen eyes sighted the forested knoll and the old Spanish mansion built by Don Carlos. Ten miles away still, it appeared to stand out with a magnificence that Starr had hinted of. A lake, blue as a gem, shone in the sun, and its circle of green let out a branch that wound down across the gray, to make a wide bend around the rocky ridge Lance had surmounted. This, of course, was the stream he had encountered below. It was a big country. How vast this country must be when here lay only a mountain-walled valley! Heading down the trail Lance thought gravely, yet somehow with exaltation, that he was won forever. He would find or make a home there, and felt that he owed Ren Starr infinite gratitude.

By midafternoon Lance rode into a pretty little Mexican village at the foot of the knoll. Columns of blue smoke arose slowly. The half-naked children, the burros and dogs, the natives in colored raiment watching idly from the low porches, all appeared to have a leisurely air. Lance ventured a question to one group. An exceedingly pretty Mexican girl, whose big dark eyes shone bright and roguishly upon Lance replied to him: *"Buenos dias, señor."*

"No savvy. Can't you talk United States?" asked Lance, mildly, smiling at the girl.

"Yes, cowboy, Mr. Stewart is home."

"Thank you, *señorita*. I think I'm going to like it here."

Her dusky eyes snapped with mischief, and quick as their flash she retorted: "It didn't take you long, *señor*."

Riding away up the gentle slope Lance cogitated that remark of the Mexican lass's. "Say! what did she mean? Can't make out, but sure she was kidding me. Some little peach! Okay by me, *señorita*. I'll be seeing you."

Lance had not proceeded beyond where the road turned up the wooded knoll when a boy overtook him to inform him that *Señor* Stewart was at the corrals, toward which he pointed. Lance threw him a quarter, and kept to the right along the base of the knoll, to

39

come at length into view of log barns and sheds and corrals, a long mossy-roofed bunkhouse, old and weathered, picturesquely falling to decay. A piercing whistle from an unseen horse brought a snort from Umpqua. Lance rode down a lane of tumble-down poles, to turn into a kind of court, at the immediate right of which stood a blacksmith shop; in front of this were several Mexican riders, and a thoroughbred black horse so glossy and well-groomed that he did not appear to belong there. Then a tall white man stepped out from behind the horse. He had a superb build, a dark intent face, deeply lined, piercing dark eyes, and there was white hair over his temples. Lance did not need to be told that this was Gene Stewart. As Lance rode up he caught first a relaxing of this stern face into a smile that warmed it attractively, and then a keen interest in both rider and horse.

"Howdy, cowboy," the rancher greeted Lance, in pleasant deep voice. "You got the jump on them."

"Who . . . what," stammered Lance. "Are you Gene Stewart?"

"Yes, I'm Stewart. And who're you?"

"Lance Sidway. I want a job."

"Fine . . . May I ask if you have been recommended by my daughter?"

"No—indeed, sir," replied Lance, recalling Starr's talk and suddenly filled with dismay. "I don't know your daughter."

"That's quite possible. But might not her return home today have something to do with your asking for a job?" asked Stewart, with a twinkle in his piercing eyes.

"It might, judging from the Arizona cowboys I've met," rejoined Lance, recovering coolness at the fun evidently enjoyed at his expence. "But in my case it hasn't."

"Indeed? Well, in your case then Ill listen."

"Here's my letter of introduction," went on Lance, producing it.

Stewart opened and read it, suddenly to beam upon

Lance. "Pard of Starr's, eh? You sure can't be all Ren says. But if you're anyways near as good . . ."

"Excuse me, Stewart," interposed Lance, hurriedly. "I'm not sailing under false colors. Starr doesn't know me any better than you do. Met him only last night! We liked each other right off. He told me you might take me on. Offered a letter of introduction."

"I see. That's like Ren. Get down and come in."

Lance stepped out of the saddle to drop the bridle. Stewart spoke to one of the admiring native lads: "Pedro, water him and rub the dust off him. . . . Cowboy, you've a grand horse. I can't see a fault in him. Any rancher in the West would give you a job to get a chance to buy him or steal him."

"Umpqua is swell," replied Lance, as the rancher led him to a seat on the porch of what appeared to be a store.

"Nels, come out," called Stewart, into the wide-open door of the old building. Receiving no answer he said plaintively: "Nels must be out back with my daughter, looking at her horses. Cowboy, you'll have hell keeping that horse."

"Oh, I see," laughed Lance, thrilled at the intimation that the rancher might take him on. "Any girl who loves horses would want Umpqua, naturally. But she'll have to take me with him.

"Old-time cowboy spirit! I was that way, once. . . . Where you from?"

Lance briefly told of his home in Oregon, his experience on the ranges there, modestly enumerating his abilities and skipping the Hollywood experience.

"Did you ever hear of this range and my ranch?"

"Only from Starr. It'd be a great place to work. Please give me a trial, Stewart."

"I'd sure like to," returned the rancher, kindly but gravely. "Once I had the best and wildest outfit on the border. But times have changed. . . . Starr says in his note that wages are no object."

"I'll be glad to work for my board."

"Are you rich?"

"Lord, no! I have a few dollars in my pocket. And Umpqua. Yes, I should have said I am rich."

"Sidway, I couldn't let you work for nothing."

"But sir, if it's money don't let that keep you from hiring me," importuned Lance.

"Tell me straight. I'll like you better if you confess you want this job on account of Madge."

"Madge!—Who's she? Oh, of course, your daughter . . . . Mr. Stewart, on my honor I swear I never heard of her until Starr raved about her last night."

"But that might have been enough. You're cowboy brand, all over."

"It wasn't enough. It wasn't anything. Women are not in my troubles."

"Don't perjure yourself. Girls are always cowboys' troubles. . . . I'll take you on, Sidway, and pay you a few dollars a month till the cattle business looks up."

"Thank you. I'll sure do my best for you."

"Did Ren mention he might come back to me?"

"Yes, he did. He wants to. I'll bet he'll come, soon as he saves a little more money."

"I hate to ask him. But with you hard-riding youngsters to help me and Danny, and my *vaqueros* we might save the herd. You see, Sidway, there's been some queer rustling. . . ."

Stewart was interrupted by a sweet high-pitched voice that came from round the corner of the porch, down the lane.

"*Nels!* . . . For Pete's sake look at this black horse! . . . Oh, what a beauty!—Oh! Oh!"

Clinking spurs attested to the slow steps of a rider.

"Well, lass, I never set eyes on thet hawse before," drawled a quaint voice. "You'll shore hate me when I say he's got yore nags beat to a frazzle."

"Nonsense!—But he *is*. . . . Nels, I want him. I'll have him if it costs ten thousand. . . . Dad! *Dad!*"

Stewart whispered: "Step around and tell her here's one horse she can't buy. It'll be fun."

"Certainly, sir," replied Lance, dubiously. It was his first order from his boss. Besides he seemed curiously struck by the situation or that sweet voice. As he moved to the corner he heard pattering footsteps. Then a vision flashed into sight to plump squarely into his arms.

"Oh!" she screamed, and staggering, would have fallen had she not caught Lance with swift hand. A girl—bareheaded—golden hair flying—lovely flushed face, strangely familiar—violet eyes widening, darkening! "Who on earth? . . . *You!* . . . Of all the miracles! If it isn't my hero!"

Lance recognized her. His girl of the campus adventure and the mad ride through the streets of Los Angeles. As she enveloped him, with gay trill, and her red lips came up nearer to meet his in a cool sweet kiss, his breast seemed to cave in.

3

It was along about sunset when Gene Stewart drove into the courtyard of his ranch. The drive out from Bolton, despite the old car, had seemed short, and for once he had failed to enjoy the magnificent range that he had loved so well for over thirty years. That day the many familiar spots, memorable of the wild past, failed to start the old dreams. Even the adobe ruins of the Mexican village where Madeline had importuned him to abandon his bad habits and come to work for her, failed for once to remind him of the turning point, the blessed uplift of his life. Trouble indeed gloomed Gene Stewart's eyes when he could not see the sage flat where, bitter and hopeless, he had pulled Madeline off her horse, and knowing that she was secretly his wife, that though she did not dream of it, she was his, and he was leaving her forever, to ride out on his old hard-shooting, hard-drinking trail to get himself killed, he had kissed her with the mocking passion of renunciation. When Gene, passing the place, did not remember that, though it had been over twenty years ago, he was indeed sore distraught with worries.

Nels, the old Texan who was the last of his great riders of that earlier and wilder day, sat on the porch of the store, smoking and waiting. Gene seemed to see that white head, and the narrow eagle eyes, the lean lined face, with a rare and shocking sense of their age. Nels must be close to seventy now. And all the West showed its life and havoc under that mild mask of tranquillity.

"Wal, you're late, Gene, an' come draggin' along like you was on a bogged hawse," remarked Nels.

"Yes, old-timer," replied Gene, wearily, as he sat down on the porch, a folded newspaper in his hand.

"What's on yore chest?"

"Things have gone from bad to worse, Nels."

"Heahed from Majesty?" queried the old cowman, eagerly.

"Letter and telegram to me. More for Madeline. . . . Madge is on her way home. For good!"

"You don't say?—Aw! Then nothin' can be bad," replied Nels, settling back with an air of beautiful relief.

"Bad news from Madge, Nels. But let that go for the moment. There are lesser evils. Lawson has gone into bankruptcy. No hope of the money he owes me. I had banked on that. My creditors are pressing. Money must be raised."

"Any better market for cattle?"

"Gone down to thirty dollars on the hoof."

"Boss, I reckon I'd sell."

"All the herd?" queried Gene, in surprise. Nels would be the last cattleman to sacrifice all his stock. There was not in Arizona a keener judge of matters pertaining to cattle.

"Every horn an' hide, Gene."

"But that is an unheard of thing for a rancher to do," protested Stewart.

"Shore. How aboot these times? Onheard of, ain't they? Never in my life have I seen the like. Lookin' far ahaid, Gene, I'll predict thet the day of the big cattleman is over."

"Unthinkable!" ejaculated Stewart. The idea somehow hurt him. "What warrant have you for such a prediction?"

"Government interference, sure as shootin'. Then the range land grows less an' less every year. Last an' wust, we already have Argentine meat comin' heah to the U.S., cheaper than we can raise it. Gene, we're in for bum years. I've got a hunch."

"I always respected your hunches, Nels," replied Stewart, testily. "But this seems preposterous."

"Gene, jest how bad in debt air you?"

"I haven't the nerve to figure it up," replied Stewart, evasively.

"Wal, if you sold oot at thirty you could pay up, an' then tide over ontil good times come again. If we live thet long!"

"I might consider selling half my stock," rejoined Stewart, thoughtfully.

"You're the boss. An' you asked my opinion. I forgot to tell you thet Danny Mains rode up today. He ain't makin' oot with his cattle raisin'. Been losin' too many steers. An' Danny is afeared thet the Mexicans air doin' the stealin'."

"But how could a few Mexicans, even if they were crooked, get rid of cattle without leaving any sign?"

"I don't know, Gene. But there's shore somethin' doin'. All of Bonita's relatives cain't be good. Some of them won't be good until they're daid. Danny's got a fine wife in Bonita, an' shore a dandy girl in their daughter, young Bonita. But thet's aboot all. And he's scared of her relatives. Asked me plumb oot what to do?"

"And what'd you say, Nels?"

"Wal, I told him to sell. An' when he bucked on

45

thet I advised him to throw in with you. Then if you hired a couple of good cow hands we could beat this game. At least the stealin' end. Thet's the profit-eatin' cussed part of it."

"Not a bad suggestion, Nels. But what'd we pay hired cow hands with?"

"Aw shucks, Gene! It cain't be thet bad with you," complained Nels, plaintively.

"I'm sorry, old-timer. But it *is*. I hate to face Madeline. And especially with this." Stewart unrolled the newspaper he had twisted in his hands and spread one over the old cowman's knees. Nels took out his glasses, and adjusting them he read slowly:

COLLEGE CAMPUS RIOT

Co-ed Expelled for Inciting Riot Between Students and Police

"Wall, I'll be . . . !" he ejaculated, jerking up his fine white head. Gene had seen those blue eyes flash fire many a time, though hardly ever like this. Nels divined the truth and his affections were attacked.

"Majesty?"

"Yes, I'm damn sorry to say. But read what it says, Nels."

"Aw!"

Gene watched that fine lined face as Nels laboriously read the half column in the newspaper. He had seen Nels face death many times and deal it often, with never a gray shade creep over his features nor a convulsive quiver, such as were visible now for a fleeting instant. And he remembered that it was Nels who loved Madge as well as her own father, it was Nels who had long years ago named the imperious child Majesty, who had put her upon a horse and taught her to ride. Nels folded up the newspaper and handed it back.

"Gene, I'd give somethin' to throw a gun on the cuss who wrote thet."

"Nonsense, Nels. Are you crazy? This is 1932."

"Why hell yes! And there's more shootin' in the

U.S. now than when we come first to this range, thirty years ago for you an' more for me. . . . He's a damn liar, Gene."

"Who? The writer of this article?"

"Yes. I don't believe a word of thet dirty part. Aboot her bein' wild, rich, an' as hard a drinker as she was a speed demon. Gene, don't you believe thet an' fer Gawd's sake, don't tell Madeline."

"I'm sort of sunk, Nels. Kind of a last blow. I don't know what to think. Madge's letter admits it. Honest, right out! And her telegrams say she's on the way home to stay."

"Gosh! Thet's the best news I've heahed fer a long time."

"It is good news, Nels. It hurts, though. Looks kind of like disgrace is responsible."

"Aw no, Gene. Why, Majesty loves this range, this house where she was born. It's home."

"I don't know my own girl," sighed Stewart. "Remember, Nels, I haven't laid eyes upon Madge for over three years. You know I was in Mexico the last time she came home. And the summer before that she went to Europe."

"Wal, I have. An' I'm gamblin' on her, Gene. Wild as a young filly, shore she was. But good as gold an' as true as steel. When she was heah last I had some jars, you bet. I had to figger oot thet times had changed since you an' me ran after girls. We've stayed right in one spot, Gene, an' this old world has moved on."

"Right. I'll bet you we have it coming to us. Madge said in her letter she was having a crowd of college friends come to visit her."

"Fine. She did thet last time an' I never had such fun."

"Nels, you're a hopeless old fool. Madge will have you eating out of her hand. But I'm her father!"

"Shore. An' I'm gonna have fun oot of you, Gene."

Gene slowly walked up the winding green-bordered path toward the ranch house. He had not told Nels all his worries. As a matter of fact he was both overjoyed

47

at the prospect of Madge's return and greatly dismayed. A crowd of college friends!

Mockingbirds and quail and robins and magpies were rustling and chattering in the thick pines. The last rays of the setting sun burned gold on the flowering vines and the open weathered walls and arches of the old Spanish mansion. The fragrance of roses mingled with that of pine, and the soft sage wind from off the range. Gene felt the fact that the grounds, the great adobe structure, were more beautiful than ever. But the evidence of decay struck Gene most forcibly this evening. The trellises were falling down; the planking of the porches had rotted through in places, the weathering of plaster showed the adobe bricks.

Passing through the high archway at the rear of the house, Gene entered the patio. It appeared a dusky jungle of dark verdure, running water, drowsy twittering of sleepy birds, and odorous fragrance. A savory smell wafted from the kitchen where he heard the servants talking in their low voices. When Gene crossed the wide porch to enter Madeline's sitting room, the newspapers to which Nels had objected did not show among the large quantity of mail. Madeline had heard his step on the porch and had come to meet him. Love for this patrician woman who as a girl had forsaken the East to make his country and his life hers, and pride in her well-preserved beauty and charm, seemed to be strong and moving emotions at the moment when these disclosures about their only child had to be made. Would Madge be another Madeline? There was gray visible in Madeline's hair and lines had begun to show in the handsome face. But the light in her lustrous eyes appeared as soft and glad as in her youth.

"Gene!" she exclaimed, kissing him. "A whole day late! . . . You look tired—worried."

"Howdy, Madeline," replied Gene, laying the bundles and packets of mail on the table. "Yes, I'm tired —and worried. Bad news, Wife. It never rains but it pours. Lawson failed, Madeline. Gone into bankruptcy. No hope of money. I'll have to sell some stock. Nels advises selling all my herd. . . . That's nothing though.

I've got a big surprise for you. Madge is coming home."

"Madge! Coming home? Why? What has she done now, Gene?" rejoined Madeline, quietly.

"Got herself expelled from college," Gene blurted out, knowing that he should have broken the news more gently, but incapable of the guile necessary to spare his wife's feelings.

"Oh, no! Not on the eve of her graduation? June eleventh."

"Yes. It's tough, but maybe not so bad as it seems. Here's her letter and telegrams to me. Read them before you open yours."

Gene went into his office, which adjoined the sitting room, turned on the lights, and laid all his unopened mail, and some business papers upon his table. Then he repaired to his room to wash and change for the evening meal. He took plenty of time about this, his thoughts under the dominance of gloom. Presently Madeline called him to supper, and he found her in the dining room. If he had expected her to be cast down he was agreeably surprised.

"I ought to be hungry," he said. "Most forgot to eat in town." And he asked Madeline questions pertaining to the ranch during his absence. Nothing had happened. The drowsy languorous summer had come and the tranquil tenor of the lonely range land had not been broken. When Gene had finished a hearty meal he suggested that they go into the sitting room and get it over.

"Dear, it will never be over until you change your habit of mind," she replied, sweetly. "You always look upon the dark side."

"Madeline, this time of trouble has brought back the Gene Stewart of other and darker days."

"It should not. You have made me perfectly happy for more than twenty years. Loss of money, for you and me, is nothing."

"Madeline, I could take my losses without. . . . But it's yours that distress me. All your life you have had luxury. You were born to it. This last year and

49

more you've been using your money to pad Madge's bank account. She keeps overdrawing her income and you keep from telling her that her income isn't one with what it was. Now through me and that spend-thrift girl of ours you must suffer. When the depression hit us you should have told Madge the truth. How much her income had fallen off. Instead of that you never told her—made up the difference yourself. And she spends hundreds like a drunken cowboy does dollars. That is what hurts me."

"Gene, I expected the shrinking of capital and income would be only temporary. I still believe, as my lawyer in New York assures me, that we will recover. Madge's capital is intact and eventually her income will grow normal. That was a wise provision of Aunt Helen's. Madge can't spend the capital. And it doesn't make so great a difference that her income has dwindled. But now we should tell her—if we have the courage!"

"We!" expostulated Gene, startled. "Not much. Why, I don't know Madge since she grew up. When she was seventeen—before she left for college I was scared to death of her. You'll have to tell her."

"That'll be hard. I'm afraid myself of these years she has lived away from us. If I had it to do over I'd not have sent her away to college."

"Well, let's forget the financial side of it for the present. You read her letters and telegrams?"

"Yes. Madge asked me to reserve judgment until I had heard her side. Evidently she became involved in some kind of a college row, for which she was not responsible, but which resulted in her expulsion. She regretted greatly that she could not graduate."

"Was that all? No regret for the—the disgrace?"

"She never mentioned disgrace. I don't believe that has occurred to her."

"Same old Majesty, eh? She couldn't do any wrong," returned Gene, and there was a tinge of bitterness in his tone. "What else?"

"She said she had invited her college friends to come out here for the summer—for the *summer,* mind

50

you. That will be after graduation. It worries me more than the fact of her being expelled."

"That's easy. Tell Madge she can't have her friends this summer."

"Could you tell her that?"

"Sure I could," replied Gene, grimly.

"Very well. That will be a relief. For the rest she wired from L. A. she was leaving. And last evening from Yuma. Gene, don't excite yourself over probabilities. The fact seems that at that rate she may get here tomorrow."

"Madeline, it—it'll be so wonderful to see her again that I almost don't care what she's done," replied Gene with emotion.

"Gene, she's our problem. She's a composite of you and me."

"Madeline, not much of me?" implored Gene.

"A very good deal of you, her father."

"Suppose she inherited some of that wild blood of mine?" ejaculated Gene, aghast.

"If it hadn't been for that, there might have never been any Madge, darling."

"Lord!—I always said Madge had your beauty, your sweetness, your intelligence. But if she's got my old devil in her, too—come out in these modern days of freedom for women—what, Maddie, what on earth can we do?"

"I don't know, Gene. Love her, trust her. Make her love her home. Let us agree on that right here, Gene."

"I promise, Madeline. But I'm scared."

"So am I. But not the way you are. I'm scared of a crowd of young college people, just freed from cramping restrictions, let loose upon us here."

"Madeline, do you remember your young crowd— that you had come out here from New York just after you bought this place?"

"Indeed, I do," replied his wife, musingly, her eyes shadowed. "My brother Alfred—his romance with Flo —my sister Helen—my best friend Edith Wynne. Oh, they seem so far away—so long ago. But Alfred has been coming back to us for ten years. . . . Gene, did

51

you ever guess that Helen was in love with you—then, when you were *El Capitan?*"

"Helen!—Why, Maddie, you're crazy," protested Gene.

"No. It's the truth. I never told you. Helen never married, you know. And she left her fortune to Madge —which after all has been such a problem—*is* so yet. . . . Gene, if Madge's friends are like her, we would have a more exciting summer than that one twenty-three years ago."

"I haven't the slightest doubt of that," growled Gene.

"If we only hád an *El Capitan* to tame Madge!"

"Maddie, we don't want a wild *hombre* like he was."

"Perhaps no other kind could ever win Madge. . . . My husband, why do you always disparage yourself so bitterly?"

"I've failed as a rancher. After raising a herd of eighty thousand head."

"But that was not your fault. Who could foresee what would happen to the cattle business? Anyway I was referring to your status as the cowboy who came —and conquered. . . . Gene, my memories are beautiful, always, eternally all-satisfying. Even to this day I can dream of that awful ride down into Mexico to save you from being shot—and revel in the sight of you striding out, as you supposed, to your execution. To meet instead—*me*—your wife, who you had no idea knew your secret!"

"Well, I find it sweet too, Madeline. The past would be enough for me. But there is you—our home—and now Madge to think of."

"Gene, it will all come out right."

"Sure it will, dear. I'm an old croaker. Wish I could be like Nels. . . . You'll want to read your mail. And I've a lot of papers to look over."

Gene left his wife, conscious of a sense of guilt and remorse. He had not told her all. The deal with Lawson had been made to raise money to pay a mortgage he had secretly placed upon the ranch. Gene had meant to confess this, but could not bring himself to it. Nels had sensed that something was wrong, though the keen old friend had not dreamed that it was so bad. It was insupportable for Gene to think of Madeline and Madge losing this beautiful ranch.

Outside he walked the old familiar path under the cotton woods that had been planted there before Don Carlos built the house. The sultry heat of day was wafting away; a fragrant incense of flowers and pine needles filled the air; the irrigation ditch in its stone-walled vine-covered confines murmured on musically like a brook.

There was strength and help in this environment, and in the solitude that hung over it. But there was no comfort in Gene's confession that he had not been equipped to cope with these modern days of bewildering changes and upsets in business. Nels was a far better cattleman than he. For fifteen years there had been too much money to spend, and he had spent instead of saving it. Then out of a clear sky, like a thunderbolt, had come the collapse of eastern securities, and the bank that had held the rest of Madeline's fortune. She did not know how poor they really were. Sober reasoning assured Gene that Madge could and probably would save the ranch. Nevertheless telling her of the straits he had brought about seemed absurdly beyond him. Gene made up his mind to sell two thirds of his stock, pay his pressing debts and the interest on the mortgage, then plan and plot somehow to save the situation.

With a mighty effort he threw off the depression, and went back into the house, to deceive Madeline with an apparent return of his old cool unconquerable spirit, and presently to bed.

In the morning there had come a change. Whether or not the anticipated home-coming of Madge had wrought the magic or a vivid realization of the sweetness of life on this glorious June morning, so rich in song of birds and blaze of purple range and golden sun, Gene did not know. A good sleep and then the light of day always worked wonders.

Gene found Danny Mains with Nels, having a cup of coffee in the old cowboy's bachelor quarters which had been his home for twenty-five years. Danny had been one of Gene's wild outfit in those long-past prosperous days. His bow legs, his sturdy build had not altered. But Danny's homely visage betrayed the havoc of the years.

"Howdy, Boss," he greeted Gene, gladly. Danny had not worked for Gene for a whole decade and more, but he always addressed him in the cowboy vernacular of rider to his employer. "I was comin' up. Nels an' me hev been talkin' over my throwin' in with you. I like the idee, Boss. Are you goin' to sell some stock?"

"Good morning, you two old *hombres*," replied Gene, cheerfully. "Yes, I'm selling two thirds of my cattle. What's your angle on that, Danny?"

"Like it, Boss. If the price is goin' up, as Nels figgers, why by the time we can round up an' drive to the railroad it ought to reach thirty-five dollars a haid."

"Shore it will," drawled Nels, as he sipped his coffee. "Danny figgers he has aboot seven hundred haid, probably more. An' he aims to sell half of them."

"Boss, with a lot fewer cattle we can keep count better an' mebbe stop this queer rustlin'."

"Who's doing it?" demanded Gene, angrily.

"I'm damned if I know. I'm shore afeared, though, thet some of my wife's lazy kin are mixed up in it some way."

"Ahuh. So Nels said. That ought to be easy to correct."

"Yes? How'n hell can I hang her relatives?"

"Danny, we don't need to hang them. Just stop them."

"An' you knowin' greasers for thirty years! . . . Gene, we're growin' dotty in our old age."

"Let's pull out of it, Danny."

"I'll drink on thet."

"Nels, I can see you've got it all figured out for us. Spring it pronto."

"Mighty simple to me," rejoined Nels, thoughtfully. "Hire a couple of rattlin' good cowboys. An' with you an' Danny an' the *vaqueros* heah you can do the job in a week."

"Hire two good cowboys, eh? Where? How? What with?" queried Gene, spreading wide his hands.

"Sech ain't to be had, Boss," declared Danny, hopelessly.

"Wal, I've an idee," went on Nels. "Gene, you an' Danny open the store while I clean up heah."

Gene took the key with its buckskin string attached, and accompanied by Danny went out by the long-deserted bunkhouse, across the green toward the store. He could hear the whistling of Madge's horses beyond the corrals.

"Danny, I'd closed up this store long ago but for Nels," said Gene.

"Aw, Boss, you can't do thet. Why, it'd kill the old feller. An' the store ain't runnin' at a loss, is it? All the Mexicans deal with Nels."

"Yes, and they owe him plenty. He must restock. And I just can't go deeper in debt."

"Hell no! We'll do somethin', Boss. I'm afraid we're down in the mouth. As if I didn't hev enough to pester me without thet girl of mine!"

"Bonita?" queried Gene, quickly, with a chord of sympathy.

"Yes, Bonita. Boss, I'm damn ashamed to confess it, but I'm afeared she's a no-good little hussy. After all your wife has done for Bonita—educatin' her—makin' a lady out of her—why, she's jest cussed."

"Danny, what do you mean?"

"Bonita has the *vaqueros* nutty. But she doesn't give a damn for one of them. She's white an' she runs with the white. Ren Starr, you know, was turrible stuck on Bonita. But her flirtin,' mebbe wuss, I don't know, querred her with him. She goes to town every chanct thet comes along. She drinks an' Lord knows what. I ought to beat the hell out of her. But I jest can't. I love thet kid like I loved her mother, Bonita, long

55

ago. You remember, Gene, 'cause you saved Bonita for me."

"Yes, I remember, Danny, old pard. It's tough sledding now for us old boys, who can't figure the present and this younger generation. . . . I've a daughter of my own, Danny. An' she's due home today or tomorrow."

"Majesty comin'? Aw, thet's grand! Why, Boss, she'll put the life in us. I'm sure glad, Boos. This time you gotta make her stay home."

"Make her?—Danny, didn't you just admit you couldn't do anything with Bonita?"

"Sure. But what the hell has thet got to do with Madge?"

"I suspect these girls are precisely the same."

"Lord help us, Boss!"

Gene unlocked the rickety door of the old supply store and threw it open. The shelves were almost bare. Some print goods, gaudy in color, and glass jars of pink and yellow candy, and gewgaws for children, and a spare supply of tobacco and cigarettes were about all the stock left for Nels. In the wintertime he sat beside the old stove, to smoke his pipe, and feed billets of wood to the fire; and to talk about the past when, at rare intervals, somebody dropped in.

"Always makes me think we're living in the past," said Gene, coming out to join Danny.

"Aw. Boss, don't talk as if it was all over," returned Danny. "We got a future."

At that juncture Nels appeared behind them, his free clinking stride belying his white locks. As he was about to step up on the porch he halted, his keen blue gaze fixed beyond the village, far down on the range.

"Look!"

Gene sighted a streak of yellow dust tailing out behind a motorcar. His heart swelled up in his throat to check his utterance.

"Car. Comin' hell bent fer election!—Boss, doesn't that remind you of Link Stevens when he used to drive Madeline's white car across thet sage flat?"

"Yes. I've never forgotten Link. A great cowboy who could no longer ride! He loved to drive and scare us all stiff. But, Danny, it's a cinch Link would turn over in his grave if he could see *that* car coming."

"I should smile. Makin' seventy miles an hour. On thet road. My Gawd, some fellers have nerve! He's young an' don't give a damn fer his life!"

"Wonder who it can be?" queried Gene, under his breath. "Important telegrams, I'll bet. Hope it's not bad news. Nels, have you a field glass handy?"

"Don't need none, Gene. Thet's Majesty!" rang out Nels.

"Madge! . . . Say, can you see? Or is it one of your hunches?"

"Both. . . . Look at thet car streak along! Gene, it shore ought to make you feel as young as it does me."

"Young! Man alive, it makes me a doddering old man," replied Gene, thickly, and he sat down to relieve shaky legs.

Somehow he knew that reckless driver was Madge and he wondered why he had not grasped the fact at once. At the same instant he had a resurgence of pride in the girl's spirit and ability. She could drive— she could ride a horse like an Indian—she could do anything.

"Nels, what color is the car?" asked Gene, whose eyes had grown dim.

"Color of a coyote, I reckon. Gene, she had two cars heah last time, both of them black, if recollect. . . . Dog-gone, but it does my pore heart good to see Madge eatin' up the miles like thet."

"Nels, you always were an inhuman monster, a bloody gunman," declared Gene. "How do you supposed it makes *me* feel to see my only child risking her life that way?"

"Boss," interposed Danny, impressively. "You an' we hev a common cause. Nels has no feelin's. I reckon we oughta git drunk."

"You said it, Danny."

"Say, you fellers air blessed among men," put in Nels. "Both got purty daughters an' you rave aboot

57

yore troubles! I wisht to Gawd they was both mine."

"Boss! Did you see her take thet wash? Must hev forgotten it."

"I'm looking, boys, but I can't see very well."

Nels had walked to the end of the porch. Gene could make out only the streaking dust-comet, blurred in his sight. Yet that appeared to grow magically closer.

"Gene, she's off the wust of the road. Be heah in a few shakes of a lamb's tail. . . . It's a low open car—shiny—with a long front—a nose like them stag-hounds Madeline used to have."

Presently car and rising dust disappeared under the slope.

"Heah thet drone? All the same airplane," shouted Danny.

Gene heard and thought that his ears had never drunk in such sweet music. Madge—his kid—his little girl—his second Madeline—come home for good! He heard Danny babbling in his old cowboy manner, and then Nels let out a: "Kiyi!" The drone gave place to hum and then a mellow roar. Then like a flash a tan car shot into sight, passed the village, to turn left at the fork of the road, and speed out of sight up the knoll into the green foliage.

"Shore, I oughta reckoned on thet," said Nels to himself.

"Boss, I'll be waitin' home when you come down," added Danny. "Welcome Majesty home fer me."

"Nels, I think I'll go up."

"Wal, I should smile. . . . Tell her my heart ain't as strong as it used to be," drawled Nels, with a hand on his breast.

That jest in earnestness troubled Gene Stewart as he made his way up the knoll. The years were flying by. This homecoming of his daughter seemed to mark an epoch in his life and Nels', too. The old cowboy had no kin; he did not remember his age and he could not have worshiped Madge more if she had been his own. Gene fought a disloyal and disturbing thought about Madge. If she turned out to be wild and flighty, undutiful!... But he conquered the incipient fear. As a child she had been warmhearted, loving, imperious and willful as her mother had been. Gene expected to find Madge bewildering, and he walked slowly up the shady path, seeking to prepare himself for he knew not what. His steps, however, led him inevitably up to the house, through the great arch into the patio and on toward the east wing. Before he stepped into the flagstone corridor he heard a strange voice, swift and high-pitched, sweet and happy. That would be Madge. She was with her mother in the living room. Gene took some long strides to reach the wide doorway. He saw Madeline in her big armchair with the girl on her lap.

". . . Mom, darling, I am wild with joy to be home. I have forgotten nothing. I am drunk with the sage. I am. . . ."

And then Gene stepped into the room. They heard his step. The girl raised a lovely face, flushed and radiant, with great violet eyes that were wet and dim. Gene knew her, yet he did not know her. This Madge had golden hair.

"Dad!" she cried, poignantly.

"Yes—if you are—Madge," he replied, a little huskily.

She sprang up, taller than he remembered her, and not so slim, to rush at him arms spread. She threw them around his neck, and swinging free of the floor she hugged him tight. "My handsome Dad! My *El Capitan!* . . . Oh, how—good to see—you!" And with kisses and incoherent words she at last let down her feet, to lean upon him breathlessly. As Gene gazed down, his breast congested and his utterance clogged, he saw that her long dark lashes lay upon her cheeks, and tears were streaming from under her lids.

"Madge, is—is it really you?"

"Yes, Dad—your bad chicken come home to roost." And she opened eyes that were like her mother's, only a deeper, darker blue, exquisite in their soft and misty lights. "Darling! You've changed somehow. Lines

I don't remember. . . . And this white over your temples!—Mom, what has grieved our *El Capitan?*"

"Dearest, the years leave their marks," replied Madeline, her voice not quite steady.

"I think he's handsomer. Can you find me a lover like him?"

"Lord forbid, Madge!" laughed Gene. "Now stand away and let me look at you."

She revolved for his inspection, like the models in fashion shows, and from the crown of her golden head to her suede shoes she appeared to be the ultimate in grace and beauty, in vivid and intense pulsing life. Then her eyes, wide upon him, brought back the child and the girl to prove this lovely young woman his own Madge. It was a profound and moving moment for Gene.

"Madge, my girl. It is you, yet not you. I recognize your eyes, your look, your smile. All else is strange—especially *this.*" And he caressed a waving tress of her golden hair.

"Mom said almost the same," rejoined Madge, with a laugh. "Both of you have forgotten your darling."

"Not much," said Gene.

"Madge, once your hair was chestnut, like mine before it darkened," added her mother.

"Well, honey bunches, we will waive that question. But really I am disappointed. I was sure you'd fall for my hard."

"Daughter, if you are one hundredth as good as you are lovely, I shall be the happiest father in all the West."

"Dubious, but eminently satisfactory." Then with striking suddenness she changed from gay to grave. "Let's get it over, my darling Mom and Dad." It struck Gene that she addressed both of them but looked at him with eyes no man on earth could have doubted. "You had my letters and wires. I hope you did not see the L.A. papers. . . . I was expelled from college, in disgrace. It was hateful—the publicity. I'm sorry I couldn't graduate, for your sakes. For mine, I don't care in the least. I learned all they gave me and yelped for more. I was secretary of the student body and I'm a Phi Beta."

"What does that mean, Madge?" asked Gene.

"Why Dad!—To belong to the Phi Beta is one of the highest honors any woman can attain in college."

"Dearest," murmured Madeline, "that makes me happy indeed."

"Madge, what did they expel you for?" queried Gene, stern despite his emotion.

"Dad, I was indirectly to blame for a riot between the students and the police."

"Indirectly? Does that mean innocently?"

"It certainly does."

"Okay. Tell us what came off."

"I like to drive fast and I didn't pay overmuch attention to laws and rules," rejoined Madge, frankly. "I never had time to poke along slowly. Several times I received tickets for speeding. Once after that I was in a rush and the officer who caught me happened to be the same one. Well, he was a sap, swelled on himself, and by making eyes at him and telling him he wouldn't pinch his little co-ed, or some such rot, I kept him from taking me to court; he said, 'I'll be seeing you, sweetie,' and the next time he saw me he was fresh. I cut him dead, of course. One afternoon I was driving up to college and saw him coming up alongside. That time I was not exceeding the speed limit. Nor did I forget to put out my hand at the corner, but he accused me of that. He followed, calling for me to stop, which I did presently along the side street halfway down the campus. It happened in between classes, and there were students everywhere. Some of my friends were right there when I stopped. They heard my argument with this policeman. And did they take my side? Students came running from everywhere. Then I noticed a young fellow in the front line, and at first took him for a student. There were two policemen in this car and a motorcycle cop came up. Both officers got out, and the mean one stepped

61

on the running board of my car—told me to move over—that he was taking me for a ride. Then the students rushed a vegetable truck, and loading up with tomatoes and oranges they just swamped that police car. The motorcycle cop called out the reserves, and the dirty bum of a policeman who had been to blame for this—he actually laid his hands on me—to push me out of my seat. Then this young fellow I mentioned, socked him in the stomach—a terrific wham! The officer began to fold up. Did I get a kick out of that? Then my champion laid him out in the street and leaping into my car he told me to step on it. We left the mob of reserves and students having a swell fight. When I got out of the crowd I *did* step on it. We escaped. . . . That's all, Dad, except the board of directors expelled me and the officers forgot to come and arrest me."

"It doesn't strike me as so terrible," replied Gene, with a reassuring smile. It was certain Madge had no idea she had done the least wrong. "What do you think, Madeline?"

"Madge was rather thoughtless and indiscreet."

"What became of the young man?" queried Gene. "I'd like to shake hands with him."

"So would I," flashed Madge, her eyes lighting up. "I drove him downtown, to a parking place where we chatted. He was the handsomest fellow. Shy. He had no line at all. Oh, I liked him. Made a date with him to meet me right there the next day. But he didn't come, the idiot! Instead, oh, never mine—that was all of that."

"If you don't feel badly over it, why should we?" asked Madeline, happily.

"Then we'll forget it. I think you are both darling. I'm going to make up for my long absence by loving you to death."

"Madge, we can stand some loving," returned Gene, fervently. "Are you really going to stay home now?"

"Dad! Don't look so wistful. Oh, how I have neglected you both! But you wanted me educated. You've had your way. I am, and how!"

Neither Madeline nor Gene could resist a laugh.

"You will stay home with us—at least once in a while?" asked her mother.

"Forever, darling. I'll have my friends come to see me. I wired you to expect a crowd after graduation. What a place this ranch is to entertain city tenderfeet! I'll have the time of my life."

"Madge, the ranch—is run down," said Gene, hesitatingly. "Hardly fit for your friends."

"But, Dad, it's so western, so Spanish. I adore the atmosphere of years and leisure. Before I left L.A., I bought three truckloads of stuff. Everything under the sun. Mom, I hope you like my modernistic taste. I'll refurnish my rooms, and all those in the west wing. Oh, it'll be swell."

"Only three truckloads!" ejaculated Gene, with a smile at Madeline. He had to laugh. His daughter was amazing, electrifying. He felt shot through and through with new life. The flush on Madeline's lovely face was pleasant to behold. "What about your baggage?"

"My car outside is full. And I expressed ten trunks and a lot of bags. They will be at Bolton today. The other stuff comes by freight. I do hope soon. We have only two weeks to get ready for my crowd. . . . Dad, will you carry in my trunk? I brought you both presents galore, when I can unpack. Mom, are my rooms ready?"

"They are clean, my dear, and exactly as you left them."

Gene went out in front, conscious of varied emotions. A good deal of the happiness that possessed him was the pent-up delight Madeline had betrayed.

"Gosh! No wonder this car could travel!" ejaculated Gene, sizing up the magnificent machine, new, glittering, apparently all engine. The back seat was packed full of bags and parcels. And there were three beautiful coats, one of them fur. All about the car and its contents reminded Gene of Madeline Hammond when she had first arrived at El Cajon, which was now Bolton. Like mother, like daughter! Still could Madge ever adjust herself to the changed times? She had a fortune but she could not squander her principal. Aunt Helen, wise in her vision, had seen to that. But Madge's income now could not support her present extravagance. Gene thought of these things and many more, in the fifteen trips he made with Madge's baggage. On the last she and her mother met him in Madge's sitting room.

"Mom! Why should you apologize for my rooms?" Madge was saying. "They are just swell. I wouldn't change them. Of course the furnishings are rather dingy and old. But I anticipated that. . . . I'll paint these walls."

"You'll what?" asked Gene, incredulously.

"I'll paint them. I bought the paint and brushes."

"You learned that in college?"

"I certainly did. See here, Dad Stewart, you give me a job I *can't* do?"

"You're on, Madge. . . . I'd like, though, that you'd run down to see Nels."

"Nels and my horses! Oh, am I happy? . . . Where's my purse? I don't want Nels to see me such a sight," she babbled. Finding the purse she sat down to open it and take out something shiny on a chain. From this she extracted a powder puff, with which she powdered her nose. This act was performed deftly and while she talked to her mother. But when she took out a small metal tube and began to paint her lips with it, Gene observed that she was careful and quiet. Her lips took on a hue still more scarlet. Madge, bouncing up, encountered her father's nonplused gaze, and she burst into mirth.

"Why do you do that?" he asked, curiously.

"You old range rider! Why do you suppose?"

"I've no idea, unless you imagine it makes you prettier. Nothing artificial could do that."

"Dad, don't you fool yourself. I just could. I'll make up really for you some day. It's an art. . . . I suppose, to answer you, that the custom grew popular through motion pictures. The most beautiful stars are those who have the artistry, or do their making up under experts. . . . Mom, would it interest you to know that I had an offer to go into the movies?"

"Yes, of course. But it wouldn't surprise me."

"There was one studio hot after me. It turned out that I had met some official or director at some function, or the Grove, I forget which. He talked me deaf, and phoned the house until I told him where to get off. I was interested, of course. Any girl in the world is keen about the movies. I'd like to have taken a fly at it. But—I decided it would cost more than I'd pay."

"Cost? Why, I read about the big salaries the companies pay their stars."

"Oh, Dad!—Mom, isn't he a darling old dumbbell? . . . I'll be back right away to unpack." She ran out, her high heels clicking.

Gene stood there, smiling quizzically at Madeline. Presently he heard the slam of a car door and the burst of engine.

"Dumbbell? I suppose I am. Poor Nels and I are in for hell."

"Gene, I'm tremendously relieved. Whatever college and city may have done to her these four years she is wholesome and sweet. And oh! so lovely!"

"I liked the way she looked when I spoke of Nels. . . . Maddie, I think, if she's got a heart, we can stand anything."

"Be assured then, Gene, and relieved as I am. She is warm-hearted. She loves us. She loves—this home."

"Why, Madeline! You're crying. . . . At that I feel sort of—weak myself. Our little girl come home—grown up—a woman! I never saw a princess, but she's one. I'm so proud of her I could burst. . . . Wife, I forgot to ask you. Don't you think we ought to patch up the telephone system to town? The wires are down in places. And there are other things." Whereupon Gene went over with her the talk he had had with Nels and Danny Mains. After that he proceeded to the room Madeline and he used as an office, and there he read neglected mail, carefully studied books, and figures that always were Greek to him, and wrote some important letters. Madge's coming had seemed to fire his energy, to make a break in the old *mañana* habit of mind he had fallen into, and to stimulate his determination to see this climax of hard times through. To Gene's surprise he was called to lunch before he had any idea the morning had passed.

Madge met him as he entered the living room, and he halted in sheer amazement. She looked like a slim boy.

"Madge, what kind of a riding outfit is that?" Evidently his reaction to her appearance gave her delight.

"Dad, I have on slacks. Don't you like them?"

"Daughter, I'm afraid I'll like anything you wear," he replied, putting his arm around her.

"Against your better judgment, yes?"

They entered the dining room, which appeared brighter than for many years. The sunshine sifted through the foliage over the open window. There were roses and Indian paintbrushes and sage in the vases. Madeline had celebrated the occasion by gracing the table with white linen and some of her old silver and china.

"Swell to be home!" exclaimed Madge.

"Disappointed in—anything?" asked Gene, haltingly.

"Not a thing. The ranch had gone to hell when I was home last. But I didn't mind the tumble-down corrals and sheds. Fits the range. But the big barn must have a new roof. . . . Dad, it gave me a shock to see Nels. I think he has failed a little. But he is the same old darling. I was so overjoyed to see him that I forgot my horses. Fancy that? Then the luncheon bell rang. I had scarcely time to change. This afternoon I'll get into riding togs, just to please Nels. What do you think he said, Dad? . . . 'Wal, Majesty, the only things aboot this heah ranch thet ain't gone daid is yore hawses. Me an' yore *vaqueros* hev seen to thet.' . . . Oh, I love to hear the old Texan talk."

"Yes, your horses are okay, Madge," replied Gene. "I hope Nels didn't talk too much."

"He couldn't keep anything from me. . . . Dad, I've known for a couple of years that your financial situation was not so hot. Mom told me when I was home last. And of course I've read about the depression going from bad to worse. Just how bad is it for you?"

Madge's direct query and the gaze that added more to it were not easy to meet.

"Pretty tough, Madge—but I'd rather not confess just what a poor businessman your dad is."

"Gene, it is not your management of the ranch," interposed Madeline. "You made it pay expenses until the bottom dropped out of everything."

"Madeline, that's darn good of you," protested Gene. "But it's not so. We had too much money and too many cattle. For ten years we ran behind, a little more every year. Then came the crash. . . ."

Gene hesitated, spreading wide his hands, looking from wife to daughter. Nels was not the only one who would find it difficult to lie to Madge Stewart.

"I get it," she said, soberly, dropping those penetrating eyes. "I've always understood Majesty's Rancho was mine. You know, just in a vain and playful way, perhaps. How about that, Dad—seriously?"

"Of course this ranch is yours—or will be someday, which is just the same. And a white elephant—my daughter."

"Not for little Madge. What do you suppose I went to college for? What did I study economics for? . . . Dad—Mom, I tell you I'm home for good. I'm crazy about my home. It has been swell to have unlimited money. Let me play around this summer—entertain my friends—then I'll hop to the job."

4

In the afternoon Gene rode out on the range toward Bolton with one of his half-Mexican riders, Manuel Mains, son of Danny, the only one of Danny's four youngsters that Gene thought was worth much. Bonita, the eldest, was distractingly pretty, to be sure, but that seemed to be a bad thing for the girl.

Gene wanted to find out how many telephone poles were down on the short cut of the line across the valley and over the ridge. From that point on in to Bolton, both the survey of the line and the necessary repair work could be done by truck. Manuel and he met some horses later, and the sum of their report was an agreeable surprise to Gene. Less than a dozen poles were down and there was only one break in the wire. Several days' labor, after the new poles had been snaked down from the foothills, would put the telephone in working order again, which Gene saw was important in view of Madge's return and the activity presaged for the summer. Then it would be very necessary to go over the road and make that safe for automobilists. The problem of help occupied his mind. That, added to his other difficulties seemed an insurmountable fact, yet somehow, Madge's presence counteracted it, and made that afternoon sojourn in the colorful and fragrant sage as pleasant as it was serious. Riding back he thought that he could not succumb to gloom and hopelessness.

Manuel turned off at the village to get his supper. Bonita, whose sharp eyes always saw everybody and everything, waved a red scarf at Gene, as if he had been a cowboy with whom to flirt. Gene waved back at her. Despite her deviltry, she was lovable. "Gosh! there'll be young fellows in Madge's crowd," suddenly exclaimed Gene. "What Bonita will do to them! But I'll gamble on her."

It was almost sunset when Gene turned his horse over to Jose. He saw Madge's golden head blazing from the top of the pasture fence. Nels' white locks appeared brighter by contrast. They were watching Madge's horses, which no doubt had been turned loose. Gene, about to join them, was deflected by the sight of a strange rider coming down the lane. Instead Gene proceeded to the square where one of the *vaqueros* and some Mexican boys surrounded a black horse in front of the blacksmith shop. Gene ascertained that the horse was lame. He examined the leg, which proved not to be badly sprained, and upon rising he saw that the strange rider had arrived. Gene's first glance at the handsome young man in his flashy cowboy attire occasioned him some amusement. A forerunner of the range contingent that inevitably would throng there to see Madge!

The rider got down, and introduced himself, saying bluntly that he wanted a job. Gene looked him over, favorably impressed. He seemed under twenty-five, tall and lithe, powerful of limb and shoulder, and he had a strong open countenance and fine hazel eyes, medium dark and very penetrating. His black horse would have been an asset for any cowboy.

Gene read a letter of recommendation from Ren Starr, and it was not many moments till he liked Lance Sidway's looks, his words, and had given him a job on the ranch.

Meanwhile one of the lads had taken the black horse down the lane for a drink. Gene anticipated results from that procedure and he was tinglingly prepared for Madge's ecstatic squeal. That girl had cowboy blood in her. Then Gene, with malice aforethought, sent the unwilling Sidway in Madge's direction. They met, so precipitously that Madge ran into Sidway and almost fell out of his arms. Astounded, plainly stunned for an instant, Madge's vivid face suddenly flashed radiance. Recognition and rapture were evident in her speaking eyes.

"*You!* . . . Oh, if it isn't my hero!" she cried in intense excitement. "Of all the surprises I *ever* had! You darling!" And with swift action that matched her voice, she lifted her gauntleted hands to Sidway's shoulders and rose on her tiptoes to kiss him warmly. Evidently she had aimed at his lips, but she missed them, leaving half of a red bow to the side.

Gene, utterly astonished as he was at his daughter's impetuous action, yet did not fail to catch the reaction in the boy. When she ran into his arms he gave a violent start and uttered a gasp. Then at her words of surprise and delight, followed by that impulsive kiss, his face turned a dusky scarlet. It receded as she drew back until he was pale.

"My God! . . . You? . . . Not *you!*"

"Yes—me!" she replied, sweetly.

"You can't be—be Stewart's daughter?" he implored. "You can't be Madge—not Majesty Stewart!"

"I am. And you know that, you clever devil," she returned, in positive admiration. "You put one over, 'n't you—meeting me *here?* No crowded noisy parking place for you, Mr. Oregon. You wanted to keep that date here, at my home, on the Arizona range. Romantic—individual—beautiful! I figured you perfectly, my campus champion. I knew you weren't ordinary. And almost I can forgive you for not keeping that date."

"I—I did keep it," he gulped.

"You did?" she echoed, her violet eyes wide and dark. "Then you didn't disgrace me by being the first fellow ever to break a date with Madge Stewart?"

"I came—Miss—Miss Stewart," replied Sidway, still overcome. "I was there—long before you came. In a car. . . . I saw you drive in. Then that—that fellow followed you . . ."

"You saw him—heard us?"

"Yes, I was quite close."

"Why didn't you jump out and let him see you were my date? He would have acted true to type—and you could have socked him, too. I'm afraid you lost a golden opportunity."

"I'm sorry, Miss Stewart," he said, in awkward though sincere regret. "But I was—sort of paralyzed. I never got over it until after you drove away with him."

"Then I do forgive you. What is your name?"

"Lance Sidway."

She touched his arm and turned him toward Gene, who had leaned against a post, taking it all in. Gene had no idea how he looked, but he felt highly amused at this clever ruse of Sidway's.

"Dad, isn't it just darling?" said Madge. "This is my hero—the young man whom I told you and Mom about—who rescued me at the campus riot. . . . Lance Sidway—my father, Gene Stewart."

"Madge, we haven't been introduced, but we've met," replied Gene, genially, and he eyed Lance as if he had been taken in a bit.

"Of course. How silly of me! He just rode in and you . . ."

"I gave him a job," interposed Gene.

"What? . . . To ride for you!—He is a fast worker. . . . Lance Sidway, I don't know just what to make of you."

"That goes for me, too," replied Gene, with a smile which softened the doubt.

"Mr. Stewart, I am on the spot," burst out Sidway. "I told you I'd never met your daughter—never heard of her till I met Starr. How could I guess she was that one? . . . I did meet her—as she told you. . . .I'm innocent of . . ."

"Sidway, don't take it so hard," went on Gene, kindly. "I was young once. It didn't turn out just as you planned. But I'd have liked you better if you'd told me . . ."

"I did not lie to you," declared the cowboy, with

such vehemence that Gene began to feel sorry for him. Then Madge claimed Sidway's attention.

"I get you, Mr. Lance Sidway. But I've been kidded by experts," she said, with laughing eyes. She was pleased with his subterfuge.

"Yeah? You get what?" he demanded bluntly, and it appeared that his awkwardness was vanishing.

"What is so obvious."

"Miss Stewart, it may look obvious that I knew who you were—that I deliberately rode out here because of you. But it is not true."

"Oh, so you are ashamed to be caught?" she taunted. "You're a pretty smooth actor, cowboy, but you can't fool little Madge."

"You may be pretty smart but you're wrong this time," he retorted, and there was plainly resentment in his tone.

"Let's skip it," she returned, without the archness. And at that moment Nels, and the lad leading Sidway's horse, came around the corner.

"Nels, shake hands with Lance Sidway," interposed Gene, glad to relieve the growing strain between the young couple. "He hails from Oregon. And I've just given him a job."

"Howdy," drawled Nels, and shook hands with the flustered lad. Gene was of the opinion that Sidway had no conception how he was being looked over by the keenest ey   in Arizona. Gene's conclusion was that the cowboy showed up favorably in a most trying situation. When Madge saw the black horse again, her swift reversal of mood eased the situation. Like a true range rider she walked around the black, all eyes, placing a careful yet confident hand on him, and never saving a word until she had made a second circuit.

"Nels!" she importuned, as if wanting him to refute her judgment.

"Wal, I'm shore sorry, lass," drawled Nels. "He's a grand hawse. He's got Cedar beat all holler."

"Traitor!" she flashed, her eyes blazing purple fire at Nels. "You're teasing me. Nels darling, you don't mean that?"

"Wal, mebbe I'm exaggeratin' some. But see heah, Majesty. Even if you been away from the range so long, you know a great hawse when you see him."

"I'm afraid I do. . . . Mr. Sidway, will you *please* let me get on him?" Her query to the cowboy was tinged with slight sarcasm, yet her desire was deeply sincere.

"Of course—if you wish. . . . The stirrups will be long."

Madge swung gracefully up into the saddle and Nels beat the cowboy to her side. Presently the stirrups were laced up to fit Madge and she walked Umpqua across the green square, trotted him up the lane a few hundred yards, paced him a little and loped him back. What a picture the black horse and the golden-haired girl made! Turning away from the sight himself, Gene saw it in Nels' worshipful eyes, and then he caught a gleam of the eternal cowboy in Sidway's.

Madge sat the saddle as if reluctant to get off, while she patted the arched glossy neck. She was flushed of face. Her eyes were soft, glowing. At that moment Gene experienced the old fullness of love for her in his heart. She was Madeline's daughter, but she was western. Presently she sat up in the saddle, the glamorous spell vanished, and she faced the three men coolly. Gene imagined he could read her mind.

"His trot does not equal Cedar's, but his pace and lope beat that of any horse I ever rode."

"Wal, lass, thet's strong praise from you," declared Nels. "Justified, I reckon."

"Madge, never go back on your own horses," warned Gene.

"I don't, Dad. But I must be just. . . . Mr. Sidway, do *you* know how fine Umpqua is?"

"Me!" ejaculated the cowboy, amazed. "Nobody can tell me anything about him."

"I'll bet I can."

"Go to it."

"What'll you bet?"

"Aw, the truth is I haven't anything. Of course I wouldn't bet Umpqua."

"No? Oh, you're a cowboy. You might some day," she returned, subtly. "Umpqua reminds me of something I read—that an Arab chieftain said. I didn't have to commit it to memory. It just stuck in my mind . . . 'If in the course of your life you alight upon a horse of noble origin, with large lively eyes wide apart, and black broad nostrils close together, whose neck, shoulders and haunches are long, his forehead, loins and limbs broad, his back and hip-bones and pasterns short, all covered with soft skin, fine hair, and his lungs wide and powerful, and his feet good, with heels high off the ground—hasten to buy or trade or steal that horse—secure him, and always afterward bless Allah for your good fortune!' "

"Wal, if thet doesn't beat me," said Nels, in rapt admiration.

"Madge, you've the high sign on us. But it was good," added Gene.

"You win," chimed in Sidway, reluctantly smiling.

"It seems superfluous to ask—can he run—is he fast?" asked Madge, tensely.

"He can beat your Cedar or any other nag you own."

"That remains to be seen, cowboy," returned Madge, darkly.

"What's more," went on Sidway, "he's the best cowboy horse ever bred in Oregon."

"Now yore talkin'," said Nels. "An Arab is no good to us riders, onless he's a cow-hawse."

"Nels, Umpqua can run over rocks as if they were level ground."

"I seen that from his hoofs."

Madge slipped slowly out of the saddle, facing Sidway: "No need to ask how you love Umpqua," she said, with a softness rounding the turn of her words. "You won't take it amiss if I—almost insult you?"

Sidway stared at her, and then with something of a gallent gesture he repudiated any possibility of her doing that.

"What value do you place on Umpqua?" she launched, suddenly keen, vibrant.

"Value! . . None, Miss Stewart."

"Every horse has a value. Tell me."

"Diamonds, rubies, gold!"

"Swell! I like you the better for that. . . . Do you know that you could sell him for five thousand dollars?"

"Humph. A movie star offered me that," returned the cowboy, contemptuously.

"Yeah? . . . I'll give you six thousand for Umpqua"

"No."

"Seven thousand."

"No."

"Eight thousand."

"No!"

"Ten thousand!"

Sidway's flushed face turned pale, either with anger or some other emotion.

"Miss Stewart, don't you know that money can't buy everything?" he queried, with dignity. "Umpqua is all I own in the world. He has saved my life twice. I love him. We raised him from a colt, and all of us loved him."

"I know I'm rotten," she cried, as if forced. "But no matter. I love him, too.'"

"That's well. I'm glad you do. But—you can't buy him."

"I always have what I want," she flashed, imperiously.

"You probably have had."

"But be reasonable." Madge stamped her booted foot until her spur jingled sharply. Tears of vexation and disappointment burned out of her big eyes and they glowed and dilated like mystic balls. You admit you're broke. I offer you a small fortune. You can get a start here on the range. Dad and Nels will help you. I will. You can still go on loving Umpqua. You may ride him—sometimes. You can make me happy. Please, Mr. Lance Sidway.'"

The cowboy gazed at her, listened to her eloquent appeal as if fascinated by something beside and beyond her offer.

"Really, Miss Stewart," he said, finally. "You may be Gene Stewart's daughter, born on this wonderful range, but you don't know cowboys."

Madge betrayed that she could not gainsay that, and it seemed a struggle went on in her between realization and selfishness. The latter evidently conquered. Anger at herself for being so little or at him for frustrating her desire burned out that momentary softness.

"You won't sell him?" she queried.

"I told you—no."

"Mr. Sidway, I can't have you riding around here on a finer horse than—a horse that I want."

"That'll be just too bad," returned the cowboy, in a tone which brought a hue to her cheeks that matched the carmine on her lips.

"You appear to be rather dense. Do I have to tell you I will not have you on this ranch?"

"You don't have to tell me anything, lady. Your father hired me and he'll have to fire me."

She looked at Gene with great luminous eyes. "Dad!"

"Madge, you're unreasonable," replied Gene, coolly, smiling upon her. "I need riders badly. Sidway has offered to ride for me at a wage I am ashamed to take advantage of. I couldn't discharge him just because he refuses to sell you his horse. Could I, Nels?"

Nels showed plainly that he was between the devil and the deep sea. Madge had been his especial joy and treasure all her life, as Gene well knew, and he had always spoiled her. Gene enjoyed his old cowman's extreme discomfiture, but knew he would extract himself somehow.

"Majesty, I shore know how you feel aboot this hawse," he began, in his slow drawl. "But, lass, you're bound to respect Sidway for his feelin's. I reckon you wouldn't be playin' the game if you fired him. Shore I never heahed of you bein' unfair. You used to give hawses to cowboys. An' I reckon, if yore happiness actooly depends on ownin' Umpqua, wal, in the nature of things on the range, you know, he'll just naturally drift yore way."

The persuasive cool voice of the old cattleman, the significant content of his last words, spread oil upon the troubled waters.

"Very well, Mr. Sidway, you stay," said Madge, loftily. "I'm sorry if I was unfair. But I will have that horse."

The dark passionate glance she bent upon Sidway had infinite and unknown possibilities.

"Thank you, Miss Stewart. But I do not want to remain under false pretenses. You will not have Umpqua."

"I accept your challenge. If you don't show yellow and ride off—we'll see." Then she smiled upon him without malice or resentment, and wheeled to start up the path.

"Hey, Madge, you're forgetting your car," called Gene. "What'll we do with it?"

She turned to call back in a sweet high-pitched voice; "Mr. Lance Sidway can use it to bed down his darling Umpqua." Then she was gone into the foliage.

"Whoopee," sighed Gene, and Nels came back with; "Doggone, old pard! Seems like old times when you fust came to Majesty's Rancho, before thet lass was borned."

Sidway had been lengthening his stirrups with swift hands. Presently he turned with pale face and hazel eyes shadowed.

"I'll be on my way. Thank you, Gene Stewart," he said.

"Hold on, Sidway. You wouldn't let my daughter's taunt. . . ."

"No, its not that, altogether. I know you didn't believe me—that I didn't come here on—on Miss Stewart's account. And under the circumstances I don't want to stay."

"No, I didn't believe you," rejoined Gene, seriously, searching the troubled face.

"See heah, cowboy," interposed Nels, descending from the porch with clinking slow steps. "Don't ride off hot-haided. Air you on the level? You didn't know

77

this was Majesty's Rancho an' thet the lass you done a favor for in Los Angeles was Madge?"

"Nels, I did not," replied Sidway, forcibly.

After a keen scrutiny of Sidway's face the old cowman turned to Gene; "Boss, he's tellin' the truth. Don't let him go."

"Hanged if I don't believe it myself."

"Stewart, I swear that I am on the level. I didn't know. It was just an infernal coincidence," rejoined Sidway huskily.

"Okay then. Let's shake on it. . . . Maybe your infernal coincidence will turn out well for me and this ranch problem. I've a hunch it will."

Sidway appeared too poignantly affected to voice his manifest relief and gladness. Gene's conviction was that the young man felt too strongly for the mere misunderstanding. There was more behind it. Gene liked this cowboy, and that Nels did also added a good deal of satisfaction.

"What'd you say yore fust name was?" drawled Nels.

"Lance. It's screwy, I know. Bad as Umpqua."

"Not so orful bad. . . . Gene, your supper bell has rung. I'll look after Lance. He can hev supper with me, an' the bunk room next to mine. . . . Whar'll I hev Jose put his hawse?"

"Not in the pasture tonight. Better in the barn. . . . Say, wouldn't it be funny if we could bed him down in Madge's car?"

"Not so damn funny in the mawnin'."

Dusk was settling under the pines when Gene mounted the slope to the house. A ruddy glow faded over the peaks in the west. Coyotes were wailing somewhere low down. Plodding up the low ascent, Gene was revolving in mind the events of the day. He had to side with the cowboy against Madge. She was willful and spoiled. That came out when she could not have her own way. He recalled the tone of her voice, her imperious look, her temper; and he shook his head sadly. But what could have been expected of the girl, their only daughter, adored and petted, born with a gold spoon in her mouth, and left a million when she was fifteen? But Gene reflected that despite these faults she seemed to be irresistible. If only one or more of his own besetting sins did not crop up in her! The cowboy Lance was in love with her—there was no doubt about that, even if he had not found it out yet. Gene, remembering that Madge had always had what she wanted, was heartily glad that Sidway had been strong enough to brook her will. He had good stuff in him, that lad. Gene's yearning for a son, long buried, had a rebirth. If Lance Sidway turned out as fine as he promised he would come somewhere near the ideal Gene had dreamed of.

By the time Gene had washed and changed, the second supper bell rang. He found Madeline and Madge waiting. The girl wore white, some clinging soft stuff that made Gene catch his breath. He thought of what little chance he had or Sidway or Nels, or any man, to resist this lovely and bewildering creature. Not a trace of the recent mood showed on her face.

". . . and he wouldn't part with Umpqua, the sap!" she was saying to her mother. And as Gene entered she extended a hand to him with a radiant smile. "Dad, I'm telling Mom about my hero and his wonderful horse. What a liar he is! He found out who I am and where I lived. I can't get what possessed him to deny that. He needn't. It was a clever stunt. Intrigued me. After I fell so hard for him that day he rescued me! . . . Well, I fell for his horse a thousand times harder. Oh, Mom, what a beautiful horse! Has it all over Cedar and Range and Bellefontaine—all of them. I wanted Umpqua so badly that I could have murdered the cowboy. . . . At first I had a kick out of it. Never occurred to me that I couldn't buy the black. But it turned out that I couldn't. Then I lost my temper. I'm afraid I reverted to feline type with claws out. Did Mr. Sidway jar me? I'm constrained to admit that he did. Made me feel selfish, mean, rotten. Which I was. But I'd do worse to get that horse. And all the time I was so mad I had a sneaking respect for

Lance, though I hated him. He's just swell, Mom. Don't you agree, Dad?"

"Rather cottoned to him myself," replied Gene to this long monologue.

"So did Nels, the traitor," she retorted.

"I am indeed interested to meet this paragon among cowboys. And see his Umpqua," said Madeline, with a smile. "Madge, in the succeeding days of trial I might be of service to you. I've had some experiences!" Madeline threw a laughing glance at her husband.

"Mom darling!" expostulated Madge. "Falling for Mr. Sidway doesn't mean a thing in the world. I've done that nineteen times this last semester. . . . But will I give that big boy a ride? It'll be a kick. And I'll have that horse if—if . . ."

"Well, if what, my girl?" taunted Gene.

"If I have to *marry* him."

Madeline neither reproved her nor showed surprise, but she remarked that cowboys must have vastly more than horses to be eligible for marriage.

"But I could divorce him next day," Madge flashed bewilderingly.

Next morning Gene was out early enough to catch Nels and Sidway at a sunrise breakfast.

"Wal, look who's heah," drawled the old cowman. "Mawnin', Gene. You ain't got oot this early fer years."

"Neither have you, old-timer," returned Gene, jocularly. "Shall we put it down to our lately acquired cowboy, Mr. Silway?"

"You shore can. The son-of-a-gun kept me up till eleven o'clock tellin' stories, an' then, by thunder, he rustled me oot before sunup."

Manifestly Nels and the newcomer had gotten along famously. Sidway appeared fresh an eager, and having donned his old outfit, he looked a lithe and striking rider.

"Don't call me Mr. Stewart," Gene replied to his greeting. "I'm Gene, or Boss, or Stewart."

"Okay, Boss. I sure appreciate falling in with you. And I'm asking if I may have the day on my own."

"On your own? What do you mean?" inquired Gene, puzzled.

"If you give me the day, I'm pretty sure I can tell you where your cattle have been rustled lately."

"Gene, he made some such crack as thet to me," drawled Nels. "Jest young hot blood. But I don't know."

"Sidway, are you hinting that you can find out what Nels and I and Danny Mains couldn't?"

"No, I'm not hinting. I'm telling you," replied the cowboy, with an engaging smile.

"You don't lack nerve," returned Gene, shortly.

"Boss, I don't mean to be fresh. I just think you men have been hunting for rustlers in an old-fashioned way."

"Old-fashioned?" echoed Gene, while Nels ha-ha'd vociferously.

"Listen, young man, rustling is rustling. Cattle don't fly. They have to be driven. On their hoofs. And hoofs leave tracks."

"Only so far. I'll bet you tracked yours as far as a macadamized road, an no farther."

"Yes, that's true. Or I should say, Jose and Manuel tracked them."

"Then what?"

"Wal," interposed Nels. "them two riders split an' rode east and west fer twenty-odd miles, an' never found the place where them hoof tracks left thet highway."

"Swell!" ejaculated Sidway, clapping his hands. "That's exactly what I wanted to be sure of. Saves me the trouble."

"Of what?"

"Bothering with tracks *on* the highway. They never left the highway short of Douglas or Tucson."

"Listen, son," returned Nels, his drawl more pronounced than ever, and very patient. "Shore you're talkin' to a couple of old cowmen, oot of date, an' I reckon pretty dumb, as you youngsters say. Will you

81

talk a language we know? These heah modern days air hell on speed, shore, but cattle cain't be drove on a cement road fer hundreds of miles."

"Sure they can. It's a cinch. Your cattle *were* so driven."

"Dog-gone!" complained Nels, turning to Gene. "An' I was kinda takin' to this lad."

"Nels, he's got something on us," declared Gene. "See here, Lance, just how were my cattle driven along the highway?"

"Simple as a, b, c.—In trucks."

"Trucks!" burst out Gene, incredulously.

Nels swore, and dropped one of his galvanized utensils on the floor. "Gene, it's shore simple. But we'd never guess such two-bit rustlin' of twenty or forty-odd haid would be done thet way."

"Well, I'll be damned. Sidway, how'd you find that out?" added Gene.

"I've seen inside one of these cattle trucks. Fact is I drove one of them," explained the young man.

"Yes? Wal, I reckon you'll be tellin' us next you're one of these newfangled rustlers," drawled Nels, dryly.

"I might have been without knowing, if the truck had been loaded. . . . On the way over here to Arizona I went broke at Douglas. Hung around for any kind of a job. Well, it came along, and it was to drive a big canvas-covered truck to Tucson. I was paid a hundred bucks, and told to expect to be held up somewhere along the road. I was held up all right a little ways out of Tucson, by a gang who expected just what I'd figured out—that the truck was full of booze. But it wasn't—and were they burned up? These high-jackers corroborated my suspicions. . . . All right now. To come short with it, by figuring and asking questions I found out that a string of trucks go through Douglas east about once in six weeks. Presumably they go east loaded with bootleg liquor and come back west loaded with bought or stolen cattle. My hunch is that this gang used to buy cattle for a blind to their real operations, but finally turned to rustling.

Just easy money! . . . On the other hand it may be that only one of the trucks is loaded with booze, and possibly it may come west, along with the cattle. We can safely gamble, however, on this—that your cattle have been stolen in this manner."

"Wal, what air we comin' to?" ejaculated Nels, scratching his white head. "Gene, shore we can look forward to be robbed by airplanes next."

"Fake rustling, likely," added Gene. "What'd the money for a few cattle mean to these bootleggers?"

"Nothing to the big shots," rejoined Sidway. "I've had a hunch that maybe the drivers of these trucks are grabbing a little money on their own hook. What I want to find out now is *who* drives the cattle to the highway. That'd have to be done on horses. . . . Boss, give me some idea where these last cattle tracks were made. I'll ride out and see if I can pick up some horse tracks. If I do I'll measure them, make sure I'll know them again, and then ride all over this darned range."

"Fork your horse and hit—No, let Umpqua rest. Tell Jose to saddle Range for you."

"I'm on my way," replied the cowboy, and he strode out of Nels' bunkhouse. Presently he passed off the porch carrying his saddle and accessories.

Nels went on wiping his utensils. Presently Gene said: "What do you know about that?"

"Gene, that feller proves how much old-time cowboys like us want to figger on new angles. Since the war, you know, we've jest been goin' back. Smart, this boy Sidway. If we only had Ren oot here now!"

"Yes. We know Ren Starr," replied Gene, ponderingly.

"Gene, did you ever know me to be fooled aboot a cowboy?"

"You mean his being straight? . . . I can't remember one, Nels."

"Wal, if this Oregon lad can ride an' shoot, he'll be a Gawdsend to you."

After that encomium from the old cattleman Gene felt himself convinced. He talked a while longer with Nels, went to the store with him, and presently set about an inspection tour of the barns and sheds and corrals, the reservoir, the lake, the irrigation ditches, the fences, and all pertaining to the ranch. He had divined that Madge would be coming to him presently and he wanted to be well posted. This survey was a melancholy task. He saw now why for years he had neglected it. In some degree verdue around the water hid the rack and ruin of the wooden structures. Those built of adobe were also damaged. And in fact repairs were badly needed everywhere.

Upon returning to the store Gene found Madge there with Nels. She wore overalls, high-top boots and spurs, and a blue sweater with a red scarf. The mere sight of her flushed and disheveled, and clad as she was, chased away Gene's gloom.

"Mawnin', Dad," she drawled. "I caught Nels drinking red likker."

"She did, at thet," admitted Nels, ruefully. "An' I'm darned if she didn't ask me for some."

That was a touchy point with Gene, which he passed by. "How'd you find your horses?" he asked.

"Cedar wild as a March hare. Bellefontaine as sweet as ever. Range was gone, and I learned from Jose that our new cow hand took him," returned Madge, and the dangerous tone of the last words were not lost upon Gene. He hastened to explain that he had told Sidway to saddle Range.

"Oh. . . . What's the matter with your own horses?"

"Sold most of my saddle stock. Your horses are fat and lazy, Madge. They need to be worked out."

"Indeed they do. That was okay, Dad. I thought Mr. Sidway, seeing he is so fresh, might have taken Range on his own. . . . Dad, his horse Umpqua came right to me. Oh, I was tickled pink. He likes me. I'll have no trouble winning him from his owner. And will I do it?"

"Madge that'd be a dirty trick."

"So it would be. But I'm crazy about the horse— and Nels said I couldn't do it. Added fuel to the flame! . . . Besides," she pouted, "Nels has fallen for that cowboy in a most unaccountable way."

"So have I, Madge."

"Et tu, Brute," she returned, reproachfully.

"I can account for it in more ways than one. Let me tell you just one . . . First thing this morning he told Nels and me how we had been losing stock so mysteriously."

"How?" she queried, suddenly intent. Gene liked that instant response.

"Driven away in trucks. That was a new one on us. It floored Nels. Sidway . . ." Here Gene briefly told her about the cowboy's experience on the trip over, and how swiftly he had put two and two together. "He's gone off down the valley to get a line on horse tracks."

"I told you he was a regular guy," declared Madge, enthusiastically.

"Yes, you did. But it turned out—you don't like him," said Gene, casually.

"Unfortunately, it did. You saw me kiss him. I was just delighted. If it had not been for him I'd have had to go to court. . . . But my feelings don't matter. If Sidway doesn't start something round here he may be a big help to you and Nels. Betwen the two of us, we will put this ranch on its feet."

"Wal now, lass. What you mean—start somethin'?" interposed Nels, greatly interested.

"Nels, you old spoofer. You know what I mean."

"He's already started somethin' with thet hawse."

"I'll say. But I meant particularly what invariably happens to fresh cowboys when I'm here."

"Ahuh. An' thet poor devil will hev to go draggin' himself off withoot his hawse—an' his heart."

"Nels! You're the same old darling!" she cried, gleefully as she left them. Presently she turned a happy face over her shoulder. "Dad, it's swell to be home!"

"Oh! that's good, Madge. It's sure swell to have you."

Madge looked in at the open shed where they had parked her car, then crossed the court and disappeared up the path. Gene observed that Nel's eyes had never left her while she was in sight.

"Gosh! . . . Nels, I wouldn't be in that poor devil's boots for a lot."

"Wal, you jest bet I would," averted Nels. "If I know cowboys, this Sidway feller will give Majesty a run for her money."

"Humph! He doesn't strike me as the fortune-huntin' breed."

"All cowboys air fortune hunters. You was, Gene. An' if I remember you, old *El Capitan,* this Oregon boy has you tied fer all 'cept drinkin' hard an' shootin' hard. I reckon no *hombre* ever beat you at thet."

"Nels, you're a sharp old rascal. I've relied upon you for years. But let's not get sold on this stranger so pronto."

"Wal, I'm sold now—same as Majesty is. Reckon it'd be a good idee for you to keep yore haid."

"Madge sold on Sidway?" ejaculated Gene.

"Shore. Only she has no idee atall aboot it yet."

"You romantic old geezer! . . . It'd just suit you now—if Madge would take to a man of our kind, wouldn't it? . . . Well, to be honest, I'd like it, too. But I think that's only a dream. Madge will marry some city man, tire of us and our simple life here on the open range—and go for the fleshpots of Egypt."

"Natural for her Dad to hev sich pessimistic ideas. But ump-umm!"

"Why natural?" demanded Gene.

" 'Cause you reckon she has inherited a lot of yore no-good blood."

"Right again, old-timer. I am afraid."

"Thet lass will turn oot like her mother. But I ain't sayin', Gene, thet we won't hev hell with her before she turns oot."

During the afternoon Gene persuaded Madge to drive him up the old road toward the foothills, where was located the big spring that fed the lake and provided irrigation for the ranch. As the road was rough they did not get back until toward the end of the afternoon. Passing through the little Mexican village, the inhabitants of which had once depended solely upon the ranch, Gene said to Madge: "Thanks, daughter. You're almost as good a driver as you are a horseman. I'll stop off at Danny Mains' and walk home from there."

"Oh—oh!" said Madge, presently. "Look who's here."

Then Gene espied Sidway, on foot, leaning on the gate talking to Bonita Mains. Range, bridle down, stood near by. There was no more denying the cowboy's demeanor than Bonita's delight. The dusky-eyed maiden radiated charm and coquetry. That Sidway was not in the least embarrassed by their arrival somehow gave Gene a tingle of expectancy and satisfaction. The car stopped. Gene stepped out.

"I'll wait, Dad," said Madge, lightly. "No need to walk home when you can ride. . . . Bonita!—*Buenas tardes.* How are you?"

"Buenas tardes, Miss Stewart," returned Bonita, shy and flushed. "I am so happy to see you. Welcome home to Majesty's Rancho!"

"Thanks, Bonita. I'm glad to see you. Introduce me to your boy friend. . . . Oh, it's Mr. Sidway. I thought I knew that horse. How'd you like him?"

"Not so much. He's cranky, contrary. Spoiled by girls, I expect," replied Sidway, coolly.

"That's fine. I'd rather you didn't ride him."

Gene spoke up: "Bonita, please call your father." And as the girl flashed toward the house, Gene turned with interest to Madge and the cowboy. She was quietly lighting a cigarette. But Gene had never seen her eyes as magnificent as now. Sidway, however, had stepped away from the gate to bend eagle eyes down upon the sage."

"Boss, look at that car," he said quickly. "Hitting only the high spots!"

Gene espied a speeding black car appearing to run away from a long trail of dust.

"He's sure coming," agreed Gene, puzzled. Drivers did not race on that rough road for nothing.

87

"Hope it's my mail," spoke up Madge. "I left orders for it to be sent out."

At that juncture Danny Mains came out, his homely weatherbeaten face wrinkled in a huge smile. Gene called his attention to the car. Mains took one look and then said, "Darn fool'll break his neck, ridin' like thet."

Then he greeted Madge and the cowboy. Bonita, bright-eyed and self-conscious, came out to join her father and gaze down the slope.

"Ren Starr!" she cried.

Gene was quick to detect a note of fear stronger than the surprise in her exclamation. Sidway must have caught it too, for he turned a narrowed gaze upon the girl. Then the group watched the racing car until it passed out of sight under the slope. Bonita, with troubled face, left them to enter the house. Gene, attending to Danny's speculation about Starr still had an ear for a byplay between Sidway and Madge.

"Awful pretty girl—this Bonita," the cowboy was saying.

"Swell kid. On the make, too. But am I telling you?" retorted Madge.

"You appear to be. I didn't get that about her."

"And you such a fast worker— Well!"

"I—I like your horse," went on Lance, evidently no match for her at repartee. Her voice had a cutting edge.

"But you said Range was cranky."

"Sure. Can't a fellow like cranky horses—and girls, too, for that matter?"

"I don't know anything about such fellows."

"Yeah? I'll bet what you don't know wouldn't fill a book. . . . When is your college crowd coming?"

"Oh, you are interested? My sorority sisters, I suppose?"

"No. . . . Just the crowd. When? The time?"

"That can hardly concern you, Mr. Sidway. But they arrive on the twentieth."

"Thank you. I wanted to know because I'd like to help your father a little. Then I'll beat it."

"Oh!—I get you. Dad thought you had taken to him and the ranch."

"I had. You see, I just left Hollywood. I was fed up on a lot of glamour gals and pretty boys. And I'm leery of a college outfit."

"Indeed. Mine would not embarrass you, Mr. Sidway. Certainly my girl friends do not aspire to collect cowboys."

"Yeah! Too slow, I suppose. Prefer gangsters, eh?"

"What? . . . You insulting . . ."

"You can't kid me, Miss Majesty Stewart. . . . Listen, let me tell you something while I've a chance. Your dad is swell. A grand guy. And if you were a credit to him you'd not have this crowd of yours out here now."

"Oh!—And—why?" gasped Madge, as if stifled.

"Because he's in trouble—deep—without your fast crowd to make it worse."

At that moment the humming car sped over the brow of the slope to draw swiftly up to the waiting group. The driver was Ren Starr. As he stopped, Gene espied the tip of a rifle barrel sticking above the door. and in the back seat a pile of duffel, topped with a saddle and bedroll.

"Howdy, folks," he said, laconically. "Heah we all air."

"Wal, Ren, you look like bizness," returned Danny Mains, soberly.

"Glad to see you, Starr," added Gene.

"Boss, you got another new cowboy. Right heah an' now. . . . Ah, Miss Majesty, I shore am glad to see you back home. Hope it's fer good. . . . An' heah's my new pard, Lance Sidway."

"Darn glad to see you, Starr," rejoined Sidway, eager and puzzled.

"Gather around, Gene an' Danny. You'll get an earful," announced the newcomer, and as the three leaned over his car he whispered, directly to Sidway: "Pard, yore trucks rolled in no more'n a couple of hours ago. Stopped at the big garage acrost the street. I got most damn curious. An' when the six drivers mosied into the lunchroom I went round aboot to peep into the trucks. *Empty!* . . . Graves, the new hired hand at the garage, was pilin' up, gas, oil, water, air. And he give it away thet the trucks was stayin' over, mebbe all night. Like hell they will! Pard, these air yore canvas-covered cattle-rustlin' trucks. Them drivers air timed fer tonight. Gene, they're gonna make one of them two-bit raids on yore cattle. An' I'll tell the world they're gonna get a helluva jar."

Gene swore under his breath, and feeling a hand-clasp on his arm, he turned to see Madge, pale, with dilating eyes of purple fire, close behind him.

"Wal, you gasoline hound!" declared Danny Mains. "Back on the job."

"Starr, you've more hunch than that. Spill it," said Sidway.

"Shore. I seen a rider—stranger—who'd been hangin' aboot all day—go into thet lunchroom. He was the go-between. An then I beat it fer heah."

5

Madges' unexpected encounter with Uhl at the parking place, where she had failed to find Sidway, made her abruptly conscious of the fact that her indiscreet affair with the gangster had lost its interest for her. She admitted this to herself while concealing her annoyance from Uhl. Her impulses were quick and she gave in to them daringly, up to a certain point. But she was just as keen to divine when a new one had superseded the old. She did not even have to see Uhl to realize that the man she expected to meet had effaced the fascination of the strange, cold-eyed and masterful gangster. Looking at Uhl, listening to him, Madge felt relief that this was so. She regretted her short flirtation with him. And presently it occurred to her that the thing to do was to get him away, drop him somewhere, and then come back.

"Jump in, Honey Bee," she said, brightly. "I'm too late for my date here and must rush back to campus. Where can I drop you?"

"But, baby, you can't flag me that way," retorted Uhl, getting in beside her. "I know where there's a speak close. Let's have a drink—and a chin."

"Indeed, I'm sorry, but I simply haven't the time. I can't even run you down town. I'll have to drop you at the first streetcar corner."

"Me ride on streetcars? That's a kick. . . . What's the dope on this newspaper stuff about you this morning?"

"Damn tough break! I wasn't to blame for that campus riot. But I'll tell you. . . . Say, Thursday. Give me a ring, and I'll meet you," said Madge, and she slowed up and halted on a corner.

Uhl left the car ungraciously, plainly against his will. That steely something about him which had appealed to Madge did not affect her again.

"Yeah? I've called you twice and nothing doing. That doesn't go with me, sweetheart. I don't wait on no girl"

"Perhaps you've found me a new species, as I you," returned Madge. "Sorry. Bye. I'll be seeing you."

"She'd better be," Madge heard, and then she had flashed across the intersection. The dumb cluck! What ever had possessed her to let him sit down beside her that day at André's? Madge reflected she was not so much to blame as Dixie Cune. But before she had circled several blocks to get back to the parking place she had forgotten Uhl. Then, half an hour late, she drove to the rendezvous, and did an unprecedented thing—she waited half an hour longer for this Oregon boy who loved his sister and his horse Umpqua. Not until Madge thought of how long she had waited, how much she wanted to see him again, did she realize that her weakness for new faces, new adventures, had this instance established an extraordinary parallel. How nice he was! How different! And evidently he had not felt that way about her. Madge suffered a new sensation akin to pique, and that melted into disappointment. Here was one fellow who would not call her up to make a date. He did not even know her name. Why had she not told him and the phone number of the house? Nevertheless on the way back to campus her injured feelings were assuaged by an inexplicable premonition that she would meet him again.

Fraternity Row appeared to be more than usually crowded with cars. All the houses had several parked out in front. Madge pulled into the driveway and ran into the living room. All her senior sorority sisters, except Maramee, were there, with two boys from the Tau Phi house. The circle did not, as was its wont, let out a whoop as she entered. They all looked pretty glum and their greetings were forced. Madge now prepared for the worst.

"That sharp-voiced boy friend of yours just called up, Madge. Uhl's the name. Has he a string on you?"

"I was foolish enough to let him think so," rejoined Madge. "You all look like death's-heads. What's the worst? I can take it?"

"Majesty, I just came from campus," replied Rollie Stevens. "They've called a meeting for tomorrow morning. Looks like curtains for you."

"I met the Dean just now," said Pequita Nelson, reluctantly. "She is afraid—because you already were on probation."

"Madge, if you hadn't pulled so many stunts this semester!" exclaimed her roommate and her closest friend, Allie Leland. "They'll hate to expel you—at this late date—graduation right at hand—and you an honor student. But ever since you were elected in your junior year you've——"

"Don't heap it on, Allie. . . . I've been a damn fool. But I had a lot of fun. For myself I wouldn't care—much—only it'll reflect on the house. And if Dad and Mom see the papers—Oh, that'll hurt. . . . After all, I didn't egg on the students to throw that party."

"I can vouch for that, Majesty," admitted Rollie gloomily. "I did. I collected some of the boys and we went to the President. He was swell. But . . ."

"Rollie, that was darling of you. I'm obliged. If it were up to him I'd come through. Mad Everett, however, has it in for me. . . . How about a bull session this time tomorrow? About my ranch party. . . . Rollie, be sure my boy friends come'"

"Humph! In that case we'll have to hold your session in the chapel. You couldn't park them here."

"Rollie Stevens, I said my boy friends," retorted Madge.

"Am I one—or just a messanger boy?"

"You're number one, when you're nice."

"It was never obvious to me, Majesty. . . . Then I'm to page Barg—Dawson—Nate—Brand?—Here my judgment, not my imagination, halts shrinkingly."

"You left out Snake!" protested Madge.

"That muscle man?—Majesty!"

"Yeah? I get you. But I like him. I wonder if I have a horse that can hold him up."

"It'd take an elephant," chimed in Allie.

"But, Majesty," importuned Pequita, eloquently. "Will footballer and cowboy mix?"

"We've got to have something beside drinks and dances," averred Madge, and then she thought of her champion. "If I had only had a chance to ask *him!*"

Rollie threw up his hands and departed, and presently Madge and her roommate were upstairs on the third floor, in their light colorful room.

"Who's him?" asked Allie.

"Him!—Why the wonderful fellow who slugged the cop and saved me from being pinched."

"Hadn't heard of him. Madge, you can dig up more romance and more trouble than any girl on campus."

"Rather a doubtful distinction, Allie, darling. If they

expel me I'll have to think about myself at long last."

"They won't. Why, they'd be afraid the senior class would walk out on them!"

Dinner that night was not the usual merry gathering. Madge seemed the only cheerful girl in the house. She felt a thickening atmosphere of disaster. Her friends knew, perhaps, what she could only anticipate and they were stricken. Soon after supper Madge phoned to break an engagement and went to her room and presently to bed. When Allie came in and crept into Madge's bed and into her arms to weep unrestrainedly—then Madge made certain of the worst. She did not sleep well until late. At breakfast she missed the girls. Summoned to the office on campus she went with her chin up and her face tranquil, but inwardly she felt a little sick. She had an interview with the Vice-President, and it was short. The directors of the college had expelled her. They had to take into account the fact of her former derelictions and that she had been on probation. To overlook this last escapade would be establishing a precedent that would have a very bad effect. Madge accepted the decree gracefully, without a word of self-defense, and left the embarrassed official to go out, and cross the campus for the last time.

For her own sake Madge did not care particularly. She was tired of college, and traditions, such as graduating and receiving a degree, had never held any significance for her. She felt she had absorbed everything that this university could give her that would ever have any meaning in her life. When she crossed the row she did not look back at the campus, and knew that she never would again.

Nevertheless, up in her room alone Madge shed some bitter hot tears. She hal loved that room, and to realize its intimacies, its joys and sorrows, its plans and stunts, were over forever struck her with her first deep grief. But in an hour Madge, to all appearances, was her old self again, and had turned her facile mind upon the problem ahead of her.

There was trouble out in her Arizona home. Long

ago she had sensed that. And it was high time she returned there to take up the burden, whatever it was, for her beloved parents. Madge knew she was going home to stay. A trip now and then to the coast, and perhaps an occasional one East, would suffice her. Before she had come to college the lonely range, the stately Spanish ranch house, the horses, and her lovely soft-spoken, stately mother, and her stalwart father, had filled her life with action and excitement and love. Now that she was a woman, they would be all the more to her. And somewhere there was a man like her Dad . . . but she dismissed that disturbing thought.

Allie came in at the lunch hour to disrupt Madge's concentration on a long-considered task, that of making a list of things to select and order for the ranch. Once given up to that occupation, Madge found it absorbing. "Honey," she begged of Allie, "fetch me up some food. Anything."

A long while seemed to have elapsed when at four o'clock Madge tripped downstairs, in a new and striking gown, to meet the bull session. Rollie had them all there, even to the hulking Snake Elwell, whose rosy cherub-like visage for once wore an intelligent expression. As Madge stood in the wide door the faces of her friends flashed expectantly and tragically at her.

"Friends, Romans, Countrymen—don't look like that!" she cried, gayly. "It's over. And I can take it! . . . I've asked you all here to talk over my cherished dream—to have you out to the ranch. Do I need to sell the idea to any one of you?"

"No!" came the concerted reply.

"Okay then. Here's the dirt. I want you to arrive on the twentieth or as near that date as possible. There are eleven of us. Allie will come in my little car, Nate driving; unless darling, you'd prefer Brand?"

"Ow! Ow!" squealed Nate. "That is a hot one. Majesty, damn your honest tongue!"

"I'll match you for that honor," spoke up Brand.

"You're on—if you got a nickel to toss."

When that dire contingency was settled in Nate's favor Madge went on, consulting her notes.

"The rest of you can come in two cars, that is, by expressing most of your baggage. Jot this down . . . Bolton, Arizona. And ship your baggage three days ahead, so it will be there. . . . Rollie's big car for one. Dawson has one. And Snake, whose big bus is it I've seen you in—with a redheaded girl?"

"Madge, it belongs to Bu—and I can't get it unless I bring her along," said Elwell, awkwardly.

"Ha! Ha! Snake's on the spot," shouted Rollie.

"Well, he can't wiggle like a snake through this field," declared Madge, laughing. "Bu who?"

"Aw, never mind."

"Madge, it's Beulah Allen," declared one of the boys, sotto voce.

"That number!" ejaculated Rollie, aghast. "Swell kid, Majesty—but I'm afraid she would disrupt the sweet tenor of our Tau Phi constancy."

"You telling me?" retorted Madge. "I know Beulah. Snake, it's up to you. Do you want her, for herself and not for her car?"

"Go into a huddle, Snake," taunted someone.

"Madge, do you like Bu?" countered the athlete, earnestness stronger than his confusion.

"Certainly I like her, or I wouldn't consider her. But, Snake, if you're crazy about her. . . . Cowboys and *vaqueros* are even more susceptible than students."

"I'll take a chance, and Madge, you're a peach," declared Elwell, in red relief.

"That's that," said Madge, when the roar subsided, and she checked her list. "You can fight among yourselves who's going to ride with whom."

"Madge, sweetest, get down to it—Clothes!—What'll we need to wear?" burst out Maramee Joyce.

"Your ruling passion, Maramee, for once will be foiled. . . . We're on a ranch you know—grand place to wear out all your old clothes. Mostly outdoor stuff, both heavy and light; your riding togs and don't forget a bathing suit. In fact, girls, I want you—if you have to come without a stitch to your backs," declared Madge, warmly.

"Suits us swell!" yelled the boys. "And Majesty—" added Rollie, "we're tired of pink teas and cakes, you know."

"I'm sending over cases and cases," replied Madge, radiantly. And when the row had subsided she continued: "I can supply anything in the world but happy hearts. You must bring them.

"I've been hours on end making up lists. It'll take two full days to shop. Oh, some job! And then I'm off. No more dates. The sooner I go the better, dear friends. . . . That's my say—for my—last bull session!"

She fled in a silence that hurt.

Early and late for three days Madge shopped in the Los Angeles stores. At night she packed, with Allie to help, and sometimes Pequita or Selma. What a relief when the expressman took her trunks away! At length all her tasks were done, even to the packing of bags in her car. Next morning when she awoke the sun was flashing on the vine-covered walls of the chapel. With Allie in her pajamas, Madge tiptoed down the stairs, passed the closed doors of her sisters, and hurried to the garage. Her last load of baggage was stowed away.

"Don't make me—cry—" she whispered, huskily, to the weeping mute Allie. "I've got to drive some. . . . Tell them all—good-by . . . darling—I'll—be—seeing . . ."

Madge drove out with blurred eyes that did not clear until she rounded the corner and turned her back to the campus forever. An early rising student halloed, but she did not look. The constriction in her throat eased as she threaded into the traffic. It was over—college and all that went with it. Madge did not deceive herself. All these lovely contacts would sever and fade away in the conflicting tides of new and wider life.

Not to press down on the accelerator seemed harder to resist than ever. In one of the suburban towns Madge stopped for breakfast and to send telegrams home. To her sorority sisters she wired: "All's well. I'll be seeing you." Soon then she faced the long orange-grove—and vineyard-bordered road, and here she drove the powerful car up to sixty along the straight stretches. Madge loved to drive, to speed, to feel the impact of wind, to see the narrow thread of road flash under her, and the blurred greens pass by. By ten o'clock she was in Banning, where she halted for fuel. The service man paid Madge and her car an admiring gaze.

A hot furnacelike breath waved into Madge's face up from the long Gorgonio Pass, as she left Banning. Once, however, under way again, the pressing air felt cool to her. At Indio she had a bite to eat and a malted milk, then leaving her car at a service station she crossed out of the copper sun to the shade of cottonwoods. These green full-foliaged trees, like the pines, were reminiscent of her ranch, and the ranges of the West. Palms and orange trees belonged to California, somehow removed from Arizona. A sultry breeze flew off the desert, tinged with an acrid dust, that felt gritty to her moist hands. Gloves were almost intolerable, and the skin of her lips and cheeks felt drying up. Nevertheless she welcomed this dry heat. Soon she would be across the desert, up on the sage ranges of Arizona, where the air was different. The sun could shine down hot, but in the shade the air felt cool. Then in her beloved home state there was never that copper sky or the blurred distance which she saw now. San Jacinto stood up shrouded in heat; smoky veils curled up from the gray weed-spotted desert; the ragged line of the barren ranges stretched south to fade in the distance; the pale expanse of the Salton Sea gleamed in the hollow of the valley, its salty shore line ghastly and weird.

Madge walked a few minutes under the cottonwoods, despite the discomfort. The next two hundred miles and more would be the most trying of this drive. To traverse a long stretch of flat country below sea level was far from a joy ride in June. Madge, rested from nervous strain, went back to her car to resume her journey. From Indio to El Centro Madge reveled in speed and the rare delight of catapulting through space. Beyond El Centro, where she halted for a little while, sunset caught her in the dunes, those exquisitely graceful curves and mounds and scallops of sand, beginning to color with opal tints, and shadow darkly away from the sun. This five-mile stretch was the only one on the journey that she longed to acquire for Arizona. Through that stately region Madge drove at a snail's pace, and rediscovered her love of color and symmetry and solitude. She felt like a Navajo at sunset, part of the nature she watched.

When dusk mantled the black lava point of Pilot Knob, and dim purple Picacho, Madge sighted the lights of Yuma and soon the broad Colorado, chafing in sullen flood away into the darkness of a bend toward the south.

In a few more minutes she crossed the bridge into Arizona, and drove to the Alcatraz, a new hotel where she had stayed coming and going on her visit home the preceding summer. Her head and eyes ached, and her body was stiff from the long drive. And hungry and thirsty as she was she enjoyed the luxury of a bath and change before going downstairs. Apparently there were only a few guests at the hotel. After finishing a light dinner Madge went out to walk up and down the street and send some telegrams. The night was sultry and warm, with no air stirring, but she required exercise more than comfort. She walked to a corner and back. Mexicans with sloe-black eyes passed her, and a group of the lofty statured Yuma Indians who wrapped their long hair in a coil on top of their heads and set a cake of mud upon it. The glaring twin lights of cars loomed and passed by. Madge did not succumb to an impulse to walk down to the main street. Yuma was fascinating at any hour, especially after nightfall.

A long black car had drawn up to the curb before the hotel. Madge, as she passed it, heard a low exclamation, then quick footsteps. A slim hand with fingers like steel clutched her arm.

"Gold-top, what you doing here?" called a sharp voice, cold as ice. Madge knew to whom it belonged before she turned to see Uhl, bareheaded under the electric light, his eyes glittering from his pale face.

"Oh!—hello—this is a surprise," replied Madge, haltingly, as her wits leaped to meet the situation.

"You alone?"

"Yes. On my way home," she said, slowly, fighting a confusion of thought. She did not like his look nor the hard clutch on her arm.

"Home! Say, what kind of a twist are you? Told me you lived in Santa Barbara."

"Did I? Will you be good enough to let go my arm? You hurt."

"Come for a ride," he returned, in a voice that brooked no opposition to his will and he almost dragged her toward the big black car.

"No, thanks," rejoined Madge, as, supple and strong, with one wrench she freed herself. "I'm tired. Drove all day. See you tomorrow."

"Like hell you will! Same as phone calls. I'm seeing you right now. Get that, baby!" He was neither angry nor insolent. His face had the clear cold chiseling of a diamond. Madge was not afraid of him, but she realized that she should be. She wavered between turning her back upon him and asking him into the hotel. The important thing was to get in off the street, and acting upon that she said: "I won't talk here. Come in for a moment."

Uhl hung close to her, hand at her elbow, and did not speak while they went through the lobby. He steered Madge into a back room with subdued lights, where several couples sat at tables, drinking. Here Uhl led her to a seat at a corner table and ordered cocktails from the attendant.

"What kind of a deal are you giving me, sister?" he began, forcefully, as he leaned toward her across the table. All about him was cold, suspicious, repellent.

"Deal?" she queried, playing for time.

"You knew I fell for you. I told you. And you met me, danced and drank with me. Then when I get stuck deep you try to pull this 'I'll be seeing you' gag. That doesn't go. See?"

"Mr. Uhl, I seem to see that you have misunderstood me."

"Yeah? Nothing doing, eh?"

"If you wish to put it that way."

He controlled what must have been a murderous fire, judging from the instant lowering of his blazing eyes and the quiver of his slim hands. Strangely, this reaction of his again restored a certain fascination he had exerted over Madge, she felt that it was almost an attraction of repugnance. She had had too much adulation, too many at her feet. There was in her, unconsciously, a primitive longing.

"Baby, I've gone nuts over some dames," began Uhl deliberately, apparently having suppressed his violent feelings. "But none ever held a copper to you. I'm horribly in love with you, sweetheart."

"Oh, I'm sorry you've allowed it to go so far," murmured Madge. "Any girl would be flattered and. . . . But, you see, I'm engaged."

"Yeah? What's that to me?"

"I can't imagine, I'm sure. But I know a girl can't accept serious attentions from one man when she's engaged to another."

"The hell dames can't. They do. They all do . . . Aw, Beauty, don't be such a plaster. I'm crazy about you. . . . If you're alone here tonight let me. . . ."

Madge felt his slim hand slide upon her knee under the table. His eyes, gray as molten metal had a hypnotic power. For a moment she felt paralyzed. Then her rigidity broke to a start, to a stinging heat, to an insupportable sensation. That tearing thing seemed to actuate Madge more than Uhl's outrage. In a fury she kicked out with all her might. And her onslaught sent the man sprawling over his chair. Madge almost overturned the table as she leaped up. Wheeling she fled from the room, and never stopped until she backed up against her locked door.

"Serves you damn—right!" she panted, passionately. "Playing with a heel like him! . . . Are you ever —going to think?"

Madge hardly had time to think then. Hurried steps

101

in the hall preceded a knock on the door. Another knock, louder, followed, and the handle of the door was tried.

"Madge!"

"Who is it?" she called.

"Bee. Let me in. I want to square myself."

"I'll take your word for it—from that side."

"I was out of my head. I'll come clean. You're not like other dames."

"Thanks, Mr. Uhl. You discovered that rather late. But I take the blame for your mistake."

"Will you let me in?"

"No. I'm going to bed."

"That wouldn't make any difference to me. I want to talk to you."

"Well, I don't want to listen. . . . But I'll see you in the morning. At breakfast. Eight o'clock," she replied, thinking that might be a way to get rid of him.

"Okay, baby. But don't string me again."

Uhl's voice had an ominous ring that jarred unpleasantly upon Madge's ruffled nerves. Uhl was dangerous. Recalling his bragging, the roll of bills he exhibited, his extraordinary intimation of some kind of power, which Madge now analyzed as underworld, she realized that she might be in actual peril and by no means should she encounter him again. She determined to be a hundred miles and more beyond Yuma by eight o'clock next morning. Following that decision her first impulse was to telephone the desk to leave a call for five o'clock, but she thought better of it. She always awakened early, provided she went to bed early. This she did at once, and eventually fell asleep.

The roaring of a motor truck awakened Madge. She hardly seemd to have done more than close her eyes. Ruddy light on the desert ridges attested to sunrise. Her wrist watch said ten minutes to five. By five o'clock she was at the desk downstairs, paying her bill. She told the night clerk, in case anyone asked, that she had received a telegram which recalled her to Los Angeles. In another ten minutes she was speeding east on the Arizona highway.

The morning was fresh and cool. A line of fire rimmed the ranges. No cars, no curves on the empty black road ahead gave full rein to her desire and her need to drive fast. Sixty miles an hour had been her conservative limit, except a few times on short favorable stretches. Here Madge had the course and the incentive to increase her speed to seventy and more. The motor droned like a homing bee. It ate up the miles. At eighty miles on the indicator Madge tasted the last complete and full elation of the speedster. The telegraph poles were almost as fence posts.

Madge never looked back once. She drove under the urge that Uhl was pursuing her and that she could run away from him. At Gila Bend where the highway forked she slowed down and took the right branch, then opened up again. Mohawk, Aztec, Sentinel—the stations that she knew well were overtaken and passed by. At Casa Grande, while the car was being refueled and gone over, she had breakfast and lunch in one. From there Madge again faced the waving colored desert, with its black buttes and red ranges, ever growing rougher. But she took little account of it or of the hours. She was bent on a record drive. Tucson for once was not interesting, only as a service station; and the quaint Tombstone and bustling Bisbee only obstacles on the road. Late that day, which had flashed by like the hamlets, Madge drove into Douglas with the most perfect satisfaction for a driving mania she had ever experienced.

She stopped at an automobile camp, had her dinner at a lunch counter, and by eight o'clock she was in bed, her eyelids heavy. Her last thought was of what she would do on the morrow to the hundred-odd miles between Douglas and Majesty's Rancho.

Next morning she was on the way by six o'clock, after having breakfasted. She would have made the run to Bolton in an hour but for the fact that she was held back by a detour, and some heavily laden, slow-moving canvas-covered trucks that simply stuck to the middle of the road. They annoyed her so that she thought that she would not soon forget them, nor one of the drivers, a swarthy visaged fellow who glared at her when at last with incessant honking she forced him over.

A Bolton Madge tarried long enough to leave orders with the stationmaster about her baggage and freight due to arrive. Then she refueled again, and drove on, beginning to feel strangely happy—with the journey almost ended, with turmoil behind her, and rest and home almost gained.

But when she struck off the highway beyond the culvert, up the old rancho road, which proved to be annoyingly full of lumps and gutters and rocks, she passed from an amused impatience to a burst of temper. She endured the jolting and the messing of her baggage and packages for some miles, then she had to drive slowly. What an atrocious road! And she with a crowd of guests due in less than two weeks! How would three truckloads of purchases ever safely negotiate that trail for steers and cowboys? Did her father have that same old loafing bunch of *vaqueros?* She would hire a gang of Mexicans to make a decent road out of it pronto. It took Madge three quarters of an hour to drive from the culvert to the summit of the slope—approximately fifteen miles.

Madge, surmounting the slope, abruptly to face the vast purple valley, with its arresting black knoll topped by the gray mansion which was her home, and the grand uplifting range beyond, stopped the car to gaze as one in transport. How astoundingly familiar! She had only to see to realize that all these blue distances and splendid landmarks were veritably a part of herself. But absence and life too full for memory had come between them, and her thought and her love, now suddenly leaping to vivid and poignant life again. The morning was still fresh; shadows still lingered under the ridges; every wash and rock shone white; the waves of sage rolled on and on, in an endless sea, dotted with cattle; the league-long slope up to the knoll had a beautiful sweep; and there peeping out of the black pines, lonely and superb, stood the mansion of the old Dons. As a fitting background the mountains loomed impressively, white-slided and black-canyoned, upflung in rock battlements to the blue sky.

"Oh, darling, darling home!" cried Madge, in rapture and reproach. "I have been faithless. But I have come back. For good! Forever, to you—to my home —to the love and life I shall find here!"

The moment of exaltation was difficult for Madge, inasmuch as she had a vague realization that she was not big enough, not good enough for this noble country, nor for the devoted mother and father who awaited her coming. But she had a clear conception that if she were true to the emotion this magnificent scene had aroused in her heart, she would grow far toward being worthy of it. That thought persisted helpfully, too strong even for her misgivings.

She drove on. The descent into the valley afforded swifter travel. She had left rocks and ruts behind. Soon she was down to a level, on a white road, six inches deep in dust; and here she cut loose again with a shriek of joy, to shoot ahead of the yellow clouds that puffed up from the wheels. The wash in the center was sand and she hit that at a fifty-mile clip, to veer and leap and plunge, the wheel lurching under her strong grip, and roar safely across to another strip of dust. Beyond that the long slope of yellow road was like a country lane, with its two narrow wheel strips, its weedy center, its hard ground. Madge hummed up that, out of the grass and sage, into the pines, and on up the shaded brown-matted aisle to the green oval before the stately mansion.

And on the porch, telescope in hand, her eyes deeply dark with joy stood her mother. Madge pressed the brake so forcibly that the great car, answering with a grinding scream on gravel, stopped so suddenly that she and the bags had a violent jerk. Madge threw off gloves, goggles, hat all in one swift action, and leaping out she ran up the steps into her mother's arms.

105

They were inside, in the living room, and Madge, wiping her eyes was saying: Fancy *me* being such a baby! But somehow it's different this time. Coming home! . . . Let me look at you, Mom darling. . . . Oh, the same lovely patrician mother!—But, darling, you *have* some gray in this beautiful hair—and a few lines I never saw before. But you're more perfect than ever!"

"Madge! How you rave!" exclaimed her mother, her voice low. "But it's worth a great deal to have you home—and hear you talk like that . . . I hope it's not all—let me say, remorse."

"Mom! . . . Come, let's not stand all day. My legs are weak. . . . I'll sit on the arm of your chair. . . . There," and Madge slipped her arm around her mother and drew the handsome head to her shoulder. "I'm the little girl who has courage to confess— but who would rather not face her mother's loving eyes. . . Let me get it over, darling . . . You had my letters— my telegrams?"

"Yes, child."

"Well?"

"I understand, Madge. You need not tell me anything. I went to college once. And all these years you've been away— these hard and changing years— I've tried to keep abreast of the times, even if it was only through newspapers and magazines and books. Most of all, your letters have told me. I know what has gone on, what has come to pass, even if I have trouble grasping it."

"Mom, I knew you'd say that," replied Madge, earnestly. "But I doubt, Mother darling, that with all your intelligence and wisdom you could realize what has actually happened to us, to my generation. Somehow I can't get it. Yet they call me brainy, Mom. You'll get some firsthand information soon. My crowd of sorority sisters and student friends will be here to spend the summer. They are normal, as young people go today. They are all radical. But I'll let you judge them for yourself. . . . My self, Mom, this contrite daughter returned to you, is an enigma to herself. . . .

106

I hate restraint. I won't be told what I should or should not do. I have no idea what I want, except that I want something terribly. I read trash where once I read poetry, history, fiction. I've read Freud and he's all wet. My favorite authors at present are Cabell and the best detective writers, wide apart as the poles. Most grownups give me a pain in the neck. But you don't, Mom! I am scared of Dad, though as a girl I worshiped him. He was my hero, my *El Capitan,* as he was yours. But will he get me—my crowd? . . . In my freshman year I went a little haywire— drinking, dancing, petting, smoking—*all,* Mom, except I didn't go the limit. I tell you that, a little ashamed, as if I were an old-fashioned virgin. But college girls, except some who are fools, work out of that worst mess in their upperclassman years. Still the pace is swift, Mom, in education, achievement, in a social way, in the modern thing. . . . For young people that modern thing seems to be to break all the laws—speed laws, booze laws. There is no such thing as modesty, as I remember you taught it to me. Pagans, I fear! I haven't opened a Bible since my religion course during my sophomore year. Lastly, Mom, don't think that *all* co-eds fall under this category. There are loads and loads of girls besides. Only my crowd, and the other sorority crowds—they get by the college courses somehow, though a few like me gain class honors and high scholarships—only for these the aim and end of existence are cocktails, dances, clothes, cars and men . . . There, Mom, darling, that's all. Will I dare tell Dad —and will he understand?"

"My dear," replied her mother, quietly, after a moment fraught with suspense for Madge, "I don't think you should tell your father—all that. . . . And there —his step in the patio!"

Her father entered, sending Madge's blood rushing back to her heart, still the stalking giant with the piercing eyes she remembered, yet somehow indefinably changed. Was it the white over his temples—the hollow cheeks and lean jaw? Then followed the greeting, the embrace, which made Madge mistress of that

107

errant and incredible weakness, leaving only the resurgence of her girlish love for her ideal of all men. During the disposal of her luggage in her rooms, so thrillingly the same, and the luncheon afterward, Madge babbled on and on, listening but little, far removed from the honest girl she had been to her mother. She divined that she thirsted for something from her father—something she knew she had, beautifully and everlastingly, from her mother. But here was a Westener, one of the old school, that daredevil *El Capitan* of the Revolution, the cowboy who had killed men! He had worshiped her mother, but would his love for his little girl survive all that the years and changes had made her?

After luncheon Madge leisurely unpacked her numerous bags and suitcases, stopping dreamily at intervals, or finding some excuse to go to her mother. During all this while the desire to see Nels and her horses grew stronger, until at length it was too demanding to resist. It need not have been anything to resist, if she had been able to put aside the strong desire to change to riding garb, and vault upon Cedar once more. Nels surely would not have liked her in these new English riding breeches, so tight and leggy, and that first day home she could not don overalls and boots. Wherefore at length she went down the old back road, now an overgrown trail, to gray ruin of ranch buildings and corrals.

Nels was her second father. He had taught her to ride, to shoot, to rope—all the tricks of the range. He had told her the terrible stories about her famous father, and that lovely and appalling romance of her mother and all about ranch and cowboy life, even before she was old enough to understand.

Meeting Nels proved to mean more, to be a deeper experience, than even her memories had anticipated. The change in him was not indefinable. Madge felt the warm blood recede from her cheeks. The years had told on Nels.

Not until she sat with him on the top bar of the

corral fence to see her horses did the zest and stir of home-coming return. What a glossy, long-maned, plume-tailed, racy and thoroughbred troop of horses! Cedar, gray as the cedars for which he was named, pranced before her, soft-eyed, whinnying, high-stepping and sensitive, knowing her yet not sure. And Range, the long rangy sorrel, red as fire in the rays of the setting sun; and Bellefontaine, that dainty proud little mare, sure of Madge, poking her nose up for sugar; and Blackboy, like shining coal in his well-groomed hide, and Sultan, the roan, and Dervish and Arab, twin whites, as perfect as the movie horses, but not so tame, and Leatherstocking, a range cow horse, loved despite his plebeian blood, and Pinto, a mustang—all her own, and the corral full of shaggy jealous horses and colts, snorting and kicking—all of them brought home to Madge the stinging truth of her return.

But it was when she walked up the lane with Nels to encounter a Mexican lad leading a black horse that Madge's emotion flooded to a bursting pitch. A strange horse, a grand horse, dusty and lame, bearing a cowboy's accouterments, in one inconceivable flash, added a bitter drop to the sweet cup which she had just tasted. Screeching to Nels, importuning the lad, this got Madge nowhere. Full tilt then she ran around the corner of the store, straight into the arms of a clanking, gorgeously arrayed—a strangely familiar cowboy whose face went white and then a dusky red.

As if by magic Madge confronted her campus champion, and under this last straw her burdened feelings burst in glad amaze and gay delight, to a welcome she did not consider and a kiss she could not recall.

Could she have paid him a more flattering compliment for his cleverness in contriving to be there at her own home? In the following exchange of words, in this cowboy's well-simulated protest and confusion, Madge experienced a reaction which inwardly she divined was something more, something deeply and inexplicably glad. And that, at his denial, submerged this sweet self. What was the matter with the fool? To be sure there stood her dad, his piercing eyes hard to meet, and his slight amused smile disconcerting. But even so, Madge argued to her ruffled vanity, her welcome, her kiss should have inspired him to confront half a dozen fathers and confess his duplicity.

It was the horse Umpqua that saved the embarrassing situation for the moment, and which precipitated a really serious one. Madge left them, furious with the cowboy. She spied upon the group below from the covert of pines, curious even in her anger to see what Sidway would do. There was no doubt about the sincerity of his purpose, when he went to his horse. He meant to ride away. And would have done so but for her father and Nels. "Can't he take it, the big handsome stiff?" muttered Madge, in her angry surprise. "What'd he beat me here for if not to make a hit with me? It did! . . . And— I was hit before. . . . Oh, the dumbell! To spoil it all! . . . Now I'll have to jolly him along and play with him to get that horse— when I really liked him . . . how much? . . . Am I burned up?"

By the time Madge had told the story, with reservations as to her own uncertain feelings, to her mother, her resentment had gone into eclipse. She could not bear ill will. And she had developed a merciless truth about herself.

"What is young Sidway like?" asked her mother, presently.

"Oh, swell!"

"That is rather an ambiguous term these days."

"Mom, I'd hate to spoil a pleasant surprise for you. Also I'd like to get your reaction to Sidway before I tell you mine. *I* may be—I must have been all wet, if you get what I mean."

"I don't, my dearest," replied her mother, with a bewildered smile. "But I'm sure you like him."

"Not on your life!—I did, yes. . . . The dirty look he gave me—what he said! . . . Such things just aren't done to *me*."

Madge leisurely changed for dinner, and after catching herself approving of the white image in the long mirror, she had the grace to be ponderingly amused at that part of her thought which conceived a possibility of Sidway seeing her thus. No telling where that Hollywood extra might bob up! She arrived late in the dining room, yet in time to hear her father say: "He'd have gone, too, Madeline, if Nels and I hadn't believed him when he swore he didn't come here on account of Madge."

"Well, Dad Stewart!" declared Madge, in mock solemnity. "So that cowboy put it over?"

"Daughter! You look like your mother—the first time I ever saw her in white!"

"Oh, thank you, Dad! Then I must look just stunning."

"You do. . . . Madge, young Sidway didn't put it over. He told the truth. Nels believed him. So did I. He hadn't the remotest idea that my daughter, the girl Ren Starr told him about, was you—the girl he'd actually met and befriended."

"Dad, he's a liar. I wouldn't believe that on a bet," declared Madge.

"I'll bet you find it out and you'll be sorry."

"Preposterous! So he put up a big bluff to you and Nels? . . . Dad, that cowboy is right up to date. He knows his stuff. . . . What I can't get is why he was ashamed of his clever stunt?"

"Madge, it's conceivable that he seemed ashamed because of his innocence when all of you believed in his deceit," observed her mother.

"Oh, my adorable parents! What you must learn about us! Mr. Sidway's ears must be burning. Let's forget him."

Nevertheless, despite her suggestion, Madge had no slight difficulty in conforming to it. She succeeded presently by launching into an account of what she wanted done to the road, and the patio and the long-deserted rooms in the west wing, and about more servants from the Mexican village—all in the interest of her guests who were to arrive on the twentieth. She was indeed not disappointed in her anticipation that both of her parents seemed heartily interested in her summer party, with no wish but to contribute in every

111

way to its success. If they appeared a little bewildered several times during the discussion, and at a loss for words, Madge put that down to her elaborate and extravagant plans.

They stayed up late, at least for them, and when Madge bade them good night, she went to her rooms thinking how perfectly splendid they were, and that she was happy, and the most fortunate girl in the world.

Next morning she satisfied a craving that had long beset her—that of getting into the saddle again. To find Range gone gave quick rise to her temper, which strangely did not greatly fall when her father explained that the cowboy had merely obeyed orders. She had resolutely to keep her eyes off Umpqua or she would have yielded to riding him again, which pride bade her forego.

That afternoon Madge found great enjoyment in driving her father high up the old road, to an elevation that permitted their gazing down upon the ranch and the house, and the flowing sage flats with their speckled knots of cattle. While her father puttered around the boxed-in spring and repaired the outlet, Madge sat at ease, lulled by the heights and the depths of this wide-spreading land.

"No wonder the lake and reservoir went almost dry," said her father, when he came back to the car. "Two thirds of the water leaking away."

"Oh, I forgot to look at the lake. Will it be full again by the time my friends arrive? We'll want to go in bathing. Dad, is there any sand near enough to haul?"

"Sand. The wash down below is all sand. Fine and white, too."

"Swell! I'll want a nice sandy beach for us to lie around on in the sun."

"That's an easy one, Madge."

The end of a perfect day just had to have a drawback. When Madge caught sight of Lance Sidway leaning over the gate, apparently deeply interested in Bonita Mains, she fell victim to a most disconcerting irritation. The cowboy, as she drove up to a halt, did not noticeably move, until Bonita blushingly drew back, to come out of the gate. Then he stared at Madge, rather satirically she thought. Was there not a single man in the whole vast earth who did not fall for every pretty girl he saw, regardless of her color? It had not taken Lance Sidway long to contact the little half-breed coquette of the range. Madge chalked up another mark against the cowboy.

The succeeding moments, outside of Danny Mains' kindly welcome—Madge did not take Bonita's to heart—should have bored Madge, if she had been running true to form. But she was off her stride and she knew the reason, and therefore looked at that reason with rather scornful eyes. Her mental alertness quickened, however, when Ren Starr's car was sighted, and Bonita precipitately fled.

The stab Sidway had given Madge, along with the look he gave her, silenced Madge, and gave rein to whirling thoughts that refused to recognize her wrath. She nursed it, yet succumbed to curiosity, and got out of the car to listen to the short talk of the men. Rustlers! Verily her home-coming had not been dull. Then the men fell back from Starr's car, Sidway to leap astride Range and gallop off, Mains to run into his house, and her father to get in with her, his fine face stern and dark, somehow recalling her fear of him when she was a little girl.

"Step on it, Madge."

"Oh, Dad! What is it? I heard some of your talk. Trucks! Rustlers!"

"You bet you did. . . . Madge, these boys have made me feel like my old self. Sidway got a line on these cattle thieves. All in a day! Won't Nels jump at that? Won't he be pleased? And Starr ran out with news of a truck raid on our cattle tonight."

"Truck raid! Who ever heard of such a thing?"

"Sidway got it, just like that. Keen as a whip, that cowboy. And Starr's a running pard for him. . . . Madge, I have a hunch things will look up for us this summer."

113

"Darling, are you telling *me?* . . . What will you do?"

"I must tell Nels first."

"That old—ranger! Oh, Dad, he'll be for guns! horses! ropes!"

"You bet. Madge, before the night is over we'll hang some of these truck drivers and cattle-raiding greasers."

"I want to go!"

"Nonsense, child. You might get hurt. . . . Let me out here. I won't be up for supper. Tell Mother."

Naturally Madge expected her mother to be greatly perturbed, but was agreeably surprised.

"This will wake up your father and Nels, too," rejoined her mother, with satisfaction.

"But, Mom! . . . Dad swore they'd *hang* some of them. They will have to catch them first. Oh, wouldn't I like to go? . . . It means a fight. Crooks these days use machine guns. Dad might be hurt. . . . And Sidway. He's a reckless devil."

"Madge, your father and Nels and Danny Mains will be a match for all the crooks in the Southwest. Don't worry about them. Rustlers will give them just the impetus they need. And cattle raising will probably be the better for it."

Nevertheless Madge did worry. She read and worried and waited until long after her mother had retired. Then when she did go to bed she could not sleep. She listened. But there were no sounds except the lonesome chirping of crickets and the murmuring of running water. This Lance Sidway had certainly injected some vim and vigor into the dead old ranch. His fine eyes, shadowed, troubled, and then blazing with scorn, haunted her as did that taunt about gangsters. She hated him, but she deserved it. Her conscience wrung that from her. Indeed he had kept the rendezvous that day, and bad luck have it! he had seen Uhl meet her, get into her car. And being Hollywood-wise he had caught the cut of that gentleman all in a few minutes. Not this fact, but his scorn was what galled Madge. Still if he had been so burned

114

up by her friendship with an underworld character, why had he learned her name, where she lived, and conceived the brilliant idea of meeting her at her own home? The answer was that no matter whom she knew, what she had done, he must have conceived more than a mere interest in her. But was that the answer? Madge conceived the idea that there was a remote possibility it was not.

6

Lance stood back in the shadow of Nels' cabin, a little abashed at his agitation, as he compared it to the coolness of these Arizonians. He did not want them to see that he was an unfledged cowboy, so far as rustlers were concerned.

"Wal, I reckon you fellers better have a smack of grub an' a cup of coffee with me," Nels drawled, as Stewart ended his brief story.

"Reckon I hed, at thet," rejoined Mains. "My two Bonitas would be too interested in thet confab we hed by the house."

"We'll all sponge on you, Nels," said Stewart. "Pitch in, fellows."

"All set 'cept fryin' some more ham. You cut it, Danny. . . . Whar's Sidway? Come heah, cowboy. . . . Gene, this truck rustlin' is shore two-bit stuff. Kinda oot of our experience. Let's get the cowboy's angle on it."

"Suits me."

"Sidway, you oughta be up on this automobile cattle stealin'. What'll we do?"

"We'll intercept this raid, of course," replied Lance, realizing that he was on the spot and forcing a calm and serious front when inwardly he was quaking. It reassured him that his wide sombrero hid his face.

"Hev a slice of ham. I can cook, cowboy. . . . Wal, how'd you intercept it?"

"I'd like Starr in on this with me," replied Sidway.

"By all means. You young bloods put your heads together," said Stewart.

"I'm with you, pard, an' I've got some ideas," returned Starr, nonchalantly. "But I cain't talk an' eat."

Lance thought with all his might. It was a situation in which he wanted to make good. But the fact that these old cattlemen, who had fought rustlers and Mexicans for over a score of years, put the responsibility up to him and Starr seemed more stultifying than inspiring.

"Starr, what hour of the night will that highway be most free of traffic?" asked Lance.

"About three in the mawnin' thar's a quiet spell. Sometimes fer two hours not a darn car goes by."

"That will be the time the thieves will load," concluded Lance.

"I agree. And even then it's pretty risky. Old-time rustlers wouldn't be that brazen," said Stewart.

"Boss, we gotta deal with a new breed of criminal," added Starr.

"Like as not the drivers of these trucks won't be regular range characters. These men will be city crooks, stealing cattle as a blind. They are gangsters. Probably hop-heads."

Stewart's leonine head swept up and he transfixed Lance with penetrating eyes.

"Cowboy, I heard you use that word hop-head less than an hour ago?" he queried, sharply.

"Yes sir . . . You—you may have," replied Lance, startled. But despite his qualm he kept his head. "I can explain it."

116

"Very well. Go on. What's a hop-head?"

"It's the name underworld characters give to men addicted to opium or heroin. They smoke or eat opium. Heroin they mostly inhale by smelling from the back of their hands. It's a powder."

"Wal, the hell you say, cowboy?" ejaculated Nels. "Them hop-heads must be kinda tough nuts, eh?"

"Brutal killers. No mercy! No respect for law. Rats, the police call them."

"Boss, they'll shoot if they're cornered, an' if they have machine guns, it'll jest be too bad," interposed Starr.

"They must be ambushed, or at least surprised," went on Lance. "They'll be waiting or driving along slow at the place nearest the highway—most convenient to pick up the cattle."

"Thet's less than forty miles from where we're talkin'," said Starr. "I spotted the blackest bunch of cattle on my way oot. I can drive fairly close. We'd hev to walk the rest of the way."

"I was going to suggest that," resumed Lance. "But not to drive too close. These raiders, whose job it is to round up the cattle, could hear a car. . . . They will be mounted—acquainted with the range—probably living on it."

"In cahoots with the truck drivers. Pard. You said a mouthful."

"Reckon he did thet same little thing," observed Mains, in dry subtlety.

"Wal, Gene, the kids ain't so pore," said Nels. "If yore through eatin' an' talkin' let's go. When we git down thar on the flat we can figger the rest."

"What's the hurry, Nels?" asked Stewart.

"Wal, I ain't trustin' them hop-haids to wait till mawnin'. Why, I reckon they'd jest as lief rob us in broad daylight."

Soon after that the five men, armed to the teeth, passed down the road in Starr's car, driving without lights. They had reached the village, passed the main street, when approaching Mains' house, Sidway's keen

117

eyes, accustomed to the dark, espied two mounted riders close to the fence.

"Hold it, Ren," he whispered. . . . "There! . . . Down the walk past Mains' house. Two horsemen! . . . They're moving."

"My gosh, I see them," replied Starr. "Gone now. Listen. . . . Heah them hoofs? Good fast trot."

"Boys," interposed Mains, "it ain't nothin' to see hawsemen around heah. They ride up bold as hell an' then again they sneak up like Injuns. Bonita's the reason."

Lance bit his tongue to keep from bursting out with the news that he had seen Bonita's dark form glide across in front of a yellow-lighted window. To his mind neither the riders nor the girl had moved without significance of secrecy. Lance resolved to make up to this pretty *señorita* for two reasons.

"Drive on, Ren," said Stewart, presently.

Below the village some few hundred yards Starr steered off the road down the slope. In the dark he had to go very slowly, a procedure difficult to accomplish on account of the grade. A vast dim emptiness stretched away under the stars. Far down, double pin points of light, moving along, attested to the presence of a car on the highway. Lance asked Stewart how long that road had encroached upon his range.

"Six or seven years, if I remember. Used to bother old-timers. But that feeling has gone into the discard with the cattle business."

"It'll pick up again and be better than ever," declared Lance.

"Ren, stop every little way, so we can listen."

It was a silent night, not yet cooled off from the day's heat. The rustle of sage and the low hum of insects accentuated the silence. Stars were growing brighter in the darkening blue. Gradually the men ceased talking. Once down on the flat Starr had easier driving. Presently he ran out of the sage into the wash where on the sand and gravel the going was smoother and almost noiseless. Starr must have halted a dozen

118

times at Nels' order and the five had listened intently before Lance heard cattle bawling.

"Reckon we've come fur enough. What say, Gene?" queried Nels. "Let's pile oot."

"I think I know about where we are," said Gene, peering about in the gloom. "Still pretty far from the road, that is, where this wash goes under. But the road curves in to the west."

"Cattle all aboot," observed Nels. "An' they ain't skeered, thet's shore. Let's mosey on till we heah somethin'."

Guardedly and slow, with senses alert, the men zig-zagged through the sage, working southwest. Grazing and resting cattle grew more numerous. After what Lance believed was several miles' travel Nels halted them near a rocky mound.

"Fur enough, till we heah or see somethin'. You cowboys climb up thar."

The eminence appeared to be rather long and higher toward the west. Lance signed to Ren that he would climb the far point. He did not, however, get to do it, for a hist from Starr called him back. Lance joined Nels and Stewart who stood under Starr.

". . . Aboot a mile from the highway," Ren was saying, in guarded voice. "Three big double lights comin' from Bolton. Trucks. They're close together. Movin' slow."

"How do you know they're trucks?" asked Stewart.

"Cars an' lamps an' such hev been my job fer a year an' more, Boss. These belong to trucks, an' you bet the ones we're expectin'. Jest creepin' along. An' thet's a level road."

"How fur away?" queried Nels.

"Cain't say. Mebbe three miles, mebbe six."

"Nels, down along here about even with where we are now there are several benches that run close to the road and break off in banks. It would be a simple matter for trucks to be backed up against these banks and loaded. In some places you wouldn't even need a platform. And my cattle are tame."

"Wal, we're some sucker cattlemen," drawled Nels,

and sat down with his back to the bank. "Set down an' let's wait fer Starr to find oot somehin'. Sidway, you got sharp ears. Go off a ways an' listen. It's a still night. Listen fer cattle thet air disturbed."

Lance did as he was bidden, conscious of growing excitement. These ranchmen evidently gave him credit for more and wilder experience than he had had. He felt that he must rise to the occasion. Presently there would be some sharp and critical work for all of them and he nerved himself to cool hard purpose. From time to time he heard Starr's low voice.

It was some time, however, fraught with suspense, before Lance's range-trained ear caught the faint trample of hoofs and occasional bawl of cattle. Whereupon he ran back to report.

"Good!" declared Stewart. "How about you, Starr?"

"I reckon I heahed but wasn't shore. I am now. Not so all-fired far, either. . . . Boss, jest wait, I'm watchin' them trucks."

Starr did not speak again, and the others listened intently. The faint sounds of moving cattle augmented. Presently the cowboy whispered sharply: "Boss, the trucks he   d—jest a little to the right of us. . . . Lights go out! . . . No, by damn—the trucks air turnin' . . . backin' off the road this way, or I'm a born fool."

"Wal, look like it's all set," said Nels, getting up. Stewart followed his example.

"Them rays of light flash across the highway," went on Starr.

" 'Pear to be linin' up. . . . Fust lights gone out! . . ."

"Come down, Ren. We'll be moseyin' along. . . . Danny, you come with us. Gene, you go with Sidway. Work straight down to the road an' foller along it. We'll aim to slip up behind the *hombres* who're doin' the rustlin'."

In another moment Lance was gliding cautiously along at Stewart's heels. They progressed fifty steps or more when Stewart halted to listen.

"But Nels didn't say what to do!" whispered Lance.

"It's a cinch we'll break up the raid. But our object

is to capture at least one each of the riders and drivers."

Lance silenced his misgivings and conjectures, and transferring his rifle to his left hand he drew his gun. Stewart, he had observed, packed two guns, and Lance thrilled at the way he wore them. So different from the movie bad man! They stole along slowly, avoiding the larger sagebrush, careful not to scare cattle, listening at intervals. The hum of a motorcar off to the east distracted Lance's attention from the now audible moving herd. Presently he saw the lights and he and the rancher watched them grow and pass not far below, and go on out of sight. That car was making fast time. No doubt it did not see the trucks. Soon Lance followed Stewart out of the sage upon the highway, black and glistening under the stars.

"We're farther this way than we thought," whispered Stewart. "That bunch of cattle are down to the road. . . . Hear that? . . . We've got to hand it to these truck rustlers for nerve. Right on the highway! Not leary of noise."

"To hell with the ranchers, eh?" replied Lance, with a little husky laugh. He felt the heat throb in his pulsing veins.

"They wouldn't put a guard out, as the old rustlers used to. . . . Let's hurry along."

Stewart strode so swiftly that Lance could not hear anything while they were moving. But presently they halted; the trample of hoofs and bawl of cattle became plainly audible. On the third halt Lance distinctly heard the thump of hoofs upon a board floor.

"——!" swore Stewart. "Loading already! Won't that make Nels snort? It should be getting hot over there. But Nels would move slow."

After another hundred steps or so Stewart led off the highway into the sage. Lance divined that the rancher wanted cover to drop behind in case the truckmen flashed their lights. Nevertheless it was not long before Stewart went down on all fours to crawl. This was tremendously exciting to Lance. The thump of solid hoofs on wood drowned all the other sounds except an occasional snort or bawl. The cattle were being moved with amazing celerity and little noise.

"Beats me," muttered Stewart, then crawled on. They had scarcely gotten even with a point opposite, where a high black bulk loomed up squarely above the horizon and marked the position of the trucks, when huge glaring lights gleamed out of the darkness. Lance flattened himself beside Stewart. A low fringe of sage on their right saved them from detection. But Lance's throat contracted. A harsh low voice, a sudden bursting of an engine, into whirring roar, a grind of wheels left no doubt that a truck was starting. It moved quickly down to the road, and turned so that the lights swerved to the right, leaving the men in darkness. Then the truck stopped and the driver called. Stewart jerked Lance to his feet, whispering: "We've got to move. Careful now. Keep your head."

His voice, his presence stirred Lance as nothing else had ever done. Stewart ran along the sage and up on the road to the truck. Lance, sharp-eyed and tense, kept at his heels. The engine was purring. Reaching the front of the car Stewart jerked open the door and commanded: *"Hands up!"*

Lance over Stewart's shoulder saw the big gun go prodding into the driver's side. "Agg-h!" he ejaculated, l lifted his hands off the wheel.

A quick grating footstep on the other side of the car caused Lance to crouch. A man came swiftly round the front.

"Beat it, Bill—we're held up!" rasped the driver.

But this man cursed and swept up his arm. Lance having him covered, had only to pull the trigger. His shot preceded the others only by an instant. Lance saw his action violently break, his gun burst red. A crash of bursting glass, a thud of bullets preceded Stewart's staggering away from the truck to fall. The driver, with hoarse bellows of alarm, shoved his power on so quickly that the cattle in the truck banged against the gate. Then the truck roared down the road.

The horror that gripped Lance at Stewart's fall

nearly overcame him for a moment. Then strident yells, the flashing of lights and roaring of engines added to his fighting fury. Nimbly he leaped beyond the broad flares. And as the second truck whizzed down upon the road he emptied his gun at the front of the first one. The splintering crash of glass, the lurching of the car, the loud yells told that his bullets did some execution. Both trucks gained the road. As they roared on shots rang out from the bank. Then Lance, resorting to his rifle, aimed above the red rear light of the last truck, and sent ten shots after it. Lowering the hot rifle he stood a moment, shaking, wet with cold sweat, realizing all shots had ceased. He caught a clatter of rapid hoofs, the crowding of cattle, then a ringing voice:

"Hey, over there," called Nels. "What'n hell was yore hurry?"

"Nels! Come—quick! Stewart's . . ." yelled Lance hoarsely.

"Keep your shirt on, cowboy," intercepted the cool voice of Stewart. Then Lance saw his tall dark form against the lighter gloom.

"Oh—Ste—wart. I was afraid," gasped Lance.

"Hello. Where are you, fellers?" shouted Danny Mains, and then followed Starr's cheery voice. "Busted, by thunder!"

"Here," called Stewart. Presently the three loomed on the road.

"Gene, you let 'um git away," protested Nels, hopping mad.

"Trucks vamoosed in spite of us. How about the riders?"

"Wal, we was creepin' up behind, all set, when you opened up the ball."

"Did you identify any of them?"

"Hell, we didn't even see them. Slick an' fast ootfit, Gene. Makes me more curious."

"I ain't so damn curious as I was," growled Danny Mains, enigmatically.

"Pard, you shore done a lot of shootin'," declared Starr, peering into Lance's face.

"Here's what happened," explained Stewart. "Sidway and I got here just as that loaded truck came off the sage. When it turned on the road, we jumped and ran. It stopped. I opened the door and stuck my right gun in the driver's ribs. He yelled in spite of that. Then his pardner came running. Bill, the driver called him. Bill sure saw me. For he came up with a gun. I threw my left on him but it struck the car door, low down. Sidway shot this fellow—broke his aim—or sure as God made little apples he'd have killed me. At that he hit me. His bullet knocked me flat."

"Gene! You shot? Whar? Not a body hit?" exclaimed Nels.

There was a moment's silence, during which the cold began to creep into Lance's marrow.

"Don't know where," returned Stewart, calmly, as he felt of his body and shoulders. "I'm bleeding. Busted glass cut me. That *hombre* saw my body outside the door and believe me he threw his gun on it. But Sidway's shot knocked him off. Maybe the bullet didn't hit me at all. Maybe it did, because I'm bleeding all over my face and head."

"Aw, then it cain't be serious," declared Nels, with relief. "An' Sidway hit this *hombre?*"

"Bored him plumb center," replied Stewart, grimly. "He stood just inside the light. I saw him drop like a sack. He's lying here somewhere."

Starr produced a flashlight and with the two men began searching the immediate space, while Lance fought the strangest, most sickening sensation of his life.

"Heah! . . . Daid, I'll tell the world!" rang out Starr. "Lousy-lookin' little bastard! One of them hop-haids."

"Search him, Ren, and drag him off the road. . . . Sidway, you're too damn good a shot. Dead men tell no tales."

"Wal, if you ask me, our new cowboy is a man after my kind. Gene, don't call him fer shootin' fast an' straight."

"I was kidding. But at that I wish Sidway had only crippled him. . . . What'd he have on him, Ren?"

"Automatic tight in his mitt . . . Watch. Knife. Cigarettes. . . . An' this wad of long green. Fellers, will you look at thet! A hundred dollar bill on the ootside!"

Lance gradually dragged himself closer to the trio, and discerned Starr on his knees beside the dead man, a slack spare figure, terribly suggestive, showing in the flashlight a crooked visage, ghastly in hue and contortion.

"Wal, you lousy hop-haid," broke out Starr, in genial levity, "bumped up agin the wrong hombre, didn't you? . . . Lay hold, Danny, an' help me haul him over heah."

The cold gripe on Lance's internals slowly lessened; and he helped it pass by a desperate effort to conceal what he felt to be his squeamishness before these ranchers. He thought he could get by in the dark.

"Sidway must have stung more than this *hombre*," Stewart was saying to Nels. "He shot the front glasses out of both cars. And be sure cut loose with his rifle as they drove away. I heard the bullets hit that last truck."

"Wal, thanks to him, it didn't turn oot so pore. Mebbe thet money will more than pay fer the cattle they rustled."

"Boss, reckon I'll hev to drive back to Bolton in the mawnin' an' report this execution to the sheriff," said Starr, joining them.

"Yes. And I might have to see a doctor."

"Lemme look." Starr flashed his light upon the side of Stewart's face which he turned for inspection. Lance saw with concern that the rancher was bloody enough to have been struck by a load of shot. The cowboy wiped the blood off, and peering closer he ran his fingers over Stewart's cheek and temple and neck. "Hell! You ain't been shot atall, Boss. Jest a blast of glass, I reckon. . . . Leastways I cain't find any bullet hole. . . . Gosh, I'm glad them glass bits missed yore eye."

"Feel here—back of my ear."

"Ah-ha!—Shore, he creased you thar. . . . Hot as fire, huh. Thet was made by a bullet, Boss."

"A miss is as good as a mile. . . . Sidway, I owe you something."

"Oh, no!—He—he just missed you. I was too—too slow," replied Lance, thickly.

"I've been shot at before, boy. I saw him jerk and his gun spurt up. He'd have bored me."

"How aboot moseyin' along? Thet's a long tramp fer a man who never trailed rustlers on foot," said Nels, plaintively.

As they moved up the highway Starr dropped back to Lance's side. He put a hand on the other's arm. "Pard, you didn't tell me you was some punkins with a gun."

"I'm not."

"Hey, you might josh me, but not these men. You pulled a fast one, Sid. An' Gene Stewart seen you. Wait till I get a chanct to tell you some stories about Stewart an' Nels. Hell, man, they've seen the wildest of western days. An' Nels was a Texas ranger before he ever hit this country. If you know yore West! An' Gene Stewart, or *El Capitan* as his handle was them days, was not only a tough cowboy but a real gunman."

"Ren, I hope this night's work will end the truck rustling," said Lance, lamely.

"Wal, it might, if them *hombres* was ordinary cattle thieves. But who'n hell can figger these hop-haids. Anyway, pard, you've cinched yore job, believe you me. An' I'm gonna ride with you."

"That'll be swell. I'm glad. We'll get along fine, Ren."

"Gosh! I jest happened to think!" ejaculated Starr, stopping in the middle of the highway to take a pull at Lance. "I'd give a heap to be in yore boots."

"Why—what's hurting? Don't you think, usually?"

"Will you be sittin' pretty with Majesty Stewart? . . . Fust stunt—right off—savin' her dad's life! Pard, she adores him. My Gawd, the luck of some gazabos!"

"Lord! . . . Starr, if you're my pard don't tell—her

126

—please," exclaimed Lance, his weakness making him prey to another emotion.

"Wal—Why, shore, Sidway. I won't tell her. But how about Gene? An' thet gabby old Nels—Pard, if I was you I'd shore want her to know."

"We've clashed, Ren. She misunderstood my coming here. Thinks I'm a liar. Laughed at me—when I denied it. . . . Vainest girl I ever met!"

"Hell! What of thet," returned Ren, bluntly. "She's also the loveliest, the sweetest, the finest an' squarest. Get thet, buddy?"

"Yes, I get *you*—you dumbbell! I see if I'd speak my mind about this glorious creature, you'd sock me one."

"Forget it, pard. You're a little upset. I ain't wonderin' at thet. You reckoned Stewart was daid an' seein' him come back to life would excite anybody, outside the fight."

Starr gave Sidway a friendly pat on the back and then let him alone. Presently they reached a culvert over the wash, and turning here, they followed the pale line of sand into the sage. The sand dragged at Sidway's feet, but the exertion helped restore his equilibrium. The distance back to the car seemed interminable and proved how, on the way down, the excitement had made it short. They found the car at length and were soon bumping over the uneven ground. Starr had no incentive now to drive slowly and noiselessly. He certainly gave his passengers a rough trip back to the ranch.

Lance went to bed at once. For half an hour Nels and Mains, dressing Stewart's wounds in the adjoining room, kept Lance awake, thinking one moment and going over the adventure the next. When quiet settled down, he soon fell asleep.

Upon awakening, Lance heard Starr and Nels talking while they got breakfast. Presently Starr pounded on the wall between, jarring the house. "Hey, Oregon, air you daid?"

"I'm up," replied Lance.

127

"Wal, you're quieter'n hell if you air. Waltz out. I gotta rustle to town pronto."

"Ren, send for my baggage."

"Shore, pard, an' what else?"

"I'll see."

When Lance entered Nels' bunkhouse to have breakfast he sensed such a great transformation in himself that he felt certain his friends would exclaim about it. But they did not notice any difference in him. During the meal they did not once mention the affair of last night. All in the day, for them, thought Lance! He essayed a cool and quiet demeanor which he meant to make permanent.

"Nels, what'll I do today?" he asked.

"Dog-gone if I know, son," drawled the other, scratching his gray head. "They're all goin' to town. Go wrangle yore hawse an' I'll ask Gene when he comes down."

Umpqua had made the most of the huge grassy pasture. Lance found him in the extreme far corner, more than a mile from the corrals, and rode him bareback to the corrals. After rubbing him down and saddling and bridling him, Lance led him up the lane to the court. Stewart, his head swathed in white bandages, stood by Madge's car talking to Starr. As Lance passed the open door of the store he heard Madge's rich voice, breaking with a singular note, and it gave him a wild impulse to run. Starr hailed him, and then he and Stewart approached.

"Hope you're okay, Boss," said Lance, eagerly.

"Mornin', Sidway. Reckon I feel like a nigger who had to have the buckshot picked out of him. Would you like to go to town with us?"

"Not on my own account, sir. Thanks. There's a lot I can find to do here." Lance said this at the same moment he heard Nels' clinking slow step behind him and a lighter pace that stopped his heart. But he did not turn.

"Starr will come back soon," went on the rancher. "It might be a good idea for you and him to fix up your quarters. Nels said they had gone to rack."

128

"How about the cattle?" asked Lance.

"They have been left free to run the range, and as you saw, have worked low down. Danny and I will be driving a big herd to the railroad soon. Maybe next week. I'll make that deal in town today. As for immediate jobs, I want you and Ren to repair the water flume and the telephone line pronto."

"Yes, sir. I'll get started on them today."

"Nels, did you make out your list of supplies?"

"Majesty writ it oot fer me."

"Say, what have you been tellin' that girl?" demanded Stewart.

"Me? Why, Gene, nothin' atall," drawled Nels, innocently.

"You old liar! Look at her!"

Lance wished to do this with an almost irresistible desire. But he sat down on the edge of the porch, dragging Starr with him, aware that the others had stepped into the store.

"Ren, you'll not forget my baggage?"

"Shore, pard. Anythin' else? Say how's yore bunkhouse fixed up? I didn't look."

"It's not fixed up at all," replied Lance. "No mattress, no chair, no mirror, nothing to wash in or with. No towels. I've been using Nels'."

"Wal, mine cain't be no wuss . . ."

"Ren, buy what you need today," said Madge Stewart, from behind them. She had not gone into the store at all. Manifestly she had heard their talk. "Whatever is this ranch coming to?"

"Aw, you heah, Miss Majesty. Good mawnin'," replied Starr, with confusion, as he stood up to turn toward her. "About the ranch—wal, I'd say things was lookin' up."

"Lance Sidway!"

Arising stiffly, Lance wheeled to doff his sombrero and greet her in apparent composure. But the tone of her voice and then the look of her played havoc with all his resolves. At this juncture Stewart and Nels came out of the store.

"Nels, do you think I dare ride in with Madge?" quizzed Stewart.

"Wall, I'd jump at the chance."

"You old traitor! Why, you never could be hired to ride in a car. Do you remember Link Stevens driving that big white car of Madeline's?"

"My Gawd, do I? But I'll bet Majesty would hev druv rings around Link."

Madge was looking down upon Lance. The fairness of her face appeared enhanced by the scarlet upon her lips. In truth Lance saw that she was pale and that her eyes were unnaturally large, glowing, dilating, with a violet fire. Then she seemed to float down the steps and entwine her arm in Lance's, and lift her lovely face to him, that in the action flushed a hue to match her lips and then went pearly white.

"You saved Dad's life!"

Lance had prepared himself for he knew not what, though not for this close proximity, the tight pressure of her arm, the quivering feel of her. "Oh, no, Miss Stewart. Somebody has exaggerated."

"Nels told me," said Madge, intensely.

"I might have known," went on Lance, trying to be cool and nonchalant. "Nels is swell, but you know he. . . . Starr told me what an old liar he is."

"Heah!" yelped Starr. "Don't you get me in bad. I never said thet . . ."

"Miss Stewart, please . . ." interposed Lance. "You mustn't give me undue credit. I was there—and I'm glad—I made myself useful. I didn't want to kill the man . . ."

"*You killed him?*" she cried, aghast. "Oh, Nels didn't tell me that."

Lance spread wide his hands to the watching men, as if to say "Now see what you've done." But it was not the revelation that distracted him.

"So you're bound to be our good angel!" she exclaimed, softly, and shook him gently.

"Really I—you . . . it was—it's not so much."

"Nothing! And you killed a robber who'd have murdered my father? I wonder what you'd consider *very* much. . . . Come away from these grinning apes, so I can thank you."

She led him out to her car and still clung to his arm. "It's impossible to think you," she went on, her voice breaking. "I can't even try. But I'm unutterably grateful. I'll do anything for you."

"Thank you, Miss Stewart. . . ."

"My friends call me Majesty," she interrupted, sweetly.

"I—I appreciate your excitement and feeling. It's kind of a tough spot for you. I hoped they wouldn't tell you. But they did . . . and I won't let you make too much of it."

"Too much! Aren't you glad?" she rejoined, incredulously.

"Glad? That I was there—with him? Good heavens! Of course, I am. Greatest kick I ever had!"

"Nels told me you were a bad *hombre* to meet in a fight. That you reminded him of an old pard, Nick Steele. But that you were different from the old-time bragging gunmen . . . modern, modest—a new kind to him, but dangerous, and just what my father needed —just what *I* needed . . ."

"Nels is a sentimental old jackass," burst out Lance. If she would only let go of his arm, move her soft warm shoulder away from his!

"It bothers you," she asserted, quickly. "We'll skip it. . . . Come into town with us."

"Is that an order?"

"Oh, no. Just a request."

"Thanks, but I've plenty of work to do here."

"I'll say plenty. . . . Lance, I hated you yesterday."

"Are you telling me? But really I'm sorry I was so rude."

"I forgive you. Let's be good friends now. You're here, I'm here—and my friends are coming. You'll like the girls. They're peaches. Full of fun—and great sports. It will embarrass me if we are at odds."

"How could that be? I'm only your father's cowboy."

"Don't forget that *I* saw you first," she taunted.

131

"You're *my* cowboy. They'll all make a play for you, especially that redheaded Bu Allen. She's a devil on the make. They'll hear of your—about you—make you a hero. I want you to be good friends with me."

"I will be, of course. A friend like Ren Starr," qualified Lance.

"But I mean more than that. Ren is swell. Only he's a hired hand."

"So am I. I won't forget my place."

"Aren't you being just a little snooty?" she inquired, subtly changing, and she released his arm.

"Aren't you kidding me?"

"No," she flashed, loftily.

"Then isn't that your line?"

"I haven't any line, Mr. Sidway."

Lance felt utterly helpless in two conflicting ways —that he simply could not help rubbing the girl the wrong way, any more than he could resist her lovely person and insidious charm. He wanted her to hurry away so that he could think. In another moment she would see that his heart if not his will was prostrate at her feet.

"I'm afraid you had better fire me right here and now," he said, glumly.

"Perhaps I had," she returned, her purple eyes glowing upon him, as if visioning afar. "But Dad needs you. And he wouldn't let you go."

"I'd go anyhow. Just you fire me."

"No. I'll not do it. . . . Listen, big boy, you gave me some dirty digs. And I've been catty. It's fifty-fifty. Here's my hand for a new deal."

"Miss Stewart—as Ren says—you're one grand girl," rejoined Lance, unsteadily. "It's unconceivable that I could withhold my hand, if you offered yours. But I can't forget so easily as you evidently do."

"I see. You can't take it?"

"Do you still believe I found out who you were— where you lived—and came out here to—to . . ." he queried, hotly, and ended, unable to finish.

"Why, certainly I do."

"When I swear on my word of honor that I didn't?" went on Lance, passionately.

"Yes," she retorted, almost with like heat. "And I'd think more of you if you'd not lie about it. This word of honor stuff! . . . I thought it was a swell stunt. I was tickled pink. I'll still think it grand of you if you'll only stop bluffing. What more could you want?"

"I must seem ridiculous to you. But I'm neither a callow college youth nor a thickheaded gangster. I'd expect a girl to *believe* me. Else I couldn't be her friend. You're just kidding me. You'd play with me in front of your college crowd—and let me down afterwards. Why, you even have nerve enough to try to get my horse!"

"Yes I have, Lance Sidway," she blazed at him. "I've nerve enough to get him, too, at any cost—unless you show yellow and ride away!"

Lance bowed and turned away toward the bunkhouses, forgetting the others and afraid to go to Umpqua. He heard her call to her father, and presently the sound of the cars wheeling away. In that moment of passion he divined if he approached Umpqua it would be to ride away from that ranch. And he flung himself upon his bunk to shut out the sunlight. Neither pride in himself nor loyalty to Stewart accounted for that victory over himself. The paralyzing and staggering truth was that he did not ride away because he could not bear to leave this beautiful and tormenting girl.

7

Early and late Sidway was out on the road job, over-seeing the Mexican laborers, while Starr and Mains, with the *vaqueros,* repaired the telephone, and then drove upwards of six hundred head of cattle to the railroad.

No sooner was the road fit for heavy traffic when it appeared all the trucks in Bolton came along loaded to capacity with the crated furniture and bales and boxes that Madge Stewart had sent from Los Angeles. There were four small trucks and two large ones. The contents, Lance calculated, must have cost the girl thousands of dollars; and the sight of them aroused an unreasonable resentment in him. What business was it of his? Yet he could not help thinking of her all the day and half the night. That fact lay at the root of his intense dissatisfaction rather than her extravagance at such a hard period for her parents. Lance was deter-mined that Madge must not know this. He was always fighting against an acceptance of her faults.

On Saturday afternoon of that busy week Lance was glad to see Starr drive up with Stewart and Mains in his car, and an empty truck behind.

The road job was finished, very much to Stewart's satisfaction, and he paid off the Mexicans, and sent them back to town.

"Well, I reckon we're ready for Madge's outfit," said Stewart, eyeing his cowboys.

"Who is, Boss?" queried Lance.

"Not me, neither," added Starr, making a wry face. "All summer long! Gene, they'll drive us nuts. . . . An' shore one of them swell college sprats will cop my girl."

"Oh, Bonita, you mean," returned Lance, laconically, as he rested against the car. "Ren I haven't noticed—so much—that she is your property."

"Sid, you double-crossin' son-of-a-gun! I might have knowed it."

"Swell kid!"

"Look heah, Sidway, hev you been after my daughter, too?" demanded Danny Mains.

"I've seen a good deal of her while you were away. I knew you didn't approve of Ren."

"Danny," interposed Stewart, "cowboys are the same now as we were. Only a good deal better. I think Bonita is better off for friends like Starr and Sidway."

"Wal, I reckon," agreed Danny, dubiously. "On'y I'm afraid they might do some mischief to Bonita's several *vaquero* beaus."

"Mischief! Say, Danny, you ain't got me figgered," replied Ren, doggedly. "I love Bonita an' hev asked her to marry me."

"Ren—So that was it?" ejaculated Lance.

"So that was what?" queried Starr, suspiciously.

"I don't want to embarrass you b⸳ ⸳pard."

"Ren, you'll excuse my cantankerousness," said Mains, simply. "I didn't hev you figgered."

"Starr, this here Oregon ladies' man is not only stepping on your preserves, but he's kidding you," rejoined Stewart, with a laugh. "Hook her up and let's go. Sidway, it's a good job well done. . . . Oh, yes, I've a message for you by phone. Madge wants you up at the house to open boxes."

"Boss! I'm a tired man," expostulated Lance. "And Umpqua needs to be worked over. Up and down this dusty road for a week!"

"Haw! Haw! Haw!" laughed Starr, fiendishly.

"All right. I'll tell Madge not tonight."

Starr grinned knowingly at Lance and drove off. From where they had caught up with him it was only a short ride to the ranch. Yet it seemed a long and thoughtful one for Lance. It began to look as if Madge Stewart either meant to try him with odd stable-boy jobs or else she wanted him to be unable to avoid her, as he had tried so hard to do. The former made him furious and the latter made him weak.

By the time he had put Umpqua away it was dark, the store was closed, and bright light shone from Nels' window and door. A drowsy breeze blew in from the range, moved down by the cooler air on high. Frogs were croaking in the lake. Lance washed his grimy hands and face before he went in.

"Jest in time, son. Come in an' get it," said Nels, cheerily.

"Pard, what say to a swim in the lake after supper? She's bank full already," suggested Starr.

"Okay by me. But, boy! that water is cold."

"An' you from Oregon!"

It turned out to be warmer water than Lance was used to at home, a he enjoyed the bath. On the way back he realized that Ren had something on his mind. Lance clapped him on the back.

"What's on your chest, buddy?"

"It's Bonita."

"Say, Ren, I was surprised at what you admitted to Danny. I had no idea you were serious. I'm sorry, old man."

"You like Bonita?"

"I'll say. She's some kid."

"Pard, did you kiss and hug her?"

"Ren! Have a heart. Would you expect me to tell?"

"Wal, in my case, yes. You see, pard, I want you to help me win thet kid. I cain't do it alone."

"Okay. Yes I did—a little. But it was no cinch. And I liked her the better. She's a charming girl, Ren. I honestly think she'd make a swell little wife. But there are a lot of guys who're after her, and not all of them with your good intentions.

"Some of them Mexican *vaqueros*."

"Yes. But town fellows, too. And I'm suspicious of them. I've a hunch some of them might know something about that rustling."

"My hunch, too. We'll find out. An' pard—listen! If you'll help me with this black-eyed little girl I'll shore play yore game with yore proud Majesty."

"My God!—Ren, have you gone nutty?"

"Nope. I'm cool as a cucumber right this heah minnit."

"But man! *Me* aspire to that . . ."

"Why, hell, yes. Pard, I seen her look at you thet day, an' if she's not stuck on you—mebbe unknown to herself—then I am nutty an' what hev you?"

"You are—Ren—you are," replied Lance, frantically. "I'll make that Bonita kid think you're a prince. But, pard, forget your pipe dream about the other."

"Faint heart never won fair lady," returned Starr, lightly.

That night Lance had a dream of a cherub-faced cowboy leading him along flower-strewn trails to a bower where a goddess with golden hair awaited him with white arms extended. At breakfast he was silly enough to tell Ren and Nels about that dream.

"Dreams come true, sometimes," declared Ren, stoutly. "Hey, Nels?"

"Shore they do. An' this one of Lance's has a pertickler bearin' heah," observed Nels, without glancing at Lance.

"Yeah? And how d'you figure that?" asked Lance, scornfully.

Nels and Ren both laughed and Lance's face crimsoned. Luckily at that juncture a message came from Stewart requesting the cowboys to come up to the house, not dressed in their Sunday clothes.

"That means work. And it's Sunday!" complained Lance, honestly and fearfully divided between bliss and panic.

"Aw, you know you're piflicated," replied Starr, cryptically.

"I am—sure, but what is piflicated?"

137

"Wal, as I remember from past mournful experiences, it's a kinda prolapsus of the gizzard. Heart trouble, pard."

Upon ascending to the ranch house the cowboys, with Nels accompanying them, found a busy and excited household. Front porch and part of the patio were packed with crates, bales, boxes, trunks, packages. Stewart, in his shirt sleeves, apparently in a trance, was helping the beaming Denny Mains carry furniture into the house. Mrs. Stewart, flushed and radiant, was bustling about with the servants. Bonita was there, red-lipped and pretty, her arms full of linens. And Madge, in slacks and a backless waist, cool and sweet and smiling, evidently was boss.

She put Lance and Ren to opening crates. For a couple of hours they worked diligently at this job, and after they had unpacked everything, they carried boards and boxes and burlap and paper out to be hauled away on the morrow. The next job was to move things into the patio rooms. Lance observed that these were light, high-ceiled rooms, with colored adobe walls, and shiny floors. He had a glimpse of Madge's rooms, and was reminded of some of the luxurious motion-picture sets he had seen in Hollywood.

At noon they had lunch on the patio porch, and it was a merry occasion. Lance, looking at Mrs. Stewart, no longer wondered how Madge had come by her beauty. She was a western girl, but her mother's eastern breeding and distinction had been augmented in her. Lance had to admit that parents and daughter made a delightful trio, and also that the girl's singular zest and enthusiasm motivated them.

After luncheon everybody worked harder than ever. Nels was wearing his long spurs, that stuck in dangerously as he knelt to hold a pillow in his teeth and slide it down into a slip. Nevertheless in housekeeping matters, Nels proved serious and efficient. Madge presently gave Starr and Bonita tasks to perform together, while Stewart carried and unrolled rugs and his wife oversaw his disposition of them, and the moving of furniture. Lance propounded the question as to

138

whether he had naturally gravitated to tasks with Madge or she had arranged it that way. But the time came when he no longer doubted. That fixed his distant exterior, but it added more and more to the tumult within.

The tasks she set him, and completed with him, would never be remembered. As the minutes sped by he seemed hardly conscious of anything besides her presence—her intense and zestful activity, her requests and suggestions, and her talk in between, the intimacy that she seemed not to notice but which he felt so subtly, the play of her lovely features and the changing expressions in her violet eyes, her laugh, her smile, her grace, her disheveled golden hair falling over her face to be brushed back with a beautiful hand.

And at last, how it came about he could not say, they had finished all present tasks, and she was offering him a cigarette.

"No thanks," he said, easily.

"Don't you smoke?"

"Sure. Once in a while."

"Lance, you're one swell assistant. I think I'll promote you if . . ."

"To what?"

"Oh, major-domo or gigolo—or just cavalier."

"It'll be all I can do to make good as a cowboy. That is—here!"

"How modest and cool you are! I'd like it, if I could be sure you were sincere. You don't ring true, darling."

He had no reply for that. They had come out into the patio, and Lance was walking slowly toward the back, with apparent composure and the respectful demeanor of a cowboy toward the boss's daughter. She walked with him, cigarette in hand. Somewhere near by Starr and Bonita were quarreling, but Madge gave no sign she heard them. Lance felt that he must escape at once, or he would betray what he knew not. Yet the bitter paradox was that another self of him longed to linger there.

"Oh, I forgot. There's a nice room at that end of the patio. I want you to have it."

"But, I—thank you, Miss Stewart. I have my bunkhouse lodgings."

"Yes. I peeped in there one day while you were out. Nels showed me. Rotten for even a cowboy. And you're a gentleman, Lance."

"Thanks again. But I'm satisfied down there."

"I expect you to help entertain my guests."

"What!" He was tremendously surprised, and could say no more.

"Why should you be so surprised? Because you've been rude to me and I've been selfish?—That's nothing. We can give, and take it, too. . . . These boys and girls will be tenderfeet. I must have some real western he-man around on occasions—especially where my horses are concerned. I'd like to trust you with that job."

"But your father wants Ren and me to ride the range, build and dig and what not."

"So Dad told me. Ren can attend to that with the *vaqueros. I* want you."

"Are you giving me an order?"

"I am inviting you—*asking* you to be a friend—a good sport," she retorted, her eyes flashing.

"You are very—kind. But in that case I must refuse."

"Don't you like me?" she demanded, incredulously.

"Miss Stewart, that is a personal matter," he replied, looking straight ahead.

"You *do* like me," she asserted.

"If you put it that way, I'm afraid I must be rude again. You are mistaken," he rejoined, and his voice sounded curiously strange to his throbbing ears. But he was telling the truth. He did not like Madge Stewart because he loved her. The silence grew almost unbearable. He steeled himself against sarcasm, anger, wounded vanity. When they reached the wide green-bordered exit from the patio, when she stopped, he simply had to look at her. The last thing he expected was to see her eyes brimming with tears. She looked by him, out over the slope to the range. Her wide eyes were softly blurred, dark with pain.

"Lance, I can take it," she said, presently, and lifted her cigarette to her lips. It had gone out. "Have you a match?" He produced one, struck and held it for her and she blew a cloud of smoke, with apparent unintention, into his face. When the blue cloud cleared away he could not have believed she could possibly have looked hurt.

"Anyone can start something. But it takes a real sport to finish."

Did she refer to an affair with him or the acquisition of his horse, or was it the passionate pride of a woman in herself? He answered by saying that he feared he, at least, had undertaken something he could never finish, and bidding her good night he left her. On the way down he took a short cut off the back road into a trail, and lingered on a secluded spot, from which he could see the flaming range on fire with sunset. The critical hour of his life had struck. He loved this girl, and the emotion seemed a coalescing of all his former fancies and loves, magnified into an incredible passion too great to understand or hate or resist. It did not require to be brooded over and analyzed and made certain. Like an avalanche it fell upon him. It was too terrible in its fatality, too transporting in its bliss, too great to be ashamed of. But it must be his secret. He swore he would die before he would let this man hunter and love taster, who like a savage princess exacted homage, this frail, spoiled, lovely creature know that he loved her.

Before dusk settled down thickly, Lance had fought out the battle, losing in his surrender to the catastrophe that had overtaken him, but victor over his weakness. Nevertheless he realized anew that he should straddle Umpqua and ride away before another day dawned. As he was not big enough to do that he did not blind himself to the peril that played and led him on.

No matter how troubled and hopeless he felt when he lay down at night, when morning dawned, with all

141

the exquisite freshness and sweetness of this country, and the golden light over the range, he seemed to be transformed, renewed, to be glad of life and youth, and the nameless hope that beckoned him on.

Returning from his taks at the corrals he found Madge and Nels puttering around her car. She wore a blue hat, blue gown, blue gloves—everywhere she appeared as blue as her eyes.

"Heah, son, come an' help," called Nels. "I don't know a darn thing aboot these enjines."

Madge's look of annoyance vanished as Lance strode up to the car.

"What's the matter?"

"The damn thing won't start," she said, smiling.

"You have a mechanic here. Cars are Starr's specialty."

"He's gone. Will you oblige me?"

Lance leisurely lifted the hood of the engine, to see at a glance what was wrong, and in a moment adjusted it.

"How easy for *you!*" she flashed. "I'm terribly grateful. . . . Won't you ride in to town with me?"

"What for?"

"Well, it might go on the blink again."

"Not a chance."

"All right. Then—just for the ride," she returned.

Lance returned her look with a feeling that he knew he was the only man on earth who could have refused her and who must suffer the anguish of despair because he had done so.

"I'm sorry, Miss Stewart. I've no time. Your father relies on me for certain things. And I'm glad to relieve him of many labors—if I can't of worries."

"Noble of you, big boy! . . . Strike a match for me. I have my gloves on," she rejoined, and leaned over the door with the cigarette between her lips. Lance had to step close, and he executed her request, but to save his life he could not have stilled the quiver of his hand as he held the match. She could not have seen it, however, for her unfathomable eyes were fastened upon his face. Then, with a merry good-by to him and Nels, she drove away. Not until she had gone down the slope did Lance realize he had watched her. Evidently Nels had done the same.

"Wal, son, she'd kinda set on disturbin' you," he drawled.

"Nels, I'll never last here," he replied, poignantly.

"Shore you will. We all like you, cowboy, an' thet applies to Majesty Stewart, too."

"Hell no!" ejaculated Lance, borrowing Starr's expressive language.

"Sidway, I've knowed thet girl since she was borned," declared Nels. "You don't figger her atall. You made her mad at you fust off. I reckon thet was good, if you're as nutty aboot her as Starr swears you air."

"Nels, did he tell you that? I'll sock him, by thunder!—Isn't there anything or anybody on this ranch but that girl?"

"Wal, she seems to be the center of things, whirlin' them like a dust devil."

All day long Lance glanced up from this and that task to see if there was a car raising the dust down on the valley road. Nevertheless he accomplished three days' work in one, so strenuously did he apply himself. When he went in to supper, Starr sat there, owl-eyed and pretending innocence. His entrance evidently disrupted some kind of a eulogy Nels was delivering to Stewart.

"Sidway, I've got to hand it to you," said the rancher, warmly. "You're a glutton for work."

"I don't hate work, sir."

Starr sat up in mild reproof. "Heah, you queer duck from Oregon, you ain't no hawg fer eatin', I'll tell you thet. An' if you keep on doin' ten greasers' work on an empty stummick you'll be an angel in heaven."

"Been off my feed lately," Lance admitted, after the laugh subsided.

"Sidway, are you any good at figures?" asked Stewart. "My accounts are in a tangle. I never was any good at them. Nels can't add two and two to make four. And Starr never went to school."

"Aw, Boss! The hell I didn't. I can read an' write some."

"Stewart, your daughter can, I'll bet. It must have cost you a lot to educate her. Why not make her your bookkeeper?"

"I wouldn't have Madge see what a poor business man I am for anything. . . . Can you straighten out my accounts for me?"

"Be glad to, Boss. I had a course in bookkeeping. I'm not so hot at it, but ordinary figures are not be-yond me."

"Nels, I'll bet our new range hand is hot all around," interposed Starr.

"Ren, he started well. But any fool can start. It's stickin' to the finish that counts."

The cowman's lazy drawl of humor recalled Madge's subtle expression of the very same thought.

"Shall I come up right away?" asked Lance.

"No. I'll fetch the books down. I had to hide them from Madge. She came home full of the Old Nick. She'd be curious, and maybe offended, if she found out about it."

When Stewart was gone, Ren stared solemnly at Lance. "Pard, did you get thet? Full of the Old Nick!"

"Are *you* going to begin again?" burst out Lance. "You're most as bad as Nels. Give me a rest about Madge Stewart."

"Rest! You cain't have a rest. Never again so long as you live! Thet's what Bonita did to me, only not anyways so bad. . . . Pard, I smelled hard likker on Majesty's breath!"

"Yeah? When did she come home?"

"Couple hours ago. She was sweeter'n a basket of roses. But I got a scent like a wolf's."

"What of that? She drinks. All these college girls drink. It's nothing. No more than cigarettes."

"Shore. I read the magazines an' go to the movies. But, pard, it's different in Majesty's case. It worries me an' Nels."

"And why? You're wasting your time."

144

"Son," interposed Nels, gravely. "Gene Stewart was the hardest drinkin' cowboy on this range. He was a drunkard. For ten years he swore off. Thet was on account of Madeline. Then he drank again—oncet in a long while—an' he does now. When he said Majesty come home full of the Old Nick, me an' Ren hed the same idee. Did he mean drink? An' is he afeared his girl has inherited his weakness for strong likker?"

"Oh, fellows, the boss didn't mean that," expostulated Lance. I'm sure he didn't. He just meant mischief. . . . My God, that'd be a tough spot for Stewart! He's one grand guy."

"Wal, you said it. Pard, if she asked you to ride in town with her how'n hell did you keep from it?"

"I've got a job and a sense of responsibility. Besides, she just wants to make a—a chump out of me."

"Son, don't you let her," declared Nels.

"Wal, I hope to Gawd you can keep from it," added Ren, fervently. "Say, Sid, there'll be high jinks goin' on if them girls air the least like Majesty. Comin' day after tomorrow."

"Lord help us!"

"Son, it shore looks like you'd hev to be the Lord. Fer all of us air under her thumb," said Nels, so very earnestly that Lance could not laugh.

"That's telling me, Nels," replied Lance, and went to his own room. He stumbled over something soft, then ran into a chair that had not been there in the morning. He could not locate his table. Even in the pitch blackness the room felt different and smelled differently.

"What in the deuce has come off?" he muttered, and taking out his matches, he struck one. This colorful clean-smelling room could not be his. Yes, it was—because he heard Nels and Ren talking through the partition. Burning his fingers in his astonishment he struck another match to light the lamp. But where was his plain, cheap, stinking lamp? Here was a shining one of brass with a big white globe. Rugs on the floor, curtains at the two windows, a dresser with a fine mirror, pictures on the walls, a new three-quarter

145

bright-blanketed bed where his bunk had been, a washstand with colored ware upon it, and towels the quality of which no cowboy before had ever felt, a comfortable Morris chair beside his table, and . . . but his roving gaze encountered a striking photograph in a silver frame upon his table. Majesty Stewart! With a groan he took the picture and fell into the chair, to stare down upon the lovely face, the speaking eyes, the bare neck of this girl who had bewitched him.

"Damn you! damn you!" he whispered, softly. It seemed a long while before he became aware of whispers and low laughs in Nels' room.

"Hey, pard, air you daid?" came through the wall.

"No! But I wish I were," shouted Lance.

"Why fer, you big stiff? . . . You oughta see my bunkhouse. My Gawd!—Pard, what's thet fairy-guy we used to read about when we was kids? Aladdin! Thet's the *hombre*. Wal, he's been here. . . . Nels told me the servants fetched all this truck down today, an' Bonita fixed the rooms up. An' a swell job she did!"

At that juncture Stewart stamped into Nels' room. Lance hid the picture, and hurried out, and into the ranchman's presence. "Here you are, Jack-of-all-trades," said Stewart, gayly, and he opened a ledger on Nels' table. "Balanced proper up to this page and date. And there's a year and more of figures. Sidway, if you make sense of these I'll be obliged."

"I'll hop to it, Boss."

It was midnight when Lance straightened out those accounts. The last entry was of seven hundred and thirty steers sold at thirty-five dollars a head—payment not yet received. Among the bank statements, papers and correspondence were a batch relative to Madge Stewart's income and expenses. Over a period of time a yearly income of sixty thousand dollars had diminished until at the present it had shrunk to a few thousands. The correspondence indicated that from time to time bonds and stocks had been transferred from Madeline Stewart's account to that of her daughter.

"Gosh! I wonder if Stewart really meant me to see

these," pondered Lance. "All as plain as print! Mother and father sacrificing themselves to the extravagance of spoiled daughter! And she doesn't know it!—Can you beat that?"

Lance's troubled mind yielded to the exhaustion of a hard day and toilsome hours with figures, and he slept. Ren's pounding on his door awakened him. After breakfast Stewart appeared and Lance brought him the ledger.

"All done, sir, and not so bad except for—for these," said Lance. "Accounts, you know, of your daughter."

"*Sidway!* Did I leave them in this book?" ejaculated Stewart, utterly discomfited.

"Evidently you did. Of course, I went over them. I'm sorry, sir."

"If she ever found this out . . ."

"Stewart, she won't from me," interrupted Lance, hurriedly, hoping to relieve the rancher of embarrassment. "And—as for your own accounts, sir—they're not so bad as you led me to believe. When you receive the money for that batch of cattle sold the other day, you can pay your debts and have around five thousand dollars left."

"No!—Sidway, you're—you're . . . it'd be too good to be true."

"Maybe you did not figure out just what you'd receive for the cattle."

"I didn't at that."

"Well, it comes to twenty-five thousand, five hundred and fifty dollars. Quite a lump sum, sir."

"I must have made a big mistake on the wrong side."

"You evidently did."

"I was thinking most of Madeline," replied Stewart, his dark eyes softening. "Sidway, I reckon Starr is right about you."

"That knock-kneed windbag! Now what'd he say?"

"I don't remember it all. One thing stuck, though. He called you a whiz."

Lance felt that he had never received a compliment

147

that had pleased him more. He went to work that day and drove Starr to distraction and dragged him home a cripple.

"Look at me, Nels," whined Ren, wet with sweat, grimy and ragged.

"Hey, Sid, who's this heah nigger you fetched in?" drawled Nels.

,"It's me, Nels. Me!—Worked to death by thet fiend. An' what I hate most in all this world is diggin' post-holes!"

"We finished that corral, didn't we? Now we can have some peace when Manuel and Jose wrangle Miss Stewart's horses. . . . Oh boy—tomorrow!"

"Me for the hills!" ejaculated Ren.

Lance was waiting for Starr the following night at sunset. Inside Nels was banging pans in unusual excitement.

"Pard, what'n hell's wrong with you?" demanded Ren, staring.

"Behold a—a—devastated man!"

"Wal, whatever'n hell thet means you shore air it. . . . So you obeyed them orders?"

"Yes. They were Stewart's."

"An' you had to ride in town with Majesty—all alone—and meet her friends—all them peaches we jest know air comin'—an' be a swell lady's guy?"

"You said it!"

"My Gawd, how tough! Jest the rottenest break ever. Wait till I bed down my hawse and I'll be ready to be deevasstated."

After supper Ren got up to help Nels with the dishes and he said: "Okay now, pard. Shoot! I reckon I'm strong enough now."

"What do you want to know?"

"Tell us aboot Majesty's outfit."

"Well, the boys are all nice clean-cut college chaps. You'll like them, especially the big football player, Snake Elwell. He's a regular fellow."

"Aw, nix on the fellers. It's the gurls Nels an' me want to heah about."

"Six of them, Ren. *Six!* And they might have been picked for a swell movie. . . . The gang arrived at ten-thirty. They stayed in town until three. Five awful hours! If I performed one job, there were a hundred. They probably were kidding me or Madge, for the whole bunch of crazy women went after me. Poor little me! While the boys hung around Madge. They ate and they drank. Can that crowd lap up the booze? I'm telling you. And they had to see everything and everybody in Bolton."

"Swell. But thet ain't tellin' us how they stacked up."

"Can't you wait till you lamp them?"

"Nope. Me an' Nels hev artistic feelin's."

"Well, here goes—the way I got it. Allie Leland first, evidently Madge's best friend, a slim styish girl with gray eyes, the peach of the bunch, I'd say, though not in looks. Next Maramee Joyce, brown beauty built like Jean Harlow, a knockout. Next a little southern girl, looks like sixteen but must be twenty-two. Dark, vivacious, with a smile that would drive any man nutty, and a sweet southern accent. Nels will fall for her. Then Pequita Nelson. Part Spanish, Ren. Creamy olive skin, great dreamy sloe-black eyes, willowy and graceful. Blue-blood, pard. . . . Then Selma Thorne, a blonde that, if you never saw Madge, would do the trick. And last Beulah Allen. . . . Whew! Ren, here's a peach that's a composite of honey, dynamite and autumn leaves of red and gold. Pretty! Why, she's so pretty I couldn't take my eyes off her. Red-headed, roguish-eyed, and a shape! What's more she's a devil clear down to her toes."

"Pard!" gasped Ren, utterly fascinated. "What'n hell are we up agin? It was bad enough with only Majesty heah. We shore air a deevasstated outfit."

"Ren, you should have heard the whoop those college tenderfeet let out when they saw Bonita."

"Ahuh. Wal, I'll be liable to shoot a laig off one of them," growled Ren.

Work on the ranch for Lance and Ren, except an

149

occasional and brief overseeing of laborers brought out from town, practically ceased. Their jobs took on manifold aspects. They had to drive and to ride, especially the latter. The only girl guest who knew anything about horses was Dixie Conn. Madge's horses were all too spirited for tenderfeet. Lance and Ren disagreed as to Madge's own ability to handle several of her mounts.

"Say, Ren, you're all wet," protested Lance. "She was a swell horsewoman once. Nels vouched for that. But she has been to college for four years. She's forgotten a lot. Besides she's out of condition. She's soft, if you get what I mean."

"Cain't you lay off yore grouch?" complained Ren. "Majesty is okay."

"So far as looks are concerned, yes. She looks grand. And that's all you see. Ren, you ought to be back at that garage."

The expression of Starr's face became so peculiar, and a giggle of Bu Allen sounded so gleeful that Lance turned toward the wide stable door. Madge had entered and she had heard him. Likewise had Rollie Stevens and Nate Salisbury, who were with her. The others appeared coming down the lane.

The purple fire in Madge's eyes was no new catastrophe for Lance. As a matter of fact, he had never seen it blaze for anyone or anything except him. Nevertheless this time, as always, it stimulated him to battle. Perhaps he labored under the delusion that he was right, but so long as he believed so he would not give in.

"Ren, saddle Dervish for me," ordered Madge, quietly.

Lance stepped forward and laid an ungentle hand on the cowboy. "Miss Stewart, please forgive my interference. But you should not ride Dervish—just yet. You—he . . ."

"I heard you express your opinions to Ren," she interrupted, in a tone that made Lance feel as if he were the scum of the earth. "You can save your breath."

"That I won't do so long as I am a cowboy on this ranch," replied Lance, coolly, as he found himself. "I have a duty here—to your father—and through him to you. . . . Dervish is a bad actor. He has not been worked out. Besides he does not like you, Miss Stewart. It's dangerous for you to mount him."

"Majesty, listen to Sidway," interposed Rollie, his fine face earnest. "That horse looks skittish to me."

Dixie Conn backed up Stevens, and the other girls apparently fell in line. This, Lance knew, was only adding fuel to the fire. He believed that if they only had advised it, Madge would have been amenable. But Lance Sidway was waving a red flag in her face.

"Ren, do as you're ordered," said Madge.

"Miss Majesty, meebe Lance is right about this."

"I know I'm right," Lance said, earnestly. "Nels agreed with me. He saw you on Bellefontaine the other day, and Bell isn't half the horse this Dervish is. May I repeat what Nels said to me?"

"Why, yes, if it pleases you so much," rejoined Madge.

"He told me to keep you off the wicked horses if I could."

"Nels! The old traitor! He taught me to ride."

"He said also that when you were sixteen there wasn't your beat in this state. . . . Coming from Nels, Miss Stewart, that is the very highest compliment."

"And *you* think sixteen is so far back in my past that I've forgotten how to ride?" queried Madge, with sarcasm. "Well, I'll show you!"

"I didn't say that. I think, though, you act like sixteen or under. . . . Will you force me to go to your father?"

"You wouldn't dare!"

"Yes, I would."

"Go ahead. It'll be a relief to be rid of you. By the time you find Dad I'll be far out on the range."

"Miss Stewart, he will hold me responsible if you are thrown."

"So that's it? Thinking of your job! It's not too sure, at that."

Lance gave up, and went back to saddling Pinto. Starr, at Madge's order, led the slender racy Dervish out of his stall. Lance heard the cowboy curse under his breath. He also heard Allie Leland, and some of the other girls, taking his part against Madge. And Lance's ears burned with something besides resentment. All these guests of Madge's had been fine to him, and Bu Allen more than friendly. Lance put Pequita Nelson up on Pinto, and hurried on to saddle Leatherstocking. The young men were having the fun of saddling their own horses. Lance liked this bunch of college boys better than he had anticipated.

At last all the girls were up except Madge and she was leading Dervish out into the open. Ren was with her. Lance hurried to get astride Umpqua. The others, except Allie Leland, rode out toward the range.

"Sidway, go with the others," called Madge.

He waited to see her put a foot into Starr's hand and go sailing upon Dervish. She was not in the least afraid of him. There was a red flush in her cheeks, a smoldering fire in her eyes. Lance had to admire her for more than the superb and lovely figure she made on the roan. Then Madge and the Leland girl passed him to join the others. Dervish acted all right, Lance thought, but Madge was holding him in. But could she hold him if he broke into a run or could she stay on if he wanted to pitch? Lance gambled that she would fail in the latter event, anyway. Starr joined him and they loped to catch up with the others.

"Ren, you four flusher, why didn't you stand by me?" queried Lance, with irritation.

"By thunder, I should of," he replied, contritely. "But Majesty always kids me along—makes me reckon I'm a helluva feller."

"Yeah? Well, if you'd come strong, we might have avoided a risk."

"She'll ride thet nag."

"Gosh, I hope so. She handles him great. But Ren, damnit! That's a horse—a mean horse! And she can't weigh more than a hundred and ten."

"Fifteen, pard, and she's strong. I'll admit, though I forgot she hadn't been ridin'.'."

"All right, let's go. I'll try to make Madge think I don't care a damn if she breaks her neck. . . . Fact is, I—I don't. But I'll keep an eye on her."

"Me too, pard. Ain't they a swell lookin' outfit? I wish Bonita was heah. Majesty said I could ask her. But I knowed I couldn't see anyone else, then . . . hey! . . ."

Lance rode away from the loquacious cowboy and steadied down conscientiously to his job. Once out in the grass and the sage there was much less danger of accidents. The girls had listened to reason, if their hostess had not. And except Dixie Conn, they were all too scared of horses to try any stunts. Dixie and Madge forged ahead, and Lance kept a position that would enable him to overtake Dervish, if he bolted. But nothing happened across the sage flat to the pine knoll five miles away. Madge led them up to the top of that, then down, and over the rolling range land toward the foothills. Half and hour of lope and trot brought them to the slope.

"Majesty," screamed Maramee Joyce. "For Pete's sake—hold on! I'm dying!"

"I've got that—awful stitch in my—side," cried Selma Thorne.

"We'll rest," replied Madge, merrily. "But how in the world will you girls ever make it up into the mountains?"

"But you're—not going soon?"

"Ah! this is swell, Majesty!"

"Majesty, let's leave these tenderfeet behind on that trip," suggested Snake Elwell, good-naturedly.

"What? You big hunk of protoplasm!" exclaimed Bu Allen, her pretty face scarlet, her roguish eyes snapping, her red hair disheveled. "Why, astride that horse you look as much like Sidway as I do like a rodeo queen."

At length when they were rested Madge gave the word: "Let's go! And step on it!"

As they swept off with merry screams and shouts

Lance, with an eye ever on Dervish, saw that he meant business. He balked. And when Madge laid on the spurs he began to pitch. Lance in a few jumps had Umpqua beside her, but as he reached for the roan's head Madge cried: "Let him alone!"

"But he'll pile you up."

"He will not!"

As bucking horses went, Dervish would have been mean for any rider. But to Lance's surprise Madge stayed in the saddle. Bent double, red-eyed and infuriated, the roan bucked all over the flat, and failed to dislodge the girl. She had her spurs dug into him and sat her saddle as if a part of it.

"You're riding him, cowgirl!" yelled Lance, carried away with her spirit and the spectacle she made.

Then Dervish, succeeding in getting the bit between his teeth, bolted away across the valley, in the opposite direction from the ranch. It took only a glance to see that the roan was a runaway horse and that he would eventually get the best of his rider. Lance spurred Umpqua after him. By now the others were a couple of miles distant toward the ranch, and they were not yet aware of Madge's predicament. The roan was fast. Lance had to urge Umpqua into his top speed to gain at all. And he saw that it was going to be a race. Madge fought her mount with all her might. If she heard Lance yell to let the horse run she gave no sign. The girl had evidently been jolted by the bucking, and now she was spending the last of her strength. She would be thrown.

Then after a grueling run Lance drew close to the roan. Madge showed signs of distress. She was beginning to sway.

"Drop your bridle!" yelled Lance. "Grab the pommel! Hold on!"

She heard him and obeyed. That saved her from an immediate spill. Umpqua thundered closer and closer until his nose passed the roan's flank. But again Madge was swaying. She was near a fall and the ground was rocky, and rough with hummocks. Desperately goading his horse, Lance gained inch by inch,

154

until he stretched out a clutching hand. She had the sense to shake her feet *loose* from the stirrups. But that loss of stability broke her seat in the saddle. She was in the air when Lance caught her in a grip of steel and swung her up before him.

"Oh!" she screamed, wildly. "You're tearing my flesh!"

Lance let her go, to slip her into the crook of his arm, and hold her across his saddle. Umpqua was excited, too, and hard to slow down.

"Whoa! Steady, old boy!" called Lance, over and over again. "We've got her. . . . There, Ump!—Easy now—easy!"

At length Lance halted the horse and then turned his attention to the girl. Her face lay high up on his left arm, near his shoulder, and it was white. The lipstick on her strained lips made a startling contrast.

"Gosh—I'm—sorry I had to hurt—you," he said, haltingly. "But I—couldn't help it. That damned—roan can run. Lucky to catch you—at all."

"How strong you are!" she exclaimed, her eyes, darkly dilated, upon him. "You had the muscles of my back. I'll bet I can't wear my new formals very soon."

"Shall I get down? Can you ride my horse?" asked Lance, hurriedly.

"I feel very comfortable where I am. . . . Lance, I deserve it. I was wrong—bullheaded—vain. You were right. . . . Now does that soothe your wounded vanity?"

"My feelings don't count. But I don't remember that vanity entered into it."

"Damn you anyway, cowboy!" she exclaimed, broodingly, passionate eyes upon him in speculation.

"That's not very kind," returned Lance, beginning to weaken under another kind of strain. She was resting in his arms, her head now on his shoulder. A little color began to creep into her cheeks. Lance almost collapsed under a terrific longing to kiss her.

"For *you* to be the one always to catch me in the wrong—do me a service! . . . It's a tough break."

"Miss Stewart, I had a hunch about this horse."

"For the love of Mike stop calling me Miss. Why don't you cuss me out?" she replied, hotly.

"To tell the truth I—I don't know why," answered Lance, lamely. He sensed that fatality for him consisted in being with her, and this close contact was insupportable. If he did not get away from it instantly he could not answer for himself. She was in his arms and if she did not like it, she was acting a part. Then Lance saw Starr approaching in a long sweeping gallop, and the others a mile or more behind.

"They're coming," said Lance, in relief, as he carefully slid with her out of the saddle. "Can you stand?"

"I can—if you hold me." And she swayed against him.

"Miss . . . Madge, you're not hurt so—bad," he protested.

"That's what you say. My back is broken."

"Nonsense!" cried Lance, in alarm, and he turned her round to feel of her. "It's just bruised—sore. I must have pinched you."

She squealed as he felt to see if he had broken a rib.

"You're a swell western girl—I don't think. Can't you take it?"

"What do *you* think, Lance Sidway?"

"God only knows!" he responded, with an inward groan. "Here's Ren. And the others are coming. Sit down. I'll ride after Dervish."

He found upon releasing her that she could stand easily enough.

"What'n hell come off?" shouted Starr, as he leaped from his saddle.

"Only me," laughed Madge.

Lance thankfully galloped off to catch Dervish, now contentedly grazing half a mile away. What a girl! He was slipping—slipping. Then his softer agitation burned away in a tumult, some of which emotion was wrath. He had not had half a chance. To save her life, or at least, a nasty spill, was just his hard luck.

All in a second to find her in his arms! Hell! What was a girl like that for? Her lying lovely eyes would make an imbecile out of a cigar-store Indian. Yet there seemed to be something so sweet, so square about her. If only she had not hated him, maybe he never would have known of her other nature! But that would have been worse. At length he caught Dervish, and by the time he had returned to the waiting group he was outwardly his cool self again.

"Did you beat him?" asked Madge.

"No. I never beat horses."

Ren glowered at the sweating roan, as he stood meekly, his racy head drooping. "Wal, I'll beat him some day, believe me."

"I wonder—why is he so kind to dumb brutes," said Madge, cryptically. "Listen, friends. Sidway saved my neck. After I refused to listen to him—insulted him! I am a cat. Now you shall see me apologize."

She turned to Lance in one of her bewildering flashes. "Lance, I am sorry. I beg your pardon. You were swell to keep your temper—and stay a gentleman. I'll tell Dad. And I'll not get on Dervish very soon again—if ever."

"That's just fine," replied Lance, heartily. "Now you ride Umpqua home. He's gentle and easy."

"What will you do?" she asked.

"I'll ride Dervish. He's worked off his edge now." He helped her mount and shortened the stirrups while the others expressed their relief in various ways. The girls, especially, had been frightened. The boys, except Rollie Stevens, quickly recovered their spirits. Then just as the cavalcade got into motion, Bu Allen said slyly:

"Lance, if I ride Dervish some time will you be a hero for me?"

8

That night after supper, when Starr, in the next room, was exaggerating the story of Madge's adventure on Dervish, and Lance sat in his big chair gazing at the beautiful photograph, there came a soft step outside and a tap on his door. Hastily hiding the picture of Madge, and with a leap of his heart he called: "Come in."

The door opened to disclose Beulah Allen on the threshold. She wore a henna gown that matched her hair, cut to expose her creamy arms and neck. Her charm appeared considerably magnified.

"Good evening, Lance. Here I am," she said, archly.

Lance awkwardly returned her greeting, then: "So I see. Who's with you?"

"I'm alone. I had a scrap with Snake, so I thought I'd hunt you up."

"Swell.—Only, what'll Snake do to me?"

"He hasn't any strings on me. We've been engaged several times and broken it off as often. Tonight is the last."

Lance had arisen, and now he stood looking at her, fully aware of her seductiveness. and half inclined to yield to it.

"How swell you are here! Madge got a kick out of dolling up these rooms. Isn't she a peach? Always playing Santa Claus!"

"Indeed, she's very kind. Which reminds me—in the excitement today I forgot to thank her."

"She hates to be thanked. . . . Aren't you going to ask me in?"

"No. But I'll come out," replied Lance, and taking his sombrero he joined her and led her off the porch. She took his arm and remarked that the night and the full moon were made for love.

"Yeah?—But how about a guy, who if he fell, would be down for good?"

"You?"

"I'm telling you. Beulah, you're one attractive kid. I like you. I'll be glad to help you with your riding—as you asked me. But don't get me in bad with Snake Elwell. He might beat hell out of me."

"I don't know about that. Snake can run with a football. But he gets hurt easily. Always crippled."

"You little devil!" laughed Lance. "Honest now, isn't Snake in love with you?"

"Yes," she admitted, reluctantly. "But he's not alive."

"Beulah, I've met a lot of young fellows. Elwell is not flashy. He's a rough diamond. He's a regular guy. If you liked him well enough to be engaged to him you oughtn't to play fast and loose with him."

"I don't."

"What do you call this? Coming to my quarters after me?"

"Lance, if you must be serious, I came because I felt a little out of it tonight. There's an odd girl, you know. Snake belongs to the same fraternity as the other boys. But I don't belong to Majesty's sorority."

"Oh, I see. . . . But she wouldn't slight you?"

"No. She's a thoroughbred—a real sport. And I'd be crazy about her if she'd let me. She's just a little aloof with me. And I'm as proud as the dickens. So when Snake made me mad, I beat it to you."

"I'm sure flattered. Let's walk down to the village cantina, and have a Mexican cone."

It was dark except for starlight. Lance thought that the ground was hardly uneven enough for Beulah to

159

hang onto him so tightly. But after a while he put his arm around her. When they reached the cantina, with its open vine-covered porch and dim lights, he did not remove his arm in time to escape Bonita's black eyes. She was there with a group of young people, and her escort was a Mexican lad Lance had never seen. He was of the *vaquero* type, a born rider, lithe of form, lean of face, and he had small glittering dark eyes. As Lance passed the table where they were sitting his keen faculties grasped Bonita's jealousy and her friend's uneasy lowering of his face. It strengthened his suspicion that some of these admirers of Bonita could have shed some light upon the rustlers.

"Hello, Bonita. Ren is looking for you," hazarded Lance, with a meaning glance. When her dusky eyes dilated widely he knew he had hit some kind of a mark. Before he and Beulah had finished their ice cream, Bonita left with her escort. The incident determined Lance to pay more attention to Danny Main's pretty daughter.

It developed that Beulah had an intense interest in motion pictures, about which Lance talked at length, and in fact all the way up the hill to the ranch house. She led him in through the corridor to the brightly lighted living room, where Madge and part of her guests sat at two card tables, and the others grouped around Stewart and his wife. Most of them were dressed in white. Lance had to bear the sight of Madge supremely lovely in filmy blue.

Their entrance put a stop to games and conversation. Beulah, flushed and radiant, made the most of the situation. It invoked various greetings, all full of fun and interest.

"Beulah, you look stunning," observed Madge. "What's your recipe for such glamour? My cowboy! ... Where'd you pick him up?"

"Oh, Lance came up after me," returned Beulah, sweetly. "He took me to the village—for a cone."

"For a which?"

"Cone?"

"You mean ice-cream cone?"

160

"Yes. It was swell. I'd have liked one of those Mexican drinks we had in town, but I guess Lance doesn't buy drinks for girls. . . . We saw that pretty Bonita. Say, she's got IT!"

"Come on, Barg," spoke up Nate Salisbury. "Let's drive down and grab a cone." And the two young men went tearing out.

"Mr. Sidway, do you play bridge?" asked Madge, politely.

"I tried it once. Didn't get the hang of it."

"Do you play any game—that is, *card* game?"

"Poker."

"Of course. Ren plays poker. We'll have you up some night."

"Thanks a lot. I'll hate to take your money. But I'll come. . . . I'm glad to see you okay, after your run on Dervish."

"I may look okay in front. . . . See, you ironfisted cowboy!" And Madge arose to turn her back. The V-shaped opening in her gown extended clear to her waistline. About half way down, disfiguring her lovely back, showed black and blue marks of a ruthless hand.

"I'm sorry!" burst out Lance, his surprise and regret checking other feelings. "That's terrible. . . . But, Miss Stewart, how could I help it?"

Madge's slow smile might have promised much. However, at this point, Stewart called the cowboy: "Sidway, I've had several versions of this runaway. Madge wouldn't say anything. From the looks of her back, though, I'd say you laid hold of her hard. Nels whitewashed the accident. Starr didn't see it, nor did the others. Come now, what's your story?"

"Mr. Sidway, take this chair here," interposed Mrs. Stewart, beckoning Lance to a seat beside her. He felt the penetrating kindness of her eyes.

"Thank you. . . . Well, really, there wasn't much danger. For a western girl!" replied Lance, deprecatingly, with a casual gesture. "Dervish began to pitch. Mad—Miss Stewart stayed in the saddle. Then he nailed the bit and lit out. Ren had gone with the outfit. I chased Dervish across the flat. He can run, that roan. I caught up with him—and grabbed her—a little roughly, I'm sorry to say."

"Did you forget my instructions?" queried Stewart, his kind eyes twinkling. "I forbade Madge to ride Dervish. And I told you not to let her get on any bad horse. You're a judge of horses, aren't you?"

"Not so good. I—I'm afraid I forgot, sir," returned Lance, not meeting Stewart's eye.

"Dad, your cowboy is a liar," spoke up Madge, in her rich voice, that now had a little ring. "In fact he's an awful liar. . . . He advised me not to ride Dervish. He insisted that I must not. He made me furious by threatening to hunt you up. But you know your little Madge, Dad. . . . Dervish worked out fine as long as I held him in. We rested a while. When I mounted again he began to pitch. He made me see red, and hurt me—took it all out of me. Finding he couldn't unseat me, the devil beat it up the valley. I stayed on somehow. After a while I heard Umpqua pounding at my heels. And Sidway yelled: 'Let him run! Hold on!' But for that I'd have gone off. The rocky ground scared me stiff. My arms went dead. I lost my stirrups. Just then, as I pitched out of the saddle, Sidway caught me. He certainly put his brand on me. . . . But, Dad, he saved me broken bones, perhaps a crushed face—maybe my life!"

Lance groaned in spirit to be thus made out a hero, yet her eloquence radiated through him, and added another link to the chain that was fettering him.

"Sidway, modesty is a becoming trait, but hardly justifies your lying to your boss to save his willful and wayward daughter," said Stewart, mildly.

"Dad, don't rub it in," called Madge, mirthfully. Then, taking up her cards, "Where was I, Allie?"

The card players settled down to their game again. Mrs. Stewart began to ask Lance about Oregon, and she was so gracious and interested that he found himself telling her of his boyhood home, of his mother and sister, about that sister's malady, and how he had left college to take Umpqua to Hollywood, how wonderfully the great horse had made good, how he loved him and would not part with him for the world, and finally how he had set out for Arizona and New Mexico.

"Majesty Stewart! You trumped my ace!" exclaimed Rollie Stevens, incredulously.

"She's transported!" declared Allie.

"Listening to Mr. Sidway," chimed in Maramee, with a giggle. "Majesty, you're not very flattering to us."

"Caught with the goods." cried Madge, leaping up with a blush, and slamming down her cards. "I hate bridge anyway. . . . Turn on the radio, you all. Or play the Victrola. Dance! What'd you come here for? . . . Mom, please surrender Mr. Sidway to me for a little. I want him to talk to *me!*" And approaching Lance she tugged at his sleeve. He arose, bowed to Mrs. Stewart, and allowed himself to be led toward the door.

"Madge, take a coat or wrap, if you're going into the patio," advised her mother.

"There's one in the hammock, Mom."

Rollie Stevens called forcefully after them. "Majesty, I'll cut in—what do you call it—pronto."

"He will, the sap!" whispered Madge. "But we'll fool him." The patio was silver-bright under a full moon. The fountain tinkled, there was a stir of leaves, and peep of sleepy birds. Madge caught up a white coat from the first hammock and gave it to Lance. He helped her into it, and turned up the wide collar, and buttoned the upper buttons, his fingers clumsy, while she stood still and gazed up at him with eyes he felt but dared not meet. Then she took his arm and led him along the wide porch, where the shadows of foliage played black on the tiles. Lance was helpless in the thrall of the moment.

"Lance, it's coming to you right now—while I'm hot under the spell," declared Madge. "Beulah Allen has fallen for you. They all saw that. I saw it long ago. What did you do to her? She sailed in positively regal. That was for my benefit, Lance Sidway. Only yesterday I told the girls you didn't neck. What a liar

163

you've made me out! . . . They all like you. Dad doesn't throw a fit over every fellow who comes along, not even a cowboy. And Mom! . . . Young man, do you know you couldn't pull a greater stroke here than that? I listened. It couldn't be a line. All that about your sister. Oh, Lance. . . . Mom likes you! That is the last straw! My lovely patrician mother!"

"She was just—moved by my—my service to you," said Lance, unsteadily.

"No. Don't start that stuff. This is serious," she rejoined, and halting beyond the last archway, she turned to him in the white moonlight. In that light, shining from the pale oval of her face, her eyes held the sum of all beauty. "Isn't it a pity—I don't like you?"

"Maybe that is lucky for me," he returned, huskily.

"Lance, are you engaged to any girl in Oregon?"

"No—indeed."

"Are you fancy-free?"

"Yes," he lied, glibly enough.

"You made a play for Bonita. Oh, I know. She gave you away—and herself. I was brazen enough to pump her. . . . Lance, do you know Ren Starr has a terrible case on Bonita?"

"I found that out pronto."

"You were only playing with her?"

"I didn't admit that."

"Aren't you?"

"Not since I found out about Ren."

"Listen, these college friends of mine, particularly Barg and Nate, are nuts over that little Mexican hussy. She's half white, yes, but the Latin blood dominates."

"Bonita isn't quite all that," rejoined Lance, stoutly.

"She is. And I'm a jealous cat. But all this is for Ren's sake. . . . You seem to be as big as that mountain there. Are you big enough to play Ren's game—to keep these college devils away from her? They're on the make. One or the other, most likely Nate, will get her."

"I'm afraid I'm not quite so—so big as that," answered Lance, led on and on by the deadly sweetness of her, and by the infernal power of his bleeding vanity.

She released his arm and averted her face. Like a cameo the perfect profile shone as if cut out of marble. The night breeze stirred her golden hair. "I'm disappointed in you—again."

"Why should you be, Miss Stewart?" he queried, stiffly, fighting a struggle almost vain. "I'm human—the same as you. Just no good!"

"How dare you!" she cried, wheeling with a startled movement. "Smile—when you say that."

But Lance did not smile. She had wanted to be serious and he had told her the truth. Without a word she left him standing there. Lance stepped into the black shadow of the wall, his thoughts whirling, his conscience stinging, his judgment at fault, his love valiantly championing this perverse and wayward beauty. A thousand wild queries did not lodge in his mind, let alone find an answer. There was not any answer to anything. Why had she asked those direct thought-provoking questions? How easy to escape from her if she were only like Beulah! But Madge Stewart had the insidious power to make men believe in her sincerity. Her look was enough to lift any poor masculine fool to the seventh heaven—to be convinced that he was the one man!

Lance's endless ravings were disrupted by approaching voices. Two people were coming down the patio path. Then Madge's silver laughter, a little mocking, froze Lance to the spot. They came clear to the inside wall.

"Majesty, you drive me mad," came in Rollie Stevens' subdued voice. "You know you have no use for that cowboy. You told me so. Yet for days now you've been rotten to me, on his account! Oh, I get it! Sidway hasn't fallen for you—and that's piqued your vanity. Besides you want his horse. Why don't you give the fellow a break? He's a real man. He's not a sap. But pretty soon he'll fall for you, even if he knows you're not on the level with him."

"Rollie, I might be in earnest," she scoffed.

"Rot! Why, Majesty Stewart, only a month ago you said you—you might marry me."

"That was a month ago, darling. An age!"

"Majesty, you can't marry a cowboy," he expostulated, incredulously.

"Rollie, I hadn't thought of that. But—why couldn't I?"

"You're a lady of quality, a talented girl. Why he's not of your class. Admitting Sidway is a fine chap—I like him, Majesty—you couldn't marry him. Oh, to talk of it is preposterous."

"All right. Skip it. . . . Rollie! don't kiss me right here in the moonlight."

"I'll bet he did," he returned, hoarsely.

"Who?"

"Your cowboy!"

"He never even thought of it."

"My word!—Majesty, can you expect me to believe that?"

"No, I don't."

A slight scuffle followed, a protest from the girl, then the soft sounds of kisses.

"Rollie, you needn't tear my clothes off. Pick up my coat. And remember, my back is too sore for hugging."

"Darling—it maddens me—to taste your lips. I'm just wafted . . ."

"New kind of lipstick! All over your face. And mine too."

"Majesty, honest to God—didn't that Sidway even kiss you?"

"No, Rollie. He didn't even try, I'm ashamed to admit."

"He could have kissed you! All the boys kiss you! It was campus talk!"

"You jealous sap! Surely he could have—and they do. I rather like it. And besides what's a kiss?"

"You know what it leads to, Majesty Stewart."

"Yeah? Well, it never led me anywhere in particu-

166

lar yet, except to muss my dress and make-up, as you've done."

"I'm sorry. But you drive me wild. . . . Kiss me goodnight, sweet. A real one, like you used . . ."

"There, little boy. Let us go back. I am cold."

Then soft footfalls and subdued voices faded away. Lance plunged down the trail like a blind man. He had his answer.

Every morning Lance awakened under the shadow of impending calamity. What was going to happen next? Or what would Madge be up to doing? It did not make the slightest difference to Lance, only he seemed to be the one doomed to encounter her in moments of stress.

Things happened to Madge's guests. Pinto ran off with Beulah; Pequita, who was a poor swimmer, fell or was pushed off the platform into the lake, and nearly drowned; Maramee was kicked in the ankle so badly that she could not ride; Allie lolled around all day on the sandy beach and was blistered by the sun. In spite of the fact that Stewart insisted on Lance's keeping a close watch upon the girls, accidents happened.

According to Starr the long-looked-for camping trip in the mountains was approaching; and that, for two lone cowboys, was a job too big. Starr told Lance that he was trying to persuade Madge to take the *vaqueros* and a cook.

The boys went off on larks of their own contrivance, and on one occasion became lost less than ten miles from the ranch. Another time they slipped off to town and did not show up at the ranch until late the next day, for which jaunt Madge called them "a lot of bums."

When, however, the least little thing or something more serious, such as Dervish's bolt, happened to Madge, Lance seemed always to be on the spot. This morning he was morosely counting the occurrences, and wondering if the last two had been strictly bona fide, yet nursing a sense of guilt because of his doubt.

There were endless jobs. He was laboring on a corncrib. Ren had taken the boys fishing. And just about the time Lance forgot his woe, there came a wild clamor of screams from the big barn.

"Sounds scary. Now what the hell?" he muttered, darkly, and strode for the barn. The first screams might have been mirth, but those following sent Lance into a run. He dashed up the runway.

The girls were in a pandemonium of fright, shrieking, pale as death and wild-eyed. It could not be an ordinary circumstance. Missing Madge from the group Lance yelled: "Shut up—Where's Madge? What's the matter?"

"Oh!—Oh!—she'll be killed!"

"Save her, cowboy—for God's sake!"

"If she falls . . . it . . . it'll be terrible!"

"Where is she? What is it?" yelled Lance.

"Girls, if you tell him—I'll hate you," cried Madge, piercingly from somewhere. "Lance Sidway, you get out—of here! Don't you dare look!"

At that juncture Beulah Allen ran to Lance. "She was swinging on the hay rope—from one loft to the other. . . . Sitting on the noose! . . . Something gave way—and up she went bang against the roof. . . . There!"

"That's out for you, Bu Allen!" raged Madge.

Then Lance saw Madge up under the roof, hard against the wheel. The noose evidently slipped from her hips, up to her armpits, and had stripped her that far. But Lance saw only those terrible eyes and the scarlet face.

"Go away!" she shrieked.

"Madge, you're in great danger," flashed Lance. . . . "Grab the wheel!"

"I'd rather die—than—have you . . ."

"I didn't look at you—directly," fumed Lance, angrily. "I didn't *see* you. I wouldn't give a whoop to . . . didn't you ever meet a gentleman? . . . hang on! —Help me, girls. Make a pile of hay right under her —so if she falls. . . ."

Frantically he began to drag huge armloads of hay

168

from the loft, flinging them to the girls. They worked with a will. Then Lance dashed to the windlass. It was an old-fashioned hay-fork contrivance, and the heavy reel, owing no doubt to a swinging rock wired on it for a balance, had slipped to jerk her aloft.

"All right," shouted Lance, as soon as he had loosened the rope and taken a strong grip. "Let go the wheel up there. . . . Down you come. . . . Hang on to the rope now."

"You're squeezing me—to death," cried Madge.

Madge reached the floor and the rope went slack. A chorus of tender and commiserating exclamations came from the girls who had surrounded Madge. Bu Allen met Lance with a twinkle in her eyes.

"She's not hurt much. I'll say she got squeezed *once* hard enough."

Lance made no effort to approach the circle around Madge who evidently lay prostrate on the hay. He had been forced to expend breath as much through emotion as effort. Bu put a sympathetic hand on his arm. Lance received the impression that the girl, despite her sophistication, was someone to like.

"Girls—is—she hurt?" panted Lance.

"Not that we can tell," replied Allie, who knelt on the hay. Maramee had Madge's head in her lap. Her abbreviated costume had been decently arranged.

"Where's that dragon killer?" asked Madge, her voice weak, but spirit apparently undaunted.

Bu Allen dragged Lance over to the pile of hay, where Madge lay, white as a sheet.

"You would!" she exclaimed, with inscrutable eyes on Lance.

"Would—would what?"

"Be the one to catch me in that stunt. I used to do it when I was little. It never occurred to me to look at the windlass. I'm an idiot. . . . Sidway, please promise you'll not tell Nels or Dad, or even Ren."

"It never happened, Miss Stewart," rejoined Lance, soberly.

"Help me to the car," she replied, and with Allie and Maramee's assistance arose painfully to her feet.

"The knot on that damned noose stuck into my back."

The girls helped Madge in, and then piled in themselves, with Allie at the wheel. Madge leaned over the door and took hold of the dusty edge of Lance's vest with unsteady fingers.

"Did I thank you?"

"No. But that's not necessary," returned Lance, hurriedly.

"I ought to be decent enough."

"Madge, you said it," chimed in Beulah.

"She's just waiting for something big," added Allie softly. "Anyway, Lance, we all thank you from the bottom of our hearts."

"Lance Sidway, don't you save me any more," said Madge, imperiously. "Not from hayforks, fences, horses, cars—from college youths or gangsters—nor from *myself*. If you do, I'll not be responsible."

"Are those orders?"

"Yes, they're orders."

"Thanks. I'll not be present next time. And I won't attend your funeral!"

The car rolled away.

Lance felt inclined to the conviction that it was his careful avoidance of the girls the next few days which kept him out of hot water. Still he had to hear about their mishaps and stunts from Ren, who had been relegated to the job, and who raved rapturously through supper, and then long afterward, to Lance's disgust. It did not help Lance's mood to realize that he listened keenly when he might have gone out of hearing.

On the third night, however, Ren, for some reason appeared very glum and silent. Nels ventured a few sly queries. And when Lance added: "Has our poodle had his tail pulled?" Ren stalked out and stamped to his room.

"Wal, he ain't often like thet," said Nels, ponderingly. "Reckon one of us ought to make a move, anyhow."

"I'll go, Nels," returned Lance, and lighting a cigarette he went out. Approaching Ren's door and seeing that the light was out, Lance knocked and said:

"Sorry, old man. I was only kidding."

"Shore, I know that. It's okay," replied Ren, gruffly.

"Little off your feed, Ren?"

"I reckon. . . . An' I was made out a turrible sucker today!"

"By whom?"

"Wal, who'd you think?"

"Bonita?"

"Thet little hussy!—Say, she's lost her haid over them boys. I cain't do a damn thing about it."

"Don't try. They're only in fun, Ren."

"Like hell they air!" ejaculated the cowboy, bitterly.

"Ren, I lay off Bonita for your sake. Maybe I shouldn't have. She liked me. And I'm your pal, you know."

"You're damn right you shouldn't. Them boys hev been chasin' Bonita an' her friends pretty hard lately, an' unbeknown to Majesty."

"That's not so good, Ren."

"Good!—It's pretty bad, if you ask me."

"Well, I'll walk down and give the kid a spiel, Ren. . . . But, I forgot. Who made the sucker out of you?"

"Never mind now, pard. I don't want to hear you whoop."

Lance strolled off the long porch across the square, and down the road toward the high wall of poplar trees that marked the village. The night was close and warm. Merry voices up by the lake attested to the presence of night bathers. The strumming of a guitar and the lilt of a Spanish love song suited the summer night. At the corner Lance turned left to go down the long avenue of poplars. Lance passed the deserted adobe houses, then the lighted store, and beyond that the noisy cantina. Here there was no one out under the vine-covered trellis. Peeping in he saw a number of Mexicans, but no girls or white men. Lance crossed the street, and in the deep shadow of the other lane of poplars, he went slowly on toward Danny Mains' house. When he got to the corner he halted in the shadow. The gate was beyond a little ways. Lance thought he would hang around a little before he went in. There were both lights and music in the Mains' cottage. Presently three bareheaded girls appeared, scarfs round their shoulders. The foremost was Bonita. They hesitated, whispering excitedly, and were evidently expecting someone. When Lance called Bonita she gave a start and then approached slowly, while the other girls hung back. He met her at the gate.

"Hello, kiddo. Where are you going?"

"Oh, *Señor* Lance!—I was afraid it might be my brother Manuel . . . I've—we have a date."

"You look it. Sweet as a wild rose! . . . Bonita, have you gone back on Ren and me?"

"No indeed. But I never see you—and him so seldom. He's jealous. Tries to boss me. I won't stand it, Lance."

"Don't blame you. Has he asked you to marry him yet?"

"He has not," she retorted. "But he did say I was so—so bad he wasn't sure he wanted me to."

"Well, that's a tough one. . . . Bonita, have you been stepping out a little lately?"

"Not so very. Tonight's the first time I've consented to go to town. Francisca and Maria have both been. I'm scared. If Daddy finds it out he'll whip me."

"Stay home. Come with me to see Ren. He's blue. Let the others go."

"Lance, if *you* wanted me for yourself I'd break any date. I'd rather. These young college men are too swift for Bonita Mains."

"Listen, honey. Now don't be a little chump. It's all right to go if you refuse to drink. You'll enjoy the movies and dancing."

"They all drink like fish."

"Right." And Lance laughed at the frank girl. He drew her close to him and kissed her. "Bonita, get a load of this. I like you myself—more than these college guests of Miss Stewart's. But Ren loves you, dearly. I know it. And I'd hate to see you two fail to make a go of it. Now be a good kid. Promise me. I'll make a date with you for tomorrow night, like this, so we can talk."

"I promise, Lance," she replied, happily, her hands on his arm. "I'll not drink tonight. If you can't patch it up between Ren and me, it'll not be my fault."

"Swell! You're okay, Bonita, and Ren is a crabby old sourdough. We'll fix it. . . . Hello!—a car?"

"They're coming. Perhaps it'd be just as well if you weren't seen."

Lance gave her dark head a pat and hurried back into the shadow of the trees. But the car did not come close to the house, and Lance could not ascertain to whom it belonged. The girls ran out and were taken in with merry greetings. As the car went on, Lance thought he saw a figure hanging on behind. Presently, being certain of this, he took to the road and strolled down the hill. He knew that if someone had stolen a ride, he would not stick on for long, not on desert roads at the speed these fellows liked.

This car, however, did not appear to open up, until it reached the level valley floor. Lance kept on, presently reaching the level, where the dry wash and the sand made rough going for a space. At length he gave up and was about to turn back when he almost bumped into someone sitting on the low bank of the road. A little peal of silvery laughter magnified his start.

"Lance Sidway! I was just gambling with myself how soon you'd arrive," said Madge Stewart.

"Well, I'm damned!"

"So am I. Fatally damned to have *you* get me out of every scrape."

"That's a tough break. You're not alone?"

"Yes, I am. Allie was in the plot with me. She was to hang onto the other side. Either she did not get on or she was jolted off. You didn't see her along the road?"

"No. She couldn't have come. I saw only one person hanging on the back of that car."

"You saw me? When?"

"When the car stopped outside Mains' house. I was with Bonita. The other girls waited in the yard."

"Oh! I see. Johnny on the spot!—Did you get who the boys were?"

"No. That didn't interest me particularly. Bonita told me these boys were too swift for her. What Bonita does is probably none of my affair, but I am interested because of Ren. So I urged her not to drink and she said she wouldn't. Bonita is easily influenced if you go about it right. I've been Ren's friend, with her, if you know what I mean."

"I didn't until now," returned Madge, bluntly. "We girls thought the boys were going to the cantina with the girls. I think it lousy of them, especially of Barg Hillcote. Just engaged to Maramee! There I go spilling my insides. . . . Lance Sidway, men are all rotten."

"Yeah!" answered Lance, uncertainly. She had begun to strike him rather singularly, as she had not moved, and she sat leaning back on both hands with one leg up over the bank. In the starlight he could see her lovely face and speaking eyes.

"Maramee would break her engagement with Barg for this. I would. And she's been so happy. . . . I hope to goodness Allie didn't get on and fall off. . . . Surely she'll come soon."

"What's wrong with you?" Lance said suddenly, and he leaned close to Madge, peering at her.

"Guess I got hurt," she replied, with great inscrutable eyes meeting his.

"Where?"

"My foot. This one. Thought at first I'd sprained my ankle. But I'm not sure."

"Let me see." Lance stepped up on the bank and knelt. She had taken off her shoe and stocking. Her white foot and leg gleamed in the starlight.

"Don't touch it!" she cried. But he went right on until she screamed out.

"All right, all right, touchy! . . . Let me see you move it. . . . Flex it!"

"Oh, I can do that. It doesn't hurt."

"Your ankle is okay. You've sprained your instep

174

—or something. But if you keep off it and use hot water frequently, you'll be all right tomorrow or next day."

"I'll have to walk back home."

"No you won't. You can't. Let me get your car."

"But I don't want anyone to know about this, and they will if I come in the car. I'll have to sneak in by the west wing to my room. I'll have to walk."

"Nonsense. I can easily carry you."

She laughed outrageously.

"But I can. I'm strong," protested Lance, earnest, amazed, solicitous. "I can throw a hundred pound sack of grain all over the place."

"Strong? I know you're a perfect Hercules, Mr. Sidway," she said, tauntingly. "But I won't have you packing me around."

Very carefully she stepped, and moved up the slope. Every time her injured foot touched the ground it must have pained greatly, Lance knew. He put a hand under her arm and half lifted her along. They came into a trail, and that appeared to be easier for Madge. When they arrived at the pines, however, she was tottering. But this girl was the kind that could not quit.

"Why won't you let me carry you?" he asked, suddenly. "You did once."

"That's why."

"If you're not the queerest, screwiest girl, I'll eat my hat!" declared Lance.

"Yes, when you haven't one!" she retorted. When she started on, Lance knew she would not make it much farther. And he bided his time, hot and perplexed. Finally she swore and sobbed almost in the same breath. Without a word more he picked her up in his arms and went on. Shifting his hold, so she would carry more comfortably for her, he said: "There. Isn't that better? I hardly feel your weight."

"Better, indeed. But I fear—riskier," she returned in a queer voice.

Lance had to look at her. Before that, all had seemed well. He was relieved to save her pain. Her face lay high up on his right arm, almost on his breast, turned toward him somewhat, and its lovely proximity grew suddenly exciting. She was looking at him with eyes whose expression he could not fathom.

"Riskier!—What do you mean?" he demanded.

"You see I am utterly helpless. You might get a cave-man notion. . . . Really that wouldn't be so bad. But you probably just kissed Bonita . . ."

"I did. For Ren's sake—mostly."

"Ye gods and little fishes! . . . And no doubt it was Bu Allen last night. She came in with her lipstick all smeared up. Radiant. Bold as the very devil. And she didn't deny it when we kidded her about you."

"Miss Stewart, I did not see her last night," protested Lance.

"Oh, for Pete's sake, can the Miss. . . . It doesn't sound natural. . . . And well, if you *had* been with Bu, you'd have kissed her, wouldn't you?"

"That would have depended entirely upon her."

"How chivalrous! If she had been suffering for contact or release—or what have you, why you'd have been a perfect necker. . . . Lance, you give me a pain in the neck."

"I know. But why—why?" he demanded, furiously.

"It must be because you're a liar."

"Well, Madge Stewart, you give me worse than that —and it's because you're no good."

"Let me down. You said that before. I'll die before I—I'll . . ."

"Bunk! You can die all right, after I get you home. I hope you do. I hope you choke on your terrible tongue."

Anger and intense mortification, and some other emotion began to augment in Lance's consciousness.

"The girls think you've the sweetest disposition— that you're the swellest fellow. My God!" And she uttered a tinkling little laugh that cut into Lance like icy blades.

"Your boy friends think the same of you. But they're a lot of sapheads. They don't know you."

"You do!"

"Bet your—sweet life I do. Better than you have any idea," he panted.

"Rest here, young Lochinvar! or you'll fall. I think, after all, you're not so strong. This magnificent frame is pithy—like your head."

Lance groaned under the excess of his burdens. Halfway up to the house, in one of the little bench parks under the pines, he sat down on a boulder to regain his equilibrium, but he did not let go of Madge. He could feel the throb of her against his throbbing. And all at once he happened to think of what she had told Rollie that last night. Under the galvanizing stress of the idea that leaped out of it he arose like a giant and a fiend. He wrapped his long arms closer about her and drew her wholly against his breast. Madge seemed totally calm. Then Lance kissed her, not with any particular feeling, but merely as a preliminary.

"I thought it was about time," muttered Madge.

Then, staggering on under the pines, he kissed her cheeks, her eyes, her hair, her neck—and when at last she protested, Lance stopped her mouth with his, in an endless passionate kiss which magnified all he had ever bestowed in his life.

"Damn—you!" she panted, as he moved a moment to breathe. And she began to pound him—to tear at his hair. "You insult me . . ."

"Insult *you!*—Good God—it—couldn't—be—done," he mocked her, breathlessly. "I heard you say—you rather liked it. . . ."

"You—*what* . . ."

"Mine ought to be—as good as any of those guys— and cleaner, by heaven! and fresher—from lack of promiscuous practice." And bending over, squeezing her face up immovably, he began to kiss her lips like a madman. His kisses choked off her scream. After one frantic and tense struggle she collapsed in his arms. And he kissed her for every step, on under the pines, out upon the drive, almost to the front archway. Keeping outside the drive he passed this, and once in the shrubbery he began again his ravenous tasting of her lips, as if his appetite grew with what it fed upon. But not until he rounded the west wing and reached her window did he realize that her face, her lips, her body had changed. Her eyes were closed tightly—heavy eyelids dreamy, long curled lashes on her cheeks; her lips bowed, open, sweet with a strange fire; her breast pressed on his. Not until Lance lifted her into the open window did he realize that she had an arm round his neck. He lowered her carefully to the floor. Then he leaned on the sill, spent and devastated.

She stirred, and sat up, and laboriously climbed upon the bed. Lance, watching her, expected, yearned for a scourging, bitter enough even for him. But she just looked at him, In the starlight he saw her face as only he would carry it in his heart forever.

"Majesty," he began, in husky whisper, "I . . ." but he could not go on.

9

Madge sat upon her bed gazing tensely out of her window into the gloom where Lance Sidway had vanished. A fringe of her senses seemed to register the drowsy murmur of water, the rustle of leaves, the chirp of crickets, as well as loud voices and gay laughter of some of her guests in the living room. But for all that her acute senses coalesced on her burning cheeks and neck, her breast, and especially her lips on fire with that cowboy's terrible kisses.

Not all at once could her wit and intelligence throw off that spell. She found herself rubbing her stocking-less leg and ankle. The tightness around her foot, the heat, meant injury in some degree, but she felt no pain. Over and above these sensations thundered the truth, clearing in her mind. She had ranged the gamut of incredible feeling—from pique, surprise, shock, fury to a sudden overwhelming tumult of love, of her willful changing moods, her wounded vanity, her temper and up-flaring hate, and her softening doubt, her endless misgivings and suspicion, that had kept her up and down for days, only to have this shameful assault leave her undone, madly in love at last, stricken forever.

"I—I can take it!" whispered Madge, with her fluttering hand on her hot lips. She did not weep. She asked no quarter. She had her just deserts. But she was not as he believed—that shot through her with a passionate pang. From the very beginning everything had worked to her detriment. Her imperious demand for that horse? No—that was not the first. Her meeting with the gangster Uhl! That had started her wrong with this Oregon boy. And every single thing afterward had gone wrong—her tempers and her tricks, her insincerity and subterfuge, her nasty tongue and open satire. He must have overheard her saying she rather liked being kissed. That night when Rollie had met her after Lance had infuriated her! But there was nothing to be ashamed of about that. It was true, only on the moment she was torturing Rollie. The cowboy had something these other boys lacked. His recent treatment of her was wholly at variance with that, and seemed inexplicable to Madge. He did not want to kiss her. He did not approve of her. He despised her. He must have possessed some kind of a masculine trait that made her kissing promiscuity intolerable and abhorrent. He was avenging the throng of boys she had kissed and forgotten. There were a thousand slants and angles to this outrageous assault upon her—only one terrible revelation accruing from them! The doom of love, that she had trifled with so regally and callously, had fallen upon her. How impossible to understand!

If Lance Sidway had entered her room that moment and snatched her up. . . . But he had not known she had been, at the last, taking his kisses and spending her soul in exchange. And suddenly Madge was possessed of an insane rage. She wanted to kill him. It would not be enough to have him horsewhipped and driven away. He must not live to kiss girls like Bonita and have the sunlight shine in his hazel eyes for some other. . . .

"Oh, nuts!" burst out Madge, baldly, suddenly sick of herself, so weary that the fury drained out of her. "I've put this day of reckoning off long enough!"

Her exclamation must have been heard, for clicking high heels sounded on the stone corridor.

"Majesty!" called Allie, in great eagerness. "Did I hear you?"

"I shouldn't wonder. I was cussing. Come in. I've a story to unfold. What happened to you?"

"Me!—I was thrown in the dust," whispered Allie. "Blinded. I couldn't see a thing. The car was gone and you with it. I felt my way back to my room and washed the dust from my eyes. After that I walked under the pines—down the road—watching for you."

"Funny you didn't see that cowboy carrying me or hear him kissing me. Must have sounded like a decisive battle of the world!"

"Majesty!"

"Be careful, darling. I'm a cripple. I fell off the car, too. Hurt me foot. . . . Help me into my bathroom."

There between the two of them, Madge boiled out the pain in her foot, and bound it up, to find then that she could walk without limping. She sent Allie out to find where everybody was, and bade her return to sleep with her. Madge found it good to stretch out in bed, in the dark, and wonder. Presently Allie came back, to feel her way to Madge's side. It was a mutual emotion that caused them to seek each other's arms.

"Your mother has gone to bed, I think," whispered Allie. "Snake was playing checkers with your dad. I told them you were tired. Your dad seemed concerned. 'Madge tired? that's unheard of.' He looked worn himself, poor dear. Majesty, do you know I've an idea he worries about you and us. . . ."

"Skip it!—Where were the girls?"

"In their rooms, lolling, fussing, gossiping. Except Bu. She's down the hill looking for cowboys, so Dixie said."

"Oh!" cried Madge, poignantly.

"What ails you, darling? You act kind of queer and talk worse. You're burning up. I'm afraid you've got fever."

"Fever!—Ha! Ha!—Yes, I've got galloping fever. . . . And the boys?"

"Down playing pool. Wouldn't take the girls."

"Frame-up to shield that trio of heels!" whispered Madge. "All in the know about that date. . . . Darling, get a load of this. Barg and Dawson and Brand were in that car. And down below they took in Bonita and two of her friends. They went to town."

"Majesty! Not really."

"I'll say. What do you think of them, Barg especially?"

"For Barg?—Lousy is too lovely a word. That dirty little bum! Just finally won Maramee, and he pulls such a stunt. Maramee is so happy. She thinks Barg is perfect. It'll break her heart."

"She must never know. Don't you breathe it."

"But, darling, they don't mean any harm."

"Who don't?"

"Why, Barg and the boys."

"No, I don't suppose they do mean any harm, but it hauls me up, Allie. I've done my damnedest to entertain this crowd. They're swell, only they want to do what they like. Suppose there'd be an accident, or a fight, or they drank too much, and got stuck out all night. That happens, when no harm is intended. What'd my dad say? I grow stiff at the very thought. He's such a peach. He believes I'm so. . . . Oh, hell! . . . What would Danny Mains say? Good old scout. Worships that black-eyed flip! What would that cowboy *do?* My heavens!"

181

"Majesty! Someone will hear you. Cowboy! You mean Sidway? It's none of his business."

"Isn't it, though? Ren Starr is his pal. Ren has been at Bonita's feet for long. And Lance has been courting her for him. Would he be sore? He was sore tonight, maybe somewhat because I . . . Allie, that cowboy would call the boys down to the barn . . ."

"But, honey, nothing terrible has happened yet. It won't."

"Yes, it has—to *me*," whispered Madge, tragically. "Death wouldn't be half so hard!"

"Majesty, are you crazy? Such talk! What happened?"

Madge hugged her loyal friend close and shook over her. "I fell off the car way down the road. Hurt my foot. I took off my shoe and stocking. Then I sat up on the bank waiting. I knew who'd come. I'd have bet my soul. And he *did* come. Sidway, the darned inquisitive rooster. We talked, and as always in a few moments we were at each other's throats. All before he knew I was hurt. When he found that out he was human for a little bit. I wouldn't let him go for a car or for help, and I started walking up the hill. Hurt? Oh, Lord, did it? Pretty soon he grabbed me up in his arms. I gave him some dirty digs because I knew he'd kiss me. No fellow yet ever got that far with me without kissing me. And I was scared of having Sidway do that. Allie, I—I-liked him too much. . . . Well, pretty soon he did. I never was so mad in my life, just at first. . . . After that I began to like it. I thought he was going to eat me alive. . . . Allie, he lighted some kind of a conflagration in me. If I hadn't been too weak I'd have. . . . Oh!—But I couldn't move. It was only after he tumbled me in my window here that I realized I'd been in a trance of bliss . . . that at last there . . . I'd been kissing him for every kiss he'd given me. It all comes to me gradually. Later I'll remember some of the things he said, and tell you. . . . Allie, darling, I've told you many stories in the dead of night—after love dates, blind dates, hells. But what do you say to this one?"

"Majesty, you *love* him!" whispered Allie, in awe.

"Ha! Ha! So you get that? What wonderful perspicacity, darling! Never mind about me—about the dual rotten nature that has turned on me . . . but what did Lance Sidway mean? Tell me that."

"Madge, it's beyond the bounds of human possibility that he doesn't love you."

"Why?"

"Because he's a man. And you've placed him on the damnedest spots. Seeing you every day and every way. . . . Why, Madge. I was sorry for him the other day at the lake. You in that indecent bathing suit— the boys wallowing you all over the sand! And he stuck there to save our lives if we got cramps!"

"Wrong again. But what did *you* see?" flashed Madge, in a passionate whisper.

"I saw the look in his eyes. You know he has beautiful eyes, when they're soft."

"You're as sentimental as Maramee, and as gullible. That cowboy hates my very insides."

"I can't believe that."

"But, sweet, listen. For God's sake use some brains. Isn't it conceivable that I should finally fall foul of a real man who sees through me—who has my number —whom I can't fool or intrigue or fascinate or seduce —who has fine ideals, and who consequently despise me?"

"Yes, it's conceivable. That'd be a horrible misfortune. . . . But if Sidway wasn't mad about you he couldn't act as he does. Actions, my proud savage! Actions! Any boy or man can rave. But it's actions that count. He's done something, hasn't he?"

"He's done me wrong," wailed Madge, fighting vainly against the sweet madness of Allie's loyal convictions.

"Take the day you were caught in the noose of the hay rope. Madge, do you imagine any man ever recovering from *that?*"

"From—what?" asked Madge, faintly.

"From seeing you—from your chin down—without a stitch!"

"Oh, no! He—he didn't see me . . . he swore he didn't."

"He *did*, Madge Stewart."

"Oh, Allie! I'm so horribly afraid he'll turn out big and fine and noble—despite all—that tonight."

"He was indicating his sex."

"Oh!"

"He was jealous. They *all* kiss you. So would he—and make one swell job of it. I think he's grand."

"You are a traitor, Allie Leland."

"No. You're that, Madge, to yourself."

"Oh, *I* couldn't be a traitor to anyone," retorted Madge, fiercely.

"You are a queen and a law unto yourself. Sidway will not bend to you."

Spent, but still unconvinced, Madge lay there in her friend's arms.

"Darling, have you *ever* been your true self to Sidway?" asked Allie.

"Yes, once. The first time. That campus day."

"Then go back to that. Even if he hates you unmercifully, he'll come around. After we are gone—and we shouldn't drag this grand vacation out selfishly. . . ."

"Gone! I couldn't stay. Yet I must. This is home. I owe it to Dad and Mom. But—alone on the range with that eagle-eyed cowboy! Mom says he is like Dad used to be! Dad is hipped on him. And Nels. . . . Oh, what is the use?"

"Majesty, it'll all work out. But I'm afraid you must suffer more."

"Have a heart, will you? For Pete's sake! I've been dying for weeks."

"Darling, compose yourself and get to sleep," begged Allie, tenderly.

"I'm dead tired. But sleep! What'll I do when I wake up?"

"You mean about *him?*"

"Of course."

"Why be just the same as if nothing had happened."

"You callous woman! . . . Allie—I think—I

guess . . ." faltered Madge, finally weakening to tears . . . "I'm licked. . . . I'm afraid—he'll go—away!"

Golden sunlight streaming in at Madge's window seemed inconsistent with the gray gloomy void she wanted to believe was her lot. Allie had gone out in her dressing gown to fetch some coffee and toast. Madge's foot felt stiff, but it was not going to incapacitate her in the least. What she wanted most right at that moment was to be down at the corrals. Would Lance be such a coward as that—to run off for fear she would betray him? What kind of girls had he known anyway? She would not have hurt him in her father's estimation for anything in the world. She was consumed with a desire to see Sidway this morning. To see if the monster resembled in any degree her conception! He should be haggard, drawn, after a sleepless night, burdened by guilt, unable to look anyone in the eye.

Allie returned, escorted by a bevy of bright-eyed girls, all of whom had been in the kitchen.

"Lazy girl! It's ten o'clock," said Maramee, whose sweet face appeared so gay and happy that Madge wondered at the credulity of human nature. They all came in, their colorful print dresses bright around Madge's bed.

"Where are Dixie and Bu?" asked Madge.

"Horse mad. Dixie loves to sit on the corral fence and Bu is crazy to ride everything."

"She'll get piled up," declared Madge, severely.

"Humph! Bu's been piled up, as you call it. But she picks herself up and yelps for more. The cowboys get some kick out of her."

After a little Madge inquired for the boys. Gone, hours before, off on a hiking trip!

"Not really?" ejaculated Madge, her cup halted halfway to her lips. "Not Barg and . . . and . . ."

"Yes, Barg," declared Maramee, happily. "He poked his head in my window and tossed wild roses

185

on my face, to awaken me. Whispered he'd rather have stayed home with me. Oh, he was darling."

"To be sure. Barg's a darling, all right. . . ." Madge was interrupted by the arrival of Dixie Conn, flushed and breathless, no doubt from a climb up the hill.

"Majesty, I thought you were indisposed or something. You just look stunning," said the southern girl.

"Yeah? Thanks, Dix. But you're looking through rose-colored spectacles. . . . Where's Bu?"

"Madge—Girls! That outsider has shown us up. She's dishonored the fair name of our sorority."

"Oh, for the love of Mike—what now?"

"Bu is riding Umpqua right this minute. You know we all tried to coax Sidway to let us ride him. Same as Majesty tried to buy him. Nothing doing! And now she's down there having a swell time on that grand horse. The cowboy is teaching Bu to jump over logs and ditches, and what have you? Was I jealous? All the same I had to hand it to Bu. She looked great. How'd she ever put that over with Sidway?"

"I've a hunch and I'm going to try it," said Thelma Thorne, subtly.

"Say, don't imagine I let any grass grow under my feet," declared Dixie. "I went up to the cowboy, raved about his horse and complimented Bu. Then I said, with all I've got, old dears, 'Lance, I'd almost sell my soul to ride Umpqua!' He said, 'Why didn't you tell me? I can't read your mind. Umpqua loves girls. I'd be only too happy to put you up on him. Hang around, till Beulah is through.' I wasn't dressed for riding as you see, so I asked if I might go down early tomorrow. Then he looked troubled. I hadn't noticed that. Why he looked just wretched. And he said; 'Yes, by all means, if I'm here. But I expect Miss Stewart to fire me this morning!' . . . Majesty, darling, what has he done now? But no matter, don't fire Sidway."

And then the other girls burst into a chorus of appeals and conjectures and wisecracks that fairly infuriated Madge. She flung pillows at them. "Beat it, you pack of imps! I must have been bughouse to invite you over here. . . . Get out!—*No!* I'm—not—going—to—

fire—Lance Sidway! Go climb on his neck and then on his precious Umpqua for all I care. That'd be the way to get there. But I'd die first."

They fled in a fiendish clamor and Madge hid her face in her pillow. It was a bad moment. There were many impetuses toward a magnificent fury, which she viewed with her mind, one after another. But she could not surrender to the one thing that had crushed her—the perfectly inconsequential and natural circumstance of Lance putting Bu Allen up on his horse. The absurdity of her childish pique gradually faded in the stern realization that her happiness, her future, and the welfare of her dear parents, so fatefully bound up in her, were at stake. Well might it be too late! But she would humble herself, crucify her selfish imperious side, absolutely refuse catastrophe. If she had been half as nice to Sidway as Bu Allen had been she would not now be in such extremity.

Madge prostrated herself before her love, which was to betray her pride and spirit. It was too great a thing to deny any longer. But by surrendering she gained some aspect of the wit and self-control she needed at this trying time. Three betrothals among her guests attested to the success of their sojourn at her ranch. That Beulah and Elwell would make a go of it there was no reasonable doubt. Madge decided to shorten and intensify the remaining stages of their entertainment and center her energies upon the trip into the mountains and the dance she had long planned.

This decision would change for her, and therefore her guests, the idle languor of the summer days. To that end, an hour after she left her room, she approached her parents, finding them in her mother's room. Evidently Madge had interrupted a serious talk, and having changed the direction of her mind she looked at them penetratingly, conscious of her neglect this exciting summer.

"Darlings, am I intruding?" she asked, halting in the doorway.

Her mother's sweet response and the light that her presence always brought upon her father's dark face assured Madge of her welcome, and that indeed she had been remiss.

"Mom, you can hide trouble, but Dad can't," said Madge, going to them, and she found that this was not a new thought only one put aside because it hurt. An unaccountable aloofness, arising from her shame, kept her from sliding upon the arm of Stewart's chair. When had she done that? How little she had seen of him for a month and more. His reserve betrayed it.

"Has my crowd gotten on your nerves?" she asked.

"They have been somewhat trying," replied Mrs. Stewart, with a smile. "But that was only because of our difficulty in adjusting ourselves to excitement and mirth and—well, the life they brought with them. I like them all, Madge. Your favorite Allie is mine, too. And the boys are fine. I'm glad you had them all here."

"Dad?" queried Madge, poignantly.

"After they're gone, I'll tell you, lass," replied her father, then hastily; "Oh, I like them all right. I just mean I must get hold of myself."

"Yeah? I'm afraid I'm answered. . . . Has Rollie Stevens been nagging you about me?"

"No. That young man steers a little clear of me. But he has approached Madeline."

"He has told me he wanted to marry you, darling. Three separate times. And has taken occasion to tell about the Stevens, their position, wealth, and all that. Very correct and a fine young fellow. But, Madge, he wouldn't care to live out here."

"I'll tell the world he wouldn't," retorted Madge, with a laugh. "And I wouldn't have him if he would. So skip that, Mom."

"Madge, then—so you intend to stay home—a while?" asked Stewart, a little huskily, gazing away from her out of the window.

"Dad!" If she had followed her swift impulse it would have been to throw her arms around his neck. But she could not do it. Her intuition grasped something strange here. "I'm going to pack this crowd off

188

sooner than I expected. And after that I'm going to stay home for good."

It was her mother Madge looked at, and she divined that whatever had been her thoughtless failings and deplorable shortcomings, they had never changed that faithful heart. If she had lost her father, through the years of absence, and his inability to understand her when she did come back, she divined that would not be a permanent estrangement, because she was kind and loving, and if she made amends for her wildness and settled down to a real love of him, and her future at the ranch, all would be well. Her quiet talks with Nels, too few and far between, had played no small part in the awakening of her conscience. Yet remorseful as she felt, her temper would admit of no reason that she knew why she should arraign herself at these odd moments. It was on account of that cowboy, and because she had been so unaccountably a prey to love for him. She had always known she must love some man with all her being, desperately, once and for good and she had always been looking for him. That might account somewhat for her endless interests.

"Dad, what's on your mind?" asked Madge, after this flashing pageant of thought had left her composed, once more in a way to win back her old confidence. "Nels told me you were worrying over money troubles."

"The gabby old woman!" ejaculated Stewart, impatiently.

"Don't be angry with Nels. I coaxed it out of him. I've intended to go at him again—but I've been so busy with these friends. Besides, Dad, I've troubles of my own."

"You have? No one would guess it. You are the happiest, gayest, most thoughtless of all these young people."

"On the surface. But never mind my trouble now. It's going to keep. . . . What I'd like to know is—when my friends are gone will you tell me everything and let me help? For five years I've spent money like a drunken sailor. It's begun to frighten me a little, Dad,

189

if I thought . . . if I found out I'd been a spendthrift while you and Mom had. . . . Oh, I'd *hate* that so inexpressibly."

To Madge's amaze Stewart abruptly took her in his arms and clasped her so closely that she could not breathe. And over her he said to her mother. "Madeline, Nels knows our girl better than we do." Then he kissed her hair, her cheek, and rushed out.

"Mom!" she cried, going to her mother. "What have I done? . . . Is it? . . . Oh!"

"Darling, your conscience and your heart have spoken," replied her mother, earnestly. "I knew they would. I have never doubted. It is no small thing for a rich and popular girl to return from college, from a great city, to the old-fashioned life of a ranch. Don't distress yourself further now. Devote yourself to your friends. When they are gone we'll face our problems. You have eliminated the only one that concerned me."

"Mother! Whether or not I loved you—and my home? . . . I'll never forgive myself."

"What is it you girls say? 'Skip it!' . . . Madge, you will not accept young Stevens?"

Madge did not need to avert her eyes, because they were blind with tears. "No, Mom. I like Rollie, and I've played with him. He has done the same with other girls while courting me. Rollie is a playboy. He couldn't stand this lonely range. But I can, Mother! . . . And I want a handsome brute who will beat me!"

"The latter is inconceivable," returned her mother, mildly. "I hope no such contingency arises. I do not want to see the ranch blown to bits or be shaken by some cataclysm."

"You overrate me, darling. I'm a very meek little girl this morning."

"You are certainly strange."

Madge's original idea had been to ask her father's advice about taking her guests to the wild fastness up in the Peloncillo Hills, famous as a stronghold of the great Apache chief, Cochise. Before her school days Madge had ridden to this place with her father and the cowboys. She had never forgotten it, and it had been one of her cherished hopes to give her friends a camping trip there. For some inexplicable reason she found that she was cooling on the project, but she was too stubborn and fearful to analyze the cause. To abandon the trip after having exalted it continually for weeks did not quite suit Madge. She would have welcomed a reasonable excuse for not going, and as she considered the plans, that idea amplified. If she remembered correctly the ride up to Cochise's stronghold was long and arduous, and not for tenderfeet. That very fact had been an incentive. She had vowed that her friends would get one experience of the real thing.

Whereupon Madge, feeling that there was safety for her in numbers, filled her car full of girls and drove down to the store. Nels was there, chipper as a grasshopper, and ready to sell the girls anything from cigarettes to calico. Three separate times Madge's contingent of friends had bought the store out, to Nel's joy.

"Where are the cowboys?" asked Madge.

"Lance is diggin' postholes. An' thet's a job he hates as turrible as any other cowboy. Ren says every time Lance does somethin' awful he goes oot an' digs postholes."

"Sort of a penance?"

"Must be. I seen Ren aboot somewheres a minnit ago. I'll yell fer him."

It developed that Ren was very easy to locate and soon stood, sombrero in hand, his sunburned face beaming, before Madge and her friends.

"Mawning, cowboy. Where's your side partner?"

"Wal, Miss Majesty, he's drunk or crazy or somethin'," replied Ren, with a grin. "Woke me up before daylight, an' heah's what he said, kinda loud an' ringin'. 'Ren, I'm goin' out to dig postholes fer thet new fence. If anybody about heah wants to hang me or hawsewhip me, I'll be out there. Savvy?'"

"How very thoughtful of him," remarked Madge, resisting a deep vibration that was more than thrill. "What's he—done now?"

191

"Dog-gone if I know. But it musta been turrible. I says 'Lance, you think you're funny?' An' he says 'About as funny as death!' An' he stamps off, without any grub. Why, he's worryin' pore Nels to death."

"How would you and Sidway like to do me a great favor?"

"Job or jest fun?"

"It'll be a job. No fun at all! I want you to truck your horses as far as you can from town toward the Peloncillo Hills. Find the old trail up to Cochise's stronghold, and fetch me a report on it and the camp site."

"I'd like it swell, Miss Majesty, an' I reckon Lance would about pass out to get away fer a spell. But, excuse me, what's the big idee? I was huntin' deer up there last fall. I can tell you most anythin'."

"Ren, be very serious now. Think of my friends. Is that trip going to be a safe and comfortable one for them?" And Madge gave Starr a look that had passed from her to him on former occasions. Ren suddenly looked blank and dropped his head.

"Hell no! it's neither one or the other. But thet's why it'd be grand." Ren hated to abandon the idea.

"I'm a little afraid of it. You see, Ren, I was sixteen when I made it first, had been riding horses all summer and I was fit."

The girls burst out into bitter lamentations. "What're we if not fit? . . . Haven't we geen riding horses all summer?—Madge, *we* don't care a damn how hard it'd be. At that, we can beat the boys." One and all they put up arguments hard for the kindhearted Madge to withstand. When they were out of breath, Bu Allen contributed calmly: "Lance told me it's a lousy trip."

"Lousy! What's he mean by that?" returned Madge, on fire in an insant, despite the fact that Sidway's inelegant remark was in line with her designs.

"Did I ask him that? He told me a lot of terrible stuff. Said we were all too weak-kneed and soft-bottomed. That's just what he said, the bum. He thinks we're a lot of swell kids, but no good for the West. And that goes for you, Majesty."

"I am quite aware in what poor opinion Sidway holds me," rejoined Madge, cool once more, and her contrariness was such that now she felt a mounting desire to go and show him how soft-bottomed she was. "Ren, you take Sidway, and leave at once. Find out all about the trail and Cochise's stronghold. Good and bad. Then upon your return you will report to me and all the crowd, after which we'll vote to decide whether to go or not."

"Very wal, Miss Majesty, I'm on my way," replied Ren.

"Madge, you're a whiz! Of course, we're on to you. But we think this investigation will make the trip irresistible."

"At least it'd be upon your own heads," warned Madge, then calling Ren back she met him halfway, to ask: "Will you let me know if this plan is acceptable to Sidway?"

Ren regarded her, comically dumbfounded. Madge averted her face slightly to go on: "You see, Ren, he may leave any minute. The more I—I need him the more contrary he grows." She managed that demurely, but she was not smiling. Starr's tanned face brightened.

"Miss Majesty, between you an' me we know Lance is daid plumb nutty, an' what it's all about. Fer a time there I kind of feared you wasn't on to him. Wal, I am an' so is Nels. If you don't believe me go to Nels. Shore I'm a pore pard to double-cross Lance this way. He'd kill me if he ever found out."

"Found out what, Ren?" queried Madge, cool and sweet, mistress of herself again, but there was an incredible and unbeliveable tumult within her being.

"Thet I give him away. . . . Majesty, Lance is a turrible bluff. He brags about ridin' away. Wal, up to this time he hasn't been able to. He's been mad an' wild, but he jest *cain't* leave."

"You surprise me, Ren. . . . And why?" went on Madge, unable to resist these precious and unreliable words from Lance's friend.

"Wal, you gotta figger thet out fer yourself. An' if

193

you cain't, why go to Nels. I've talked too much. Thet son-of-a-gun has eyes like gimlets when he's close an' telescopes when he's far. He might be seein' us right now. Anyway all he does is watch fer you, Majesty."

"Ren! What on earth for?"

"It's not because you're nice to look at. . . . I've peeped through a crack in the wall between our rooms —an' seen him porin' an' sighin' over a picture. He acted like a man who couldn't help lookin' when he hated to. Thet picture is one of you, Majesty, fer I sneaked in an' took a peep. He keeps it under a book in his table drawer. Now don't ask me no more. I feel pretty yellow. But I'd never give him away onless fer my hunch thet you like Lance a little. Don't you?"

"Like—Lance?" repeated Madge, and all her blood seemed rushing to her head. "Ren, if Lance cannot trust you, how can I?"

"Doesn't make sense. But you can."

"I'll trust you. Yes, I do—like Lance," returned Madge, and to save her life she could not have made it casual. She went back to the house with the girls, playing her gay part, but there had come a complete reversal in her emotional reaction. Ren had vindicated her own deep convictions—that even if Sidway did hate her, he liked her too, against his better judgment and will, surely. Once more alone in her room she endeavored to stem this tide of overwhelming love, that was so great and so humble at the mere words of a sentimental cowboy. It frightened Madge— that flood of feeling. The sweetness of it warned her that this was not the time for surrender. But she had a tiny nucleus of hope around which to build. If she could only clasp to her breast this humble spirit! Time, days and days, would be her ally.

It was getting along into August, with touches of color beginning to show on the hills. Stewart advised Madge that if she was contemplating a camping trip up in the Peloncillos not to waste any more time. And she confided that she was pretty sure that would fall through. Snake Elwell had to return to college soon for fall practice; Allie had planned to motor east with her parents; and the rest of the party were beginning to think of the city. Nevertheless they were enthusiastic over the prospect of that horseback ride.

It chanced that Madge's wish to see Sidway and Starr upon their return, before any of her friends, was denied her, much to her concern. She had been alone with her mother when word came up from below that the boys were in. Madge rushed out the patio way and down the trail. A confusion of bright colors decorating Nels' porch attested to the whereabouts of the girls, and where they were the boys would be also. It was a good long run, and Madge had to halt to catch her breath before she half crossed the square. The horses had just been unloaded from the trucks, and the packs thrown out. Ren was surrounded by her excited friends who were evidently besieging him in unison. Sidway stood a little apart, conversing with Nels and her father. The *vaqueros* were attending to the horses. Umpqua nickered at Madge, and she flew to stroke his dusty neck, while he nosed at her for sugar. She had never ridden him since that first day, but she had won his affection, and she felt a sense of guilt to look up and see Sidway's piercing eyes upon her. Ragged and dark, dusty and unshaved, he appealed so powerfully to Madge that as she approached them she wondered how she could hide it.

"Majesty, they won't say a darn thing," burst out Maramee, and the others chimed in with gay sallies.

At last Madge reached them, and with a hand on Stewart's arm, she faced Sidway, and the grinning Starr. She was keen to feel something proven in them.

"Boys—it took you—long enough," she panted, and smiled upon them.

"Wal, Miss Majesty, you gave us all the time there was," replied Ren.

Sidway's hazel eyes, dark and intent, appeared to pierce through Madge. Not for weeks had she met his full gaze like this, and despite the scattering of her

195

wits, she realized the searching nature of his look, as if he were striving to divine her wishes.

"Miss Stewart, it was well you sent us," said Sidway, simply. "I'm sure it spared you and your friends a real ordeal!"

A groan ran through the listening party.

"Real ordeal! What do you mean?"

"Too severe a physical strain for tenderfeet. A motionpicture crowd would shy at this one—and they do things. . . . But it can be done, Miss Stewart, and I'm bound to admit, it'd be the trip of a lifetime."

"You don't advise it?"

"I do not."

"Would you take the responsibility if I insisted?" asked Madge.

"Yes, if your father insisted, too."

"Dad, are you with me?"

"Daughter, this issue is between you and Sidway. He has not told me a thing. My advice is to listen *before* you make up your mind. You know how you are, Madge."

Madge transfixed Sidway with a troubled passionate gaze. She did not want to undertake this trip. She rejoiced that Sidway was making it impossible. But there was something about him that dared her to see if she could prevail upon him. She realized that until she could conquer such weakness, she would never be at her best with him.

"Lance, you're on the spot," she said.

"Heavens, when haven't I been?" he ejaculated, and joined Stewart in a laugh. Their understanding and good feeling seemed manifest. Then he bent a glance upon Madge, so clear, so frank, yet so supremely doubtful of her, that she writhed inwardly under it. She divined a thrust aimed at what must be his conviction of a vulnerable point in her which she had no idea she possessed.

"Shoot!" she said, with all her disdain, but she felt dismay before she had been attacked. This cowboy must know something about her, to her discredit, or he could not have affected her that way.

196

"It may seem superfluous—to you," he said, coolly. "But have you considered the expense?"

"Expense!" echoed Madge. That was the last question she would have expected.

"Yes. Perhaps you have not thought of that."

"I had not. Usually I don't consider what my plans cost."

"Exactly. That is why I presume to mention it. . . . This trip would cost a great deal. A gang of laborers would be needed on the trail. Two weeks' work at least. The cabin up at Cochise's stronghold has gone to rack and ruin. It would have to be repaired. There are no tents and tarpaulins at the ranch, nor cooking utensils. You would require a complete new camping equipment. We have packsaddles for only few horses; and, well, would you expect to have this camp on the scale on which you do everything?"

"I'm afraid I would."

"Of course. Then it would be necessary to buy twenty new packsaddles and at least ten pack animals. That would entail hiring half a dozen extra riders. . . . So you see, Miss Stewart, it is quite a big undertaking."

"I see all right," replied Madge, dubiously. To the credit of her friends, they at once turned thumbs down upon the whole proposition, and were so nice and fine about it that Madge regretted her subterfuge. But what was Lance Sidway aiming at? She believed his report implicitly. A half or a quartter of these obstacles would have sufficed. He believed that no matter how unfavorable his report or how exorbitantly the trip would cost, she would decide to go willy-nilly. Then he believed other things that mystified Madge. For an instant she had a bothersome thought that he might feel contempt for her because expense had never meant anything to her. A rebellious impulse to do the very thing he expected died in its infancy, somehow hastened to its death by the singular, almost mocking light in Sidway's hazel eyes. In a flash she saw how she could amaze and undeceive him.

"Thank you, Sidway. I'll abandon the camping trip

197

solely upon your report," she said. "You have been very conscientious and dependable. I appreciate it."

If Lance's scarcely veiled surprise proved Madge's intuition close to correct, his relief and gladness, that warmed out the coldness of his face, augmented the thought-provoking power of that moment. Madge conceived, too, an impression that Sidway's feelings were reflected in her father's dark face. Could these two possibly have an understanding? Madge drove the perplexing thought away.

"Friends, it's off, our mad ride up into the wilds," declared Madge. "Some other summer! Instead I'll throw the biggest party ever."

Pandemonium broke out among the boys and girls. When they ceased mobbing Madge she suddenly found Sidway towering over her, a stranger to whom her whole being seemed to leap.

"Thank heaven, I won't have to make a report on *that,*" he cried. "But, come, here!" And seizing her hand he led her aside. "You don't know what I thought and I'll never tell you. Only I'm begging you to forgive me. You are one swell sport! You're a thoroughbred! It's no wonder . . ."

He broke off and squeezed her hand and strode away toward the bunkhouses. Madge stood a second, aware of the cramped fingers she could hardly straighten, and wondering what were the words he had left unsaid. It was not her fault if he had not had a glimpse of all her sides. Madge went back to her father.

"Dad, have you and Lance framed me?" she asked.

"My dear, I've had no part in this—this, whatever you'd call it," he laughed. "Honest, Madge. It looked as if I might have been in cahoots with Lance to queer your trip. But he never told me a thing. Nor did Ren. I think he carried it off very well indeed. Your mother will be pleased."

"Yeah?—What's this Machiavelli mean by pleasing you and Mom? Looks like deep stuff to me."

"Madge, he's just a nice boy, who disapproves of you a lot."

"Dad, he said some strange things, for him. Nearly crushed my poor hand. Look! Then he beat it. He ran off before I could even answer."

"Lass, if this Machiavelli and your dad, or better, old Nels, could get you locked in a room and starved or beaten or loved into *listening* for some hours, you'd come through like your mother did when she decided some momentous questions twenty-five years and more ago."

"Dad!—Starved or beaten or . . . You are as mysterious as *he!*" And Madge judged that the better part of valor would be to flee. But not until she had plunged deeply into plans for her party did she recover from the confusing thoughts resulting from that surprising contact with the cowboy and her father.

Madge set the date for the party. Invitations were sent to all the range people her father knew from Douglas to Bolton. All the *vaqueros* and *señoritas* known to Bonita and her brothers were invited. It took a whole day to put up the decorations. That night when Madge tried out the colored lights and lanterns the glamorous effect transported even her. Next morning the caterer rolled in with his trucks and minions, and Majesty's Rancho hummed like a beehive. Last to arrive were the sixteen musicians. That was early in the afternoon. Madge went to bed to rest, but she could not sleep. The girls could not even rest. They were in and out all afternoon, and finally when Madge asked Allie to get out a new gown none of them had ever seen, and which she had reserved for this occasion, there ensued a perfectly rapt silence. Bu Allen, of course, broke it. "My Gawd!" she gasped in uncontrollable excitement. "Majesty, you must be married in that!"

"Bu, a girl has to have something beside a gown to get married."

"Not that one. You don't even need a slip."

And so mad were they all that only Madge noted the omission of a man. The thing struck a fatalistic chord in her. She had everything—wonderful parents, lovely friends, wealth, education, ranch, horses, cars, all to make any girl happy—except a man to marry.

But that was the last thing in the world to occupy her mind now. Anyway it was a calamity she could remedy this very night, provided she beat down her obsession for one unappreciative, unresponsive cowboy. Still it had been ingrained in Madge's girlish dreams that no one save a cowboy like her father could ever have her.

Toward the end of that long day Madge slept, and was awakened by Allie and Maramee. They informed her that the lights were lit, the many tables set, and guests were arriving. Madge sent them off to dress and flew to her bath. She was in the midst of her make-up task when they returned, formal and elegant, to draw encomiums from Madge.

"Girls, we'll knock 'em for a loop tonight," said Madge, gleefully.

"We?" chirped Maramee.

"Yes, us," declared Madge.

"Darling, I think you mean him," retorted Allie.

They brushed her hair until it sparkled with glints of fire, and then by some magic of deft feminine hands they incased her in the blue and gold gown. For jewels Madge wore a string of pearls, the gift of her Aunt Helen, so beautiful and valuable that she had not risked it out of the safe for years. Allie was silent, gazing raptly at her, but Maramee raved on and on.

"Once in my life!" was all Madge whispered to the image shining from her long mirror, and either she meant that she was satisfied or that she would play that beauty to the limit. Madge went to her mother's room, to be admitted. Her father was there, lean and dark and handsome in his black suit.

"Oh, Mom, but you are a lady of quality!" cried Madge, a rush of warm sweetness piercing her trance. "Dad, isn't she just stunning?"

Both her father and mother appeared incapable of speech on the moment, but their eyes would have gratified a far vainer girl than Madge. "I wanted you to see me first." And she whirled for their benefit. "Now, darlings, this is my party. I've had it coming to my crowd for a year. Unknown to them it is my farewell to them—to college—to that kind of life. Whatever we do, don't be shocked."

And she ran out, through the living room, into the corridor where she encountered Sidway. In his dark garb he looked so slim and different that she did not recognize him at first glance.

"Oh!—how stupid of me! It's Lance." And she halted under the colored lights.

He started and backed partly against the balustrate, while a dazed and frowning expression altered his face. Then it vanished as he leaped erect, to utter a queer little laugh and make her a profound bow.

"Lance. Do you—like me?" she queried softly.

"Majesty, I used to believe you were a mistake of evolution, but now I know it was God."

"Is that a compliment or a slam?"

"Pardon me. I'm in urgent search of your father. I just found out that the balance of his cattle herd were just rustled. And I'm going to find out who stole them and where they were driven."

"Oh, Lance, how dreadful. But must you tell him tonight?" wailed Madge.

"Come to think of it, no," he returned, brightly. "I haven't even told Ren. Poor kid! It's going tough with him. Love is a terrible thing!"

"It is indeed," agreed Madge, fervently. "But *you* have merely heard or read about that."

She left him, sailing with a swish down the corridor to her room. She had no time to deduce sense from Lance Sidway's queer remarks, and she was glad of it. If she spent ten minutes with that cowboy there would be no triumph for her tonight. What a devastating effect he exercised over her! Some of the girls were in her rooms and the others soon paraded in. Every last one of them had on a new gown! And had they planned for this *pièce de résistance* of Madge's? They were interrupted by the caterer, a handsome Italian in immaculate white. Madge admitted him and drove out the girls. "Find the boys. I'll be with you in a moment."

"I hope you please," he said, rubbing his hands together.

"Corvalo, I'm bound to be. Remember, serve champagne to my party in the living room. Wine to the other tables. As for the punch, it must have an awful wallop. But not an immediate kick. Use creme de menthe to flavor only—to make them like it—leading them on. A soft sweet tasty punch—flowers and music leading to a precipice. Get me, Corvalo?"

He departed with shining eyes and beaming face, as if that order had been one to his liking. Madge went in search of her friends. They had rounded up the boys, who looked cool and natty in white flannels. Their various comments were incense to Madge's heart. Rollie Stevens said: "Murder in the Rue Rancho this night!"

"Come, let's make the rounds," said Madge. "At least I can speak to all these strangers."

"Lamping you will be enough," declared Barg.

Madge found it easier to be courteous and friendly than she had anticipated. The delight of the Mexicans especially pleased her. There were ranch people she remembered, and apparently all the cowboys on the range.

"Pack of wolves!" averred Rollie. "They'd eat you alive. Good thing you're under my wing."

"Are you sure you can be trusted to think of *me?*"

The long patio made a colorful and beautiful spectacle. A row of tables extended down the center. Benches and chairs lined the walls. The waxed floors, built in for the occasion, shone iridescently. Colorful lanterns hung from the center of the arches. The gorgeous Spanish and Indian decorations lent a richness and legend to the old rancho. Madge slipped a hand over her heart to still its beating, its muffled pain. What was this pang stealing into her happiness?

Moments for pondering had passed by. The great dinner gong pealed through the corridors and the patio, and was followed by a merry hum. Then the

orchestra upon which Madge put such store pealed its
exotic music through the house. It heralded the Spanish *fiesta* that was to last until dawn.

Madge, with her college guests, and her father and
mother, sat down to dinner in the living room. That
table from its hot-house orchids, its silver plate and
crystal, to the rare and savory dishes of the sumptuous
dinner, excelled anything the ranch had ever known.

Stewart appeared to be staggered with its magnificence. But as the dinner wore on he fell under the
spell of his wife's pleasure and Madge's rapture, and
the continuous merriment and wit of the college
crowd. Snake Elwell and Bu Allen were the first couple to begin dancing. Bu looked ravishing in a white
gown that threatened to split at every move. Allie,
usually the sweetest of girls who never made a criti-
cism of caustic comment, spoke right out: "Some hot
little cookie!" And Madge's father, who heard it, surrendered unconditionally to this group of young mod-
erns.

Madge's keen eyes did not miss anything. Once she
saw Sidway and Starr, flushed of face and fire-eyed,
peep into the living room. She also observed that her
father did not drink his champagne. With dinner at an
end, the dancing set in continuously, with only short
intermissions. Madge loved to dance, and the first
hour passed by on wings. When her crowd happened
to congregate, someone remembered the punch, whereupon they flocked to the living room. The long table
had been cleared, and moved back to the wall. In the
center an enormous bowl of silver and crystal shone
resplendent, full of a twinkling liquid that had life
and color. An attendant stood ready to serve. Curious and gleeful, Madge drained her cup, tasted and
wondered, and listened for comments. She alone knew
that innocent-looking punch was loaded with dynamite.

"Say, Madge, where'd you hit on this concoction?
Pretty nifty," observed Rollie Stevens, who considered
himself a connoisseur.

"New to me, Rollie."

"Soft and minty," interposed Brand. "I'll bet it'll lead you on."

"Tame, if you ask me," said Allie, loftily, and that from her was a source for mirth. Allie could not stand liquor at all.

"Swell punch," observed Elwell. "What do you say, Bu?"

"Hand me another," replied the redhead.

"Majesty, are you kidding us with this stuff?"

"I'm sorry, Brand. But this is my home, you know. And remembering your capacities I wanted something weak."

"Weak or not let's have another."

Madge finally dragged her friends out. While dancing and resting the next hour she contrived to keep tabs on that punch bowl. Just as she had suspected, her friends were succumbing to this insidious drink. Once with Rollie she almost burst in upon her father, Nels, Danny Mains, Starr and Sidway, but she drew her escort back behind some decorations in the corridor. With intense interest and fiendish glee she watched them and listened, holding Rollie back with imperious hand.

Manifestly this group of gentlemen had been in there before.

"Gene, we shore lived too soon," drawled Nels, regretfully.

"Shades of Monty Price and Nick Steel!" ejaculated Stewart. "Nels—Danny, what would our old pards have thought of this drink?"

"My Gawd, I dunno. . . . Fill me up another, waiter."

"Boss, this heah punch is nectar an' honey an' hell all mixed up together," said Starr.

"Where does the hell come in?"

"Wal, I hadn't noticed thet until this last drink, which was my sixth. . . . Pard, how many have you had?"

"Enough," replied Sidway, tragically.

"Why, you dawg-gone kill-joy! Cain't you hold your likker?"

"Ren, I can't hold this liquor—and I can't take it!"

"Lissen, pard. I'm gonna put a couple of these under Bonita's belt," whispered Ren, behind Danny Mains' back.

"Don't. You'll lose her right then."

"Umpumm! Thet's when I'll win her. Pard, Bonita is funny tonight. Been cryin' an' turrible upset."

"Come here, you geezer!" And Sidway dragged Ren out of the room.

"Gene, any drink that can make an old man young again is one to tie to," said Nels.

"I agree with you. But, pards, even if my daughter hadn't sprung some destroying drink on us, I'd have to get drunk with you for old times' sake."

"Wal, ole *El Capitan* again!" ejaculated Danny Mains. "If the ootfit was only heah!"

Madge had heard enough to give her a twinge of conscience. But only gay and rapturous thoughts could abide in her mind. She went back to dancing. Rollie with more drinks than were good for him had begun to grow demanding and bossy. Soon came an added interest in Sideway's presence upon the floor. He was taller than her college friends, slim and erect in his black suit, broad-shouldered, quite the handsomest boy there. He had started in dancing with Bonita, and from her to Bu Allen was only a short step. Then he cut in on the boys and apparently enjoyed thoroughly her girl friends. Naturally she expected him to gravitate to her. But he did not approach her or look at her, an omission that did not go unnoticed. It was rude of him, Madge thought, as she was his hostess, but it seemed between them there was no observance of rules. From that hour Madge's feeling of happiness underwent a change. Visits to the punch bowl kept up her spirits. By midnight some kind of climax seemed imminent. Her father and his friends, despite their visits to the living room, were still steady on their feet. Stewart appeared to have lost his gaiety. Madge saw her mother apparently remonstrating with him, to no avail. Thereafter Madge did not see her Mother. Madge was glad and she hoped her father would retire soon. There would be no fights such as Stewart had known in the early days, when he was *El Capitan,* but Madge knew something was bound to happen, and she repented now that she had been responsible for it.

It came in the nature of a surprise. Bu Allen sat down on the floor, a cup of punch in her hand, and turned a somersault. She did not spill any liquor. The boys and girls howled at the sight. Thus encouraged, she turned somersaults all across the living room. Nels and Danny Mains were in hysterics; Ren Starr whooped like the cowboy he was; Sidway strode out of the room. Stewart, his face like a thundercloud, threw up his hands like a man who had been vainly fighting facts, and lunged out into the patio.

Madge, frightened at the lightning of his eyes, watched him disappear with a sinking of her heart. Had she gone too far? But she had not known Beulah Allen would disgrace her party. And if Snake Elwell had not violently jerked the girl to her feet and dragged her out Madge felt that she would have had to adopt extreme measures. That event saw the disintegration of the party. The dancing grew desultory, except in the patio where the range quests still held forth.

Finding Barg and Maramee asleep in each other's arms in a corner, and some of the other couples fading from the living room to the benches, Madge realized her party was about over. And it had been a failure. She knew when she had had enough to drink. But in her bitterness, she overstepped her habit. With Rollie she drank two more cups of punch. And as she went outdoors with him, wrapping a mantle around her bare shoulders she realized two things—that Rollie was pretty drunk and that a gaiety had overcome her gloom. Good to have the blue devils fade away! Lance Sidway had not come near her! To hell with him! Rollie was a pal, and on the way out under the pines, Madge not only permitted his extravagant embraces but returned his kisses. She felt just on the verge of being giddy and dizzy. But she did not want to think. After all she could do worse than marry Rollie Stevens.

In an open space, shaded by spreading pines and surrounded by low foliage, they found a bench covered with blanket and pillows. The moonlight streaked through rifts in the branches to lend a silver glamour to the glade. Rollie sat down and drew Madge upon his lap. At first she felt silly and soft at his love-making, and experienced a pleasant glow of excitement.

"You're going to marry me," he said, thickly, between kissed.

"Is that so? Who told you?" laughed Madge.

"I'm telling you," he replied, more violently.

"Rollie, you're drunk."

"If I am it's your fault."

"You all fell for that punch. My secret, Rollie!"

"Yeah? . . . Your line, Madge—secrets! I'll give you another one."

The edge on his voice, accompanying some rough handling of her awakened Madge to the situation. But her lackadaisical good nature was such that she made only feeble resistance to his ardor.

"You love me—don't you?" he demanded fiercely.

" 'Course I love you—Rollie—as a pal—old friend, and what have you? . . . but . . ."

"Nuts! I'm tired of that dope." And the hot kisses upon her mouth and neck grew more violent. Madge was no longer returning his kisses. From that to remonstrating with him was only a short step. It appeared to inflame him. Locked in his arms she was at a disadvantage. A rattling of her pearls alarmed her. The fool would break the necklace.

"Let me—go! . . . You're drunk—boy. . . . this is . . ." "So're you—drunk," he panted, and pushed her back off his lap upon the cushions. Madge's utterance was stifled by his kisses. She twisted her face away. But Rollie only grew more violent.

Furiously she flung him aside, and sprang off the bench. In the dark she fell over someone she took to be Rollie and had to clutch his arm to regain her balance. He appeared to be sitting against a tree trunk. But there at the end of the bench was Rollie, mumbling and cursing.

"Oh!—What?—*Who?*" screamed Madge, leaning forward on her knees to peer at this man she had fallen against. He had his hands over his eyes and ears. They fell, and Madge recognized Lance Sidway.

She managed to arise despite a paralyzing dismay, that gave place to a terrific shame and rage.

"*You!*" burst out Madge.

He rose rather slowly and pulled himself erect. A slant of moonlight fell across his face. It was ashen white, and out of it glittered eyes as black as coal and as sharp as daggers.

"Yeah, it's me. Who else in hell could have such rotten luck?" he returned, with exceeding bitterness.

"Lance Sidway! you waylaid me!"

"Don't flatter yourself," he flashed, hotly. "I'd left your drunken outfit. On the way to my lodgings, I stopped here to—to smoke. But after I'd finished, I lingered, like the sap I am. I saw you coming and made sure you'd pass. But you didn't. Ha! Ha!"

"Oh, you lie! And you laugh at me!" exclaimed Madge, beside herself with rage.

"No, I don't lie," he retorted. "But I've the laugh on you, Madge Stewart."

Rollie had clambered up, hanging to the bench, evidently more than ever under the influence of liquor.

"Whosis?"

"Rollie, it's Lance Sidway. He was sitting here all the time," declared Madge.

"That cowboy cad? Conceited jackass! . . . Look here, sir, you spy on *me*. I'll cane the hide off you," shouted Stevens, and he struck openhanded at Sidway.

"Keep your hands off me," ordered the cowboy, shoving him back. "I'm sorry. But I wasn't to blame. I didn't spy on you. You get that?"

"You're a liar, Sidway. You're always spying on Madge. You're stuck on her."

Sidway jerked as if he had been stung. "Stevens, if I were you, I'd be a gentleman about it, which you're

208

not. I wouldn't try to take advantage of her when she was drunk. Somebody ought to beat you good. And by God, *I* will, if you don't let me out of this."

Rollie lunged at Sidway who avoided him, backing against the bench.

"Let him alone, Rollie. You're drunk," cried Madge.

Sidway had no recourse but to stave off Stevens' blows. Finally a hearty slap in the face changed the cowboy's tactics. He seized Stevens by the arms and shook him violently. Then he shoved him back. "Stevens, I warn you. Lay off me, or I'll sock you."

"I'd shoot you if I had a gun."

"Yes, if my back were turned. You're one swell flop, Stevens. . . . Stay away from me, I tell you."

"Lance, get away from the fool!" implored Madge, who was if anything more infuriated with Stevens than Sidway.

"Sure, you would ask that. Me run, to save this guy's face."

"It might save my good name."

"You can't save a rotten egg, Madge Stewart. I tell you I'm the insulted one here and I'm getting sore."

When Stevens belligerently confronted Sidway again, it was to meet no resistance. The cowboy stood motionless in the moonlight, his arms lowered. But to Madge he looked formidable.

"You—insufferable cow hand!" shouted Stevens, furiously and he struck Lance twice in the face.

"Okay, Rollie. Now let's see if you can take it," rejoined Sidway, grimly, and he swung hard on the collegian. The blow sounded solid, meaty, and Stevens went down with a thud and did not move.

"There! Sorry to mess up your lover, Miss Stewart, but as you saw, I couldn't avoid it."

"He lies so still . . . he's so white," cried Madge, in alarm.

"I hope the sucker croaks," rejoined Sidway, brutally.

"What'll I do?"

"Well, you might hunt up your dad and Nels, tell

them what this guy tried to do to you—and watch them hang him."

"What a beast you are, Lance Sidway! It was bad enough to sit there, like a cheap eavesdropper, and listen, let alone . . ."

"Hell! I tell you I'm innocent. I didn't look. I didn't listen—at least until you got so raw in your lovemaking . . ."

"But you should have made your presence known at once," cried Madge, poignantly.

"Right. I'm damn sorry. But I was scared, confused . . . It wasn't easy—for me—Madge Stewart."

He choked over the last utterance, and gazed down upon her with eyes of terrible reproach, which might have softened Madge, but for her own insupportable emotions.

"That's no excuse for a gentleman," she retorted.

"No! But for God's sake, do you think you were a lady?"

"Lance Sidway, I *was* and I *am!*" she rejoined, imperiously.

"And I'm a poor, miserable, crawling louse!" he ejaculated, in desperation.

"I regard the appellation as fairly felicitous."

"And you're Majesty Stewart, a law unto herself, a lady of quality, a princess who can do no wrong?" he burst out, passionately. "Listen, you!—That college bum there was not drunk. But his decency, if he had any, was gone. And you were not drunk, either, but your dad would have despised you if he had been here in my boots."

"Rollie forgot himself—I confess . . . But I didn't . . ."

"Bah! Why, for a real man you'd have been a push-over," retorted Sidway, hoarsely.

Madge slapped him viciously across the lips. The next instant his open hand cracked along her cheek and head, and but for the bench would have upset her. Nevertheless, almost blinded by stars and shock, Madge slapped him again, with all her might.

"Regular cat, eh?" he burst out, huskily. "But you can't make a dog out of me."

"I—don't—have—to . . ." panted Madge.

He seized her in powerful hands, hard and hot, and dragged her into a ray of moonlight.

"Majesty—what a travesty that name is!—Madge Stewart, you're going to hear the truth once in your life."

He was suddenly so strangely different, so grimly righteous and ruthless, so white and fire-eyed that Madge sustained a sinking of her heart. She tried to retort with some further insult, but failed of coherence. He shook her as he had shaken Stevens.

"Majesty Stewart! One swell girl, they all think. Proud, blue-blooded, rich. What a mistake! Why you are as false as hell. It was low-down enough before I caught you tonight. Thank God it was I instead of your dad who caught you. He's had enough of you to stand."

"Sidway, what do you—mean?" whispered Madge, and slipping out of his nerveless grasp she sank upon the bench.

"I mean your splendid father and your loving mother are too damn good for you, Madge Stewart."

"Lance, I—I know that."

"But you don't know what you've put them through."

"Oh!—Not—not money trouble?"

"Yes, money!" he bit out, bending over her.

Madge moaned. This it was then that had vaguely haunted her, the conscience which she would not face. She felt it in this man's intensity, in the bitterness of his voice, the fire of contempt in his eyes. This something had given him power over her, and her spirit seemed to be fainting.

"It's fate that I have to tell you this," he went on, swiftly. "Your dad gave me his books to straighten out. He did not know that in the book he had left your bank statements, checks and what not. I went over these, too. And that is how I learned of your rot-

211

ten extravagance and the way your parents have ruined themselves for you."

"Oh! Lance!—don't—*don't!* You are furious with me. I—I don't blame you. But for mercy's sake, don't say any more . . ."

"Listen, girl, I couldn't say enough," he interrupted, adamant to the piteous fear in her appeal. "I love your dad. He makes me remember my own father. And your mother—how sweet and loving and thorough-bred!—All for Majesty. That has been the whole story of this ranch. . . . Madge Stewart, you're not rich. You have no income any more. Three years ago it flopped. And these parents of yours have let you go on, spending like a drunken sailor, deceiving yourself, sacrificing them for your college career, your clothes and cars, your cocktail dates with gangsters— My God! that is the limit. . . . And this party of yours, Miss Stewart, this rare and exotic *fiesta* to your glory —you have pulled it when you were broke. And your dad rounded up the last of his cattle to sell—to cover your debts . . . And tonight when the whole country was doing you honor, dancing to your jazz, drinking your wines and punch—that last herd was rustled."

Madge sank down to hide her face in the pillows. The blow had fallen. And of all blows it was the mortal one which could crush her.

"And now, angel-face," whispered Sidway, almost spent, "your father is ruined—and who'll pay for this party? Would you like Nels and Ren and me to chip in our savings. . . ."

Madge stretched out a shaking importunate hand that silenced him. And it seemed amidst the knell of pride and happiness that had fallen in ruins about her, she heard Sidway's swift footfalls fading away.

10

Halfway down the slope Lance halted in his blind hurry. The Spanish music floated softly on the still air; the moon soared pitilessly white. What was it that he had done? He sat down under a pine and battled with his conflicting emotions.

Brutally he had made impossible any longer stay at Stewart's ranch. That long-deferred break seemed an unutterable and immense relief. But his conscience flayed him. "What for?" he whispered, huskily. "Why do I feel this—this. . . . It was—coming to her!" He was glad that he had had the courage to tell her. If she had a grain of good in her the truth would bring it out. Then why this stab in his heart, this clamor of furies in his ears, this still small voice? He would have wanted to tell her like an impassive destiny, letting the iron consequences fall. And he had sunk to the level of a man like Uhl. Perhaps even that philanderer would have been more of a gentleman. Lance struck the low of misery.

Then attending to his smarting lip he found it cut and bleeding. How about that? And the stinging blows might as well have been re-enacted. He had struck her, a hard openhanded slap that had staggered her. Suddenly it all flashed clear. Jealousy had been at the root of that incredible passion. Loving Madge Stewart to distraction, his damnable fate had been to be compelled to cower there in the shadow, seeing, hearing the kisses she had lavished on that college fellow. Lance tried to blot out the sight. That had seemed a sickening mortal blow, but it was his vile speech to her that stuck like a hot blade in his side—the jealous false word for which she had struck him across the lips. At last Lance uncovered the real trouble.

"Rotten of me!" he muttered, under his breath. "My God, how terrible she made me feel! . . . But even half drunk she could take car of herself. I saw that. Yet I . . . Jealousy made me low-down. If she had been kissing *me* . . . it would have been heaven. A tough spot for Lance Sidway! . . . Well, Madge, whatever else you are, you're straight—and I can climb out of hell on that."

Lance stood up, shivering a little at the cool air and the indifferent stars. This was the end of his secret love affair. And there would never be another, he was certain. It did not seem possible that any man, much less he, could see Madge Stewart as he had seen her, and carry her in his arms, and kiss her with such abandon, and then fall in love with another woman.

Lance strode down to the bunkhouse, his mind trying to take up the threads of the information he had forced from Bonita. There was a light in Nels' cabin. Lance's watch said that morning was less than an hour away. He burst in upon the old cattleman, who was in the act of undressing.

"Nels, are you sober?" demanded Lance.

"Hello, son, what's ailin' you—all white an' eyes aburnin'?"

"Hell to pay, Nels. Are you sober enough to get me straight?"

"Sober?—Dog-gone! I don't know. Thet shore was some punch. I jest couldn't stop drinkin' it."

"Swell drink, all right. What'd it do to Danny and Ren and Stewart?"

"Wal, they cleaned oot the bowl. Gene said it was an act of charity on their part. *He* was sober. Gene used to hold more bad likker than any man on the

214

range. But Danny an' Ren were lit up some. . . . Say, what you got on yore chest?"

"Plenty! Now, listen. Pack me some biscuits, meat, dried apples—anything you can dig up pronto. Put it in a saddlebag. I'll wrangle my horse. And you be sure you sober up while I'm gone."

"Son, I reckon I savvy," drawled Nels.

Lance went into his cabin, and hastily changed into his riding garb, buckled on his gunbelt, and hurried out, to jerk a bridle off a peg on the porch. The night before, because of the strange horses that had arrived, Lance had put Umpqua in the barn. The moment Lance's step sounded on the runway, Umpqua nickered, and stamped his hoofs. Lance looped the bridle round his neck, led him out, and filling a nosebag with grain, he put that over Umpqua's head. Then leading the horse he hurried back to Nel's cabin. There he saddled Umpqua, but left the cinch loose. He decided before seeing Nels to go into his cabin thinking hard what to take. It was necessary to light the lamp. A blanket, his fleece-lined coat, his rifle and some shells, his gloves, money and matches—these he thought would be about all. Then he remembered Madge's photograph. He would take that, for the chances were against his returning, or ever seeing her again. Fortunately the picture fit inside his coat pocket. He wrapped it in a silk scarf and carefully put it away. Funny, he thought, if a rustler's bullet pierced that lovely likeness of Majesty Stewart before it pierced his heart! But even so it could not hurt any more than she had hurt him. Then he extinguished the lamp and went out. The east was breaking gray. Dawn was not far off.

Umpqua was pitching the nosebag to get the last of the grain.

"Nels, come out," he called.

"Heah I am. Been waitin', son, kinda worried."

"Thanks, Nels," replied Lance, receiving the saddlebags. "Nothing to worry about—much."

"No. Wal, you act kinda queer. I've spent my life

215

with range fellers. An' if you're not drunk on thet punch, you're shore drunk on somethin'."

"Yeh? Well, what, old wiz?" rejoined Lance, his swift hands at work over the saddle.

"You're leavin' Majesty's Rancho."

"Ha! Gee, Nels, you're keen. I rather snicker to snort that I am."

"An' on account of Majesty?"

"Yes, on account of Majesty!" ejaculated Lance, flippantly.

"Aw!—Did you quarrel?"

"Look where she split my lip. That little lady has a sock."

"Son, don't tell me she—she hit you?"

"I'll tell the world she did."

"What in Gawd's name for?"

"Nels it's too long a story. I deserved it and I took it."

"Lance, you're uncommon bitter. . . . I don't mind admittin' thet I had it figgered you—you was in love with Majesty."

"Nels, damn your lunatic hide!" burst out Lance. "You don't mind admitting!—Say, you lying old matchmaker, you've been driving me nuts! You haven't given me any peace for weeks. You wouldn't even let me sleep. 'Ain't I kinda in love with Majesty? She shore is sweet on you!' . . . What kind of talk!— Now, listen, for once, for good and all. 'Kinda in love with Majesty?' Ha! Ha! Ha! . . . I love that good-for-nothing angel so terribly I'm dying for her. Do you get that? I'm stark staring mad about her. I'd shoot myself if I hung around here any longer. So I'm beating it. Now, take a load of that."

"Son, it'll be the turriblest mistake if you run off now," replied Nels, awed and moved. "Fer Majesty's jest as turrible in love. . . ."

"Skip it. You're balmy. You're nuts. You're crazy," retorted Lance, wrenching the words out. It was insupportable to listen to such raving from this simple old man. "Listen to this. All the cattle Stewart had

216

left were rustled last night, right after dark. Must have been rounded up in the daytime."

"What?" roared Nels, changing magically. "Why'n' hell didn't you tell us?"

"Your darling Madge begged me to keep it till tomorrow. Well, that's today."

"Who told you?"

"Bonita."

"Ahuh. How'd you drag thet oot of her?"

"I threw a couple of those punches into her, danced with her, took her out. Well, she spilled the beans, on conditions."

"What conditions?"

"Never mind them, Nels. I won't tell you. And you're not to give Bonita away to Stewart or Ren."

"Humph! You cain't fool them."

"That's not important. The cattle have been rustled by *vaqueros*. Bound across the border. By the Gray Ridge Divide. Where's that?"

"It's thet long gray hill southeast of heah. Aboot ten miles, closest. Separates the range from the foothills of the Peloncillos. There's a cattle trail straight down the valley across the border. Rustlers used it years ago."

"Stewart's cattle ought to be around that divide by now."

"Shore, an' then some. What's yore idee, son?"

"I'm going to find out."

"Good. But don't let yourself be seen from the ridge top. Those rustlers will figger thet the cattle won't be missed right off. But they've got sharp eyes. With two days' start they'd aboot get acrost before we could haid them off. . . . I'll get Stewart an' Danny, an' Starr drunk or sober, an' hit this cattle trail. Meanwhile you locate the rustlers, then ride on in to town. Don't lose no time gettin' an ootfit of cowboys—or any kind of a posse, an' ride hell fer leather to haid these greasers off."

"Use my own judgment as to where I'll cross the ridge?"

"Shore. But if you're snart an' lucky you can cross

217

by the Cochise Trail. Only don't ride down into thet valley onless you're ahaid of the rustlers."

"Okay, Nels. I'm on my way," replied Lance. "Nels, that outfit might get suspicious or something, and hit up the Cochise Trail. Tell Gene and Ren to look for my tracks on that trail, crossing the valley." Then vaulting astride he rode across the square, down by the sleeping village, out upon the shadowy gray range. It was almost daybreak when he struck the wash. By the time a ruddy light showed over the dark mountain barrier Lance had struck the fresh cattle track. It crossed the highway and headed straight for the low slant of gray that marked the northern end of Gray Ridge Divide. Satisfied and thrilled, Lance swerved off the trail to make a short cut, intending to climb the ridge ten miles or so toward the south. It was then only that his mind reverted to the tragedy of his leaving. Madge haunted him, her lovely face white and tragic, her big eyes, and most of all, after he had told her that she had ruined her father, the way she sank down, crushed by amaze and shame. Lastly that imploring hand, mute appeal for mercy. Would she like him and Nels and Ren to donate their wages?—those had been his last words. Too late! Lance writhed in his saddle. As the dawn slowly flamed to a glorious sunrise and the broad daylight drove away his morbid thoughts, he could not understand how he had been so base. He felt that he would be driven to go back to the ranch and explain to Madge how his jealousy and passion had made him a coward and a cad. That would be a betrayal of his love, a refuting of all his scorn. As he rode along, his brooding self-reproach and remorse augmented his error and mitigated Madge's faults. If it turned out that he was to be the means of saving her father's cattle, and perhaps getting himself shot in Madge's interest, that would be all right with him, if only she could know of his repentance.

Lance crossed the valley obliquely and headed up the ridge about five miles south of the point. The sun was high in the heavens when he gained the summit. He took care not to show his horse or himself on top

218

of the ridge. There were rocks and scrub cedars all along, affording good cover. Lance dismounted to reconnoiter. He had to walk a long way north on the ridge before he discovered the cattle. They had been driven into the head of the narrow valley between the foothills and the ridge, and were grazing. The distance was not quite too far to distinguish horses and riders, but Lance had to wait a good while before he made sure he saw them. They should have traveled down the valley to a point almost equal with his position. Lance lingered there until he saw the herd move down the valley toward him. Then he retraced his steps.

Vaqueros had almost as keen eyesight as Indians. But if these rustlers had anticipated immediate pursuit they would not have traveled so leisurely during the night. They had probably calculated upon the cowboys and riders sleeping all this day after the excitement and disturbance of the *señorita's fiesta*. The raid would not be discovered for several days, which would give the thieves time to get across the border. It was a clever and nicely timed move on their part.

Arriving at the spot where he had left his horse, Lance sent a keen gaze back across the valley toward the ranch. He espied puffs of dust some miles out from the highway, about on a line with the cattle trail. He concluded Gene and his riders were in pursuit of the rustlers.

"Okay," soliloquized Lance, with satisfaction. "Pretty lucky for me to worm this out of Bonita. Poor kid! All to save her good-for-nothing brother! Well, I'll keep my word."

Lance mounted and rode along a rough summit trail, which Umpqua had to walk. Lance calculated that he was forty miles from the highway, and close to forty from town. The hour was short of midmorning. He had all the rest of that day, and longer, if need be to carry out Nels' instructions. Recovery of the cattle looked easy to Lance. He tried to conjecture unforeseen circumstances. If the *vaqueros* discovered they were being pursued they would take to the foothills and escape. Lance eyed those formidable hills, rising

219

and swelling gradually to the rough black summits of the Peloncillos.

"My best bet is to go down to the range and look for a cattle outfit between here and town," Lance told himself, and after thinking of every angle possible he decided to put his idea into effect. There were several ranches along that slope of the ridge, and he might be fortunate enough to meet some riders. To this end Lance headed down the slope.

Lance had enough on his mind to make the miles and hours seem short. Umpqua walked and trotted under the hot sun. As long as he had soft ground to travel on he would not tire. Late in the afternoon Lance arrived at the last ranch along the ridge, and ascertained that an outfit of cowboys had left not long before to round up some cattle south of Bolton. This was good luck, indeed, and Lance set off with high hopes. These riders would very likely camp outside of Bolton.

It was sunset when Lance caught up with a trio of cowboys leading three pack horses, and half a dozen extra mounts. Lance joined them with a greeting and pulled Umpqua to a walk.

"Howdy," returned a lean towheaded rider, fastening penetrating eyes upon Lance. "I seen you coming 'way back. Jest about in a hurry, wasn't you?"

"I'll say. You're the Bar X boys from Spencer's ranch, aren't you?"

"Wal, we're some of them."

"I'm Sidway, riding for Gene Stewart."

"I reckoned you was. My handle's Tim Sloan, an' my pards are brothers, sons of Spencer."

"Your boss told me you were bound south of Bolton to round up some of his cattle."

"We air, if we can locate them. But I reckon they're rustled across the border. Some two-bit outfit been workin' the edges of the range lately."

Lance lost no time accounting for his presence, and the lean rider was so interested that he reined his horse, and halted the cavalcade in the middle of the road. "Hell you say!—Boys, you hear thet? . . . How far back air these raiders with Stewart's cattle?"

"Over the ridge in the valley, halfway at the least."

"An' when was it you sighted them?"

"This morning around ten. Stewart will be behind them, keeping out of sight. And it's my job to get some riders to head them off from this end."

"We're with you, Sidway. . . . Boys, like as not this same outfit has been runnin' off our stock."

"Purty shore, I'd say," replied one of the brothers. "But we'd help you out if there wasn't a chance."

"Thanks, fellows. I'm relieved. . . . And now, Sloan, what do you advise?"

"Wal, them stolen cattle won't get nowhere near this end of the valley tonight. My idee is to camp here outside of town, an' be off before daylight in the mawnin'. How's thet suit you?"

"Fine. It's just going to work out great."

Before dusk settled down the riders halted just on the edge of Bolton near a clump of trees Lance remembered having passed on the trip to the Peloncillos.

"Sloan, will we eat in town?" queried Lance, as he dismounted.

"No. Boss won't stand for thet. We'll throw up some grub here. But we're out of coffee an' butter."

"I'll buy some. Do you think I ought to notify the sheriff?"

"Hell no. This deal is a cinch, an' thet old geezer would hawg all the credit."

Lance strode off into town, his mind thronged with thoughts. He seemed on the verge of an adventure much to his liking. Stewart and Nels were sure to like him better than ever. And proud, wild, volcanic Madge Stewart would surely be indebted to him, whether or not she ever confessed it. Lance had a desire to telephone the ranch. At that hour, with Stewart and his men absent, it was ten to one that Madge would answer. How coolly he could make his report, not omitting subtly to augment the dangers! Did that violet-eyed girl have a heart? Lance had to admit that she had, but he had never touched it. His bitter and final resolve of last night still held, yet he was conscious of a rending of spirit at the thought of keeping it, and leaving Majesty's Rancho forever.

At Smith's Store on the highway Lance purchased butter and coffee, and several cakes of hard chocolate, one of which he put in his pocket. While the clerk was wrapping Lance's purchases the proprietor accosted him.

"Hey, Sidway, when did you leave the ranch?"

"Before daylight this morning. Rode down the ridge looking for cattle."

"Then you don't know Stewart's phone is out of connection? I suspect it has been cut."

"Indeed I don't."

"Well, something's wrong. This morning Mrs. Stewart phoned in an order. I expected some things she wanted by express, so did not call until after they arrived. Then I couldn't get an answer."

"That's not strange. One of the old telephone poles may have toppled over," replied Lance, thoughtfully.

"Yes, it might, but it didn't," returned Smith, bluntly.

"Yeah? How do you know?"

"Mike Scanlon was in not ten minutes ago. He'd been out for a load of dead aspen wood. He said that when he was cuttin' it, out there along the creek, he saw a big black car dustin' along toward down hellbent fer election. An' it stopped down the road eight or ten miles. Mike forgot about thet until he got near to the highway. Then he tangled up in a wire thet turned out to be Stewart's. It had fallen across the road. Hadn't been cut long, for Mike saw the bright end, where it had been clipped. He thought somebody in thet big black car had done it. Not half an hour ago! Damn queer, don't you call it?"

"Where does this Mike Scanlon live?"

"Up at the end of town, on the other side of the highway. Ask Meade, the garage man."

Lance, hurrying along past the bright red and yellow lights, pondered this news. It clamped down upon him with a presagement far out of proportion to probabilities. Apparently Stewart's telephone wire had not been

222

cut until late in the day. That seemed to preclude any possibility of the rustlers being accountable. A big black car! Lance wanted to talk to Mike Scanlon about that car.

He passed the last bright neon lights. Meade's garage appeared to be deserted. Just at that moment a big black car, with headlights dark, moved slowly down the back road. Lance wanted a look at that car. It was strangely familiar in line and build. He swerved off the highway, crossed the open space to the back road.

"Hi there. Hold up," he called boldly. Manifestly the driver heard him for the car came to a halt. The street lamp behind Lance caught the gleaming faces of men in the front seat.

"Stick 'em up, cowboy!" cut the air with deadly menace. As Lance threw up his hands he recognized that voice. It belonged with the car.

"Okay, Uhl. Up—they are," he replied quietly.

"Come close."

Lance walked to the automobile halting abreast of the front seat. Uhl had his hand in his coat pocket and he was leanin over the door. Lance knew that he faced a concealed gun and that he had to think quickly and right. Uhl was bareheaded. His clean-cut visage shone pale and cold in the light. The driver hunched down over the wheel, as if ready to race. The engine purred. Then Lance caught the gleam of a machine gun on the lap of a man in the back seat. Between him and another man shrank a girl with a face as white as chalk and great dark eyes. Lance recognized her with a terrific stop of his heart. For an instant he seemed to reel dizzily, then the cold sickening freeze of his very marrow quickened to a hot gush of blood, and his faculties cleared to a magnified intensity.

"Cowboy, you've been here on Cork's snatch racket?" queried Uhl, sharply.

"Yes."

"What held him up?"

"I don't know."

223

"We beat him to it! Who wised you and why're you looking for me?"

"Want to tip you off. You cut the wire too late. Sheriff here has blocked you as far west as Tucson and as far east as El Paso. Posse down the road waiting to blow your tires into smithereens."

Uhl burst into vehement curses: "Raggy, —— —— your dumb soul! You —— —— —— hop head! I ought to bump you off for that loss of time back there. . . . What'll we do?"

"Shoot our way through," rasped the driver.

Lance interrupted in ringing low voice: "Might be okay for Bolton but points farther on the highway will be blocked. No chance in a million. Just as bad east. The wires are hot."

"Fox, what's the dope?" flashed the leader.

"Are you asking me?" curtly retorted one of the men in the back. "Didn't I warn you against this racket? I advise hiding along the railroad track and hopping a freight."

"You're no fox. You're a rabbit. . . . Cowboy, what's your tip?"

"Beat it for the hills pronto," exclaimed Lance, hurriedly. "You can't get through this town by car."

"Hills! . . . I get it. But horses, food, blankets— where can they be found?"

"Cowboy outfit just out of town. You can buy what you need from them and be on the trail in a jiffy."

"Good. Where'll we go?"

"Up in the Peloncillos. Rough wild country. You couldn't be tracked. You can hide for days. As soon as you get your dough you can ride down across the border into Mexico."

"Good tip, cowboy. What about this bus?"

"Send your driver on the ridge road. Give him water and grub. When morning comes he can drive off the road into the cedars beyond the point. And hide there. He could get out later."

"Oke. Will you guide us?"

"Sure. If you slip me enough."

Uhl's gun gave out a metallic clink as he drew his

224

coat over the door. Producing a roll of bills he handed one to Lance.

"Here's a grand."

"Make it two, Uhl. And promise of more if I get you through," demanded Lance, lowering his hands.

"Okay, you chiseler. Jump on the running board and tell the driver where to go."

Lance ran around to the other side of the car and caught on. He directed the driver down the road and away from the town. A campfire blazed among the trees. In a reaction of feeling Lance could scarcely hold on. He imagined he was in a dreadful nightmare. But the car was moving. In the back he saw a gangster on this side with a machine gun across his knees, the same as the other. And on the floor lay another man. Lance puzzled over that. By sheer luck and wit he had met a tremendous situation. Anything to keep Uhl from carrying Madge off to the cities! She would be worse than lost or dead. He divined that Uhl would never release her. If he could steer them up into the hills, Stewart would be on his trail in another day. It was the only chance.

"Here we are," called Lance, as the car approached to within fifty feet of the campfire, out in the shadow.

"Fox, you and Flemm get out and stick up this bunch," ordered Uhl.

It was done almost in the twinkling of an eye. Uhl got out and faced the cowboys. Sloan's comrades, especially the cook, looked comical in their maze, but Sloan himself grew pale and grim.

"No holdup, cowboys. I want to buy horses and stuff to go up in the hills. Here's a grand."

"What's thet?" queried Sloan.

"Ten hundred smackers—a thousand dollars, you dumbbell."

"What do you want fer thet much?"

"Five saddle horses, some packs, and whatever else we need."

"It's a deal."

Uhl stuck the bill into the cowboy's shirt pocket.

"Line them up, Flemm, and keep 'em covered. . . . Come here, cowboy."

Lance strode into the campfire light, quite prepared for the profane ejaculations of Sloan and the Spencer brothers.

"Pick out what we want damn quick."

"Uhl, we'd save time by having these cowboys help me saddle and pack. Two of your men can keep them covered," suggested Lance.

"Oke. Step on it," rejoined Uhl, then repaired to the car. He opened the back door. "Come out, baby."

Madge descended from the car, clad in white slacks and a white sport coat. She made a step toward the campfire, when Uhl seized her roughly.

"Say, you move only when you're told," ordered the gangster, harshly. "Honey Bee Uhl talking—and you get it."

"All right. But keep your hands off me," flashed Madge, with a passion that told her spirit had not been weakened. And she twisted free.

"Oke, baby. But you might as well get used to them. . . . Raggy, throw that college bloke out. Then you grab some eats and drink and beat it."

Lance was as amazed as the other cowboys to see a limp young man pulled out of the car. He appeared dazed or injured, but he sat up, to disclose the handsome pale features of Rollie Stevens.

"Get up and come to the fire," ordered Uhl. And he pushed Madge along ahead of him. "Now sit down, both of you. In a minute I'll talk ransom money to you. . . . Raggy, don't forget to put our bags out of the car."

Lance tried to see and hear everything from where he saddled Umpqua. The other cowboys were saddling and packing with extreme celerity under the guns of the two gangsters. Lance, thinking to have Madge ride his horse, shortened the stirrups. If a chance offered he might shoot one or more of these fellows and leap up behind Madge to make their escape. In a very few minutes six saddle and two pack horses were ready to travel. He searched for an extra rope and canteen, to tie them on his saddle. He heard the car roar and roll away up the ridge road. Hurrying back to the campfire he said crisply: "Ready, Uhl."

"My God!" cried Rollie Stevens. "It's Sidway. Madge, look!"

"I've had the pleasure," returned Madge, with infinite scorn.

"Kidnaper!" shouted Stevens, incredulously. Then it appeared a kind of joy came over him. That infuriated Lance, whose nerves were taut.

"Fetch those cowboys here," called Uhl.

When Sloan and his two comrades were lined up in front of the gangster, he asked, indicating Sloan, "What's your name?"

"Tim Sloan."

"Get this dope, cowboy," went on the gangster, deliberately. "In the morning you notify Stewart I'm holding his daughter for fifty grand. . . ."

"My father can't raise that," interposed Madge. "He is practically ruined. But I can raise half that."

"Baby, will you keep out of this?" retorted Uhl, then turning to Sloan again he resumed. "Notify Stewart I want fifty grand for her, and the same for her boy friend. If my orders are not obeyed, we'll rape the girl, and then kill them both. No bluffing. Send one man on our track with the money. Get that, cowboy?"

"Shore—I get it," replied Sloan, huskily.

"Fox, you keep these fellows covered until we're all in the saddle and out of the light. . . . Sidway, you lead the way with the pack horses. I'll follow with the dame. Fox, you and Flemm drive Stevens between you. Let's go."

"Uhl, I've selected an easy-gaited horse for Miss Stewart," spoke up Lance. "It's a tough trail."

"Yeah? Bet she'll stand it better than any of us. I haven't been in a saddle half a dozen times in my life. . . . Which horse? Come on, baby."

Lance led them over to Umpqua, and took from the saddle the fleece-lined coat he had untied.

"Get into this. It'll be bitter cold when we're high

227

up," he said, and held the coat for her. If he had not
been under stress of strongly suppressed emotion he
might have recoiled from her convulsed white face and
magnificent eyes. But her look of horror and hate
strangely changed.

"It can't—be true!" she cried, poignantly.

"What can't be true, baby?" interposed Uhl.

"That Lance Sidway is a side partner of *you,* Bee
Uhl!"

"Miss Stewart, it happens that I am," replied Lance.
"Hurry into this coat. . . . You'll find gloves in the
pocket."

Lance blindly held the coat for her and then
plunged away. Mounting Sloan's horse he drove the
two pack animals into the road, and headed for the
dark hills. In a moment or more he recognized
Umpqua's gait behind him, and presently heard the
other horses following. It was done, and his heart
seemed to descend from his throat and settle where it
belonged. A cool wind blew down from the heights.
The stars blinked as if incredulous. His jumbled
thoughts began to straighten out. No use to marvel at
where he found himself—at the unaccountable fate
which had finally placed it in his power to save Madge
Stewart, her honor and her life, and the happiness of
her parents. Somehow he would do it. All these dove-
tailing angles could not be merely coincidences. They
fitted, and he felt that he would solve the problem.
But he must be governed by cool judgment instead
of emotion. To this end he brought sternly to bear all
the mentality of which he was capable. And out of
the welter of thoughts he fixed upon a determination
to be alert and ready on the instant to seize any opportunity to escape with Madge. It would come inevitably. These tenderfoot gangsters, unused to horses and
pains, climbing into the wild rugged hills, would
sooner or later provide that opportunity. But if it did
not come before Uhl resorted to violence with the girl
then Lance must be quick to kill him, and call upon
her to run for her life while he fought it out with the
others. That settled Lance into a cold and calculating

mood which transformed him into another man. He was dealing with a matter of life and death—with vicious degenerates from the underworld of crime.

Tim Sloan had a rather complex problem to solve, as far as Lance's connection with Uhl was concerned; but any cowboy would obey the gangster's orders, and then let Stewart decide. Lance knew what would happen and he would not have been in Uhl's boots for a million dollars. Stewart and his men would be Indians on the trail of this gang, and they would shoot them down from ambush or surprise them and hang them from the pines. All Lance's faculties must be concentrated on his task of saving Madge from these merciless fiends.

Several miles out, the road swung to the south, and the Cochise Trail branched off around the lower point of the ridge. The black hills loomed high. A brightening to the east heralded a rising moon. Lance did not need the repeated calls from Uhl to "step on it," and he led across the valley at a trot. The pack horses, with light burdens, did not hold up the progress. In short order Lance reached the point where the trail started up the slope. He dismounted here to wait for the others. Umpqua was close behind. Lance broke the tip of a cedar bush with a vicious twist. He prepared this first sign to make his trail easy to follow.

"How you riding, girl?" queried Lance, as Umpqua came up.

"Swell. I like Umpqua in spite of the bum who owns him. It's going to be some romantic ride," replied Madge, mockingly.

Uhl arrived next, straddling his horse as if he were on stilts.

"What you gassing about?" he demanded.

"I asked Miss Stewart about her saddle cinch," returned Lance.

"Yeah? And what did that little dame say?"

"Ask her."

Uhl did and was promptly told to go where it was hot and that if he wanted to keep her from talking he would have to gag her. Stevens rode up then, accompanied by his captors. He appeared to have recovered somewhat and sat his saddle upright. The other gangsters, packing their bags and machine guns in front, looked as if they would have been glad to get down and walk.

"We begin to climb here," said Lance, "and I'll tighten your cinches." When he worked back to Madge and made a motion at her cinch she interrupted him.

"Keep your black hands away from me. I don't want to be soiled. If my cinch needs tightening, I'll do it," and her voice rang with contempt.

"Black? . . . Oh, I see. Gosh, how dumb I am!" declared Lance, lowering his bare hands. "Listen, you all. This trail is steep. Give your horse his head. Lean forward in bad places and hang onto his mane. When I stop to rest my horses you do the same. That's all."

He slapped the pack animals up the trail, and mounting he followed them. Umpqua, with a loose bridle, kept right on the heels of Lance's horse. When Lance turned to look back he saw Madge almost close enough to touch. The other four riders came on in close single file.

Lance zigzagged after the pack horses, and forbore gazing back again. But he thrilled at her nerve. She was not in the least afraid of Uhl. Lance let the pack horses initiate the rests. They were well-trained animals. Beyond the first foothill yawned a shadowy cedar flat, which led to another slope, long and gradual. When he surmounted it to the summit a full moon soared white above the black domes, transforming night into a silvery luminous day.

"Beastly trail," declared Madge, sarcastically. "I'll have to send a gang of laborers up here for two weeks to work on it. Big expense, though."

"I'll say," replied Uhl, taking her literally. "Tough as nuts. But, baby, you ride like one of those circus girls in tights."

"Miss Stewart, you'd better not go to such expense," interposed Lance, satirically.

"Oh, are you a monumental liar?" burst out the girl.

"Shut up gabbing to him," ordered Uhl.

That significant speech for once silenced Madge, and it almost drove Lance into throwing his gun on the egoistic crook. He had kidnaped Madge for more than ransom.

Lance rode on into an up-an-down cedar country with an occasional pine tree heralding the approach to the heights. The air began to have a cool edge. The moon climbed toward the zenith. Presently the trail led into a narrow canyon. It was long and tortuous, heading at last into a mountain meadow, where traveling was comfortable for a while. A black belt of pines loomed ahead, shining in the moonlight. Lance kept eye and ear keen for his followers. Madge appeared to ride easily, but the others were growing crippled. They shifted from side to side in their saddles, let their legs hang, and grumbled intermittently.

Once, under the dark pines, Lance was seized by a savage and desperate impulse. Here was the place to shoot Uhl and ride off with Madge. He almost surrendered to it. He was sure of killing the gangster, sure of Umpqua, but some hitch he could not anticipate might give the other gangsters a moment to rake forward with those machine guns. Lance refused the chance. A better would offer, and he importuned patience.

The forest belt gave way to rough rocky country where Madge, if she had not bestrode a grand horse, would have suffered considerably. The horses labored slowly over shale and up loose slides and through thick brush that tore at them. The moon reached a point overhead; the air had a bite in it; coyotes mourned lonely cries; the night grew far advanced. Here Uhl at last fell off his saddle and walked behind Madge leading his horse. The other gangsters cursed and raved for a halt.

"Sidway, for God's sake, have a heart!" yelped Uhl, finally. "Aren't we far enough? Can't we camp here?"

"No water. No grass. You must go on," replied Lance.

"But we've rode—a hundred miles—already," panted the gangster.

"Seems like, maybe. But we're not twenty miles from town. Better get on your horse again."

Uhl obeyed groaning. Lance would not let them rest, and presently divining that Uhl was dependent upon him and knew it, he turned a deaf ear to appeals and curses and threats alike. And he led on and up through increasingly rough country, until Uhl, with a bellow, fell off his horse.

"Sorry, Uhl," said Lance. "You almost made it."

"Made what?"

"Camp at Cochise's stronghold. Not much further. And a swell place. Water, wood, grass. A log cabin."

"Gimme a—drink—Fox," panted the gangster. "I can walk—the rest."

"I wouldn't ride no furder for Al Capone," retorted Flemm, doggedly.

"Well, you can rot here—for a little shot," snapped Uhl, and he labored to his feet.

"Beat it, cowboy."

Lance led on, riding with his hands in his pockets. On the heights it was cold. Madge would be warm, all except her feet. Stevens appeared to be sagging in his saddle, but Lance could not summon any sympathy for the collegian. After more weary miles of travel Uhl burst out:

"Baby, what kind of liar did you call Sidway?"

"Monumental. But that's weak. He's a colossal liar!"

"Shall I bump him off?"

"Nothing could delight me more, except to see *you* bumped off."

"Say, you're a hellcat, ain't you? But I'll tame you. . . . Hold up, you guide. I want to get on again."

The last miles of that uphill ride were dragging and cruel to the gangsters. Even Stevens, hurt at the outset in some way, endured the ordeal better. When Lance led into the beautiful wooded park, which inclosed Cochise's stronghold, the moon was low and dawn not far away. He halted the cavalcade under some spreading pines.

Lance's hands were so stiff from cold that he could scarcely start a fire. But that once done, he gathered firewood, and soon had a blaze. White and silent now Madge leaned against a tree. Lance threw his saddle, then flew to the packs. In a few moments he had them off the horses. He carried one to the fire and threw out blankets. Uhl knelt, his shaking hands to the fire. The other gangsters stood over the blaze, guns in hands, still wary and watchful. Their chief might have trusted Lance, but they did not.

"Majesty—aren't you—frozen?" asked Rollie, his teeth chattering. "Come to the—fire."

"My feet—are ice," she whispered.

"Here," cried Lance, sharply. "They can't be frozen. It's not cold enough. . . . Sit here, on this blanket. Lean against the pack. Put this blanket over you. . . . Never mind, I'll take off your shoes."

Her thin shoes and stockings afforded little protection against this frosty air. Her little feet did feel like blocks of ice.

"Rollie, throw a blanket round you and sit close to her," went on Lance. No one seemed to oppose him, and he caught Madge's great dark eyes upon him.

Then Lance leaped to throw the other pack, and unsaddle the horses. He turned them loose. The luxuriant grass and good water in the mountain park were the equal of any pasture. There was not much likelihood of their straying soon, and Umpqua at least would stay. Lance went back to the fire. Madge was asleep, her fair face drooping upon Rollie's shoulder. He too had sunk into weary slumber. On the other side of the fire Uhl lay covered with his head on a log, dead asleep. Fox appeared to have crawled under a pack canvas. Flemm sat on his guard, his machine gun at rest, his eyes like gimlets.

"Cowboy, stretch yourself right there," he said. "Me an' Fox will have a go at this job."

Lance dragged his saddle close, and wrapping himself in his blanket he lay down to make up a little for

233

the loss of two nights' sleep. His last thought was a wondering if he dared risk a snap shot at Flemm, and then kill Fox and Uhl as they lay. Sleep claimed him before he could decide.

Daylight had come when he was awakened by a sound of wood being dumped upon the fire. Fox had taken Flemm's place on guard. The others were locked in slumber. Lance fell asleep again and when he awakened the sun was high. Uhl sat huddled near the fire, his pale face showing the havoc of extreme exertion and privation. Behind him the fox-featured guard paced to and fro, gun in hand.

Lance threw off his blanket and arose to his feet, cramped with the cold.

"Good morning. Kind of brisk up here on top," he said, cheerfully.

"Brisk?—Ha! I damn near froze to death," ejaculated Uhl.

Lance spread his hands to the blaze, and casually looked about. The third gangster evidently was hidden under the tarpaulin. The two victims of the kidnapers were asleep. All Lance could see of Madge was her disheveled golden hair.

"Uhl, it's only a little way to the log cabin," said Lance. "Much better place to camp. Hadn't we better move over? Then I'll cook some meat and make some hot coffee."

"Oke, cowboy. Step on it. I'll follow with these duds. . . . Fox, kick Flemm out of his sleep. . . . Baby, wake up and get wise. This is the last time you'll ever sleep with any man but me."

Lance, with murder in his heart, lifted a pack upon his shoulder, and stepping into the trail he strode for the clearing. He could see it through the big pines, a beautiful glade, with its frosted grass glistening under the sun. Sight of deer made him think of his rifle. That was in his saddle sheath. There might come a chance later to use it. Umpqua whistled from some point near at hand. Lance saw no sign of the other horses. A huge pine tree with wide spreading branches, and some high gray rocks marked the site of the log cabin. Its open

234

door stared like a black curious eye, wondering what was to happen there. All around the stately pines stood up and beyond them rugged crags. This spot had once been the stronghold of the Apache chief, Cochise, at which time the trail was known only to the Indians.

Depositing the pack under the pine, Lance hurried back for another load. Halfway he met the gangsters. Lance swerved off the trail into the brush. He had a reluctance to meet Madge Stewart face to face. Yet the part he was playing sustained him with a kind of rapture. Perhaps he was afraid she might see through him. Most certainly he must look a queer kind of villain. Returning to the glade with the second pack, which he had opened, he set that down with the other, and then proceeded to build a fire. This done, he went back to fetch his saddle and the blankets that had been left.

Flemm, the meanest looking of the gangsters, manifestly distrusted Lance, and for that matter, the situation itself. He sat apart, holding the machine gun across his knee.

Lance spread the tarpaulin on the grass and proceeded to empty the contents of a pack.

"Rollie, you're one of these worthless rich guys, I know," said Lance, not without sarcasm. "But if you'd condescend to help me, we'd have breakfast sooner."

"I'd starve to death before I'd associate with you in any way," declared the collegian.

"Yes, and you'd let Madge starve, too. If you and she were left alone on your own, she'd soon get your number."

"Don't address me again, you two-faced scoundrel. You're a dirty rat, Sidway, and your pleas won't get you anywhere with Miss Stewart or me."

"What would you call yourself for night before last?" queried Lance, in bitter scorn.

Stevens' pale face flamed red, but it was fury more than shame that strangled his speech in his throat.

"Cowboy, you said a mouthful," interposed Uhl, caustically. "What'd this swelled-up sap pull on my baby?"

"I don't know whom you mean," snapped Lance.

"Well, then, Miss Stewart."

"That's none of your business."

"Yeah?—See here, cowboy. Don't let this dame work on you. Flemm swears you're sore because we beat you to this snatch."

"Bee, I tell you he's not on the level," interposed Flemm.

"Sidway, you're not on the spot with me," went on Uhl. "You've done me service and I'm for you. But don't strain things on account of a pretty skirt. That doesn't go with me. . . . What'd this swell sap do to Madge Stewart that burned you up?"

Lance was quick to see how jealousy and heat had imperiled him, and therefore the girl. Despite his calculations he had erred.

"Chief, you wouldn't think it much," Lance said, with an outright laugh. "I happened to see Stevens trying to take liberties with Miss Stewart."

"Did he get away with it?"

"I'll say he didn't."

The gangsters' explosion of mirth was no compliment to Madge. Lance resisted a strong impulse to look at her then. No doubt she would be something unforgettable to see.

"Skip the dirt about me, you poor fish!" she interrupted shortly.

Suddenly Lance felt her close to him, and then heard her light step. He was on his knees on the tarpaulin fumbling among cans and parcels, and he was aware that his hands shook.

"Did anyone see the sack I had with me last night? Coffee and butter."

"If it was a snake, it'd bite you," spoke up Madge sweetly. "There, under your nose!—Lance, can I offer my services as assistant cook?"

Lance sustained a slight start. "Are you—any good?"

"Pretty good—in *that* way."

"Can you mix biscuit dough?"

"Swell. Nels taught me."

236

"Go to it. Here's flour, salt, lard, pan. Fetch some water. I'll heat the Dutch oven."

Uhl showed interest in the proceedings. The other gangsters grinned sardonically. Stevens sat dejectedly with his face in his hands. Lance cut strips of bacon into a skillet all the while bafflingly aware of the going and returning of the girl, and then her agitating presence close beside him, on her knees. The shine of her hair, the fragrance of her, the vitality of her, and more than all that nameless and irresistible attraction seemed propelled into his senses. Hurriedly he arose to rake red coals out of the fire, to put on the oven to heat, and the coffeepot to boil, to fetch more firewood, and to find other tasks. It was the eyes of Uhl and his allies fixed upon the kneeling girl that drove Lance to look at her. She had thrown off the heavy coat, and knelt in her thin slacks, her round, gold-tanned arms bare, her beautiful voluptuous form revealed in all its devastating allurement. Lance cursed under his breath. This gangster was a ghoul for both money and flesh. Madge was in deadly peril, yet seemed oblivious of it. Lance's calculation had been that by midday Stewart would be on his trail. That would fetch him to the mountain clearing late the coming night or at dawn. What might happen before then? No matter what happened, Stewart and his men could be expected to waylay or ambush the gangsters and kill them. No doubt Tim Sloan and the Spencer boys would be with them. It was all up with Uhl right that moment. They would not escape these relentless rangers. Gene Stewart would experience a throwback to his wild frontier days. But they were hours and miles away. And Lance had to escape with Madge before nightfall. These thoughts revolved in his mind as he perfomed the tasks of cook around the campfire.

Presently breakfast was ready, and it was Madge, not Lance, who called: "Come and get it!" Kneeling over the fire had caused her cheeks to burn red, and it was only in her deep somber eyes that there was any sign of physical or mental distress. They all sat or knelt to eat and drink, except the cursed Flemm, who partolled his short beat. Fox brought him food and drink.

"Baby, I didn't think it was in you," declared Uhl, devouring one of the hot biscuits.

Then Lance discovered that as she did not reply, nor deign to glance at the gangster, he took offense at her indifference. Evidently he had a tremendous egoism. "Get this, baby," he flashed, in cold passion. "Soon as I thaw out and get some sleep, I'll change your damned snooty manner." With that he stamped away into the pine brush beyond the clearing. Stevens appeared to shrivel up at the significance of that threat. Madge gazed intently at Lance, her wonderful eyes, hypnotic effect, searching his very soul. She was delving into his depths. What did she imagine she saw there? She was strangely uncertain of her convictions about him. Her present bad conceptions might be warring with good ones of the past. Lance nearly betrayed himself before her tremendous appeal. But he was aware that the beady and fox-eyed gangsters were watching, too. Kneeling once more, Lance bent over the utensils, and began collecting them preparatory to washing. Presently Uhl returned.

"Flemm, I'll give you a rest for half an hour. Then I want to sleep. God, that sun feels good!" Then he turned to Madge.

"Baby, you can go into the cabin."

She hurriedly acted upon the order.

"Uhl, hadn't I better look up the horses?" queried Lance.

"Horses? I forgot them."

"They've strayed. I didn't see any tracks going down the trail. So they must be around. You realize how important horses are, don't you?"

"By God, I do now! . . . Here, Stevens, you wash up that mess. Cowboy, find those horses."

Lance, making a show of anxiety and hurry, strode off. Circling the clearing he found Sloan's roan and near by his own horse Umpqua. No sign of the other animals. Lance did not bother to hunt tracks. He made a detour and came up within sight of the camp, and sat down on a log to peer through the foliage. He could see the cabin. There, watching intently, he brooded over the situation. Presently he saw Flemm rejoin Uhl. The three gangsters held a colloquy, which was unintelligible to Lance. But they did not appear concerned. Once Fox pointed at Stevens, who knelt with his back turned, laboring over his task. Again Uhl made a passionate gesture toward the cabin, at which Flemm threw up his hands in resignation. Then Uhl lay down on a blanket in the sun and went to sleep.

Lingering there for some time Lance finally retraced his steps.

"Found only two horses," he informed Flemm. "The rest have wandered off. I'll have to saddle up to find them."

"Wait. If we waked up the boss now he'd bump you off."

"But every hour they may stray father away."

"Okay by me. I'd a hell of sight rather walk."

Whereupon Lance proceeded to wipe the utensils for Stevens. "Rollie, this is a tough break," he said. "Don't take it so hard. You'll come out okay, except for loss of some dough you won't miss."

"I don't mind the money. I fear for Majesty. It was all my fault—that we were caught by these ruffians. I persuaded her to come out—lied to get her, in fact. And we were held up."

"Sidway," interrupted Flemm, sarcastically, "you don't strike me as a snatch scout. . . . Cheese it!"

Lance wisely refrained from further talk, though he gnashed his teeth. When the chores were finished he cut and packed firewood, mostly bark from dead trees. After that he cut great armloads of spruce boughs and dragged them to camp.

"Sid, there's somethin' rotten about you, but it ain't in this camp stuff," commented Fox.

"Ha! He learned all that in Chi," laughed Flemm.

"Say, tenderfeet, if you're stuck up here for a week, you'll appreciate soft beds," replied Lance.

"Week! What in hell's eatin' you? Two days is my limit," retorted Fox.

Lance strode off, ax in hand, groaning over a thought of what complications would evolve among these violent men in another day. He cut armloads of spruce, and packing that back he approached the door of the cabin, and without a glance at the gangsters, made bold to enter.

To his amaze Madge had been waiting, surely watching for him, for she leaped at him.

"Lance—*darling*," she whispered, and circled his arm with two steellike hands.

He let the load of spruce fall with a sodden swish. Her extraordinary loveliness must have been due to intense spirit and emotion. Her face was like a pearl —her eyes glowing purple.

"Are you crooked or honest?" she added.

"Crooked—as hell!" he gasped.

"I fear it. . . . But still you must save me from *him* —and get the ransom. I'll pay anything. . . . He means to attack me—keep me! . . . For God's sake—for Mother's—for mine—save me from that!"

"I'll try. . . . Keep your nerve. Watch!" he whispered, huskily, and turned to stride out. Before facing the gangsters he thought it best to go into the woods and cut more boughs. Recovering his poise he packed another huge load back to camp. Presently he said to Flemm.

"It's getting late in the afternoon. I ought to be wrangling the horses."

"Yeah. An' what's that?"

"Hunting them."

"Set down an' keep your shirt on. Or you might peel potatoes an' what have you."

"*Uh!*" yelled Lance, suddenly.

The gangster leader roused out of his slumber with surprising quickness, and sat up, blinking.

"These guys won't let me hunt for the horses. I found only two. I ought to ride around these woods and find them."

240

"Hop to it, cowboy. But don't forget we want supper soon."

Lance ran to get his saddle and bridle and blankets, tingling with the vibration of his nerves. All day he had pondered over the need to saddle Umpqua. Once astride the horse he felt that the critical hour was near at hand. Riding off out of sight he returned to the point where he could watch the camp. The heat of the day was waning, and sunset burned in the west. Lance saw Uhl, bare headed and coatless, get up to go toward the cabin. And he went in!

That was a signal for Lance to ride back toward the camp. He had to meet the crisis. Terror and panic gave way to fury, and by the time he had reached the clearing he was steel—cold and tight in mind and body. Boldly he rode to the big pine opposite the cabin, and there halted. Flemm and Fox were watching him curiously. With warning gesture, Lance pointed down the trail toward the opening into the clearing. Both gangsters were impelled to leap up and look. On the moment Lance heard Madge's ringing voice: "No! . . . Bee Uhl, I'll pay the ransom. But. . . ."

"Baby, you started it. You got to come through. No dame who ever lived can play with me," he replied, in cold passion.

"I *did* play with you," she protested. "But I didn't mean what you mean!"

"No matter now. You'll come across."

Lance leaped off Umpqua and ran over to the excited gangsters. His manner would have struck anyone into amaze and fear.

"Where's Uhl?" he queried.

"He said he was goin' to love his baby," replied Fox. "What's eatin' you?"

"I rode up high back there on the slope. And I saw two horses down where the trail comes up. First I thought they were our horses. But they had riders and were coming this way."

"Riders! You mean men on horseback?"

"I sure do. . . . There may be more than two. Looks

damn bad. You better sneak down the trail, keeping out of sight, and make sure."

"What of?"

"Who it is and what they want."

"Fox, you go," ordered Flemm.

"Okay. But what'll I do!"

"Hold them up. An' use your gray matter."

Fox looked to his machine gun, and ran out to the trail, which he entered, and glided along till he reached the green foliage where he soon passed out of sight.

Lance stepped up on the pack beside Flemm.

"There! Look!" he whispered, tensely. "That little open place, beyond the yellow pine. See!"

"My eyes must be damn poor. I see nothin' but green," growled Flemm.

"Okay! then see stars," hissed Lance, and swung his heavy gun on the gangster's bare head. Flemm fell soddenly. Whereupon Lance sped across the space to the side of the cabin, listening, watching the door.

He heard a scuffle, then swift light footfalls, then panting breaths, and—: "I'm not—afraid of you—Bee Uhl!"

"Swell! I like my dames to be wildcats," replied Uhl, with something exultant in his voice, no longer cold. "Make me fight for it, eh?"

"You lousy bum! Fight you? I can whip you," cried Madge, hotly.

Lance made for the door. He heard thudding footfalls, a cry, and then a rip of cloth.

"Let go!—Oh, you beast!"

"Baby—I'll strip you—right now," panted the gangster.

Lance leaped into the doorway, gun leveled. Uhl had Madge backed against the wall. The gangster's clawing hands held strips of her clothing. The girl, half naked, was warding him off, like a tigress at bay.

"Madge! Duck! Get away from him!" shouted Lance.

The gangster froze a second, then sprang into convulsive action, to catch the girl and get her in front of him. But she was as strong as he and far more supple. A short struggle ensued, the end of which came when Uhl made the blunder of striking her down. Then, even as he half turned, his thin face gray, his eyes hot and clear as molten steel, Lance leaped to get in better line. When his gun boomed the gangster appeared to be propelled against the wall. It upheld him a moment. A great bloody blotch came as if by magic. Lance thought he had shot away half of Uhl's face. He stuck there an instant, a ghastly spectacle, then slid sideways to the floor.

Madge lay apparently unconscious, a bruise on her white temple and a red welt across her bare shoulder. Lance snatched up a blanket, and lifting her flung it around her and carried her out the door. Flemm lay as Lance had last seen him. Far down the trail Fox appeared running toward camp. Lance took a long shot at him for luck, then sheathing his gun, he stepped to the snorting Umpqua, and kicked the stirrup around.

"Steady, Ump! It's me. Hold, you fool horse!"

With Madge in his left arm Lance mounted and drew her across his saddle. Umpqua needed no urging. As he plunged away a rattle of gunshots blended in a continuous volley, and a rain of bullets whistled and ticked through the trees, and pattered on the cabin. But in a few jumps the horse was behind the cabin, and out of danger. Lance held him to a lope along the wall of foliage, into the woods.

11

No sooner had Gene Stewart lain down and dropped to sleep, some hours after midnight, than he was assailed by nightmares. It was just as well that he had not gone to bed in his own room, for he kicked around pretty violently. And he was in the thick of violent events when someone not a hobgoblin or demon thoroughly aroused him. Dawn had come. He made out Nels standing over him.

"Wal, Boss, you was loco. Never seen you so oot of your haid."

"Hello, old-timer. Been having crazy dreams. Must have been that punch concoction Madge sprung on us."

"Wait till you see Ren. . . . Pile oot, Gene, an' throw on your riding things. We've got work on hand."

"Uhuh. So that was the big idea. What's up?"

"Sidway just left on the trail of your cattle. Rustled last night before the ball opened."

"By jacks!—He wanted to tell me last night. But Madge wouldn't let him."

"Might hev spoiled her party. . . . We're to hit Sidway's trail pronto. Danny is wranglin' the hawses. An' I've throwed some grub together. Come along, Boss. We hev Sidway to thank fer somethin' like old times."

Nels clinked out into the patio where his musical footsteps died away. Gene quickly dressed in his range garb, and slipped a comb and toothbrush into his pocket. His gun belt had ample shells, and his rifle was down at Nels' bunkhouse. Then he went to his wife's room and poking his head in the door he awakened her: "Sorry, dear. Nels just called me, We're going after a bunch of strayed stock. May not be back for a day or two."

"So this is what young Sidway had to tell you?" she replied quickly.

"Good guess, Mom. Go back to sleep, and don't worry about what that cowboy starts. He's a finisher."

Going out through the patio Stewart saw two of Madge's guests, boy and girl, asleep in each other's arms in a hammock. They were half covered by a colorful blanket. It was a pretty picture, and Gene thought the girl was Maramee. "Some party!" he muttered, as he strode on. "But dog-gone-it! I had a good time watching them. . . . Only—my girl worries me!"

Clear daylight had come when Stewart reached the bunkhouses. Four horses saddled and briddled stood at the rail. He found his men inside eating. Danny looked grim and dark as he bent over his plate. Starr appeared drunk.

"Boss, throw some hot cakes under yore belt. . . . Ren, you drink thet hot coffee or I'll pour it down you."

"Nels—old manz—I want drink."

"I gave you a bracer."

"Ren, you're drunk," said Gene.

"Whosh drunk? I ain't so. . . . It wash just thet peach juice las night."

Nels forced the cowboy to drink the coffee, and stuffed some biscuits and cold meat in his pocket.

"Boss, let's get goin'." interposed Danny Mains, darkly. "If I don't miss my guess we'll hev hell catchin' Sidway. Thet boy's another Nick Steele."

"Right," agreed Nels.

They dragged Starr outside and threw him on his horse.

"Can you stick on?" queried Stewart.

"You insolt me," protested Ren, swaying in his saddle.

245

"I'll hold him on, Gene," said Danny, "till he sobers up."

"Bosh, whash in 'ell was thet punch as night?"

"I don't know, Ren. It sure gave me a hell of a nightmare."

"I'm agonna get thet mixtoure from Miss Madge—an' make million bucks. Washen thet heavern best drink ever?"

"A most deceiving one, Ren. It led you on."

"Whash wuz in it?"

"Dynamite, greased lightning, sweet cider and aqua fortis."

"Hell you shay?"

They rode down past the village, Stewart and Nels gradually drawing ahead, while Mains came along behind steadying Starr in his saddle.

"Nels, what's the deal?" asked Stewart.

"Wal, some Mexicans sloped off with the rest of yore an' Danny's cattle. Gosh, but Danny is sore! They was slick aboot it, when every last person in the country was heah last night. I've a hunch how Sidway got wise to the deal. He's a clever boy, Gene. But how he found oot ain't nothin' to us. The thieves drove the cattle acrost to the valley behind Gray Divide. An' they expect to work them by easy stages down acrost the border. It'd been a cinch but fer Sidway. . . . Wal, he's goin' to locate them, then ride on into town an' get help. In the mawnin' he'll haid the rustlers off in thet narrow valley. Our part is to ride in behind the ridge an' trail them down, keepin' oot of sight. By this time tomorrow I reckon we'll be smokin' them up."

"Hardly, in that open valley," replied Stewart. "They'll see us and slope. Which suits me, though I'd like to throw a scare into them."

"Wal, we'll get the cattle back, an' mebbe thet'll end this two-bit rustlin'.' "

"Nels, as long as westerners raise cattle out on the range there will be stealing."

"Kind of a disease. . . . Look, Gene, heah's the trail, plain as plowed ground. An' there's the track of Sidway's hawse."

"I see. . . . Nels do you remember when I gave my great roan Majesty to Madeline and beat it for Mexico to get myself shot?"

"My Gawd, yes," declared Nels, fervently. "All thet past seems to be gettin' clearer in my memory. . . . Gene, I'll bet Sidway gives Umpqua to Madge."

"Not that cowboy. He's got too much spunk. He's onto Madge," replied Gene, a little sadly.

"Wal, I reckon thet won't make no hell of a difference. There ain't a man in the world who could resist thet girl long."

"If you put it that way," agreed Stewart, pleased with the old cattleman's hint.

Once across the highway the four riders settled down to a steady trot, and in two hours had reached the rocky point of the ridge. They rode around cautiously. The gateway to the valley was wide, and on the ridge side thick with sage and brush.

"Let's hold up heah," suggested Nels, and reined in. "Ren, air you so bleary-eyed yet you cain't see nothin'?"

"Nels, I can see a hawse ten miles an' a steer more'n thet—an' a gurl with a red bonnet twice as fur," declared Starr, swaggeringly.

"All right. Climb up the slope heah an' see if you can spot the cattle down the valley."

"My Gawd!—Climb in these high-heel boots?"

"Come on, Ren. I'll go, too," offered Stewart. They did not ascend the rough brushy slope more than a hundred feet when Starr made good his brag. Then Gene saw a long black band, moving like a snake, down the valley.

"Eight or ten miles?" asked Gene.

"More'n thet, Boss. Jest moseyin' along."

They retraced their steps and reported to Nels. "Wal," said that worthy, "I reckon we better keep travelin'. We want to be on their heels when Sidway haids them back in the mawnin'."

"Ren, don't I remember there's good water down this valley?" asked Gene.

"Shore you do. Nice rocky creek haids aboot where them cattle air now."

"That'll be far enough for us. We'll camp there. . . . Walk your horses and keep your eyes peeled."

They rode on in single file, somewhat separated. The sun rose hot; a flock of buzzards circled high over the locality where the herd moved, indicating death to a calf or heifer. Coyotes slunk through the sage, another indication of meat on the move; the black domes of the Peloncillos sank behind the gray foothills.

Stewart's memory was busy. He recalled his early days with Nick Steele and Monty Price, and others of Stillwell's famous cowboys. And that reminded him of Madeline's brother Al, who had married Florence Kingsley, and had moved to Colorado to take charge of a ranch she had inherited. They had prospered. Stewart wondered if it would not be a good plan to ask financial assistance of Al. Something had to be done as soon as Madge's guests left, or he would lose the ranch. Madge would have to be told of the impending ruin, and Stewart hated the thought. But he must do it. Madge was wonderful, adorable, irresistible, but she was on the wrong track. Hours wore away while Stewart revolved memories and problems and hurts over and over in his mind.

Some time late in the afternoon Stewart and his men arrived at the head of the creek and halted to make camp there. It was an ideal spot, with grass and sage, and cottonwood trees, and dead cedars near by on the slope.

"Wal, I'll boil a pot of coffee," drawled Nels, "an' what with our meat an' biscuits we won't fare so bad."

"Rustle then, for I'm almost asleep this minute," replied Gene.

"We ain't none of us had a damn wink of sleep," added Starr.

"Why, Ren, I had to kick you onmerciful this mawnin," protested Nels.

"Thet wasn't sleep. I was unconscious from Majesty Stewart's punch. . . . Boss, don't you never let thet

248

gurl make thet drink again. My Gawd! if college eddica-
tion is responsible fer thet—wall, when I marry Bonita
an' we hev a dotter, she ain't goin' to get any modern schoolin' atall."

"Ren, your philosophy is sound," declared Stewart,
ruefully after the laugh had subsided. "But it can't be
adopted."

"An' why'n th'ell not?"

"Because these days girls will do as they please
whether they have education or not. They are going to
have equal rights with men."

"Wal, Gene, thet'll make a better world," interposed
Nels.

"Nels, never in yore born days, did you know anythin' aboot wimmen, much less a dotter," observed
Danny pessimistically.

"Dan, do you mean a dotter is a turrible burden?"

"More'n turrible'n awful."

"An' if you had it all to live over again would you
kept single, so you couldn't hev no dotter?"

"I ain't sayin' thet."

"An' you, Gene, would you rather never hev had
Madge?"

"Nels, old pard, ten thousand times no," burst out
Stewart, somehow glad to express himself. "Madge
has been a joy. And will be forever."

"Thar yore talkin'. She's life—beautiful life—an'
thet cain't be perfect."

They talked and had their leisurely and frugal meal
round the little smokeless campfire, while the sun set,
and shadows appeared under the slopes. Stewart made
his bed with saddle and blankets, and scarcely had he
stretched himself when a subtle glue touched his eyelids. Late in the night he awoke, saw Danny replen-
ishing the fire, fell asleep again, to be roused at dawn
by an ungentle boot.

"Come an' get it," said Nels, cheerily. "I've a hunch
we've a day ahaid of us."

Before broad daylight they were on the move. When
the sun arose, Danny and Ren rode up the slope to
locate the cattle, but failed to do so, owing to a project-

249

ing cape that ran down into the valley. This was some miles ahead. Before they reached it Ren sighted dust clouds.

"On the run already," declared Nels.

"Looks like it," admitted Stewart.

"They're pretty far yet, Boss," added Ren.

"Wal, there ain't no use in our haidin' the cattle off, when we want them to come this way."

"No. But how about the rustlers?"

"If they got haided off below, we won't see hide nor hair of them."

They rounded the cape and rode at a trot fully five miles farther before Ren sighted cattle. They were headed up the valley and evidently had been running, but had now slowed down. They rode on, keeping sharp lookout for riders on the slopes, and presently had to take to higher ground to let a scattered herd pass.

"Aboot seven hundred, I'd say," observed Nels. "Reckon thet's all of them. Not winded much. They'll be home tomorrow."

"Wonder where'n hell them rustlers rode?" complained Ren. "I ain't feelin' swell, an' I'd shore like to shoot at somebody."

"Suits me," replied Danny, relieved. "Killing Mexicans even from acrost the border wouldn't set good with my family."

"Danny, we don't know them rustlers was greasers," declared Ren, too casually.

"No. But I was afeared they might be."

Stewart suggested they ride on to meet Sidway, and whoever he had with him. Very soon Ren sighted three riders, whereupon Stewart ordered a halt.

"Lance ain't in thet ootfit," declared Starr, presently. "Say, they see us, an' air ridin' to beat the band."

Stewart was curious about the three horsemen who were evidently in a hurry to reach them. In very short order they arrived, three lean cowboys, ragged and dusty and hard-eyed. Stewart recognized them.

"Howdy, boys. Where's Sidway?"

Stewart thought Sloan's intent eyes searched his with undue fire, and he wondered what was coming.

"Mawnin', all," returned Sloan. "Stewart, you don't 'pear all het up aboot this raid—or nothin'."

"I'm well satisfied, thanks to you boys. Did you get a line on the rustlers?"

"They seen us far off an' bolted. We couldn't make them out."

"All right, that's that. Where's Sidway?" rejoined Stewart, sharply, suddenly sensing some untoward circumstance.

"By now Sidway must be at Cochise's stronghold, guidin' some gangsters who'd kidnaped your girl Madge an' a young fellow."

A blank silence ensued. But amaze did not long obstruct Stewart's faculties. He had sensed catastrophe. Sloan's tan had lost a shade. His eyes smoldered.

Nels flung a clenched hand at him. "Sloan, what you sayin'?"

"Listen, all of you. But don't waste no time restin' here. Come on. Ride close an' let me spill it. . . . Yesterday a little before sundown, Sidway caught up with us on the road to town. He told us about this cattle steal an' asked us to help him haid them back this mawnin'. Me an' the Spencers was glad to help, of course. We made camp jest outside of town. Jest about dusk, Sidway walked in town to get some coffee an' butter. Not long after, but it was dark, a big black car came up, an' Sidway was on the runnin' board. We was held up by two men with machine guns. Then their boss got out an' bought my hawse outfit fer a thousand dollars. They was a gangster outfit an' Sidway 'peared to be on good terms with them. I didn't get wise to the kidnapin' till Miss Madge an' the young feller was dragged out of the car. Then I seen it plain as print. . . . Now, to make it short, one gangster drove the car away, up the range road. Sidway an' us fellers, under them guns, saddled an' packed. Then thet pale-faced gangster ordered me to wait till mawnin', an' notify you to send one man up the Cochise Trail with fifty thousand dollars fer Miss

251

Madge an' the same for the young feller. An' if his orders was not carried out Miss Madge would be raped, an' both of them killed. . . . It was hard fer me to wait till mawnin' but with your telephone wire cut, I couldn't find out if you'd left, an' I knew you'd be comin' along here after the cattle. So here we are."

By the time Sloan had concluded, Stewart's horror had mounted to a ruthless and terrible wrath. Starr's face had grown a leaden white, and he appeared incapable of speech. After a brief paroxysm of emotion Nels interrupted Danny Mains' curses with a terse query: "Gene, what do you make of Sidway?"

"What do you?" countered Stewart, huskily.

"I got it figgered. When he went in town he seen thet car with Madge in it. He must hev been slick enough to scare them kidnapers off the highway, to take to the hills."

Sloan interrupted impatiently: "But, Nels—Stewart, it looked like Sidway was one of thet gang."

"It shore did," corroborated the Spencer boys in unison. "Their boss *knew* him."

"You all think Sidway was in with the gangster?" queried Stewart.

"I'm afraid, sir—we do. Why, we stayed awake half the night talkin' it over. These kidnapers are pretty smart. They take their time. We figger Sidway must have been sent on ahead—planned the job— rode away the day it was done. But we jest couldn't figger this cattle steal in the job at all."

"Sloan, I'll grant it looked that way to you," rejoined Stewart, tersely. "But you don't know Sidway. I tell you the idea is preposterous."

"All right, sir. I only hope an' pray you're right."

Then Ren Starr exploded. "I ought to throw my gun on you," he roared. "Sidway's my pard. He's as true as steel. He *couldn't* be in a deal like this. How in hell he ever got mixed up in it I can't guess, but you bet your life it's damn lucky for the girl an' us. He'll *save* her. An' you'll have to apologize to me fer thinkin' him a crook."

"I'll do thet now, Starr," returned Sloan. "But be reasonable. Things looked queer. Circumstantial evidence, you know. . . . An' Miss Madge!—*she* believed Sidway was one of them. You should have seen her—heard her call him."

"My—Gawd!" gasped Starr, totally overcome by that information.

At last Nels broke silence: "Gene, I knowed thet cowboy would hev his chance. It jest worked oot thet way. An' I'd gamble my bunk in heaven on his honesty, an' his nerve an' sense to beat thet gang. He *knew* we'd be on his trail. Why, the last thing he said was, in case, look fer his tracks. Them gangsters air tenderfeet. Once up in the hills they'll be lost, an' easy fer thet slick cowboy. He'll lay fer his chance, an' as shore as we're right heah he'll hold them somehow till we come, or get away with her, or do something to save her from them."

"Boss, thet's it—one of Nels' hunches," affirmed Starr. "But, my Gawd, we got to rustle!"

"Sloan, you boys will go with us," asserted Stewart.

"You bet your life!"

"Nels, we'll cut off the trail halfway up, and work round to the west side of Cochise's stronghold. We might get there ahead of them. It'll be a drill for tenderfeet. They'll be all in. We've got time. We *must* make it before dark. . . . Now, all of you—ride!"

Riders and horses were wet with sweat, and practically spent when that long climb up the mountain had been accomplished by sundown. A halt was made in the deep forest west of Cochise's stronghold, at a point they all agreed was scarcely a half mile from the clearing.

"Ketch your—breath, fellers," panted Nels, as he removed his chaps.

"Men, in case they're here . . ." began Stewart.

"They air heah," interrupted Nels. "Didn't we foller their tracks over two thirds of thet trail? Didn't Sloan ketch two of his hawses makin' fer home? Sidway

253

would make the gang stop heah, even if it wasn't the logical camp."

"All—right, then," Stewart rasped. "We'll slip up on them. Then what?"

"Stewart, they're gangsters with machine guns. I'd say shoot 'em down on sight."

"Hell, yes," agreed Starr.

"Wal, I don't know," added Nels, ponderingly. "Shore we never—dealt with any of this ilk—before. I'd say hold 'em up. If they don't hold up pronto then bore 'em."

"By all means before they can turn machine guns loose in our direction," replied Stewart, grimly. "But I want to talk to these *hombres* first—and then see them kick at the end of a rope."

"Boss, it's a better idee at thet," agreed Ren, savagely. "But my gun finger is shore itchin'. . . . If we only find—Madge alive an' unharmed."

"We will—shore," declared Nels, passionately. "I may hev lived to be old an' soft, but somehow I gamble on Sidway. He loves thet girl an' he'll ootwit the slickest kidnapers there ever was."

"Nels, that faith has kept me from collapse. Firs' time in my life I've weakened. But it's—my girl!" exclaimed Stewart, low and thick under his breath.

"Come on," ended Nels. "Keep even an' in sight of each other. No noise!"

A pine-thicketed slope led up to the gray crags. They entered the mountain enclosure through a gateway between the huge monuments of stone. The clearing lay beneath Stewart's strained eyes, a green and gold park marked by great pines scattered about, and shining with appalling beauty under the sunset glow. A thin column of blue smoke halfway across made Stewart's heart leap. Ren pointed to a roan horse grazing in the open meadow, and Sloan whispered that it was his horse Baldy.

At a motion from Nels they stealthily began their approach down to the level. Every few rods Nels halted to listen. Stewart could hear only the sough of the wind in the pines, and the murmur of distant running water. The place seemed locked in an unearthly silence.

Suddenly Ren startled Stewart and all of them. He held up a pregnant hand.

"I heah voices," he whispered.

He must have possessed extraordinarily sharp ears, for all of his companions shook their heads. Hardly had they started forward again when the boom of a gun made them statues. They listened with bated breath.

"No forty-five Colt," whispered Stewart.

"Sidway packs a forty-four Smith an' Wesson. Sounded like it," replied Nels. "Come on, we gotta see this."

Before they had taken a dozen swift steps a rattling biting volley halted them.

"*Machine gun!*" whispered Sloan, in great excitement. "Have I heard them? I'm tellin' you!"

The continuous volley appeared to come from their right down the trail. Accompanying the rattling was a swishing cut of bullets through foliage and then a pattering on solid wood. It ceased. And Ren leaped up in the air, trying to see over the green brush.

"Heah 'em?—Hawse hoofs!"

"Shore as Gawd made little apples!" ejaculated Sloan.

Stewart was quick to catch a soft rapid thud of hoofs, a crash of brush, a cracking of dead twigs, then thudding hoofbeats dying away.

"Thet was when, Gene!" hissed Nels, his gray eyes like points of flame, and he motioned them on.

Despite the intense suspense, Nels had the cool judgment to advance very slowly, without the slightest sound. Stewart swallowed his harrowing fears and doubts. Then swift footfalls close in front made him, and all of them, aware of the nearness of the trail. Nels crouched down and stealthily separated the small pines to slip through. Starr followed suit, as did the others to left and right. Stewart saw the roof of the old cabin over the tips of the brush.

"Flemm!" shouted a hoarse voice. "What happened?"

"He crowned me," replied another man, hotly.

"Who? Not Stevens?"

"No. It was that two-timin' cowboy. He lied about seeing horses down the trail. Ruse to get rid of you. Then he beaned me."

"That shot in the cabin?"

"I didn't hear any."

"You know Uhl went in the cabin to the girl?"

"Yes. I saw that."

"Well, there was a shot in there, all right. Sidway went in and bumped Bee off. That's it. For I saw the cowboy come out with the girl in his arms and jump on his horse. I let loose my gun, but I was running—and didn't connect."

The faces of Nels and Ren appeared to shine upon Stewart, a singular transformation from grim dark passion to an ecstasy of gladness. Stewart felt the same so powerfully that he was overcome. But his tremendous relief was counteracted by a hateful query—had Sidway gotten in that cabin in time? Again Stewart's passion to rend and slay dominated him. He crawled softly after the others, until he bumped into them.

They had arrived at the edge of the clearing. Ren's hard hand pressed Stewart's shoulder. Peering through the foliage he saw that they were scarcely fifty yards from the campfire. Two bareheaded young men, with corded livid faces, stood facing each other. Both held machine guns. The taller, a dark-haired individual, was bending his head to the other, no doubt for examination. Beyond them on the ground sat young Stevens, apparently uninjured, but plainly shocked with terror. Then on the moment the gangsters whirled at a piercing shout from the cabin. A third man appeared, a slim-built fellow, with a bloody face. He staggered toward them, a ghastly spectacle, but assuredly instinct with life and desperation. His curses rang through the forest clearing. Then he confronted the astounded gangsters.

"That ——————— fake cowboy shot me . . .

got away with her!" he yelled, wildly. "I'll kill you both— you ———————— hop-heads! What in hell were you doing?"

"He fooled us, Bee," replied Flemm. "Made us believe he saw horses. Sent Fox down the trail. Then he crowned me."

"I wish to God he'd smashed your empty pan!"

"Looks like he emptied yours. Better let us wash you off. Looks like what you used for brains is oozing away."

"It's only blood. He grooved me . . . here . . . Christ, how it burns!—Wipe me off."

Fox laid down his gun and picked up a towel from the pack. He dipped it in a water bucket, and wiped off the blood to disclose to the watchers the visage of a white, hard-faced criminal whose passion and experience seemed greatly beyond his years.

"HANDS UP!" thundered Nels.

"Stick 'em up, gangsters!" rang out Starr's voice.

Uhl and Fox lost not a second in elevating their hands. But Flemm whirled with his machine gun bursting into flame and rattle. Almost instantly his distorted visage went blank and he pitched forward. The machine gun sputtered into the ground, scattering gravel, then fell from the gangster's stretching hands. Stewart saw smoke issuing from Starr's rifle. Then Nels, gun low, ran out, to be followed by the cowboys. Mains came out from the right. When Stewart emerged from the foliage Sloan was disarming the gangsters.

"Heah, gimme thet rope, Spencer," yelped Starr. Receiving it he spread the noose, and pitched it deftly over Uhl's head. The gangster had courage or else he did not get the significance of Starr's move.

"Wait, Ren!" ordered Stewart, and strode over to Stevens. "Are you all right, boy?"

"Yes—sir. I—guess so," faltered Stevens. "Thank God. I was about—dead of fright."

"Sidway made off with Madge?"

"He did, sir, but—but . . ."

"Was she—all right . . . too?" queried Stewart, hoarsely

"I'm afraid—not. . . . I heard her fighting—*him!*" And Stevens pointed a shaking finger at Uhl. "She'd fainted—or was dead—when Sidway got on his horse with her. . . . But, Mr. Stewart—even if she was alive—she's as bad off with him . . . for he's one of —these gangsters!"

"Yeah, that's correct," interposed Uhl, darkly. "Sidway belongs to Cork's snatch gang. He tricked me. He wants the ransom and the girl for himself. I'll get him for that if it costs me a hundred grand."

"Haw! Haw!" burst out Sloan, sardonically.

"Gangster," added Stewart, coldly. "If you knew Westerners you would not concern yourself about that."

Ren Starr confronted Rollie Stevens. "Say, did I heah you make a crack about Sidway bein' one of this outfit?"

"Yes, you did. He's hand in glove with these kidnapers. And he has betrayed them. He's . . ."

"Shet up, you white-mugged college dude! What'd you go to college fer? Haven't you any sense? My pard *saved* the girl."

"You're a thickheaded fool."

"I reckon I'll have to bat you one . . ."

"Hold on, Ren," interrupted Stewart, sternly. "Make allowance for circumstances. It does look strange. But we'll clear it up presently."

The gangster Flemm was dead, shot through the center of the forehead. Stewart ordered Sloan to take charge of the machine guns, and Starr to search the gangsters. Nels stood with his gun on Uhl, and not for many years had Stewart seen such an expression on that lean face. Then Stewart strode to the cabin and went in. There was a pile of spruce brush on the floor, but it had not been disturbed. Searching around Stewart saw tracks of Madge's little feet in the dust, and he could read from them that she had run and fought. He also found a splotch of blood in a depression, where no doubt Uhl had fallen, and had lain

"He was going to kidnap Madge himself," snapped Uhl, but his certainty seemed weakening.

"Your mistake. Why would he want to kidnap her when he's going to marry her?"

That random shot of Stewart's broke down the gangster's stubborn convictions and betrayed the terrible nature of the man. If he were capable of love for a woman, he must have felt it for Madge Stewart. At any rate Stewart decided the gangster had been obsessed with some violent passion for Madge and that an insane jealousy possessed him.

"Marry her—yeah?" he choked out, his face purple, his neck convulsed, his eyes not those of a human. "He's welcome—to the rag—I made her!"

Stewart knocked him flat, but had the self-possession to turn aside Nels' quivering gun. It seemed impossible, however, to control Starr, and suddenly Stewart had no desire to. Starr dragged the gangster to his feet.

"You bastard," he hissed, his visage gray and set. "You'll never live—to brag of thet again!"

"Stand aside, Ren," ordered Nels, piercingly.

"No, Nels, you ain't gonna bore him," shouted Starr, hoarsely. "An' we ain't gonna hang him. We'll hang his pard, an' make him look on, but by Gawd, I owe somethin' to myself heah!"

Starr slipped the noose over Fox's head and jerking it tight he threw the end of the lasso over a sturdy pine branch, and caught it coming down. "Heah, Sloan, an' you Spencers! Get in on this. An', young feller, grab hold of this rope behind me, an' pull, if you're half a man. . . . If you don't I'll beat hell oot of you. . . . PULL! . . . Ahah! Them yells choked off! Yellow clear through! . . . There, tie the end, Sloan."

Stewart averted his eyes, but he could not escape the grotesque jumping-jack shadow on the ground, or the expulsion of breath from the condemned and executioners, the scrape of boots and jangle of spurs, and lastly the incredible spectacle of Stevens hauling on the lasso. For the moment the collegian had answered to primal instincts, and his red visage was as beastly as those of his fellows.

But suddenly Stewart swerved his attention to Uhl. The gangster had watched the hanging of his lieutenant, and his face, his look, his mien were vastly but incalculably transformed from what they had been.

"What do you think of our necktie party, gangster?" demanded Ren, leering at him. "Thet's how we do things in the West. . . . I'm jest damn sorry I cain't hang you an' watch you kick. But yore swagger gets my goat. So Mister Bee Uhl, kidnapin'—bootleggin' gangster gunman, you're gonna go up agin my game!"

"Heah, Ren—none of thet. Hang him," said Nels, speaking for the first time.

"Umpumm, old pard. I wonder you ask it. . . . Where's thet popgun of his?" Ren snatched it up from the pack and held it gingerly in contempt. "What do you think of thet toy, Nels? These guys in the movies shoot through their coat pockets. Okay! . . . Where's his coat?" Starr took that up and slipped the little automatic into the right coat pocket.

Stewart had answered to the same strange antagonistic passion that beset Starr. No doubt Nels also was under his influence or he would have shot the gangster and made an end of the thing. Nels had been a gunman in his day; and later cowboys, who packed and shot guns, were wont to view with contempt the exploits of the modern killers with their automatic and hidden firing. They were simply murderers. An even break was Greek to them. But Ren wanted the test.

"Listen to reason, cowboy," importuned Stewart. "I savvy you. But even a little risk . . ."

"Risk, hell? There won't be none. Anyway, Boss, neither you nor Nels must hev this crook's blood on yore hands."

"What's the difference whether it's you or me or all of us?"

"On account of Madge. An' if you elected to take him to jail—why Sidway would ride down there an' shoot him in his cell. Thet wouldn't do either, Boss."

Nels appeared to be struck mute and Stewart had no ready answer. At that moment Starr reminded Stewart again of Monty Price. The advance of time did not change the hearts of these firebrand range riders.

Starr drew his gun, and kept it in his hand while he helped the gangster into his coat.

"There! . . . Stewart, you fellers get back pronto. . . . Now Uhl, don't move a hand." Starr backed away from him for perhaps twenty feet. "Turn around, Uhl."

The gangster did as he was bidden, exposing a front that was sickening to men who held courage and nerve as Stewart held them. Blood had again begun to stream down the side of Uhl's temple and cheek.

"Ten—grand—if you'll . . ."

"Bah!" interrupted Starr, piercingly. "You're talkin' to an American cowboy." Starr sheathed his gun and held his hand out, his fingers clutching at the air.

"Nels, you give the word. . . . Come on, kidnaper! Let's hev yore game."

"Ready!" rang out Nels. *"Shoot!"*

Stewart's gaze was riveted on the gangster. In a flash he jerked his right hand down into his coat pocket. As the corner of his coat suddenly pointed out to bark and smoke, Starr's gun crashed and in a second again. The gangster's bullet sputtered up dust and gravel. Between the shots his visage underwent an indescribable change, and as he fell the terrible instinct to survive left his body.

Darkness found Stewart and his men around a campfire in another spot, several rods from the cabin. Nels was cooking some supper. And he was speaking:

"Wal, Gene, I cain't see any sense in tryin' to trail Sidway in the dark."

"Hawses all in, Mr. Stewart," interposed Sloan. "We'll have to rest up tonight at least."

Stewart endeavored to subdue his impatience and dread, knowing how right his comrades were.

"Anyway, wait till Red comes back," added Nels,

263

and presently called them to supper. While they were sitting there the cowboy returned. In the campfire light his face showed white and set, without the violence that had distorted it.

"I found Lance's trail," he said, eagerly. "Used my flashlight. He had Ump goin' some when he struck into the trail. But he soon slowed down. I follered the tracks till they turned left off the trail."

"What'll he do?" queried Stewart, sharply.

"Beat it fer home. Thet guy an' thet hoss—nothin' to it, Boss, if Madge is okay."

"Does he know how to get down out of here?"

"Wal, we rode all over when we was up heah."

"Ren, you take his trail at daybreak," suggested Nels.

"Shore. I'd thought of thet. But mark my hunch, Sid will beat us home half a day."

"Set in an' hev a bite."

"Nels, I sorta ain't hungry."

"Wal, eat an' drink anyhow. It's been a tough day."

"You boys go after our horses and hobble them out for tonight. And Sloan, you'll hunt up the rest of your horses tomorrow," asserted Stewart.

"They'll be around close. Seldom thet stock will leave this grass an' water."

Stevens set propped against a pack, with a blanket around him, his hair damp on his pale forehead.

"Rollie, you had a hand in that lynching," said Stewart. "How you feel?"

"Pretty scared—and sick yet," he replied, weakly. "But it—isn't my part in that hanging. That was great."

"Fine. Brace up now. Everything is okay. And we're d——lucky."

Very little was spoken after that and nothing at all about the tragedy. The cowboys brought a pile of firewood to last out the night. Stewart asked one of them to fetch the cut spruce in the cabin, and he made his bed upon that. Starr was the only one who did not smoke. He stood back to the fire, his head bent. Stewart appreciated how he felt. The night wind set up its dirge in the pines and coyotes barked off in the distance. Despite his extreme fatigue Stewart could not sleep at once. The stars seemed to mock his troubled mind.

12

Uhl's striking Madge down had less to do with her collapse than the appearance of Sidway in the cabin, with his darkly stern visage, his deadly voice, and the bursting red boom of his gun.

She did not wholly lose consciousness, for she felt him lift her and wrap her in a blanket and carry her out. More clearly then she heard a string of shots and the spang and thud of bullets all about, and felt herself swung upon a horse, and the violent jars of her body as he plunged away.

A vague, almost blank interval succeeded. When her mind cleared again she was being carried comfortably upon a pacing horse over a level trail. Through the big black pines she saw the stars shining, and then a dim outline of Sidway's face and bare head. That thrilling reality brought back vividly the fight with the gangster, his half stripping her, and the brutal blow he had dealt her, and then Sidway's startling and fatal intervention. Sidway, no matter why, had saved her again, and this time from a horrible fate—an insupportable shame and inevitable death. Her thoughts grew so wildly whirling that she had to disrupt them by talking.

"Lance," she whispered. Apparently he did not hear her.

"Lance! . . . We got away." She felt a strong vibration pass through him.

"Hello! You've come to?" he returned, hastily.

"Yes. But I wasn't altogether out."

"I haven't had time to see. . . . Did he hurt you?"

"Lance, I was holding my own with him—when he struck me. I wasn't afraid of him—till then. . . . I suppose he could have beaten me helpless?"

"Then . . . Uhl didn't—harm you?" queried Sidway, in a halting husky voice.

"No, not outside the blow. Lance! You—*killed* him?"

"Yes."

"You *saved*—me?"

"Yes."

"From something hideous. He never meant to let me go for ransom. He'd have kept me. . . . Merciful heaven! What an idiot I was—to flirt with Honey Bee Uhl!"

"It takes a lot to cure some girls' egotism," returned Sidway with an intonation she could not define. He seemed far removed from her, somehow.

"I'm cured—Lance."

"Listen, baby!—Excuse me. I fell into Uhl's way of speech. . . . The day will never come when you won't look at a man."

"But for goodness sake! I have eyes. I can't hang my head—never look."

"A look from *your* eyes is enough."

"Yeah?—For what?"

"To incite a man to madness—kidnaping—outrage—murder."

"Oh!—Not a *real* man. What do you mean?"

"I mean, Miss Stewart, that whether you have guilty intent or perfect innocence, when you look at men with those eyes, you play hell."

"I observe, Mr. Sidway, that my marvelous eyes failed to play hell with you," she returned, sarcastically.

"Only because I was wise to you."

Madge had no quick retort for that, mainly because there seemed some hope for her with this young man of dual nature. They rode along the trail in silence. But she watched him from between narrowed eyelids. If she had not been spent and in pain she would have found this situation vastly intriguing. At length Umpqua exchanged his pacing gait for a walk. Evidently the mountain clearing had been passed. Presently Sidway turned off the trail to the left, and had to pick his course. The forest gradually grew less dense, and therefore lighter. Thickets of pine and spruce reached above Sidway's head, and in places had to be carefully threaded. It became evident to Madge that they were traveling downhill. At length the cowboy halted as if undecided how to proceed.

"Lost?" inquired Madge.

"I'll tell the world," he replied, with a queer laugh.

"I'd just as soon you made a halt till morning. I'm about done for."

"My idea exactly. . . . Soon as I hit a level spot."

He zigzagged down the slope for a while, and eventually stopped, to slide out of the saddle. Madge could not help feeling that he handled her as if she were a child. He set her down, back against a tree, which Madge observed to be a cedar. There were still big pines about, but scattering, and the presence of cedars denoted lower altitude.

"I'm freezing to death," she said.

He stripped the horse and haltered him to a sapling. Then from his saddle he untied a blanket, and other trappings. This he doubled and wrapped around her. Then he tore sheaths of bark off the cedar, and snapped twigs and dead branches, with which he started a fire not far from her feet. The crackling of wood and leaping of red flame changed the moon-blanched gloom. While Madge stretched her hands to the heat, Sidway opened a saddlebag.

"Here's some meat, biscuits, dried apples, and a piece of chocolate. . . . Yes, and a little salt. Are you hungry?"

"I could go for a *filet mignon* in a big way."

"Daresay you could. Sorry I can't furnish one."

"Very well. I'll have a biscuit and a piece of meat. . . . Thanks. Where are we, Lance?"

"Up in the Peloncillos."

"How far from that camp?"

"Miles, I'd say."

"I wish you could have gotten Rollie away from them."

"Well, I expect trouble enough, without your boy friend."

"Trouble?—You'll not have any with me," she returned, all at once cognizant again of the double role he played. "Lance, you're after that ransom yourself!"

In the light of the fire she saw a dark tide sweep across his face. His somber eyes regarded her as if somehow she had recalled to him her true character. He let out a mirthless laugh.

"You guessed it, Majesty," he replied, grimly.

"I will gladly pay you. . . . What will those gangsters do with Rollie? His people are rich. They will pay. But it'll take time. Meanwhile Dad and Nels will be on the rampage. That demand of Uhl's will drive him crazy. He can't pay it. I'll bet they are on our trail now."

Sidway had averted his face and he made no reply, facts that excited Madge's speculation. Suddenly a wild conviction bore crushingly upon her. *"Lance!* Ransom or no ransom—you mean to—to keep me?"

"You sure are some guesser," he declared, bitterly.

"My—God!—You can't—be so low."

"Men as a rule are pretty bad *hombres.* Don't you think you deserve it?"

"Yes—yes! Oh, I've been a heedless, vain and selfish thing! . . . But, Lance, I—I haven't been rotten . . ."

"Are you telling me?" he queried, turning his back on her.

"Yes, I am. I never. . . . Oh, what you must think me! . . . Lance Sidway, you killed that devil Uhl just so you could have me—take me yourself?"

268

"You said it, baby."

"Don't call me *that*. I'll hate you."

"I thought you did already."

"I didn't. But I shall."

"Okay by me. More sport if I have to beat you."

"Beat me! You've already done that."

"Miss Stewart, I think you hit me first."

"Yes I did. For the dirtiest remark any fellow ever dared make to me."

"Struck me at the moment as strictly merited."

"Oh, the way we quarrel! It gets my goat! . . . What do you intend to do with me?"

"You're so damn smart—why don't you tell me?"

"I can . . . You've fallen for this temptation, Lance Sidway. Too much easy money in sight! And a chance to get even with me . . . I suppose you'll tie me in a cave—starve me—beat me . . . till you get that money."

"I declare," he interrupted, as she choked over her words, "you grow better all the time. Wise girl! College girl, you know!"

"Oh, damn!—Lance Sidway, you'll have to marry me!"

She might have struck him, judging by his shrinking start. "I'll refuse to pay that ransom or move out of my tracks unless you swear you'll marry me."

"Very well, if you think that important," he returned, in a queer voice.

Madge, in the wildness of that agitation, thought she must make the best of a bad bargain. She loved him, whether he was a crook or a cowboy, a Dr. Jekyll or Mr. Hyde, a strange combination of virtue and vice. It ran through her mind that he could not forever stay immune, that she could win his love, and reform him. That might be the retribution meted out to her for her imperious and willful ways. After all he had saved her. She could not hate him. If he beat her she would fight back, and perhaps, womanlike, love him the more for his brutality. There was a queer streak in her, she feared, or at least one strongly primitive.

"You are fagged out," he said, presently turning. "I'll make a bed for you."

He broke an armful of cedar brush, laid it flat, and put a saddle blanket on that. Then he arranged his saddle for her head. As she moved over, half crawling, the folded blanket fell, and the one wrapped around her half slipped off. Madge made no great haste to wrap it around her again.

"What's the odds?" she said, moodily. "You've seen me almost naked twice." And she lay down to stretch out wearily, her eyes upon him as he bent to cover her with the extra blanket. She made the discovery then that if the moonlight did not deceive her, his face was white.

"Now it's settled, let's talk . . ."

"What's settled?" he interposed.

"Why, I suppose you'd vulgarly call it my hash. . . . I intend to make up for the ruin I unwittingly brought upon Dad and Mom. I suppose you'll block that."

"Too late! I'll need the money."

"But you needn't be a hog. You seemed to like them. Can't you be sport enough to let me make amends?"

"Sure, I liked Gene. And your mother is . . . swell! . . . But they won't need the money after you've gone."

"Mr. Sidway, when you were snooping over my securities and bankbooks, did you get a line on what I was worth?"

"I did, you bet. It used to be about a million!"

"Yes. But that won't do you much good now. I can sell my pearls and other jewels for a hundred grand—as your gangster pards call it. I'll do that on one condition only. You let me split with Dad and Mom!"

"Okay! Fifty grand will do for our honeymoon—at least until the dicks get me.

"Oh, you were wanted by the police even before this," cried Madge, despairingly. Then she grew enraged and flung at him: "How can you be so—so fine —so— Oh, so many things, and still be such a beast."

"Mystery of life, baby," he retorted. "How can you

270

be so sweet—have such an angel face—such soulful, eloquent, lovely eyes—such a winning way with everyone, when at heart you are just no damn good?"

"You've about convinced me," she said, darkly. "Perhaps this will either kill or cure me. . . . But beating me, as no doubt you will, depriving me of the home I'd just begun to love, packing me off like this to misery and—and God knows what else—perhaps it'll reform me. . . . Yes? No?"

"I wouldn't limit your possibilities any more than I'd believe one word you said," he returned, passionately.

"We're certainly two of a kind," she retorted. "But let's not be fourflushers. If you're not big enough to reform yourself, and me, then be big enough to be outright bad. And not a two-faced liar such as you are!"

That stinging speech appeared to wither him. Presently he began to gather firewood and pile it conveniently. Madge had an intense curiosity in regard to him, and tried hard to keep awake. But she was utterly exhausted, and felt her eyelids falling again and again until they shut for good. She seemed scarcely to have slept any time at all when she was awakened. Sidway was shaking her, and not gently.

"Are you dead?" he called, with something besides impatience.

"Oh!" . . . The gray dawn, the piercing cold, the ghostly pines quickly regulated her bewildered senses to actuality. "*Buenos dias,* darling. No, I'm not dead —yet."

"Don't call me that," he almost shouted, most unreasonably. "I'm liable to slap you good."

"Well, you put one black and blue brand on me. Why not another?"

"Get up. Move around. Eat something," he ordered, peremptorily.

Madge found the first desperately hard to accomplish, and the second no easy matter, and the third impossible. Her hands were numb and her feet blocks of ice, until she almost burned them in the fire. Sidway went off somewhere in to the woods, presumably to hunt his horse. Madge could easily have escaped from him then. But that would have been absurd, even if she had wanted to. She walked away from the fire and back again, and presently found that exercise relieved both cold and cramp. At length the cowboy returned with his horse, which he saddled and bridled.

"You'll have to ride," he said, brusquely.

"Thanks. You're very kind to your squaw—darling."

"But not in that blanket. Here, put on my coat."

"No. You'll need that yourself. I can ride with this blanket around me. Only my hands and feet are cold now."

"Warm them pronto, while I tie these things on."

When presently Madge mounted into the saddle she found the stirrups had been shortened to fit her. Without a word Sidway took hold of the reins and led Umpqua down the slope. He took long strides and a slanting zigzag course, down through the cedars. Broad daylight had come and gradually the nipping air and the frost lessened. Madge kept her hands in the folds of the blanket and endured the acute pain of cold feet. Gray shaggy foothills appeared to surround them; the heads of ravines slanted down between these, to widen into narrow valleys; through the trees Madge sometimes caught glimpses of a hazy void. When the sun rose it appeared to be in the wrong direction to her, and if her calculation was correct, Sidway was taking her down across the border into Mexico. He never spoke, never glanced back at her, but strode on, down and ever down, like a man who was lost and did not know nor care where he was going.

Madge's thoughts did not change materially from those which had had their inception in the dark hours of the night before. She could not save herself, or help herself, and any romance or thrill she might conjure up were welcome. In the sunlight of day, however, her disappointment in Sidway and her disillusion grew more bitter hourly. She felt her strength failing, and a consequent gloom and sadness wore on her antagonistic and unquenchable spirit. The time came when she would not have cared what happened, if she could only rest. The cedar trees gave place to brush, which offered no protection from the sun, now climbing high and growing unendurably hot.

"Lance, I'm—spitting cotton," said Madge, at last breaking silence. "Must have—a drink."

"So am I. But hang on. I see green willows below. There's water."

When at last Sidway found water it was none too soon for Madge. There was nothing to drink out of and Madge said if she got off the horse she could not climb back. Whereupon the cowboy, regardless of the fact that she had let the hot blanket slip down, lifted her out of the saddle, and after she had slaked her thirst, he put her back. Madge had never known before the sweetness and life in cold pure water. There were many things she had never appreciated.

Sidway led on tirelessly, always down, but it appeared to Madge that the slopes were less precipitous and the zigzags far longer. She grew so weary that she sagged and swayed in the saddle, and so hot she wanted to fall off and perish, and so miserable that she had hardly strength left to hold the remnants of her garment around her. Nevertheless she woul have endured more before entreating him to find some shade and let her rest. She hated him now. She could have killed him. To make her love him hopelessly and terribly, to heap the shame of her horrible selfishness upon her head were indeed enough, without adding this endless insupportable ghastly ride. Madge clutched the pommel and her blanket with sore and hot hands, and sat with closed and burning eyes, wearing to collapse. Minutes or hours dragged by until she seemed not to feel any more. Still she was aware when the horse stopped.

"Look, Madge!" rang out Sidway's voice.

Madge seemed impelled by more than his command. Opening her eyes she saw that they had halted upon a promontory, a level summit of the last foothill. A blue and gray range land not far below, clear and

273

close in the sunlight, appeared to leap up at her. Across its sage-spotted floor moved a long line of cattle, wearily wending their way. Like a black ribbon some miles out stretched a road with speeding automobiles, flashing sunlight from their glass windows. And beyond, over the blue sage loomed a green timbered knoll, from the top of which, half concealed, peeped a white ranch house that Madge knew.

"The cattle herd you see working back belong to you father and Danny Mains," said Sidway, imperturbably.

"That's the highway! . . . there's—my home!" faltered Madge, fighting a sudden dizziness.

"Thought you'd recognize it," he drawled, lighting a cigarette. "I'm sure tickled with the way I came straight down, in a swell short cut, from Cochise's stronghold."

"Lance!" She could not hear her own voice.

"Okay. What now?" But he never turned to look at her.

"You're taking—me *home?*"

"Certainly, you poor fish!"

"You're not—what I took you for?—Liar—two-faced—cowboy—kidnaper . . . gangster?"

"No, Miss Stewart. I hate to disillusion you—spoil your pipe dream. It's just too bad, for you're such a swell romancer. You concoct such lovely things about me and my motives. But they didn't pan out, as you see."

"Oh, my—God!—Then you didn't kill Uhl—to—to abduct me, but—but to save me?"

"Right. Your comprehension is at least encouraging. You may be a bright girl yet."

"You don't want—a ransom?"

"Madge Stewart, I'd starve to death before I'd accept a dollar of your money."

"Oh—oh—I . . . What you've done—for me, for Dad and Mom! . . . And I?—Oh, how little—how miserable—you've made me! Oh, the shame! . . ."

Uttering a sharp cry she swayed in the saddle.

"Madge! Hang on!" she felt pierce her fading sense, and then, as she fell into his arms, all went black.

When Madge recovered consciousness she found that Sidway was carrying her in front of him, and traveling at a fast pace across the range. Only vague thoughts accompanied her sensations of faintness and pain, and these faded. Then she went through stages of sleep or semiconsciousness, until at last she recovered sufficiently to make out that it was sunset and that she was almost paralyzed.

"Lance . . . how far?" she shispered.

"Almost home," he replied, cheerily. "I'm glad you came to . . . Brace up now. So you won't scare hell out of your mother and the girls. . . . Here, I'll have to wrap you up again, for you're sure in a state of nature."

"Oh—you cowboy!" And she turned in his arm, to sink against his shoulder, reviving anew to life and pain and love, and realizing that there would be nothing worth living for without him. Wide-eyed she lay there, her cheek against his hot dusty vest. They began to climb and entered the pines. A little later Sidway halted the horse in front of the house and yelled: "Hello, inside! It's Sidway! . . . And here's Madge all in, but okay!"

He stepped off with her in his arms, and mounting the porch, encountered a group of wild screaming and questioning boys and girls, and behind them her white-faced mother and the servants.

"Mrs. Stewart, she's *all* right," Sidway assured her. "Let go, girls." He carried her into the house and to her rooms, finally to lay her down on her bed. *"There!"* he ejaculated, poignantly, and straightened up as the others flocked in, eager and wide-eyed, all talking at once.

"Mom!" And that was all Madge could say as her mother knelt to envelop her in loving arms. But she gazed with blurred eyes up at the faces of her friends, crowded around the bed. It was a little while before Madge could answer coherently.

"Mother!—Darling! I'm well—and safe. You're to

thank Sidway for that. . . . I'm just done up. Oh, what an adventure! . . . About Rollie?—I don't know—I don't know. . . . Lance, tell them what it's all about."

Sidway turned away from the window. "Stevens was all right when we left. I'm sure Stewart with his men will have rescued him by now. They'll be back tonight, or tomorrow surely."

"Rescued!" they all cried in unison.

"We were kidnaped," whispered Madge. "Rollie and I went down to the village. That gangster Uhl!— I *knew* him. I'd met him in Los Angeles. He'd found out where I lived. He and his gang kidnaped us . . . And that night Sidway bobbed up—to perform another miracle. He also knew Uhl—and he fooled Uhl —tricked him to leave his car—and ride into the mountains. . . . Lance was the guide—and I thought —but never mind that. He led us up—to Cochise's stronghold. Uhl had sent word to Dad to—pay ransom. . . . Uhl meant to—to . . . he was vile—and Lance had to *kill*—him—to save me! . . ."

Sidway interrupted the chorus of wondering and awed exclamations. "Her voice is gone. Stop making her talk, and fetch her something to drink," he said, hastily. "Mrs. Stewart, Madge is naturally excited about all this." He briefly outlined the history of the adventure, ending, "Now, it's a sure bet that Sloan joined Stewart and they cut loose after us. I think you may expect them back with Stevens by tomorrow."

"Sidway, how can we ever thank you for this?" exclaimed Madge's mother, fervently. "What a relief! . . ."

"Mom, don't let him leave!" cried Madge, frantically, as Sidway started out. "He'll ride away . . . and never—let me thank him."

"Why, child!—Sidway would not do that."

"Wouldn't he? Much you know! . . . Lance, promise me . . ."

Then the girls added their entreaties to hers, until Sidway, red of face, assured them he wanted only to go down to his bunkhouse to clean up, and that he would come back.

"You'll have supper here," added Mrs. Stewart.

At this juncture Barge elbowed his way to Madge's bed with a silver flask, and a glass.

"Nothing doing!" cried Madge, her voice still weak. "I'm on the wagon—for good. . . . Get me some water first—then hot coffee. . . . And I'm starved."

But despite the assiduous attention of her friends and mother Madge could not keep awake very long. She slept until late the next day, to find that a relaxation had set in from her strenuous and harrowing experience. She was too weak to get out of bed. Allie, who had slept with her, told Madge she had never before looked so lovely and languid and fascinating.

"That bruise, though—I think you'd better hide it," added her worshipful friend.

"Not on your life!" retorted Madge. "That's where Bee Uhl socked me. . . . It might serve to soften the heart of a certain callous and soulless person."

"Majesty! . . . Is it *that* bad?"

"Oh, Lord!—Allie, it's terrible. A million times worse than before—before . . ."

"Before what?" whispered Allie, intensely excited.

"Before he slapped me the night of my party. Oh! wait till you get an earful of that. . . . Before he saved my life. . . . Before I took him for a gangster and a crook—and God only knows what else I called him! . . . Allie darling, I'm terribly afraid it's hopeless."

"Moron! Of course it will be, if you persist in this inferiority complex. But if you *get* to HIM . . ."

The other girls trooped in, clad in colorful pajamas and slacks, and made much of Madge. The boys hung at the door and out in the patio, and then her mother entered. Madge, for once in her life, was coddled and nursed, and paid enough compliments to last a month. But the one person Madge wanted most to see did not present himself. She was too proud, too hurt to ask for him. Why could he not be kind enough to come to see how she fared after the long ride? No doubt Sidway was anxious for the return of Stewart and the others. Madge hardly expected them so soon, and not at all without Rollie Stevens. Late in the afternoon, however, when gold shafts from the setting sun filtered through the foliage at her window, Madge was greatly excited to learn that Rollie had returned safely.

"Drag him in—no matter how he looks," cried Madge, who knew Rollie's weakness.

"He's a sight," replied Nate. "But we'll get him."

Presently there was a merry hubbub outside. Then Rollie came in, supported between Nate and Snake Elwell. Allie, who sat beside Madge on the bed uttered a shriek. Madge was too overcome for mirth. The collegian's appearance presented grim evidence of the hardship and fright he had suffered.

"Oh, Rollie!—I'm so—so glad! . . ." burst out Madge.

"I'm glad myself, especially to see you home safe. . . . That blighter turned out a hero instead of what you and I took him for?"

"Yes, Rollie."

"He's one swell fellow—I'll tell you," gulped Stevens, galantly.

"But, *Dad!*"

"Your father is all right, Majesty. He's coming up, with Sidway. The boys drove me. . . . Excuse me now, Majesty. I'm a mess."

Then, as Rollie left, Dawson Metcalf called in at the door. "Steady, Madge! Hold everything! Here come your dad and the hero!"

The clinking of spurs on the stone patio path sent strange little shivers all over Madge. She squeezed Allie's hand and she felt her heart weakly swell in her throat. Then her father entered her room, followed by someone Madge saw only vaguely. Sight of her father stalking in, dusty in his rider's garb, dark of visage, somehow recalled Madge's earliest memories. What a piercing gaze he bent upon her! Never had she met his eyes like that. What thought had been in his mind?

After that strange look, his eyes and face softened, and he held her shaking hands and kissed her.

"Well, lass, I'm happy to see you safe at home," he said, with deep feeling.

"Oh—Dad!" And Madge sat up to cling to him and hide her face. There was more than the aftermath of her adventure in her instinctive action. Had she nearly lost him?

Stewart laid her back upon the pillow. "You're pretty white, Madge. And that's a nasty bruise on your temple. How'd you get that?"

"Honey Bee Uhl paid his respects—that way." Her eyes fastened upon Sidway, who stood at the foot of her bed, looking with grave eyes down upon her. It was not only his clean shave and change of garb that made him look so different. Madge thought she had never seen him so handsome, so fine, so disturbing to her heart and mind. She had wit left to realize that she should control her spoken thought, but so great an emotion that she did not care what she said. Her remorse seemed insupportable.

"Lance," she said, beseechingly, "come here—beside Allie—and let me thank you."

"What for?" he asked, smiling.

"Well, saving me from Uhl—killing him, for *one* thing."

"Madge, you and I were mistaken. I didn't kill him."

"No!"

"Daughter, though you both thought so, Sid isn't responsible for that," interposed her father. "Or I either. It was Ren Starr. That cowboy seemed unusually wild, even for him. Effect of that punch you served the other night! . . . Well, Ren shot Flemm when he held them up. That gangster turned on us with his machine gun spitting fire. Then Uhl came out of the cabin, all bloody. Sid's bullet had grooved his scalp. I had some words with Uhl. He was a queer duck, quite beyond me. While Nels held a gun on him, Ren and the other boys hanged the third gangster. And they forced your college boy friend to help. What do you think of that?"

"Heavens!—Rollie help hang a man—even a gangster who had kidnaped *me?*"

"It's a fact. He pulled on the lasso like a regular cowboy."

It would have been extremely embarrassing then for Rollie, had he been present, to hear the outburst.

"We intended to hang Uhl, of course," resumed her father, presently. "But Ren wouldn't hear of it. He forced Uhl to fight—gave him his gun and an even break. Killed him, Madge! . . . Well, I've told the sheriff all about it, and that lets us out. . . . Madeline," said Stewart, addressing his wife, who had come in to stand with Sidway, "it's a good thing this sheriff is not like Pat Hawe, my enemy sheriff of our early years here. . . . And to conclude, we will have out cattle back in another day. All's well that ends well. Let's forget it."

"But, Dad," said Madge, her voice soft and low, "it—hasn't ended well, yet."

"How come? Sure it has."

"I haven't thanked Lance," rejoined Madge, turning the full battery of her eyes upon Sidway, knowing she did so, but deeply sure of her sincerity.

"Well, do so, then," declared Stewart, with a laugh, as he arose.

"I don't need—want to be thanked," said Sidway, with inscrutable eyes upon her.

"Darling!—I . . ."

"There! Let that do," interrupted Sidway, holding up an appealing hand. "It's an inconsequential word for you, Madge. You call your friends 'darling,' both boys and girls. You call Nels and Ren darling, and your parents, even your horses. So, evidently it's just a convenient word that places the lucky one within the charmed circle of your intimates. I accept that gratefully as your thanks for my little service. And it's enough."

Madge stared up at him while the others laughed

and made mirth out of it. What a speech for Lance Sidway! He was keener, wittier than she had ever realized. Had he the faintest conception of her remorse? Could not the cool smiling enigma see how she regarded him? There came a culminating rush to Madge's uncontrollable emotion.

"Beloved!" flashed Madge, with a passionate defiant eloquence. "Is that less impersonal?" she added trying to make her tone flippant although she felt her face burn red.

Sidway appeared very far from being prostrated by that exquisite epithet. Turning to her father he spread wide his hands: "Gene, I told you she is flighty. Out of her head! I noticed it yesterday toward the last of the ride. No girl ever pulled a gamer stunt. That night ride up on the mountain, then half another night down, then all day in the hot sun—why, it was a grand performance. Not to say fighting off that thug in between! It's no wonder she's cracked under the strain. . . . I think we all ought to get out of here. She needs rest, nursing, quiet."

"Right you are, Sid. Come, beat it, all of us, except one or two of the girls to care for her."

They filed out, except Allie and Maramee, who piled back upon the bed. Someone shut the door.

"Oh hell!" cried Madge, wildly. "Was there *ever* such a man? . . . So I've cracked!"

"Majesty," murmured the incorrigibly romantic Maramee. "It's the most delicious love story there ever was in all the world."

Madge made the following day a quiet and recuperative and thoughtful one. Her guests were due to leave next day and she felt that she would be both sorry and relieved to see them go. The truck loaded with baggage departed early the following morning. And at one o'clock three cars took aboard a hysterical bevy of girls and a merry wisecracking complement of boys. Farewells were prolonged. And at last, when it seemed all had been said, Bu Allen hailed the somber Sidway in a high-pitched penetrating voice.

"Lance, old darling, if Snake Elwell gives me the gate, I'm coming back to go for you in a big way."

That sally elicited a roar of mirth, in which Lance had to join. Madge's rather weak response was a little insincere.

"But, old red-top, that will be swell," retorted Sidway.

"Cowboy, you don't think anyone else around here has a look-in with you?" went on Beulah, demurely anxious, with a sly glance at Madge standing big-eyed and disconsolate on the porch.

"Not a chance, Bu."

Then with a chorus of: "We'll be seeing you!" they were off. Madge watched the cars wind into the green pines and disappear down the slope.

"That's over," she said, with a sigh.

Sidway, with Nels and Ren, had slipped away unobserved. There were tears in her mother's eyes. Her father bent an abstracted gaze below, watching to see the cars come out from under the slope.

"Darlings, let's get it over," said Madge, and locking arms with her parents she led them in.

"Get what over?" queried Stewart, with a start, and her mother looked suddenly concerned.

"Now, Dad! Don't try to fool your little Madge." Forthright then, she plunged abruptly into a confession of how it had come about that Sidway had told her of the impending ruin, if she did not retrieve the situation. She tried to spare the cowboy, but not herself. The quarrel they had had, and the vicious slap she had given him, surely justified him in losing his temper to bitterly flay her.

"You slapped that cowboy, Madge?" queried Stewart in surprise and concern.

"I'll say I did. You may have observed his cut and swollen lip."

"Yes. . . . What did Sidway say to that?" asked her father curiously.

"He slapped me back."

"No!"

"I thought he'd jar my teeth out of their sockets. But I hit him back with all my might. Then he said he refused to let me make a cat and dog fight out of it. . . . Well, that, of course, happened before he told me where to get off. . . . Dad, dear—Mom darling, this pass that my extravagance and stupidity—and selfishness—have brought you to, has almost broken my heart. I shall make amends. I'll pay it all back. I've wired L. A. and New York, too. I can raise a hundred grand on my jewels. I don't need them. . . . Dad, will that money save us, with plenty to spare?"

"It would—lass," he replied, a little huskily, and his arm tightened round her.

"Madge, dearest," spoke up her mother, her poise for once broken. "I *knew* you would do just this. If Gene had let me tell you long ago!"

"Dad was trying me out, Mom. It's settled then. . . . I've had a ghastly lesson. I'll make up for it, my darlings. . . . Dad, I never could hope to be your ideal western girl, nor ever in Mom's class as a lady of quality, but I can be a square shooter and I will be."

"Lass, we might argue over that western girl idea," returned Stewart, his dark eyes alight. Her mother folded her in loving arms, and by these simple things Madge seemed to grasp a great joy that had almost eluded her.

"Oh, yes, Dad . . . there's one other thing," said Madge, turning in her mother's arms. She essayed to be composed and casual, with dubious success. "Can I rely on you—on your keeping Sidway here? He— I. . . . At least I can thank him—reward him some-how."

"Madge, I don't think that'll be at all difficult," replied Stewart, but he did not make clear whether he meant keeping Sidway there or rewarding him.

"I'm almost—happy again," said Madge, yielding to tears, "but still feel kind of wobbly and I'd better —lie down."

"It might be a good idea to talk that matter over

with Nels," added Stewart, smiling. "He and Sid are thick as hops."

Madge fled, yearning to ask just what matter her father meant, but she did not dare. How perilously close was she to betrayal of her secret! Her father's evasive eye and significant words, her mother's softened face and restrained sympathy—these were hard to resist. But Madge had a little pride and spirit left. In her room, which had again taken on its old tranquillity and speaking silence, she salvaged something of her old self.

Next morning, biding her time, until she had seen Lance and Ren ride away, Madge waylaid Nels in his bunkhouse.

"Wal, Majesty! I shore was wonderin' when you'd remember your old Nels."

"Darling, I've never forgotten you," she said, tenderly. "It's just that I've been knocked out—and lots on my mind. . . . And I knew when I *did* see you I'd have to talk turkey."

"Aboot who, lass? Wal, I reckon I know. An' it's aboot high time."

"Nels! He's not leaving?" queried Madge, hurriedly.

"Wal, he talks aboot it a lot. An' he's purty sad these days. Ren rags him all the time aboot you. Lance says he'll stay till Ren an' Bonita air married."

"Oh, Nels! Is that settled?"

"It shore is. An' Ren is one dotty cowboy."

"I'm happy over it. . . . Oh, what shall I give them? It must be something wonderful."

"Wal, lass, if I had my say, I'd want to see another marryin' pretty pronto."

"Nels!—You're so sudden. Have a heart! . . . You mean. . . ."

"Lass, I'm confessin' something'," replied Nels, earnestly. "I'm gettin' along—close to seventy. An I've had a long full life. Lately my heart has been warnin' me thet I might not hev long to be heah. An' I couldn't go satisfied an' happy if you wasn't . . ."

"Oh, Nels!—Don't! don't!" implored Madge, poignantly, and she flew to throw her arms around his neck and lay her face against his hollow bristling cheek. Don't think such a thing—It'd break my heart.— Nels, you're my second dad. You taught me everything. . . . You must not go away—and leave me."

"Wal, honey, I reckon there ain't any reason to be onduly scared. I was jest preparin' you. . . . An' thet fetches me to the somethin' nearest my heart. It's this turrible love affair between you an' Lance."

"Turrible one-sided. . . . Yes," choked out Madge, hiding her face.

"One-sided?—Not onless you don't love him."

"Oh, dear old Nels!" was all she could say, clinging to him.

"Majesty, the boy is dyin' fer you. He's got it wuss than I ever seen any boy in all my life."

"How do you know?" she cried, desperately.

"Wal, a blind man could see. But, lass, I'll give him away—double-cross him—if you say his case is not hopeless."

"Nels—darling . . . it's not—*quite* hopeless," she whispered.

"Aw, thet's fine!—Wal, Lance has told me time an' again, an' this last time, the other night, he jest cried in his misery. It seems you hurt him turrible by believin' he was a gangster—a kidnaper—an' Gawd know what. . . . Lass, I cain't understand how you— so smart a girl—could ever make thet mistake."

"I did!" I'm not smart. But I know *now*—and *that's* killing me."

"Wal, he's the finest youngster yore Dad an' me ever met. Thets all of thet. An' he loves you so much he suffers awful. I could tell you the things he does thet'd make you ashamed an' sorry. But this is enough. He told me thet he loved you so much he couldn't stay heah an' he couldn't leave. Now Majesty, I've told you—I've betrayed him. What do you say?"

"I can't say—much—when—I—I'm crying. . . . But I—I love him more—than he loves me—and I'm dying of longing—and shame. . . ."

285

"Thet's enough, lass," interrupted Nels, vastly disturbed by her weeping. "It's gonna be all right. . . . What you must do is be clear enough to break his pride. He's stubborn as a mule."

"Break his pride! You mean—make him confess—he loves me?"

"Sartin I mean thet. An' you've gotta do somethin' onheered of an' powerful sweet thet won't give him no chance on earth."

"Nels, I'll do—anything," cried Madge, wildly. "But what?"

"Wal, thet's more than I can tell. You'll hev to figger thet yourself."

"I'll do anything—anything . . ." Madge repeated.

"Wal, thet makes me happy," burst out the old cattleman. "Majesty, run home now an' cudgel yore pretty haid fer a grand idee. Somethin' onheerd of—turrible lovin'—amazin' an' sweet thet won't give Lance no chance atall. An' spring it on him pronto."

"You darling old match-maker—*I will*," promised Madge, and almost blind with ecstasy, she ran away, up into the solitary pines.

After dinner that night, during which she had been rapturously gay, to the wonder and delight of her parents, Madge put on one of her flimsiest, most shimmering gowns, with high-heeled white slippers to match. Wearing a long dark coat over this she stole forth upon what seemed to her the most momentous and thrilling venture of her life.

She went by the patio and down through the pines by the trail. At this hour she knew Nels, her father perhaps, and surely the cowboys, would be at the store. As if by magic all her old imperious confidence, tempered this time by a secret humility and gratitude and love, returned in full force. She could not lose, and that gave a tremendous zest to her venture.

Her blood raced with her thoughts and her heart throbbed high as she gained the level, and like a shadow glided across to the bunkhouses. Lance's was next to that occupied by Nels. She tiptoed down the porch, close to the wall until she came to Lance's open door. The yellow lights of the store cast a glow out upon the open. She heard low voices and Sidway's laugh. That gave her pause. Could he be so deeply and miserably in love, as Nels had sworn, and laugh like any other fancy-free cowboy? What if that sly Nels had framed her? The thought was terrible. But nobly she cast it aside as unworthy of a chastened and humble girl. Anyway the die was cast.

Madge took off her clicking high-heeled slippers and stole into Lance's room and laid aside the long coat. Feeling around for his chair she found it and curled up in it, shaking with excitement. Presently she dimly espied her picture on his table, and that overjoyed her.

It was done. She was there, in his room. Beyond Lance's finding her there she had not thought. This was far enough. Of all the things in the world, this was the last Lance Sidway would think of. It did not matter much what he did, when he found her there, unless he took her by the heels and dragged her out. He was capable of that, Madge thought.

Voices and jingling spurs enjoined silence. The men were approaching. Madge would have preferred that Lance came alone. For a moment she fought a wild need to laugh. How her blood was gushing through her veins!

Heavy footfalls upon the porch jarred the log cabin. Madge sat as quietly as a mouse, her heart pounding. She hoped Lance would not come to his room while the other men were in the bunkhouse. Still, no matter! She did not care what happened. Nels had cured her malady. She had all the cards in her hands.

The men, apparently three in number, filed into Nels' room.

"Strike a light, Nels," said Stewart.

"It's pretty darn warm," rejoined Sidway. "I won't light my lamp."

"Wal, Sid, you won't need to," added Nels. "Reckon you got kind of a glow aboot you."

"Nels, I've a mind to bounce something off your dome," declared the cowboy, irritably, and then he laughed.

"Son, I'll smoke one of your cigarettes," said Stewart.

How Madge shook at that laconic epithet given Sidway by her father! Poor Lance! They were all in league against him not a ghost of a show to escape!

"All right, we're set," went on her father, seriously. "You're determined to ride away tomorrow?"

"Yes, Gene—I am," replied Lance, sadly.

"There's a future here for you. This ranch will pay again some day. I'm glad to tell you that I'm going to pull through this tough time. Madge is helping me."

"By God! I *knew* she would," cried Lance, passionately, as if verifying something to a doubtful side of him. "I'd glad, Gene. It's worried me a lot. Not that it's any of my business. . . . She's swell. She's a Stewart, all right."

"I had that hunch myself."

"Wal," drawled Nels, "I always told you *hombres* that Majesty was true-blue, a western girl at heart, an' one grand thoroughbred."

There ensued a momentary silence, during which Madge feared they might hear her heart beat, so thickly and swiftly did it pound in her ears.

Then Stewart spoke: "Son, please tell me why you dont' want to stay here at Majesty's Rancho?"

"Gene, it can't be possible you don't know," retorted Lance. Then his laugh cut a little coldly, with a hopeless note. "Gene, to come straight out with the truth—I'm so mad over your beautiful daughter that I can't stand being any longer where I can see her."

"That's blunt and to the point," returned Stewart. "I'll speak the same way. I'd like you to be my son. . . . Have you asked Madge to marry you?"

288

"Good heavens—no!" ground out Sidway, apparently tortured.

"Why not? Faint heart never won fair lady! I don't recall being very shy with Madeline. Was I, Nels?"

"Hell no!"

"Madge hates the very sight of me," declared Lance, abjectly.

"Don't believe it," declared Stewart, vigorously.

"Son, I reckon you air wrong aboot thet," drawled Nels.

"Oh, you fellows will drive me to drink. Let's make an end of it. I know you like me, and you've been swell to me. I love you both. But that has nothing to do with it. Madge is the one. And she loathes the ground I walk on. It's no wonder. I've had the rotten luck to save her in humiliating circumstances. She is as proud as a princess. I've rubbed her the wrong way. I've bucked her in everything. Perhaps the last straw was her finding out that I had seen her bank statements and credits. But that wasn't my fault. Worse than that, my knowing about her flirtation with that gangster, Uhl . . ." Suddenly Lance broke off, panic in his voice. "I didn't mean to tell you that—to give her away. I could kick myself."

"Son, you're not giving Madge away. I savvied that. And then she told me."

"She did? Holy cats!"

"She just casually spoke of it, as if for her it was okay. That has been bothering me. . . . Just how far it went!"

"Wal, Gene, thet doesn't bother me none," drawled Nels.

"But it should," flashed Stewart.

"Gene, one day Majesty talked to me for a long while. She was in one of them bare bathin' oofits, an' I jest couldn't look at her atall. An' she got to tellin' me aboot the girls an' boys, an' these new modern ways. We air old-fashioned, Gene. An' this world has moved along. It's changed. Somehow I seemed to savvy Majesty, an' since thet day nothin' she ever did or might do could bother me."

"Why didn't she confide in her father, too?" asked Stewart, jealously.

"Gene, you may not believe it," put in Lance, "but Madge was afraid of you. Loved you—craved your respect. I know."

"All right. You and Nels are hipped on this girl. You just can't see anything wrong. . . ."

"There wasn't anything wrong," interrupted Sidway, with heat, "unless we except her flirtations and extravagances. Not in this day!"

"What's the age to do with it?"

"I don't know, but it has a lot."

"Sidway, speak right out, will you?" importuned Stewart. "It seems we three all worship this strange girl. Well, Nels is set and safe in his worship. I don't want to embarrass you. I know you'd lie like a gentleman to protect her. And so would I if I were in your place. I love Madge and nothing can change it. Still I wish. . . . Oh, hell, I don't know *what* I want. But it's a deep and bitter need, I assure you."

Again there ensued a silence, except for Nels' cough, and the tapping of his pipe upon the table, while Madge sat there, strung and tense, her heart bursting.

"Gene, I get you," spoke up Lance, with finality. "You want your old idea of respect back for Madge. I tell you, on my word of honor, that you may feel that respect. Madge Stewart has never done one single thing that she would hide from you—that she could not look you in the eyes and tell. Sure she is modern, sophisticated. She's a college girl. A radical, when it comes to mid-Victorian standards. . . . But, get this, both of you. Even if she had been what you old fogies would call bad, it'd make no difference. Not to me! Not to anyone who knows her! Madge Stewart is like Helen of Troy. Their value is as incomparable and incalculable as their beauty, their minds and souls, their great power to create love, to give, to be a joy to all who come in contact with them."

"You win, son," came Stewart's quiet voice, a little

husky. "Then, even if Madge were what you swear she is not—you'd make her your wife, if she cared for you?"

"My—heaven! Gene, you're thickheaded," declared Lance in despair. "Yes! *Yes!* And consider myself the luckiest fellow in the world—as I'd be the happiest."

Madge could not bear any more. Slipping out of the chair she picked up her slippers, and softly went outside, to appear in the open doorway of Nels' room. She paused a moment, then entered.

The smile of beatitude that shone resplendent on Nels' visage, the sudden sinking of Stewart into a chair, as if his legs had suddenly grown weak, and Sidway's backing into the wall for support,—these reactions sustained Madge in this emotional climax of her life.

"Dad—Nels—Lance, did I happen in opportunely?"

"Madge! Where did you come from?" demanded Stewart.

"From Lance's room. I've been in there listening to you."

"For God's sake! . . . Are you crazy, girl?—What were you doing there?"

"Waiting for Lance. I'd framed a little stunt. But you've upset it."

"Yes. And what were you going to do—when he came?"

"Dad, I hadn't the slightest idea. But I know now."

She approached Sidway, in so poignant a joy and surety of her power to bestow happiness, that his pale and working face did not deter her from prolonging his torture a little longer.

"Lance, if I don't put on my slippers I won't be so tall, and I can look up to you better. See!" And dropping them she stepped closer, to look up into his eyes.

He stood like a statue, his gaze somber and unbelieving. But her glance quickly descended to his vest, where her hands, quivering almost imperceptibly, touched the frayed edge, and a spot that lacked a button. She was not quite ready yet to let him read what her eyes would surely say.

"Cowboy, you need someone to look after you," she went on, sweetly. "Did you know I could make buttonholes and sew on buttons?"

"No. I couldn't imagine it," he returned hoarsely. "Did you learn that in college?"

"Mother taught me. . . . I can mend socks, too. And make my own clothes, and I know how to cook and bake, too."

"You're—a—remarkably accomplished—young lady."

"Thank you. I wondered if you had found it out. . . . Are you interested in my waiting for you—in your room?"

Evidently it was utterly impossible for Lance to answer that. He divined something his intelligence repudiated.

"Well, as a matter of fact, I forgot. You and Dad and Nels spoiled my plot. Let's skip it."

She began to slide her gold-tan hands up the edges of his vest, and her eyes traveled with them. Then, in a flash, her arms encircled his neck, and she gave him her eyes, with all her heart and soul in them.

"I have much to thank you for," she said, eloquently. "But even more than for my very life. I want to thank you for what you told Dad just now."

"Madge, please—don't," he rejoined, unsteadily. "You're excited again. . . . I don't want thanks.

"Wrong again, darl . . . No, darling is out. I must find another word. . . . Lance, I'm not excited. Just in a transport," and her hands slipped by one another, so that in another moment her arms were clasping his neck.

"Did it ever occur to you that I might have fallen in love with you at first sight—that day at the campus in L.A.?"

"It—certainly—didn't!" he gasped.

"Well, I did. And then wondering where you were, and if I could find you again, and then discovering

WESTERNS
THAT NEVER DIE

They pack excitement that lasts a lifetime.
It's no wonder Zane Grey is the bestselling
Western writer of all time.
Get these Zane Grey Western adventures
from Pocket Books:

———83102 BORDER LEGION $1.75

———82896 BOULDER DAM $1.75

———83422 RIDERS OF THE PURPLE SAGE $1.95

———82692 DEER STALKER $1.75

———82883 KNIGHTS OF THE RANGE $1.75

———82878 ROBBERS ROOST $1.75

———82076 TO THE LAST MAN $1.75

———83534 UNDER THE TONTO RIM $1.95

———82880 U.P. TRAIL $1.75

———83022 ARIZONA CLAN $1.75

———83105 BLACK MESA $1.75

———83309 CALL OF THE CANYON $1.75

Clair HUFFAKER

Westerns

"Move Huffaker onto your list of great storytellers!"
—*Chicago Tribune*

_____ 83142 GUNS FROM THUNDER MOUNTAIN $1.75

_____ 83030 SEVEN WAYS FROM SUNDOWN $1.50

_____ 83033 GUNS OF RIO CONCHOS $1.75

_____ 80711 CLAIR HUFFAKER'S
           PROFILES OF THE
           AMERICAN WEST $1.95